GONE FISHING

Also by Sion McCabe

Evil Reawakened
The Book of Matthew

GONE FISHING

Please leave your reviews or comments at Amazon.co.uk
or at sion.mccabe@outlook.com
or on Twitter @SionMccabe
Thank You

Copyright © S.McCabe, 2023

This book is a work of fiction.
All names, characters and incidents portrayed in this book have been created by the author's imagination.
Any resemblance to actual persons, living or dead, is purely coincidental.

Acknowledgements
During the writing of this book, I reread and enjoyed the following:
Slaughterhouse-Five by Kurt Vonnegut.
Brighton Rock by Graham Greene
Great Expectations by Charles Dickens
Lord of the Flies by William Golding
Heart of Darkness by Josef Conrad
The Ragged Trousered Philanthropists by Robert Tressell
Animal Farm by George Orwell
The Spy who came in from the Cold by John Le Carre
Thanks for the valuable references available at www.marxists.org

THE LAST DAY

1

They walked out together through the wedged-open double doors.

○ ○ ○

Michael, the school's unhappy, overworked, and underappreciated caretaker, had wedged the glazed doors open. Some would believe that the rare July heatwave was responsible for triggering such a dynamic response, but Michael's action was petulantly enacted after a command from on high.

'I'm sorry, Michael, but I insist you wedge them open. It's far too hot in the reception area and adjoining corridors.' The Head, Dawn Harrison, found that using her haughtiest voice and immediately walking away worked best when instructing the bothersome caretaker. It provided concise instruction and negated Michael's inevitable doom-laden response. Despite being ignored, Michael clung to his belief that such an action would result in an unavoidable catastrophe, for which she would be solely responsible.

○ ○ ○

The joke concluded; James had heard it numerous times as Ollie perfected his delivery, but despite the practice, the audience's forced smiles indicated that either the joke required more work or should simply be binned. As the three critics turned to leave, they each raised a hand to bid James farewell. James, head slightly bowed, nervously reciprocated, then took his position on Ollie's left as they turned to walk the extended distance home. As their bus, transporting them away to start six school-free weeks, drove past James and Ollie, the three critics helplessly observed Ollie snarling into James' face and knew their next six weeks would be far happier than that of their tormented classmate.

James' heart sank as he watched the bus disappear. He often imagined sitting on that bus; the dream always made him happy, but reality quickly vapourised the transient state. 'What the fuck was that about?'

'What?'

'That stupid little wave of yours. Do you think they give a flying fuck about you?'

'Uh, no. I just waved back because they waved to me.'

Ollie turned and punched James hard on his right arm.

o o o

PUNCH:

- *Verb - Strike with a clenched fist.*
- *Noun – a blow with a fist.*

On paper, punch only serves to convey a physical outcome. Ollie punched James, or James felt the well-aimed punch. These comply with the definition perfectly. However, in the, as yet unpublished, "James Smith Dictionary 1974/5", the definition differs slightly.

PUNCH:

- *Verb – To reinforce the dominance (physical or psychological - I haven't worked it out yet – see future edition for update) over another soul.*
- *Noun – a physical reminder to the recipient that confirms he/she is worthless.*

James Smith had secreted "The James Smith Dictionary 1974/5" in his bedroom and had been adding to it regularly since Tuesday evening, May 14th, 1974. He always remembered the first entry.

TRAUMA (Noun)

- *My emotional reaction to Ollie Jenkins sitting at the desk in front of me, turning around, smiling at me, and then punching me on my left cheek.*
- *2nd Edition – My ongoing emotional reaction etc.*

o o o

The latest punch was observed by those walking behind Ollie and James.

'You'd think he'd hit him back by now, wouldn't you?'

'Why the hell does he just take it?'

'I wouldn't put up with that shit! Acting like a punch-bag? Mental.'

'Cruel bastard.'

'Poor bastard.'

'Stupid bastard.'

○ ○ ○

Ollie and James kept walking, the throbbing arm still sore. 'Come get me at around six; we'll have a walk around town.'

'What do you fancy doing? A kick about, or what?' James asked.

'Not sure yet; yeah, maybe a kick about would be a good way to unwind,' Ollie conceded. 'Remember to bring the ball, okay?'

James nodded, and the pair kept walking until they arrived at Ollie's house. The house, or rather the door to the house, was attached to his father's DIY hardware shop on the town's High Street. The shop, with its brown painted window frames, faded and crazed by sunshine and neglect, was squeezed in between an Oxfam shop and a bookmaker's. The town had seen better days. The shop had certainly seen better days. Jenkins' Tools & Hardware Store did not reflect its contents' ability to refurbish, renew or refresh. Instead, the dusty window housed faded boxes housing screws, nails, grout, fillers, and tools from renowned makers like "Spear & Jackson", "Roebuck", "Britool", "Challenge", "Stanley", "Record Tools", "Draper", and Ollie's favourite, "King Dick". James always believed, should they ever enter this sorry excuse for a store, that those noble manufacturers would insist Mr Jenkins immediately remove their products from such a ramshackle establishment.

'See you at six then, Ollie,' James confirmed as Ollie let himself in and disappeared into the gloom. James didn't expect an answer; he turned and trudged back towards his home, number five, Cromwell Terrace, where he lived with his parents and older brother Edward.

Situated on Cambridge Road, the twin terraces of Cromwell and Cambridge ran inline. The ten houses of Cambridge ran uphill and, separated by a narrow road at the apex, the ten houses of Cromwell ran downhill. Facing the terraces were two prominent buildings housing the activities of the town's WI and the YMI. Just beyond these decaying bastions stood the fence and gate to Ailsworth Secondary. Despite his parents' foresight to start their family with the school's proximity as a qualifying factor, James nowadays undertook a circuitous route to accompany Ollie, who lived much further away.

People aware of James' situation would be surprised he regarded the unaccompanied walk away from Ollie as a trudge. Wouldn't the walk away from his tormentor be undertaken with the lightest of steps, his body carried along by the breeze of freedom? No, James Smith trudged.

o o o

TRUDGE

- Verb - To take slow steps because of the weight of shame I carry.
- Noun - Any distance I cover by foot.

o o o

Instead of taking the small back alleys home, as he usually did, possibly because it was the last day of term, James turned down New Road, past the post office and the small grocer's opposite. As he trudged, dreading how the next six weeks would pan out, James heard a familiar shrill voice.

'James!' He turned. 'Well, bless my soul. Doris! Look who's here.'

James forced a tired smile as he beheld the sprightly proprietor. 'Aunt Maude, how lovely to see you.'

Miss Matilda Wilkinson, Maude to her friends, the Aunt prefix added by James because he felt it showed respect, put down the sturdy box of outspan oranges. She walked briskly over to James and gave him a generous hug.

Her smell.

He'd forgotten about her liking for saturation perfumery, but the sea of earthy green moss notes that invaded his nostrils reminded him of Maude proclaiming her love for Avon's "Moonwind" to enthralled customers. It was evident from the hug that "Moonwind" was still very much in favour. Releasing him, the seventy-two-year-old looked into his face and smiled. 'You look tired, James, my boy. Has school finished now? For the summer?'

Before he could answer, the pair became three. From the darkness beyond the open shop door, a tiny woman with tight curly white hair rushed out. Her mauve polyester-cotton housecoat, Maude's was blue, had been hemmed to negate the original garment's obvious potential to become a tripping hazard. 'James, James; come here and give your auntie Doris a squeeze.'

The request was clearly rhetorical because two short arms immediately clamped James before he had a chance to blink. "Moonwind" was instantly forgotten as Yardley's "Lily of the Valley" smothered James' senses; even his eyes started to water. It was clear that Doris had adopted and possibly exceeded Maude's dosage philosophy.

James couldn't help but smile, reciprocating the smiling faces of his ex-bosses.

∘ ∘ ∘

One evening, three years ago, as John Smith settled in his armchair, his postman's jacket hanging in the understairs cupboard, he turned to twelve-year-old James. 'Maude and Doris are looking for a delivery boy.'

James, sitting with Edward on the sofa, was watching the latest episode of The Goodies and didn't seem to hear the statement. John Smith waited for the, in his opinion, annoying closing tune to start before trying again. He was a calm and patient man. 'James! Maude, the grocer, told me she's looking for a delivery boy for Friday evenings and Saturday mornings. Do you fancy it?'

James looked at his father. 'My bike hasn't got a rack to hold anything.'

John Smith leaned forward, unperturbed by his son's negativity. 'As it happens, we've upgraded our stock of bike racks at the depot, and Mr Hepton, the Post Master, allowed me to liberate one of the older ones. We can fit it to your bike this Saturday if you like?'

Now concentrating on his father, James felt a sudden panic, realising that his knowledge of Ailsworth's street names was limited to those where his friends lived. 'I don't know about addresses like you do, Dad.'

'You'll soon learn, son. After all, I know Maude only has a few regular customers. Yes, you'll soon learn, *and* it'll do you good.'

So the ex-PO bike-rack was fitted, and James started working for Aunt Maude on Friday evenings and Saturday mornings. Despite his initial concerns, James quickly learned the customers' addresses and was often given a few pence tips to add to his princely salary of £1.20. Most customers seemed to be of similar ages to Maude and Doris. They would ask James to carry the box of carefully distributed produce (Doris delighted in the physics of balance) into their kitchen and place it on the table. The tables were of various designs; dark wood, teak, square, round, or oblong. However, all the tables did have one thing in common; they were all covered with oilcloth tablecloths, albeit displaying disparate patterns. James' favourite tablecloth, he'd reflect on this strange fixation after hanging up his bicycle clips, was Mr Taylor's, which depicted four London landmarks in a repeating pattern of Guardsman, Big Ben, red double-decker, and Hackney carriage. It wasn't that the design was dazzling; it found favour with James because of what it wasn't, namely flowers or brown and orange geometrics.

○ ○ ○

'Yeah, school's just finished, and we've got six weeks of freedom,' James lied to the kind, expectant faces. He'd become proficient.

'Oh, how lovely for you, eh Dor?' Maude turned to Doris, who seemed transfixed, staring at James.

'You look tired, James,' Doris said as if she'd conspired with Maude. 'Is everything okay?'

James flicked his gaze between the two. 'Of course, I'm fine, Aunt Doris. I suppose I'm just a bit tired after all the activities this week. A lot of sports and stuff, you know,' without taking a breath, he continued. 'How have you two been? Not seen you for a few months. Is Eric still delivering?'

Maude seemed to close her eyes and become inert as she digested this. When she opened them again, she did so with an accompanying smile. A kind smile. A knowing smile. 'Eric is fine, James, but many of our regulars still ask about you. They always do, don't they, Dor?'

Doris smiled and nodded but did not or could not answer. She reached out and squeezed James' left hand, and he couldn't fail to notice the tears waiting to trickle from her pale blue eyes and run down her crinkled rose-flushed cheeks. She gave a subtle shake of her head and returned to the shop in silence. James was feeling awkward.

'I best be getting home, Aunt Maude. It was lovely seeing the two of you again.'

'You too, James,' now Maude held his hand and looked into his face. She wasn't tearful; she seemed stern. 'Six weeks is a long time, James. Remember that.' She gave his hand one last squeeze and released.

'I know Aunt Maude. See you around, eh?' She nodded as James trudged towards home.

○ ○ ○

SHAME (Noun)

- *My go-to emotion whenever I tell everyone that I'm okay.*
- *The loss of all self-respect for allowing this to happen.*
- *What I will bring to my family – when they learn of my patheticness.*

○ ○ ○

James knew they knew. As he trudged, he wondered if they knew knew or if they kind of knew based on rumours and suppositions. Ailsworth was, after all, a small town. He thought it over. What did Maude mean when she said six weeks is a long time? Did she think that he couldn't cope with Ollie for six weeks? He knew he could. He'd been coping with Ollie Jenkins, on his own, for fourteen long months. Six weeks was nothing.

He arrived home.

He'd have two hours.

2

It was five to six as James approached the entrance to the back alley that bypassed New Road; he didn't much fancy meeting Maude and Doris again. Before turning off New Road, he stopped to watch Eric tie down a cardboard box with three bungee straps. James smiled as Eric adopted the method he'd shown the young replacement last June. He could imagine the carefully distributed potatoes, carrots, cauliflowers, and suedes. Doris was a master. James enjoyed working for Maude and Doris, but Ollie told him to stop. His smile became rueful.

James, carrying his football, hurried along the narrow back alley until it made a sharp ninety around a coal shed. Not expecting anyone to be standing there, James barged into the side of Brenda Johnson, dislodging the football from his arm and the lighter from her hand.

'What the fuck!' she shouted as James scrambled for his ball. He looked up and saw that Brenda was with two other girls from his class, Sally Jordan and Maureen Knowles.

'Sorry, Brenda, sorry. Didn't see you there. Sorry,' he bent down to retrieve her lighter. She was the only one without a lighted cigarette. He made to hand over the BIC disposable.

Brenda was a sturdy individual, a formidable presence in their class and not someone to be messed with. The other girls were not as fearsome, and James was shocked to see Maureen smoking. He always assumed she wasn't the smoking type or even the type to hang out with Brenda Johnson.

With her hands on her hips and the unlit cigarette hanging from her lips, Brenda made no attempt to take the lighter. She stared at James and then used her lips to flick the cigarette up and down. She nodded, and James knew she wanted him to light her up. Panic coursed through his body.

Holding the football under his left arm, he reached up with his trembling right and flicked. Thankfully the lighter worked first time, but Brenda had to grab James' trembling hand to have any chance of lighting up. Once lit, Brenda held out her hand for the lighter and blew the first smoke into James' face.

'Where yous going, turd? Seeing your boss tonight, eh?' She stepped forward, and James retreated until his back met the brick wall opposite. 'Well? Is that where yous going, little mouse?'

'Uh, I'm going to see Ollie and play some footie,' he managed to say. Suddenly, Brenda whipped her right hand and slapped James hard on his cheek. The noise was far worse than the pain, but it still made James nauseous.

Sally Jordan was shocked and pulled at Brenda's shoulder. 'Don't do that, Bren; he'll faint,' she looked at James' humiliated expression. 'Let's go; he's got more than enough to deal with.'

Brenda shrugged and walked away with the others. James Smith was insignificant. The three walked away, but Sally and Maureen glanced back. As James leaned back against the wall, breathing hard, he didn't know if the shared expression on Sally and Maureen's faces was sympathy or disgust.

○ ○ ○

They'd all try to take turns.

Once it became known that Ollie Jenkins had a punch-bag, they all wanted a go. All doesn't mean everyone. In reality, all, in this case, meant a small minority of like-minded individuals. The issue for James was that Ollie's other acquaintances did seem to be like-minded. So, on some quiet evenings, Ollie would demonstrate the art of how to hit someone hard enough for effect but not too hard that it showed any after-effects.

'You see, lads,' Ollie would begin. 'If he's wearing long sleeves, I can fill my boots; I can't go wrong. But I must be careful if he's wearing a stupid tee shirt, like today. So with tee shirts, it's better to go for the back of the torso for two reasons. One, I know the bruising will be hidden, and two, it makes the little shit think twice about wearing a tee shirt to minimise his punishment.'

The audience of like-mindeds listened and watched, enthralled. Strangely Ollie wouldn't allow anyone else to practice the art on James. That didn't mean they didn't try.

One evening, three of Ollie's acquaintances came across James walking home alone. They pushed and poked him, thinking it would lead to a full beating, but James jumped on one of them and started to pummel his face. The other two dragged James off, and although James did get a beating, they never bothered him again.

He often thought back to that incident. Why did he fight back? Why fight back when faced with three assailants and yet meekly accept Ollie's punishment? It made no sense. Having steeled himself to have-a-go when next he met Ollie, his resolve dissolved the instant Ollie snarled in his face. That evening, in bed, he stuffed his homemade bookmark into his then-current reading companion and placed it on the floor. He turned out the light and lay on his side. The throbbing reminders of Ollie's medicine came to the fore, as they did at night, and he cried again.

James Smith didn't hit girls. There was never a chance he'd retaliate against Brenda Johnson.

○ ○ ○

DREAD:

- *Verb - To anticipate my punishment.*
- *Noun - The feeling I have whenever I meet Ollie.*

○ ○ ○

He knocked. He saw the distorted figure through the privacy glass move towards the door. His dread made his heart thunder and stomach lurch.

The door opened, and Ollie filled the frame. 'Where the fuck have you been, you little fucking toad? I told you six.'

Before anything else passed between the two, a woman's shrill voice echoed down the tiled hallway. 'Be sure to be back for eight, Ollie. Your uncle David and his family are staying for a few days. I want you here when they arrive,' the voice trailed off, and Ollie slammed the door. He grabbed James' arm and led him along the pavement. They stopped and sat at a short wall beyond the bookmaker's.

'Well?'

James was conflicted. The short-lived joy he'd experienced hearing Ollie's mother's command reduced the dread he'd felt watching Ollie's distorted shape stomp towards him, but now, facing Ollie alone, the dread was back. 'I stumbled across Brenda. I almost knocked her over, so she belted me,' he turned his left cheek, hoping it was redder than the other.

Ollie brightened up immediately, his face breaking into a menacingly grotesque grin. Still grinning, Ollie jumped off the wall and stood before the still-seated James. 'Let me see,' so James turned his left cheek again. 'Fucking hell, Shmitsy, nice one. Now, look straight ahead,' so James looked straight at Him.

The slap wasn't unexpected. Ollie had this innate ability to assess the level of adult human activity in the vicinity of his planned actions. In the few seconds it took Him to jump off the wall and face James, Ollie knew that no one would notice before delivering the slap with his left hand. 'There, a perfect match,' he smiled, pleased with his skill. Ollie took his place on the sandstone chair next to James, who was now sitting, head bowed, holding the football in both hands by his knees. He knew more was coming. 'If I tell you six-o-fucking-clock, then I mean six-o-fucking-clock; not seven minutes past. Do you understand why I had to punish you for this, Shmitsy?'

'Yes, Ollie, sorry.'

'Right, go to Gordon's and get me a Marathon and some black jacks and fruit salads. Mum was keeping the dessert until my fucking uncle arrived.'

'But I only have 10p to last till the end of the week.'

'More than enough. Now go over there and get me some sweets, okay?' James nodded, handed the ball over to Ollie and crossed the road to Gordon's sweet emporium.

As James pushed open the heavy door, the most pointless of doorbells sounded to announce his entry. The bell, struck as the door opened, worked fine; that was never the issue. James believed it pointless because the shop was more like a narrow corridor, and the shelves on either side left an aisle precisely the same width as the door. At the far end of this gallery of confectionary stood the serving counter, housing a more exotic collection of goods like Turkish Delight, Old Jamaica, and Grande Seville, alongside the different varieties of cigarettes, cigars, matches, and BIC disposables. Gordon sat behind the counter. There was no room at the back, so Gordon brewed his tea, ate his sandwiches, and smoked from behind the counter. James asked him once how he got there, and Gordon proceeded to show him the surprising way the serving counter hinged open towards the back, thus allowing him enough space to squeeze in and out. The shop was open twelve hours six days a week from eight to eight in the evening, closing only for an hour at lunchtime (an early break so as not to clash with the school's lunchbreak) and for a few minutes here and there when nature called upon Gordon's bladder. Yes, James concurred with his previous assumption; the doorbell was pointless.

'Hi, James dude, what's the lowdown?' Gordon asked when he saw him enter. James inwardly cringed when he heard Gordon's attempt to be cool.

'Not a lot, Gord. School's finished for the summer hols and stuff. That's about it,' James felt awkward talking to a single forty-year-old that the kids knew had suffered a breakdown after his wife left him six years earlier, taking their two daughters with her to live in Spain. He didn't run the shop then. He used to work in an independent furniture shop and, besides transporting furniture, Gordon could fit carpets to a very high standard.

Everyone in Ailsworth and the surrounding district knew Gordon's skill. It became even more widely known as a consequence of the subsequent gossip after his wife left him for a carpet salesman from Chester. His parents bought the shop as part of his rehabilitation, and it worked well enough for Gordon to have some kind of life. James felt sorry for him. His sunken eyes betrayed the grief Gordon experienced, and James knew that jokes circulated about him. After getting paid for Maude's delivery work, James started spending some of his tips at Gordon's Emporium. After talking to some older boys outside the shop one day, James returned home and asked his father, 'Dad? Why could Gordon lay carpets better than he could lay his wife?' After being scolded for talking like that with boys like that, James had to wait until someone at school eventually explained.

○ ○ ○

Walking out with a Marathon, four black jacks, and four fruit salads, James wasn't surprised that Ollie was no longer there. He'd gone to the pitch.

The "pitch" was a small field opposite the large Norweb maintenance depot and in front of the walled gardens to the rear of a five-house Terrace. Bracken Terrace was known locally as Slagheap Terrace, the nearest housing to the looming waste heap extracted from the local coal mine. James always liked Slagheap because, despite its nickname, it had an expanse of common separating it from the detritus, the remains of man's blinkered drive to extract every last resource from the earth's womb.

Mining and the Cotton mills were aspects of life where James' world and that of the other Ailsworth residents diverged. The majority looked at the last remaining colliery and run-down mill with pride, even though their present-day influence on the local employment level and economy was negligible. The National Coal Board had been cutting back production and would have closed the mine already had it not been for the pressure applied by the NUM union. The old mill had been running down in James' lifetime, and rumours about its impending closure were rampant. So, even though not many were employed, coal miners, in particular, held a form of kudos in the town, and townsfolk wouldn't hear a bad word against the industry.

John Smith, local postman, held very different opinions about the mines; his weekly visits to his widowed mother, Joanna, before she died were a memory of why. Watching helplessly as his forty-seven-year-old father coughed out his phlegms and fought for every last breath of Ailsworth air created a deep mental scar. And, when the NCB announced the colliery's record year of production in the week following his father's funeral, sixteen-year-old John's hatred for the industry became cemented.

The town was now seeing new units being built, but these were small and employed fewer people than the more significant industries. There were small units for double-glazing windows, sewing, and biscuits springing up, but the overall feeling around town was one of decay rather than rebirth.

Ollie was waiting, sitting on one of the small boulders that bordered the small field. To call it a field was stretching it; plot being a better description. It measured roughly twenty yards by thirty but wasn't perfectly proportioned. The angled access road had the effect of extending the southern boundary by at least three yards. As the field sloped up from the access road, they positioned the goal near Slagheap's walled gardens at the highest end. The bare patch bore witness to the frequent rain-affected knockabouts.

'Here, numb nuts. Let's get some energy before I trounce you again,' James handed over the confectionery. While Ollie tucked into the Marathon, James took the ball and started to run up and down the pitch, practising his not-insignificant ball control, a skill he never dared use against Ollie. As he returned up the field, watching Ollie devour the chocolate bar, he never understood why his master even bothered with the kickabout; he was useless, ungainly. The usual scenario would see James pretending to miss a tackle and allowing Ollie to shoot at the open goal. His conversion rate was running at around forty per cent.

○ ○ ○

'Is that you, Smithy?'

James and Ollie had earlier noticed two boys heading towards them up the access road from the town centre. Ollie muttered at one stage as James feigned another missed tackle, 'What the fuck are these two looking at?' It was clear that the new boys were interested in their knockabout. James ignored them and continued to pander to Ollie's vain belief that he was a proficient football player. When the two strangers reached the pitch, they stopped, and the tallest one asked the question.

Ollie Jenkins stood at least two inches taller than James and was bigger. He wasn't fat, but there seemed to be a layer of something between his skin and his muscles, giving him the appearance of a tall, well-fed toddler. He had short lank dark hair and matching eyebrows. Whatever the substance was that filled the space between skin and muscle gave him flushed, rounded cheeks that seemed to force his eyes to narrow. His full lips operated symmetrically, so both sides of his upper lip moved in unison when he sneered or snarled. The two strangers were as tall as Ollie, but nothing lay between their muscles and skin. They looked athletic.

'It is you, isn't it, Smithy?' the tallest boy confirmed.

Ollie and James stopped and looked at them. James studied the two boys, and slowly a smile of recognition swept across his face. 'Is that you, Nigel? And you, Thomas? Bloody hell, I haven't seen you two since the summer we left primary.' James noticed that Ollie looked uncomfortable. 'This is Ollie Jenkins; we're in the same class.'

'Hi, Ollie,' the greeting issued in unison. Ollie nodded, but his expression seemed to suggest he needed an explanation.

'We used to be classmates of James' back in primary, but we went on to Brinsley Grammar while he chose to stay at Ailsworth,' Thomas said.

'Chose?' Ollie loved gaining any extra information about James.

'Yeah, he never sat his eleven plus; said it was against his parents' beliefs,' Nigel filled in.

James felt a rare warm glow as he saw his two former friends. 'God, you two have changed so much,' James observed.

Thomas and Nigel looked at each other for confirmation before Nigel spoke. 'You haven't, though, have you, James? You're still the same size as you were back then,' he turned to Ollie. 'Can you believe he was the tallest in our year?' Ollie smiled and shook his head.

'He was head boy and captain of our footy team,' Thomas added.

'Who, James?' Ollie laughed. 'I don't think he can play now without tripping over the fucking ball!' The smileless boys stood still, and Ollie's cheeks flushed. James felt nauseous at the awkwardness of the situation.

'Can we join you for a quick kickabout?' Thomas asked, thawing the frostiness.

Without thinking about the repercussions, James threw the ball at Nigel, who caught and rolled it out in front of him and passed it to Thomas. The two passed and ran up to the goal before Thomas drove it sweetly into the open goal. James' smile disappeared when he caught the frown on Ollie's face.

After finding that two versus one defender was too easy, they settled on a single striker against two defenders and the goalie. It was a great workout, and cheeks quickly became flushed. James started slowly, always allowing Ollie to beat his attempted tackle. However, as the game wore on and became more competitive, something long forgotten reawakened his old football instincts.

After seven rotations, where no one had scored a single goal, James stood and faced Nigel and Ollie with Thomas in goal. Despite his smaller stature, James could move quickly and easily beat Nigel as he feigned right, his favoured side, but deftly moved the ball to the left beyond Nigel's tackle. This time, instead of weighing up Ollie, he rushed towards him, passed the ball between his open legs, and rounded him. He squared up to shoot at Thomas, allowed him to dive, calmly dragged the ball to his left side and slotted the ball between the two piles of jackets with the outside of his right foot. James felt the rare rush of adrenaline that happened at that beautiful moment. Everything his mind had planned, his body had managed to manifest, and it was a fantastic feeling that had not gone unnoticed.

With his hands on his hips, Nigel, looking on as James completed his move, shook his head and shouted, 'You beauty, James boy!'

After his futile dive and brushing himself down, Thomas grabbed James by the neck and ruffled his hair. 'You haven't lost it, have you, cap?' Thomas then turned to Ollie. 'Trip over the ball? This little genius? Fucking hell, James; that was awesome.'

Ollie, who has a robust self-preservation mode, chipped in, 'yeah, that was good, James.'

NUTMEG:

- *Verb Informal*
- *A stupid thing to do (under current circumstances).*

Example: I nutmegged Ollie and knew that retribution would be inevitable.

o o o

James could no longer feel his throbbing arms, but he wasn't bothered; something else was occupying his thoughts. Dust! James was desperately trying to understand dust. Its lightness, irregularity of density, chaos, and haphazardness were abstract propositions. This new, strange, never-before-experienced encounter with dust was confusing his senses. Everything else had gone; everything revolved around dust. His mind raced, trying to quell or confirm his rising fear. *Is dust carcinogenic? Does dust host rare diseases?* His racing heart was an insignificant by-product of the jumbled emotions running through his body as he fought against the pressure Ollie was applying to the back of his neck, introducing him to dust. The goal line dust. The dust that Thomas had to brush off as he stood to acclaim James' dormant skills. Ollie relaxed the angry grip, his fury sated, turned, and sat down. James lay there as the dust stopped dancing and settled once again. He turned over and sat up beside his avenged "friend".

'Don't you ever even fucking think about doing that again, okay, shitbag?'

'Okay, Ollie,' James had a well-practised look of remorse.

'And wipe your stupid-looking face; it's embarrassing,' James lifted his tee shirt and dry-wiped his forehead, nose, and cheeks. He looked down at the previously random dust that had left the chaos and settled on his face. The captured dust was primarily light brown, but three dark-brown oases of wet dust indicated where his eyes and nose had added moisture. Ollie seemed satisfied by the clean-up; the last thing he wanted was for James to carry home any telltale signs. The two continued to sit silently, Ollie finishing his Black Jacks and Fruit Salads.

To anyone looking at the two from afar, Ollie and James looked like two good friends passing the time of day together. This false impression would inevitably continue, sustained by Ollie's ability to detect prying eyes and James' inability to tell anyone.

The evening fizzled out, as their evenings usually did, and they walked silently to Ollie's front door. As they walked, James once again wondered what Ollie was getting out of this relationship. Was Ollie trapped just like him, trapped by his control over James? Did it mean that he had to use it every day? As they walked along, James was horrified as he realised he was feeling sorry for Ollie. It didn't last long.

Standing outside Ollie's door, waiting to be dismissed, James felt exhausted. 'Right, fuck off home then, you little shit. Don't come here until oneish tomorrow, okay? I've got to do some stupid family stuff with my uncle in the morning.'

'Okay, Ollie, see you at one.'

James turned and trudged home.

3

The walk from Ollie's took longer than usual. James was exhausted.

∘ ∘ ∘

EXHAUSTION: Noun

- *= me every day.*
- *What I feel at the end of every day, brought about as a consequence of being me.*
- *The daily cumulative realisation of what my life's become.*

∘ ∘ ∘

Once past their small iron gate, James opened the door to their old coal shed, now used for storage, and threw the football to its usual spot. As he was about to turn away, he saw his Dad's fishing gear. He smiled. Although James no longer fished with his father, he remembered the long days spent together at the small remote lakes dotted around the hills surrounding Ailsworth, beyond the waste heaps. A different world.

'There's leftover chips and half a fish in the oven; if you fancy, love,' Martha Smith shouted from the living room when she heard James walk in.

'Thanks, Mum,' James picked up the plate with the dishcloth hanging on his father's chair and sat at the table to eat.

'Are you okay, love?' she asked, 'Dad's gone the club, and Edward's gone to see his mates; I'm just watching this thing on the TV, if that's okay?'

James smiled. 'Don't worry; I'll finish this and join you afterwards.'

And that's what he did. After washing and drying his plate and cutlery, James changed his tee shirt and sat on the sofa. Martha paid scant attention to her son and sat absorbed as someone documented the pilgrimage to Santiago de Compostela. James stuck it out for twenty minutes.

'Is it okay if I have a bath, Mum?' James asked.

'Uh, yeah, I think there's enough hot water, but I'd put the immersion on, just in case.'

'Thanks, I won't use too much.' As he left his mother to carry on watching the TV pilgrimage, he wondered if she was planning something similar. He dismissed the thought.

∘ ∘ ∘

There was enough for half a bath. As their scarce supply ran in, James stood in his underpants and looked in the mirror. He managed this by opening the mirrored cabinet and standing on the toilet seat. The bruises on his back and above the tee shirt line were bad. These were as bad as he'd seen for a while. With him standing on the toilet, the cabinet door allowed a view from his chin down to his navel; he was scrawny. He jumped down and stopped the water. Slipping out of his underpants and into the warm water, James lay back and started to worry. *Will I be this size forever?* Lately, there had been signs of change, with James noticing hair growing where it didn't previously and certain physical developments that, once the initial panic was over, indicated he was growing. If only he could be taller.

Seeing Nigel and Thomas today was great and terrible. He used to have friends, good friends, but they had become men while he remained a boy. He dipped under the water. Emerging, he lathered his hair and washed his neck and thin face, paying close attention to his eyes and nose. Dipping again to rinse, he re-emerged and failed to contain a huge sneeze. Using his hand to shield the bathroom, he felt the discharge on his palm. Looking at the gooey mess, James was horrified by how black it looked and, having no obvious alternative, he stepped out of the water to wipe his hand clean with toilet tissue. He blew his nose again to finish the de-coke before returning to the tepid water.

He added more water now that the immersion had had enough time to do its work.

James looked down at his body and slumped in shame. He was fifteen and, despite the recent sprouting, practically hairless. The football tonight had been great, but Nigel and Thomas didn't know that James changed modestly at the end of every PE or swimming lesson, minimising the time he spent naked as his hirsute classmates paraded about, joking in their deep voices. He slumped and closed his eyes. Lying back in the water, it now covered his nose and eyes; he looked up at the distorted ceiling.

○ ○ ○

He feels calm and in control of his life. *Why should I return to my world? This world is serene, painless, shameless, and mine.*

He holds his breath, and everything changes.

He has control.

He has choice.

He has life.

James splurts out of the water and breathes in the precious air he's just depleted. As the awful reality of what tonight signified, forty-four days in the service of Ollie Jenkins, he remembers Madge's words, *"Six weeks is a long time, James. Remember that"*. There, contemplating how he'll cope with forty-four terror-filled days, he understands what she meant with her words. He jumps up and, still dripping, goes straight to his dictionary to add *Nutmeg* and *Plan*.

○ ○ ○

PLAN:

- *Verb – Planned – James forms a plan.*
- *Noun – a method to rid myself of Ollie Jenkins – James devised a plan (with assistance from Maude) that could save his life.*

GONE FISHING

1

I hadn't used my old alarm clock for years and wasn't sure it even worked, the alarm part, that is. I knew it didn't keep time all that well, but I reckoned if it lost or gained up to ten minutes overnight, then that would be neither here nor there. I set it down on my bedside locker, ensured it was wound up and switched off the light. To dare to dream and dream to dare.

It worked fine, brutally waking me from a night's broken sleep. It was half past six, give or take ten minutes, and it was a lovely Saturday morning. With basics ticked off, face and teeth, I selected my country attire for the day's planned activity; fishing. Sifting through my only piece of bedroom furniture, a dark wooden set of drawers given to us by Elsie, my grandmother, I chose a pair of brown cords, two tee shirts and a crew neck jumper.

Layers. I'd chosen the Black lakes for my first trip, and I guessed they were at least four hundred feet higher than Ailsworth. I'd seen pictures from my Dad's National Geographics, and even at the height of summer, those climbers who ventured to the Alps and such places wore layers, including a heavy jacket. I had my trusty navy anorak with its sporty yellow lines down the sleeves.

I snuck downstairs, not wanting to explain stuff to Mum; Dad was already at work. Unfortunately, our house is terrible for sneaking. While I was confident that Edward would be oblivious to my activities – he camped in the converted attic – I felt sure Mum would hear the creaking and the groaning that the staircase emitted even when someone as light as I was descended. The kitchen clock showed ten to seven; perfect! I planned to leave at seven, and the cornflakes wouldn't take long.

'And where do you think *you're* sneaking off to, young man?'

Mum's voice is soft. It's neither shrill nor booming, but this soft voice, this morning, scared the hell out of me as I sat there slurping my cornflakes. She stood at the doorway with arms folded and her head tilted, wearing her quilted dressing gown, more apt for the depth of winter than a summer's day.

Emptying my mouthful, I splurted, 'I thought I'd go fishing; start the holidays by doing something new.'

'Is Ollie going with you?'

'No, I thought I'd have some alone time. Maybe read a book while I'm there,' I pointed to my copy of "Slaughterhouse-5" on the table.

'Are you coming home for lunch?' She inquired, and the look on my face and accompanying shrug must have answered her. 'So, what time do you think you'll be back then?'

'I thought I'd make a day of it. Get back around eightish,' I ventured.

'So, Marco Polo,' Mum always threw in names of random famous people if she thought they fitted the bill, 'is that all you're having to eat all day?'

Shit, food; I'd forgotten about food. My plan was falling apart like my mushy cornflakes. It had started out firm and resolute but now looked weak and half-hearted. Everything was turning to mush, and it wasn't seven yet! 'Uh,' was all I managed before Mum shook her head and marched to the bread bin.

'If you're going out for the day, you need food. Go and sort out the fishing gear while I sort out your food.'

I quickly polished off the mushy cornflakes and washed and dried the bowl and spoon; I wasn't going to push my luck. Leaving Mum humming "morning has broken", I found that Dad's fishing gear was in good nick with a good selection of flies, bubble-floats, and spinners; enough for my first adventure. I closed the coal shed door and rested the rod against the wall, taking the canvas bag inside to face Mum.

I love my mother, as I love my father and brother, but she's different. While Dad wants to be my mate, Mum is the one that looks after me. She's my Superman, coming to my rescue without me asking for help. As I watch her, I feel sick. After all she's done to nurture me, be there for me when I'm ill, help me with school work, and stop Ed from teasing me, I let her down. I know I've let her down. I've allowed a scumbag like Ollie Jenkins to undo everything she's ever wanted for me. All she ever wanted was for me to be happy, and as she busied herself trying again to make her son happy, I knew what I'd allowed to happen. I could feel my cheeks burning as I fought an overwhelming need to walk to her and hug her tightly.

'Thanks, Mum; they look great.'

She turned to me, holding a light-blue Tupperware box with an opaque lid. 'It's salmon paste and some strawberry jam.'

'Ugh, that sounds gross,' I deliberately teased.

'Hilarious, James Smith; so, you've enough here for a full day, and take these crisps with you in case you need a snack,' she looked at me like I'd imagine a detective looking at a thief banged to rights. 'What about drink?'

As plans went, mine sounded incoherent, but I had to tough it out as a politician would. 'I'll be okay, Mum. After all, I am going to a lake, aren't I?'

Look, Mum *has* told me off, even slapped me a few times, but most of the time, she just pretends to tell me off, like she's doing today. 'No son of mine is going to drink unfiltered lake water! You'll stop at Bill's garage and buy a drink; he's open at seven.' Shaking her head, she walked to her shelf to pick up and open her purse. She handed me ten pence. I looked at the money in her hand and, remembering what I last did with ten pence, I simply looked up, staring mutely at her, ashamed. I knew she was right, so, despite my shame, I took the coin with my grubby deceitful little hand.

I'm never sure if Mum knows what's going on, but knowingly or unknowingly, she does manage to magnify my shame. Seeing how she asked about Ollie, I guess she doesn't know. After a quick kiss on my head, she turned to wipe the breadcrumbs into the bin. I looked at her, and my stomach lurched. She knows there's something wrong, I can see that, but I think Mum puts it down to growing up issues that boys go through.

Mum wanted me to be a girl; I have no doubt about that. This may seem a strange thing for me to say, but it's a fact that keeps me going despite her pain. So, while I've been disappointed with myself for fifteen months, Mum's carried her disappointment for fifteen years! And now that I've hatched this fantastic plan, I've given myself hope. The plan may well fail, but at least I've given myself hope. Mum will never have that. She'll continue to look at the three of us - Dad, Edward and me, watching cowboy or war films on TV or talking about football, like last year's world cup – and dream of having a heart-to-heart with Jane (the name she'd planned for me) and share in her journey to be a woman, a journey that she could help shape.

We have a Kodak Instamatic, and you can find evidence of its use in various shoeboxes scattered around the house. These random memories get an airing from time with the sole purpose of embarrassing Edward and me. They mostly show Edward and me growing up, and, weirdly, it appears we did so at random seaside resorts like Rhyl and Blackpool. They also show Mum looking motherly, dressed to cope, and looking tired. While her children looked cute, the way children should in photos, she looked dowdy and old, not how a young woman would like to look. Today, years after those Kodaks, Mum still looks elegant, is not particularly overweight, and has black hair with stray whites darkened by some form of magic performed at Pauline's salon. She may have put on *some* weight, but not much, and her face is elegant, with prominent cheeks but spoilt slightly by what I call a smoker's mouth; that is, her mouth is surrounded by little crow's feet from the cigarettes I know she smokes on her nights out to the Bingo and after her sons had gone to bed. So that's Mum, an elegant woman who dresses to emphasise status rather than show how young she is. I'm not afraid of repeating myself; I love my mother.

○ ○ ○

MUM:

- *Superman*
- *A heavy burden I carry created by my SHAME*

○ ○ ○

I set off with the fishing gear, sandwiches, crisps, layers, anorak, and ten pence. I sped through the back streets; I gambolled, strutted, marched, strode, stormed, but didn't trudge. Today was a new start, and by taking the back streets; in reality, they were tarmacked footpaths weaving between houses, Streets, Terraces, and coal sheds, I quickly reached the National Garage at the north end of town. The four white and blue petrol pumps stood vacant, looking like jukeboxes waiting for action. Guarding over the four was Mr Mercury, with his yellow wings protruding from his helmet, majestically framed on a blue background. This is what a garage should look like; guarded by a god.

I'm not stupid, as many children in our school believe; I take a lot of interest in many things, and even during this current episode in my life, I make a point of reading Dad's National Geographics. I know they're two months late by the time we get them, but it's only then that Mr Peter Crabtree gives them to Dad to keep his house clutter-free.

○ ○ ○

Last September at school, I opted to drop History in favour of double Biology because I was concentrating on the sciences, but I had a miserable time. Ollie sat next to me and made clever use of the long continuous bench to carry out his personal experiment of seeing how my pain threshold stood up to his twelve-inch wooden ruler coming into contact with the knuckles of my right hand. I made the mistake once of moving my hand from harm's way, and the ruler clattered the bench. Consequently, old Bluerinse, our passionate and unhinged teacher, his tinted whitish hair falling wildly over his dark bushy eyebrows, instinctively threw the blackboard duster at Ollie, narrowly missing his cranium. To be fair to Mr Eckley, he *was* concluding his description of "Nutrition of animals: ingestion, digestion, absorption, and assimilation of food in Amoebas" with his usual theatrical flourish. It was only natural he reacted as he did, and it was only natural that Ollie reacted the way he did later. My hand never moved from the bench after that lesson. So, because of the setup at the Biology lab and the dread it instilled, I decided to do something about it.

○ ○ ○

HISTORY: Noun

- *The best subject in school.*
- *My oasis*
- *Happy time.*

○ ○ ○

We have three terms at school: Winter, Easter, and Summer. Winter Term starts in September, Easter in January, and Summer in April. I'm not sure who came up with this naming convention, but I'm sure it's confused a lot of children over the years. Towards the end of the Winter term, I asked Mr Neil Willams, the red-haired History teacher, if I could change my choice of subject for the start of the Easter term. I knew that only six pupils were sitting History at O level. None of them was Ollie.

'See, I'd love to have you join, James, but you've already missed a full term. So, now it would mean you having to copy the previous term's work from one of the other students while still picking up the current work. I cannot not progress the syllabus, or everyone would suffer, so you see my problem.' I remember thinking he showed genuine concern, and his Welsh accent perfectly matched the subject.

'I can cope with that, sir; what I can't cope with is studying a subject with which I have no affinity.'

'Very well, James; I'll ask Stephen Sheret if he'll lend you his exercise book over Christmas; to give you a flying start, okay?'

'Oh, thank you so much, Mr Williams; you can't begin to understand what this means to me.' My gushing left him blushing.

∘ ∘ ∘

Stephen Sheret is the number one boy academic in our year, the only boy in the top ten, but he was surprisingly supportive of my decision to change subject. 'It's a genuinely exciting syllabus, James, covering 1815 to 1914. That's from the end of the Napoleonic Wars to the start of the First World War and includes Peterloo, the Great Reform Act 1832, the repeal of the Corn Laws, the Indian Mutiny, the Boer War and the build-up to the First World War.' Stephen had outgushed me. He duly lent me his book, and the cleanly written words hooked me after the first few pages. It was mesmeric, and History became a passionate obsession instead of simply an escape plan. I'd always thought that History was about kings, queens and weird battles, but reading this stuff was more akin to politics.

How the hell could anyone vote for the Tories? Even back then, they were the baddies, but this time fighting the Whigs (I'd never heard of them before). Over Christmas and beyond, Dad and me had long chats about politics; he was dyed-in-the-wold Labour and volunteered to help the local Labour Party and Doctor Arthur Clarke, our standing MP at Elections. I genuinely enjoyed everything I copied across from Stephen's book, and by the end of February, I was up to date with the syllabus and contributing enthusiastically to the lessons.

So, I am pretty bright when I apply myself but don't bother doing well in subjects shared with Ollie, including PE, because of possible repercussions.

∘ ∘ ∘

Since the National was the petrol filling station at our end of the town, I'd asked Mum and Dad what Mr Mercury represented. Neither knew, although Dad thought old Mercury was related to the Roman or Greek gods. The following Saturday, after meeting Peter Crabtree in the Railway Inn, the local scholar explained that he was the messenger to the gods and was known as the god of speed in the Roman system. Unfortunately for the National garage, Mercury also escorted people to the underworld, not a trait you'd like advertised for a company providing fuel for fast cars.

'What do you…. Oh, it's you, James.'

'Good morning, Mr Graham; I'd like to buy a drink for my fishing trip. I've got ten pence,' I stated optimistically.

'Right, I can give you a couple of cans for that. Will one Coke and one Fanta be good for you?'

'That would be brilliant, Mr Graham; I wasn't sure how much they cost,' Mr Graham smiled and walked back to the booth with my ten pence before returning with the cans.

'There you go, James,' he studied me as I placed the cans into my bulging canvas bag. 'Black lakes?'

'Yes, Mr Graham, I'll make a day of it.'

'Greenwell's Glory and Butcher always work well there, as do Black Gnat and the Bonddu fly.'

I might be pretty bright, but I only had a sketchy knowledge of the names of fishing flies and hoped Dad had a better understanding. 'I'm sure Dad has them in his collection, Mr Graham. I was going to use "bubble-and-fly" with three flies on the leader,' I offered.

'Not the proper way to fish, James, my boy, but if you're ignorant to the finer points of fly fishing, then your method is the next best thing. If you're using three on the leader, I'd put Greenwell's furthest from the bubble.'

'Thank you, Mr Graham; I'll remember that and let you know how I get on.'

'Don't expect a big catch today, James; you've no wind.'

I nodded my appreciation and set off on the gradual climb to the lakes.

2

After crossing the High Street and away from the filling station, I had to navigate around the last two terraced rows of this part of Ailsworth. A rock outcrop to their north and north of the garage has created a hundred-and-twenty-yard gap before the houses of the smaller North Ailsworth begin. The footpath for the lakes starts at the edge of the upper Terrace's northernmost house. Valeview Terrace has one strange characteristic. Although the Terrace comprises eighteen similar houses, a gap exists between nine and twelve. While Lower Valeview Terrace, which runs along the High Street, consists of two rows of ten houses with the link road to Valeview dissecting, Valeview Terrace has a detached house where the town planners envisaged numbers ten and eleven.

The road from the High Street was steep, and as I made my way between ten and eleven Lower Valeview, I saw that the owner of the detached house ahead of me was taking the trash out. I always resented delivering to Villa de Pomme-de-Terre because I always had to dismount and push my bike up the steep hill.

Peter Crabtree, known locally as Pete Pots, Potato Pete, or Pervy Pete, waved in my direction, so I went over. Quite a few locals carried an unfounded opinion about Peter. They believed it strange that a man lived alone in a sizeable house, resulting in those people labelling Peter as a homosexual or child molester. I've heard kids at school calling him a bent bastard, not from their personal experience but from hearing gossip from parents or siblings old enough for the pubs. I knew that Peter tipped well when I delivered his groceries, and he never said or did anything untoward. As I also knew that Dad frequently passed the time of day with Peter, I felt sorry that he'd been labelled a child molester but wasn't bothered about the first label because I believed my brother Edward was probably homosexual.

'How are you keeping, Mr Crabtree?' I asked.

'Not too good, young James; my esteemed physician has completed a thorough examination and presented me with the awful news that I have an ingrowing toenail, I'm afraid.'

It was the kind of statement that worried me; made me panic. Do I laugh or console, ignorant as I was, about the pain and misery that an ingrowing toenail could engender? 'Is that a serious condition, Mr Crabtree?' I played it safe. He smiled, and I relaxed as I watched the short, ruddy-complexioned gentleman – he was a gentleman rather than simply a man – glow with happiness as he started to answer.

'No, it's not serious, James, but the look on your concerned visage did make it appear so.' He lifted the plastic household bin and emptied it into the galvanised rubbish bin at the side of the garden gate. He then emptied the ash bucket over the household stuff and replaced the bin lid quickly before the dust became a pollution incident. 'And may I ask to where are you venturing this morning?'

'I'm going fishing….' he cut me off.

'No? Really? For some strange reason, I assumed you were attending football practice,' he mocked.

I became riled. 'If you'd allowed me to complete my sentence, Mr Crabtree, I was going to add….'

'The Black Lakes,'

I couldn't help but smile. 'Touche, Mr Crabtree,' I said.

'Good for you, James; after all, six weeks is a long time to be twiddling your thumbs, don't you think?'

'Yes,' I agreed, 'it's far too long to be doing nothing,' I said, thinking back to what Maude had said yesterday and wondering if the two had attended a public meeting to discuss my issue.

He seemed to consider something. 'Your father tells me you partake in that most wonderful of pastimes, namely chess; is this correct, young James?'

I blushed. 'No, I only know the moves; I'm certainly not an experienced exponent,' I answered, worried that my choice of words mocked him.

'But you have taken books from the library about Fischer and Spassky, have you not? And played out the matches on your plastic WH Smith chess board?'

I was still blushing, but the little jibe about WH Smith rankled, focussing my answer. 'Yes, I did do that, but I didn't understand what the moves meant or what was coming next.'

'I'm asking these questions because I relish the wonderful pastime's intricacies, but no one will play with me at the Railway.'

'Is that because you're too good?'

He burst into a bout of laughter that rocked his shoulders and wobbled his tummy. 'Good god, James. I so wish that was true,' he started to laugh again. I instinctively smiled at the sight of this man enjoying the moment and waited for him to compose himself. 'No, no, James, although I wish it were so. They will not engage in battle with me because they do not understand the subtle nuances that chess demands. To be brutally honest, I don't believe they understand the moves. It's draughts or dominoes in the Railway; always has been. So if you have some time to spare, you're more than welcome to come here.'

I wasn't sure how to respond. Despite thinking I knew Peter, having attended his house previously to set down Doris' boxes of expertly packed groceries, I felt uneasy accepting an invitation to play chess. It conflicted with the parental instruction I'd received throughout my life. 'I'd love a game, Mr Crabtree, but it's best that I ask Dad first; if that's okay?'

It looked as if a bolt of lightning had struck him. 'Oh god, no, no; of course, you need to ask your Dad. That was stupid of me to ask you like that. Sorry, James.'

I felt terrible. Peter looked mortified and seemed to have lost all the confidence he'd shown earlier. 'It will be fine, Mr Crabtree. I'd enjoy a game because nobody plays it at home, and I'm sure it will be okay with Dad,' I smiled, but Peter had become flustered.

'Oh, okay, I best be getting on now; I've already taken up too much of your time. Bye, James.' He turned and scurried back, carrying the plastic bin and ash bucket.

I felt awful.

∘ ∘ ∘

Having walked away from "Pomme de Terre", named after Mr Crabtree's former wholesale potato business, I wondered why I liked a man such as him. His flowery use of English was unique in Ailsworth, and while many found him tiresome and pretentious, I found him entertaining. I believe this was because I admired how he stood out and persisted in his uniqueness in the face of the male norm in a northern industrial town.

At the end of number twenty, Valeview Terrace, I found the footpath and walked up the hill, leaving Ailsworth below. I hadn't been here for a few years, but it all became familiar as I ascended from the town, and the silence of the countryside descended, smothering me with a forgotten sense of comfort. I knew this plan could well be futile, but at least I was enjoying it today.

Soon the tarmacked footpath petered out, and the route appeared to stop, penned in by stone walls and fences. Edward and I were familiar with this, so I knew I could continue by using the stile provided. But this wasn't the usual bridging wooden type stile. This stile was a set of three long stepping stones inserted through the wall, allowing the trekker three robust steps up and three equally robust steps down. Someone had historically provided a rusted pole at the top of the wall to allow the intrepid traveller the opportunity to turn through one-hundred-and-eighty degrees and descend facing forwards; my preferred option. Once on the other side, Ailsworth could have been in another county; the transformative effect of going over the wall was profound.

I walked on, and even though we were on our third consecutive day of sunshine, the lower, gently rising field was still soggy, and I needed to follow the haphazard trail of carefully placed stones to avoid getting my feet wet. Marco Polo would never start his adventure with wet feet.

That thought made me think of Mum and her random choice of historical and sporting figures. If Dad drove too quickly, he'd be Stirling Moss. Edward became Henry Cooper after getting involved in a fight. Several women shared the name of Jezebel, and I was once called Einstein after getting an A in Physics homework. Columbus would surface if Dad managed to find his way to a new holiday destination, and Edward was Michaelangelo when he brought home a painting depicting a local landscape. When Dad suggested that Constable was a more apt analogy, she dismissed it immediately by asking if Constable had ever painted any ceilings of note. I smiled at the memory and moved on.

After leaving the wetness of the lower fields, my footpath continued upwards, hugging one of the earliest spoil heaps. It was my favourite in the whole of Ailsworth. It's probably strange to have a favourite spoil heap, but I've known it all my life, and the only thing that has changed is the amount of greenery it supports. It's like a good rash, making me happy to see it spread. Green does that, I think. To be able to grow out of the dead blackness and proclaim life gives us all hope. Anyway, it's my favourite spoil heap.

After rounding the spoil heap, the path levels out, and the land becomes greener with small bushes, ferns and tall wispy grasses threatening to hide the footpath. They have little chance as not only do humans use the path, some sheep use it as well, as evidenced by the black pea-like waste left behind on the path, keeping it open against the wishes of nature.

I could now hear the trickle of water from the stream that, a hundred or so feet higher up, exited the smaller Black lake. Before this point, it was as if the stream percolated beneath the surface, unsure it was safe to show itself. Here, it was a confident stream, about eighteen inches wide, and Dad told me that fish actually swam in these waters, although I'd feel foolish fishing such a small waterway for fear of someone seeing me and telling me that Dad was one hell of a joker. Since I knew he did have a reputation for being a jester, a puller-of-legs, a comedian, and a lover of "Candid Camera", I was never going to take the chance.

A plant proliferated on the banks of the stream, and Ailsworth kids called it "bamboo". Dad taught Edward and me to pull one up from as close to the ground as possible to create a boat. This entailed creating a long oval coil, starting at the base and tightly coiling the bamboo. After making an oval base, you'd wind the rest of the bamboo around the middle of the flat coil before finally pushing the pointy end through the bottom of the coil and the last wrap of the wound centre. This was the crux of the construction. If the bamboo was too dry, it would snap at this point because of the sharpness of the final bend, but if you got it right, the pointed end would appear, and you'd pull it tight, locking the construction in place. You'd now have a boat with the pointy end looking like a furled mast.

Edward and I would place our boats in the water at the same time and see which one reached a specific stone first. Edward won most of the contests, but once, after I had created a dream vessel, my boat was in the lead, and I was still screaming at it to defeat Edward's poor attempt when suddenly a rock smashed it and covered me in water. 'It's a stupid game anyway,' he said and walked back to catch Dad. As he caught up with Dad, I caught up with him and threw my body across his back. We fell in a heap, and I started to pound his back with my puny fists.

Knowing nothing about Edward's nuclear option, Dad grabbed my wrists and pulled me up, smacking me hard across my legs. Edward turned over and laughed.

As I walked past the bamboo again, I felt embarrassed, not because of my reaction to Edward's skullduggery but because I later learned from books that these plants were not even bamboo. They were and still are a soft rush. Not bamboo at all, even though Dad let me believe bamboo was their correct reference. I didn't bother to stop to make a boat today.

○ ○ ○

PERFECT DAY: Term

- Any day when I don't see Ollie Jenkins and not dreading to see him.

○ ○ ○

Today was starting to feel like a perfect day already. It was eight-fifteen, and I felt truly happy. I felt light, and there was a different beat in my heart. Ha, if only I'd not dropped Biology, I might know what was causing it. I smiled, and then my perfect day became even perfecter. I stopped the instant I heard it. I carefully placed the rod and canvas bag on the path's opposite side and listened again. There! It was coming from a clump of tall grasses.

It was during a walk with Dad and Edward when I first heard this noise. Dad was leading us along a similar path when he stopped abruptly and raised his left hand, indicating for us to be quiet. I was afraid. He looked like one of the scouts I'd seen in cowboy films who's heard the telltale sounds of an ambush up ahead. My eyes darted around frantically but saw nothing. Dad then crouched low and moved towards some grasses just off the path. He seemed to study each long blade carefully before inching forward again with his hands cupped, about an inch apart. Dad stood stock-still, and I had hardly breathed, let alone asked him what was happening. Suddenly, in a flash, he brought his cupped hands together in a blur of speed, and it looked as if he'd caught a small ball. He smiled and turned to face us. Edward and I gathered around the cupped hands and waited as he slowly opened them, our hearts racing. As light flooded his palms, I could just make out something green, like a clump of grass. Proudly spreading his hands further, I saw my first grasshopper; its alien-shaped head, large eyes, long antennae, and powerful legs. It was brilliant. As Dad opened his hands a bit further, it disappeared! I now know it jumped, but, at the time, my brain didn't expect it to move that quickly, so it disappeared.

Now, on my own, I'd heard the sound that Dad explained was the signature sound of the grasshopper. Because of my interest in words and stuff, I asked Dad how he'd describe the noise.

'Well, James, I think the correct term for it is chirping.' I accepted this in the same way I bought bamboo. Later, probably after finding out about bamboo, I looked for a better word for the sound a grasshopper makes. I didn't particularly care for the word chirping because birds chirp. I initially liked the word chirrup, as the double r gave it a resonance that suited the sound. However, I have now superseded chirrup, and my favourite word for their sound is chirr.

I once again heard the distinct chirr of the grasshopper to my left and crouched at the tall grasses to see if I could make it out. Focussing on each blade, it took me some minutes to see it. It was silent again now. I moved forward, but before I could get within a foot of it, it sprang forward and disappeared. Undaunted, I stood in the tall grasses until I heard fresh chirrs and managed to visually locate an elusive grasshopper. I took my time until I got into position with my cupped hands surrounding my prey, tensed, ready to pounce. I must have had an involuntary muscle twitch or something before I sprang into action because my target bounded away, and I had to start again.

It took me a further four attempts before I could gently drag my cupped hands up a blade of grass with my prize hopefully locked between my palms. I daren't open my hands for two reasons: firstly, there may be nothing there, and secondly, if it is in there, it may jump away immediately. I waited, and I suddenly felt the gentle movement of something alive between my hands. I'd caught a living thing and wished my father was here to see it. He wasn't, I was alone, and I held this life dearly, not wanting to let it go. I slowly prised my two thumbs apart and peered inside the chamber. I saw it looking at me with its alien head and high eyes. It stirred, so I slammed shut my thumbs, entombing it again. I wanted it to stay there forever, but then I heard more grasshoppers chirr around me and realised how cruel I was for keeping it to myself. I opened my hands, and the grasshopper perched on my right palm for less than a second before it bounded towards its friends and family. It disappeared. I felt strange.

If I was in Ollie's palms, he must feel that I crave to be free, yet he keeps me entombed in my darkness. Now, standing on that footpath on a perfect day, listening to the grasshoppers' chirr, I realise that my double History lesson was my lever to prise open his cruel thumbs to see some light, and this plan is the mechanism by which I force open his hands and set myself free.

3

Due to the delay in capturing the grasshopper, I arrived at Small Black at around twenty-past-nine. I'd seen it ahead of me for about ten minutes as the small stone-built dam revealed its whereabouts between two small hillocks. I kept to the right and ascended the shallow rockface that connected the dam to the ground. Once up, standing on the right edge of the dam, I stopped, as I assumed all explorers did when they reached their intended goal, to take it all in.

Small Black is dull, a simple fat oval, almost a square, held captive between the hillocks on two sides and two dams on the east and west. The western dam segregates the two lakes and owes its existence to the fact that Small Black and Great Black once served different mines run by the NCB. The only river into the lakes flows begrudgingly into Great Black, so depending on the output of the mines, the mine people could isolate the water to the Small if ever they needed to increase the head at the Great quickly.

The northern hillock, the right where I'm stood, is a rounded rock outcrop standing only fifteen feet above the west dam. I stride heroically up to the uppermost point of the outcrop, and below me, I could see a vast swathe of land that included the last Terrace of North Ailsworth. Ailsworth itself remained hidden behind the hills and spoil heaps that protected the path.

Across the lake, the southern hillock rises, ominously growing darker, until it towers some fifty feet above the western dam. Then, after a slight dip, it continues rising slowly to a plateau, dominating the south side of the Great Black above the lake's crooked elbow. The plateau then swings through ninety degrees to slope down and away towards North Ailsworth. The Great Black is L-shaped and is very, very dark.

I chose to start my day's fishing from the rock outcrop of the Small Black. I chose. Yes, James Smith chose. I seldom do that anymore, so today was turning out to be a most perfect day. I dug through Dad's canvas bag and decided to spin, knowing that not much existed below the surface at this point to snag the submerged lure. I tied it up using the old faithful hangman's knot (my angling book calls it the uni knot – but because I use it to bring death to a creature, I prefer hangman's) and pinched three lead pellets to the four-pound line that Dad always uses, directly above the Mepp.

Mepp! I remember hearing that word for the first time and how it threw me into a state of confusion. New words do that to you, I think. Like when I was in the last year of primary and heard two older boys I knew, who'd been two years in secondary, start to use the word wank. I didn't understand the context in which they were using this word. It sounded like a physical something you owned, yet I'd never heard it used before; not in my books, on TV, or from my parents. It then became apparent that it was both a verb and a noun, and I had to ask Edward for an explanation after I returned home. That wasn't very comfortable, but Edward found it hilarious. Mepp was another word that local kids used, but this word was only associated with fishing. When I asked what it was, they opened their tackle box and pulled out what I'd always called a spinner. I argued as such, but they outnumbered me by whatever to one. So Mepp it was until I discovered that Mepps is a manufacturer of spinners, probably the original. Like a vacuum cleaner is always called a hoover. I tried to think of other things we've adopted but only managed Biro, Lilo, Coke, Sellotape, yo-yo, Tupperware, and Airfix. Fishing is great.

The first cast of the day is a significant moment. You've done all the hard work to get to this moment: found time to fit it in, prepared your gear, worn layers of clothing, carried food, walked whatever distance it was to the lake, and assembled the equipment, including the Mepp or spinner. For me, this cast was a symbolic gesture. I pinched the line against the upper handle, pulled back the bail and faced the dark waters of Small Black, my left leg two feet in front of the right. Holding the lower handle with my left hand, I moved the rod past my shoulder and waited until I felt my muscles synchronise before casting the rod forward and releasing the line at the perfect split-second. The Mepp flew forward - it must have been a new world record - and splashed into the water. I immediately turned the handle and heard the reassuring clunk of the bail returning to its engaged position. I reeled it in, feeling the familiar resistance as the Mepp's dog-tag began to spin. The faster I reeled it in, the greater the resistance and the shallower it returned.

It all sounds good in theory, but in practice, after the first thirty casts, it becomes very monotonous. I decided to take a break and sat down on the rocky surface, gazing across the still water now that the wind had died. Was that first cast symbolic, or was its symbolism just pretentious? Did I believe that that cast signified me casting away Ollie's control over me? Of course not; I'd be stupid to think it was that simple. Even though I was miles away, I still carried the dread that Ollie would come storming up the hill to sort me out.

I was out on a beautiful day, surrounded by lovely scenery and nature, yet I felt timid and vulnerable. I knew Ollie was cruel and wrong, but for some reason, I thought *I* was doing something wrong and felt guilty for doing it. I lay back and looked at the delicate clouds appearing like performers on a stage from behind the tall outcrop, presenting themselves as surreal shapes for my brain to create a recognisable form. I wasn't playing that game today; instead, I tried to analyse whether this plan would work. Could I go fishing every day during the school holidays? Was that feasible? I sat up and decided that I, James Smith, would do this. No one would ever record this as a significant human achievement. I don't think there's a category in the Guinness Book of Records for what I was doing, but it would be the most significant achievement of my life.

I promised myself I would not see Ollie Jenkins until school restarts.

Right, I'd analysed enough; it was time to start fishing.

○ ○ ○

I'd forgotten how boring fishing was. It was almost three o'clock, and I hadn't had a nibble on the line since around one. It was different with Dad and Edward; we'd have a respite for a chat to break the monotony, and Dad usually caught fish to inject some excitement. I'd made my way around Small Black, stopping at different points and spinning mainly, but during a break, when I saw the smug trout breaking the surface and the wind pick up, I decided flies may be the way to go. So, after lunch (the sandwiches were excellent), I started to use bubble and fly. After casting the bubble float, the rewind is far slower than spinning; more relaxing but tedious. By the time I'd reached Great Black, my enthusiasm was waning, and, even after getting a bite at two, I was struggling. I made my way around Great Black and ended up at the far corner beneath the tall hill that dominated the southwest corner. It was a great place to fish because it offered a full view of the Great Black lake and the two small dams that contained its waters.

At three, I gave up on fishing and dragged out my book, Slaughterhouse-Five or the Children's Crusade (having now read it, the former suits it best). I'd already read over half the book and was now finding out what happened to Billy Pilgrim on that fateful night in Dresden.

Books are my sanctuary. Since it's dangerous for me to wander around freely in my natural habitat, I need a sanctuary, and books are where I go. Since I couldn't express myself physically, yesterday evening's nutmeg being such an example, I needed my mental sanctuary to survive. If it wasn't for my books, I don't think I could have endured Ollie for this length of time. Despite all the psychological damage he'd inflicted, I could still escape into my books and learn about different aspects of the human condition. I loved books. I needed books.

Books are clever. Well, I think they're clever because I don't understand them; they have a complicated meaning that I sometimes don't get. I don't go along with this notion of waiting until I'm grown up; it makes no sense. If I don't understand something now, I should try my best to understand it because who's to say I'll understand it when I'm older? Slaughterhouse-Five is clever, I think, because it says things about the effects of war on the brains of people, in this case, Billy Pilgrim. I sat at that quiet corner of the Great Black Lake and tried to understand this book and how I felt about it.

War must be surreal to any normal human being, but to experience it first-hand must be mind-blowing. The trouble I had with Billy was that he's a coward. Even before he witnessed Dresden, he was damaged. I'm scared of war, but I like my way of life, so if someone decides to invade us, I think it is worth fighting for your way of life. What would happen if the country was full of Billy Pilgrims?

I threw a stone into the water and realised an uncomfortable, inescapable truth.

'I'm Billy Pilgrim!' I shouted. Because, like Billy, I retreat into my head and allow the physical world to wash over me and cope in whatever way I can. I was a coward and didn't have the mental resolve to change my world to protect my beliefs, so I put the book back into the canvas bag and held my head in shame.

○ ○ ○

BOOK: *Noun*

- *The door to Other Worlds*
- *My Fire Exit*
- *My Sanctuary*

○ ○ ○

After feeling sorry for myself, a regular occurrence, I decided to restart my fishing. There was a light wind ruffling the surface. I duly cast the bubble away and slowly rewound the line while sitting on a rock. As I watched the slow return of the plastic bubble, I felt my plan unravelling. *I can't do this for six weeks! It just isn't feasible*, and even if I managed it, I'd still be Billy Pilgrim at the end, cowering in corners. Even though I was out in the open, I felt the hills closing in on me and found it difficult to breathe.

That's what time does. I started today in a positive frame of mind and was just as optimistic when I began fishing. Time, I thought, could do one of two things depending on what type of person you were. If you're confident and get into difficulty, your head will tell you that it's only a matter of time until you find the solution and happy days will return. If you lack confidence, even after finding a solution to a problem, time will erode your confidence in the resolution, and doubts will emerge. Having spent seven hours up here on my own, I felt foolish. What kind of answer was this? Was there an opposite to "house arrest"? Because that was my solution; sentence myself to six weeks of "outdoor arrest". It was stupid.

As I sat there pondering the stupidity of my once beautiful plan, I looked up and saw the dark outline of someone walking along the west shore of Small Black and making his or her way to Great Black.

I was trapped. I had nowhere to run, and a wave of panic overwhelmed me.

My heart beat so hard that I felt myself moving each time it thumped inside my chest.

My head pounded.

I wanted to cry or scream. I had to release the pressure building up inside. I wasn't coping.

It stopped getting worse, and I slowly began to focus.

If it was Ollie, the worse that could happen was that my plan, such as it was, would be binned, and I'd have to put up with six weeks of obeying his inane instructions and following his pathetic whims as a subservient, worthless coward. In a way, I deserved it.

If it wasn't Ollie, I should start to appear as if I'm trying to catch something, so I cast the bubble with its attendant and underemployed flies out again. I decided to stand to give the appearance of being anglerish, and started the slow rewind of the bubble float with its attendant flies. I kept an eye on the figure, and it seemed to be ignoring Small Black and walking directly to the Great. I was desperately looking for signs of fishing gear, and as the figure stepped around the dam, I saw the glorious outline of a rod case slung over his left shoulder. It was a fisherman, and I knew Ollie was never one of those. As my heart slowly calmed, I closed my eyes. Suddenly, a new surge of adrenaline grabbed my heart as I felt a distinct pull from the line and saw the rod tip bend down towards the lake.

About fifteen yards ahead of me, a thrashing, bucking silvery-yellow missile exploded out of the dark waters of the Great Black Lake and crashed back in after gravity overcame its weight. It was pulling hard, so, trying to remember what Dad had taught me, I released the pressure at the spool to allow it to pull more line out. As it pulled more line out, I was reeling him in, allowing the resistance of the spool to limit the drag on the fly. The fish's brave fight for life gradually subsided as I reeled it closer to shore. I saw it coming towards me and suddenly realised that I hadn't picked up Dad's net; it was still hanging on its hook inside the shed. I guided the fish to beach it on a flat gravel area between two large rocks. I pulled it in slowly, taking it out of its environment and into mine.

With it thrashing on the hard gravel and holding the rod high with my right hand, I bent down and grabbed it. It was a brownie, well over the seven-inch minimum size stipulated by the angling association. Holding it in my left hand and leaning the rod against my shoulder, I used my right to dig out the fly from the side of its gaping mouth. I reckoned it was about three inches over the minimum, a nice size for these lakes. Brown trout are lovely fish; silver underneath but then freckled along their flanks with black spots surrounded by a whitish halo. The top of the fish was a muddy brown and graduated from the dorsal fin down to just past the centre, where the spots also die away, and the silver scales start to dominate.

I looked at its face and felt a sense of guilt that I was about to end a life. Heart pounding, I placed my thumb into the inverted fish's mouth and wrenched it down until I heard its neck snap. Dad said this was more humane than knocking its head on a stone, and I was in no position to argue; I didn't want the fish to suffer. I gently placed the lifeless fish in a plastic bag, filled it with lake water and put it into the cool lake with a stone to keep it in place.

'Well done, lad!' the fisherman's voice boomed across from the opposite bank. 'Is that your first?'

'Yes,' I shouted in reply, ' it took Greenwell's Glory.'

'Good choice; I'll let you carry on,' with that, he continued to walk until he stopped at what was probably one of his favourite spots. That's what anglers do; they remember where they once caught a fish and return to it. I don't quite understand that tactic. I found it difficult to imagine that an unrelated fish would consciously take the lure at the same spot where once one of their own, probably a friend or relative, was hooked and dragged out of the peace and calm of the lake to the thrashing world above. I thought the opposite would be true. I could imagine people walking the pavement on Ailsworth High Street consciously avoiding the manhole cover from where Tiny Tim or whoever was whisked away by aliens. Indeed, if it happened a second time, people would give that manhole cover a very wide berth.

As I cast out again, I held my breath and realised that not only did I consider myself similar to Billy Pilgrim, the coward, but I also imagined alien abduction. I slowly rewound the line, unfocusedly staring across the lake, and felt slightly sick. I've not been anywhere near war and haven't the right to compare myself to young men who had.

I started to shed silent tears.

I realised I was damaged and panicked about the long-term effects, gently convulsing as I tried to control my feelings. I had to understand why this had affected me like this.

Aliens? Why on earth did I think about aliens? It was Edward's stupid book. If I hadn't begun to read it, then Billy Pilgrim wouldn't exist, nor would the Tralfamadorians and their stupid planet Tralfamadore. So, therein lay the answer; if I hadn't read the book, it would have been an acceptable metaphor for me to substitute the removal of a fish from its lake with a human abducted from Ailsworth High Street! So had I become that weak? That a work of fiction could make me doubt my sanity? As I felt the line jerk into action once again, I remained calm and smiled as I realised that, bad as it was, the plan had to work.

4

The fisherman, Thomas Renshaw, a local carpenter, eventually made his way around the Great Black Lake to my corner. After identifying himself, I was pleased that he knew of my father. I'm not sure why that is, other than a sense of reflected pride when he used "a good man" as part of his sentence.

'I hope you don't mind, but I couldn't help but notice that you've just caught your third, and I haven't had a single bite,' he ventured after our introductions.

'No, it's not a problem, Mr Renshaw. My only concern is that my bubble and fly system may interfere with your fly-fishing,' I said after observing his undoubted skill in the art.

'That's okay, James. If you continue to cast straight ahead, as you're currently doing, I'll work the bank to the left of here. Is that okay with you?'

I felt myself blushing. 'That's perfectly fine, Mr Renshaw, perfectly fine,' he smiled broadly at this, although I didn't think I'd said anything amusing. I blushed during my answer because of the strange feeling that swept over me. He was treating me with respect.

When my life is at its darkest, I think that everyone in the world looks down on me, that I'm just a worthless shadow standing behind Ollie. For someone to talk to me on an equal basis is a shock to my system, and I have difficulty dealing with it. But after my emotions calm down, I'm left with a beautiful warm feeling that there are genuinely lovely people in the world and that there may be a place for me in their midst.

I checked my Timex and saw that it'd gone seven. 'I'm packing up now, Mr Renshaw, if you'd like to take my place,' I said as my bubble arrived back from what was to be my last cast.

'Well, thank you, James; I might just do that. But I doubt I'll be as successful as you've been today. Three! And by the look of them, they seem a pretty decent size; I'm sure it will be a lovely surprise for your Dad.'

I smiled, nodded, and picked up the plastic bag from the lake to empty the water. I ensured that the fish didn't drop out (that would be embarrassing), rolled up the plastic bag and placed it at the bottom of the canvas bag. After dismantling the rod, reel and leader, I packed everything away and stood up to leave. 'All the best, Mr Renshaw: I'm sure you'll catch at least four after I've gone.'

'Thank you, James, but I'm not so sure about that. Tell me, has your Dad never tried to teach you fly-fishing then?'

'Well,' I thought back, 'he did tell me a couple of years ago that once I'm a bit stronger and taller, he'd do so. As you can see, I'm still pretty small for my age,' I answered.

'He may be right about strength, James, but next time you come to the lakes, bring a fly rod with you and practice using a floating line. I noticed you studying me, so you know the basics. Practice is the best way to strengthen your arm, so set aside half an hour during your day, and you'll soon be able to cast a fair distance.'

'I might just do that, Mr Renshaw, when no one's watching; thank you for the advice; bye.'

He nodded an acknowledgement, and I set off along the footpath towards the first dam. After twenty or so yards, I heard the sound of a large splash from the lake; it made me turn. I saw Mr Renshaw holding his arcing rod high as he carefully drew back the fishing line.

'Do you want a hand with the net, Mr Renshaw?' I shouted.

He turned to me. 'No, James, I'll be fine,' he answered. 'But thank you for offering; I appreciate it very much.'

I smiled at him and felt very pleased on his behalf. 'I told you you'd catch four!' I shouted, and he waved in acknowledgement.

I set off for home feeling optimistic but unsure how long the alien feeling would last.

○ ○ ○

It was just gone eight when I arrived at Valeview Terrace. Because of the western hills, some of Ailsworth was already in shadow; I knew all of it would be in shadow before nine. There were people around, but not many. I worked my way down to the High Street and stood on the pavement, wondering what my safest route home would be. By safest, I meant what route would be the least likely for Ollie to patrol to intercept me.

I was aware of a pretty old film called "Billy Liar" and saw it once on TV. I learnt there was a book, so I read it after seeing the film. Because I'd seen the film, I had less patience with the book, but I'm not sure why that should be. It was about a weird young man who couldn't live in the here and now and how he coped. What stuck in my head was that the eponymous hero had two additional ways of thinking besides the regular thinking system! While one of them was paranoia and stuff, the other thinking system was about imagination, where he hid when things didn't suit his way of thinking. I read the book pre-Ollie, but, even though I probably have more reason than most, I never resorted to creating my own fantasy world that I controlled. Thinking about it now, I could see that escaping into a fantasy world would be pointless because my real world would render any escape futile and counterproductive. I was not Billy Liar; I was James Smith trying to face up to the truth. Where I am similar to Billy Liar is in the paranoia stuff.

Standing there on the High Street, I imagined Ollie hiding around every corner of every possible route or combination of routes I could imagine. Indecision leads to inaction, but on what do I base my decision? Was this me becoming Buridan's Ass? I remembered, from primary school, Mister Galloway telling us the story of a donkey or mule (I'm not sure what the difference is, if there is a difference at all) that died. According to Mister Galloway, I put a lot of trust into what primary teachers told me;

the starving donkey found itself standing equidistant between two identical hay bales. Apparently, (that trust thing again) hay to a donkey is like fish and chips to us, but the donkey couldn't decide which hay bale to choose and consequently died of starvation. I disagreed with Mr Galloway's conclusion; I believed the donkey died of procrastination.

We have two fish and chips shops in Ailsworth, and from our house, I'd guess the distance to each establishment would be similar. We use the "Blue Star" fish and chip shop, but I don't know why that is. Did Dad, on his first hunting trip, stop at the junction, toss a coin and then go left? Or was the wind blowing in such a way that his nose made the decision for him? I don't know why he chose the "Blue Star"; I only know that he didn't stop at the junction and starve to death from procrastination.

Anyway, the donkey (or mule) differed from my Dad, and the poor animal couldn't decide between the two options. So, because of its procrastination, it starved to death! Mister Galloway called this a paradox.

I tried to enter paradox in my dictionary, but I wasn't sure if it was applicable. I kept thinking of phrases like, "my friend's enemy is my friend" or, "I must end the friendship to find friends". They seemed like paradoxical statements, but they would only apply to me; they wouldn't convey a paradox to anyone else, leaving them confused.

I needed to make a decision. If Ollie knew I'd been to the Black Lakes, he'd guess what route I'd take home. If Ollie didn't know, he'd probably be keeping an eye on the High Street. Ollie had no qualms about knocking at our door and asking me to come out; he was supremely confident in his power over me. Therefore Mum may well have told him my intended destination. I shrugged and walked toward home, guessing that Ollie hated waiting as much as he hated walking and that he would unlikely be hiding in wait in the backstreets of Ailsworth at this time of day. My decision had taken five long minutes, but I enjoyed these little discussions with myself; they proved that I had options. As I walked, no longer trudging, I smiled as I thought of a paradoxical example. "For one's sanity, it isn't an option to not have options".

5

'What do you mean, he's gone fishing? James hasn't fished for ages,' John Smith was standing in front of his wife, who was sitting down trying to watch her idol Tyrone Power in a bullfighting film alongside Ava Gardner. John Smith had just finished his six-to-three shift and was responding to his wife's answer after he asked where James was.

'I thought you knew about it.'

'James hasn't mentioned fishing for over a year! I had no idea he wanted to go fishing.'

'Don't shout at me; it was you that bought him the fishing permit in April, as I recall. Besides, he looked happier than usual, so I made him some sandwiches and off he went,' her interest in Tyrone was beginning to wane.

'Was he going to pick up Ollie on the way?' John asked.

'I don't think so because Ollie came here to ask for him just before two. He seemed taken aback that James had gone without him,' Martha added. She got up and switched the television off. 'Are you worried about him? Is that why you're angry?'

'I'm not angry; it just seems a bit odd, that's all. Don't you think it's odd?'

'It was unexpected but not odd; I don't understand your reaction, John. He was happy and said he'd be at the Black lakes all day.'

He paced around the small living room, Martha watching, intrigued and worried. John stopped and looked at his wife. 'I'm worried about him, love, that's all. On my way home just now, I stopped for a quick chat with Maude, and she asked me if James was okay, that she was worried he looked tired and that she didn't much care for that Ollie Jenkins boy.'

'Ollie? That doesn't make sense. He's always very polite when he comes here to ask for James, and I've never heard James say anything bad about him; have you?'

Her husband still looked pensive. 'No,' he eventually answered, 'James has never said anything negative about the lad, but I know what Maude means. Whenever I talk to Ollie, he can't seem to hold my gaze and seems furtive; sly if you like.'

'Did Maude give any reason why she doesn't like Ollie, or was it just a gut feeling?'

'I asked what she meant, and she said that Ollie had a dark soul and had once seen him walk behind Laurence, imitating his walk and body shape to entertain a couple of younger boys.'

'Oh, that is cruel! Poor Laurence is a lovely lad. I hope James doesn't do that kind of thing.'

John bowed his head as if looking at his feet before looking into Martha's eyes. 'What upset me was when she said that James always looked unhappy when he was in Ollie's company, that they don't look like two friends.'

'But they're inseparable, love; James is always with him.'

John shook his head. 'If they're so inseparable, then why did James go fishing without telling Ollie anything about it?' He dearly wanted his wife to have the answer, but all she did was look at him, unable to do so.

∘ ∘ ∘

An hour later, John Smith was sitting on the floor in James' bedroom with his back against the small single bed. His eyes were red-rimmed sore, and his cheeks flushed. On his lap lay the James Smith Dictionary 1974/75.

6

It took me twenty minutes to circuitously walk the ten minutes from the High Street home, and I felt relief when I eventually arrived at the front door.

'Hi, it's me,' I announced as I lay the canvas bag on the kitchen table.

Mum came through from the living room and looked at the bag. 'Well?'

With pride, I opened the bag's flap and pulled out the plastic bag with the three lifeless fish huddled together.

'Three? That's brilliant, James! Hand them over so I can clean them and put them in the fridge. We can have them on Monday as a treat.' I did what she asked, and soon she was rinsing them in the kitchen sink. 'Are you hungry? There's a bit of leftover sausage and chips if you don't mind them cold.'

That sounded brilliant to me, and I quickly devoured the leftovers as Mum cleaned out the fish, ensuring that Bambi, our cat, didn't miss out. 'That was lovely, Mum; I was starving,' I said as I carried the plate and left it beside the sink. I leaned toward her and gave her a peck. It felt like the right thing to do. 'Thanks.'

'Did you not enjoy the sandwiches then?' she lifted her smiling face from the thoroughly rinsed sink, although the piscine smell lingered.

'They were lovely, Mum. But it was a longer day than I intended, so that was just what the doctor ordered.'

'Ollie came by, you know.'

'Oh?' My heart pounded.

'Yes, he came by at around two. He seemed shocked that you'd gone fishing without him,' she was studying my face for a reaction. My stomach lurched when I first heard his name, but now I was back in control.

'That's strange; I told him yesterday that I was going. He must've forgotten,' I lied. Lying had become second nature to me, and if I was calm and in control of my emotions, I could reel off lie after lie to cover my shameful secret.

'That's good. I'm glad you haven't fallen out. Six weeks without a friend would be terrible for you. He said he'd come by again tomorrow.'

Now, I wasn't calm, so I decided to shrug rather than say anything else. 'I think I'll turn in, Mum; That hike to the Black lakes was shattering.'

'You do that, love; I'll finish in here and catch what's on telly. See you in the morning.'

'Night, Mum. Oh, has Dad gone to the Railway?' I thought to ask.

'It's Saturday night, isn't it?' she tilted her head to indicate that it had been a stupid question. She usually answers that question with a question about the Pope's religion, but tonight it was a silent tilt of her head. I smiled and ascended to my bedroom, unsure about the next phase of the plan.

○ ○ ○

As I lay on my bed, the only thing I could envisage was Ollie's anger, an anger of unimaginable magnitude focused narrowly on me. I'd read about scales such as Richter's, Beaufort's, Decibel's, Kelvin's, and Moh's, but never heard of a specific scale for anger. If there were such a scale, probably called Jenkin's Scale, Ollie would be registering a ten. He would also be registering a ten on the Anger Retention Scale.

When you've witnessed venting, or, more accurately, felt the venting of someone's anger, it's not something you ever forget. It's the eyes mainly, the hatred they contain. Apart from their function of holding in the aqueous humour and vitreous gel, I never thought of eyes as receptacles for feeling and emotion, but

I can vouch for their presence. I've seen eyes unable to control the hatred within and bulging and distorting under the pressure of such incandescence. When those eyes reflect your fear, the combination is overwhelming, and as I wearily lay on my bed, they were all I could see. I turned around, pulled the cover over my right shoulder and tried again.

I started to calm down and closed my eyes once more. The hateful eyes were still there but seemed more distant, less important. Suddenly, Mr Renshaw stepped in front of the eyes, followed by Mr Crabtree, Mr Graham, Doris, and Maude. With my eyes closed, I smiled at my new defensive wall, and despite their average age being in excess of sixty, I felt so much safer that I quickly fell asleep.

7

I experienced an alien sense of well-being when I opened my eyes on Sunday morning. Ollie's eyes were a distant memory, and I kept getting flashbacks of the happiness I'd found yesterday through chatting, walking, listening, grasshoppers, bamboo, fish, and the tranquillity of the lakes. I felt safe and happy in bed and then allowed myself to start focusing on the day ahead. I stretched the sleep out of my bones and sat up. I looked at my watch; it was half past eight! My plan!

My bedroom window, located directly above the back door, was always cracked open during summer. As I jumped up and found that my alarm clock was missing, I heard a determined knock on the door. I froze, not daring to move from the edge of the bed. Another knock, and after a brief delay, someone opened the door.

'Good morning, Ollie. How may I help?' Dad asked jovially. Despite my panic, I was confused about why Dad was up so early. Sunday morning was his lie-in day, especially after a night at the Railway.

'Good morning, Mr Smith. I was wondering if James was coming out to play?' the disguised voice still had a powerful impact on my stomach.

'Oh, but he's gone fishing, Ollie. Didn't he tell you?'

'Uh, no sir, I, I didn't know. Did he say where he was going, by any chance? I forgot to ask yesterday.'

'Yes, Ollie, he said he might try the Black lakes. Do you know where they are?'

'Uh, not really, Mr Smith. I'm not much for fishing, as it happens,' Ollie answered.

'So, do you want to know where they are, or will you wait for him to return? I think he said he'd be back for eight,' Dad still sounded upbeat.

'No, it's okay, Mr Smith; I'll catch him tomorrow,' I felt Ollie stare up at my window and heard steps moving away. Our door closed, the house secure again. I rolled back onto the bed, pulled the blankets over me, and stared at the ceiling.

What had just happened? Why did Dad lie and do it so convincingly? I lay there pondering.

My Dictionary!

I jumped out of bed and kneeled to pull Grandad's old leather case from underneath. This was where I kept old schoolwork, exercise books, homework, and test papers. I stored the Dictionary under all the documents and books, and to my relief, it was still there. I tidied everything up, pushed the case back, and lay back in bed to analyse the morning's turn of events. Before I could delve into my thoughts, the bedroom door opened slowly, followed by a light knock; it was Dad.

'Morning, sleepy head. I thought Mum told me you'd be fishing again this morning?'

I smiled. 'That was my intention, Dad, but I was so tired after yesterday that I didn't wake up in time. And for some reason, my alarm clock's gone walkabout.'

'It's a tough old walk up to the Blacks, isn't it? I thought you'd be tired, so I decided to remove your alarm clock. You needed the rest.' He placed the alarm clock back on my set of drawers. 'Good fish, by the way, impressive sizes for the Blacks. Was it Minor or Major?' he asked.

I smiled at his use of different names. 'All three were from the Great, Dad. Two were on Greenwell's and one on the Bonddu.' It was great talking like this to my hero.

'Wow, I'm so pleased for you, son. Did you see anyone up there?'

'Yes, I met a Mr Renshaw, said he knew you and suggested I start practising fly-fishing if I have a spare half-hour or so during my next expedition.'

Dad nodded. 'I know Tom quite well. He lives on Dover Terrace with his wife. They don't have kids, but they're a lovely couple, and he's a keen angler. I think he's the treasurer of the AADAA.'

The Ailsworth and District Angling Association has been well known to me since I joined when I was eight; Dad and Edward were already members. There are quite a few members around Ailsworth, and I know of some keen as mustard kids, following in their Dads' footsteps. 'He did seem keen,' I added. 'And I saw him catch one just as I was leaving,' the conversation was now becoming strained.

Dad seemed to think the same thing and fell silent as he struggled to restart our chat. After a while, he seemed happy to resume. 'Last night, at the Railway, I had a conversation with Peter Crabtree. He said he saw you yesterday.'

I looked into Dad's eyes to try to understand what was happening. This chat was great, but it was still weird, uncomfortable, and strained, like two people talking in a stuck lift. I wanted to scream into Dad's face, but I didn't; I carried on talking to my fellow lift passenger. 'Yeah, he was taking the rubbish out, said he knew you.'

'Well, he made a strange request last night.'

'Oh?' My heart beat faster.

'Yeah, he asked if I'd be happy for you to go to his house to play chess. Did you two chat about chess or something?' he asked.

Now, this explained some of Dad's weirdness; I'd struck up a conversation with an older man, and Dad must be wondering about the implications. I felt relieved and relaxed immediately. 'Don't blame me,' I chided. 'Apparently, it's you who's been telling him about me. Now he has an inflated expectation of my chess skills that is sure to disappoint him.'

Dad smiled broadly.

He has a kind face, but Edward and I have seen the other side and have suffered a few open-handed slappings to our legs and arms. The beatings were fairly regular and usually came about after we'd disobeyed an instruction for the third time. Most of the time they happened as we tried to settle for the night.

○ ○ ○

DAD: noun

- *My Hero*
- *My heaviest burden.*

○ ○ ○

The scene always began with Dad shouting from the bottom of the stair. Edward and me shared the same bed in the second bedroom at the time. Since then, Dad has adapted the attic, and that's been Edward's den since he was thirteen.

'Edward and James! Stop teasing each other! Go to sleep.' We ease off, but inevitably we start up again.

'Edward and James! I told you two! I'm not telling you again!' We'd look at each other and lower our voices to the barest whisper. We'd continue to tease but soon forgot about the volume, and the next thing we'd hear was Dad pounding up the stairs. Edward and I would immediately separate and turn our backs on each other. The serenity Edward and I tried to convey made no difference to the outcome. Dad would crash through the door and lift the sheets to slap Edward on the thighs before going over to my side and slapping my thighs to complete his message. Thinking back, being second was worse because I knew what was coming; Edward and me should've swapped sides. It's funny how you solve a problem when the problem's not there to solve anymore; I suppose that's what they mean by "in the cold light of day" or "easy in hindsight".

'Why don't you two listen? If you think I enjoy doing this, you're wrong!' We never answered at this stage; our stinging thighs reminded us to keep quiet. 'Your mother and I have had a very long day, and all we ask is for peace during the evening. Is that too much to ask from you two?' We remained silent as he walked back down.

If Dad was having a late one at the Railway, it would be Mum stepping in like an apprentice leg slapper. The scene would play out much the same way but with one significant difference – Mum's slaps were more painful. I tried to analyse why her slaps hurt more than Dad's and could only put it down to the lack of flesh on her palm. Her slaps were open-handed like Dad's, but the skin of her palm was shiny smooth, whereas Dad's palm was pudgier and kinder to our flesh.

While on the subject of slaps, parents weren't the only ones dishing them out. Teachers regularly meted out various forms of slap punishment, but on the whole, I avoided their attention because I was quiet and unremarkable. One exception happened this year, and it still makes me embarrassed.

After our double Physics lesson in the lab, it was customary for our class to wait outside our form room to await the conclusion of the sixth-form students' maths lesson. I don't know why they used our room, but use it they did. For some reason, I found myself at the front of our queue, waiting for Mr Murdoch to finish. Ollie was directly behind me.

'Put your ear to the door, James; they may have already gone,' Ollie instructed. This seemed a reasonable thing to do, so I put my ear to the door and heard voices. Before I could report back, Ollie shoved me against the door.

The door to our form room was temperamental when it came to staying closed, and Mr Murdoch had placed a chair against the door knob to guarantee against such a variable. As I hit the door, I overcame Mr Murdoch's Heath Robinson solution, and the force propelled the chair against the first row of desks. My poor, unbalanced body followed and ended up in a heap on the floor with my physics exercise books resting under a student's shoe in the front row. I jumped up and bent to pick up my books amid total silence. Mr Murdoch walked menacingly toward me.

'Uh, sorry, sir, I tripped and fell against the door. Sorry, sir.'

He stopped in front of me and stared silently into my face. Mr Murdoch was red-haired, and his head had somehow grown through this hair, leaving a few strands that bridged from right to left and others that bridged left to right. He was a good maths teacher and an excellent footballer, always starring for the teachers at the end of year match against the sixth-formers.

After quietly studying me for a few seconds, he magically whipped his right hand and slapped me hard against my left cheek.

It was like the grasshopper! One second, his hands were by his sides, and then bang! I never saw the transition, but I'll keep this new comparison to myself; Mr Murdoch won't like being compared to an insect.

The slap was deafening, and my cheek tingled hot. As Mr Murdoch was standing with his back to his class of maths students, I could see them all laughing silently at my misfortune.

'Get out, and wait patiently out there until we leave. Is that clear, Smith?'

'Yes, sir, very clear,' I think I gave a little bow and walked out as Mr Murdoch slammed the door shut behind me.

Outside in the corridor, everyone in the class was doubled up laughing. That was Ollie's crowning moment because even I could see it was funny. What my laughing classmates ignored in order to justify their merriment was far from entertaining and far more sinister.

○ ○ ○

I love my parents and know that they love us as well. And, apart from having to control our indiscipline, they are kind and gentle. Dad was smiling, and this made his face look very thoughtful. He's sort of overweight, but not if that makes sense. His face, arms, and legs look slim and athletic, but his belly is a bit more rounded, and his chin is difficult to distinguish. His hair is dark, but some white bits are showing at the ends despite using Brylcreem. I always think of Dad as hard, probably because he regularly describes the fights he used to get into as a kid and how Seargent Burns, the local bobby, slapped him whenever their paths crossed. If I expressed horror about Seargent Burns' treatment, Dad shrugged it off, saying it was Burns' way of punishing him for the inevitable crime he was sure to commit as soon as the policeman's back was turned. I was even more shocked when he explained that he'd only told his father once about Burns' system because his father suspected that Seargent Burns must have had a good reason for administering the slap. So, in support of the local constabulary, his father gave him an additional beating and sent him to bed early.

'I have no issue with you going to Peter's to play chess. It will do you good to challenge yourself, and more importantly, you can tell me how good Peter actually is.'

'When did he want me to go over? Did he say?' I asked.

'Peter's not the religious type, so he asked if you could go over to his house by around ten if that fits in with your plan for the day?' Dad was giving me options. The idea of playing chess was great, but all I could think of was the journey to Valeview Terrace and the chances of not being spotted by Ollie.

As if reading my mind, Dad continued. 'I'm going over to fill up the car this morning. I can drop you off on the High Street if you like.'

'I'm not so tired that I can't walk to Mr Crabtree's house, Dad!' I mocked outrage.

'Not saying you are, son. I'm saying that I'm going for petrol at around ten, and you're welcome to share a lift, and if that insults you in any way, please refuse the offer.'

Damn, he called my bluff, so I pretended to think for a few seconds. 'Oh well, if you are going that way, then it would be silly not to keep you company. Thanks, Dad.'

'Right, get yourself ready, and I'll see you downstairs for breakfast,' he turned and left.

After getting myself ready, I sat on the edge of my made bed and tried to assess what remained of the plan. I realised that the initial plan was to make myself disappear by going to remote lakes for whole days. In retrospect, that initial plan hadn't considered the British summer, the inevitable rainfall, and the tediousness of a full day's fishing. So, now that Dad had given me an excuse, I could metaphorically go fishing by playing chess with Mr Crabtree. So, in addition to my fishing expeditions, I could fill my days doing other stuff, so long as Ollie didn't know. I smiled and left my bedroom feeling very optimistic.

8

Dad's red Hillman Avenger was his pride and joy. It wasn't new when he bought it, but it was a considerable step up from our old Vauxhall Viva that had seen much better days. The Avenger was far cooler but didn't go that fast, and that didn't matter; it was the best car we'd ever owned.

Dad is a postman - Mum tells everyone he's a PHG (Postman Higher Grade) because he's in charge of the sorting office at Ailsworth Post Office. Despite being a PHG, I don't think he's well paid, and Mum works part-time at the Post Office counter, selling stamps and dealing with people's Giro's and stuff – don't ask me what Giro is; all I know is that it's something to do with money. Mum works Tuesdays and Thursdays, and on those days, Grandma Elsie looks after the house, including the cooking!

Because we live close to the school, we always walk home for lunch. I love lunch at home because it gives me a break from Ollie. The problem with Tuesdays and Thursdays was Gran's cooking. I don't know why that should be because whenever we'd go to her house in North Ailsworth, her home was filled with the beautiful aroma of slow-cooked lamb and homemade rice pudding. In our house, however, she just burned everything. We have a fixed menu for the week, Tuesday is sausage and mash, and Thursday is liver, onions, and mash. These sound like easy meals, even to me. In Gran's hands, for some reason, the diametric ratio of sausage meat to skin dwindles from the usual forty to one down to three to one. The skin was so thick that I'd swear the sausage meat had made a run for it, knowing who the day's cook was. Gran could also convert the usually moist liver into one of the most hygroscopic materials known to man. The moment I started chewing, my entire stock of saliva was drawn to my mouth, only to disappear as Gran's liver absorbed every moisture molecule thrown at it by my inadequate salivary glands.

The one good thing about the liver was that it made me enjoy the lumpy mash a bit more.

I felt guilty about moaning to Mum about Grandma Elsie's cooking, but I couldn't help it. Food is an emotive subject. Also, whenever Ollie didn't demand my immediate attendance after school, I'd rush home, hoping to watch a cartoon to relax. However, if Gran Elsie were covering for Mum, we'd have no option but to sit through an episode of Crossroads and miss the start. Edward gave up trying to change her mind, but I tried my best by demeaning the Crossroads characters she loved so much and took them to be real people. Despite my nastiness, Gran ignored me and stayed focused on her motel people, and I, too, have now given up trying to change her ways. When we did complain, Mum and Dad always told Edward and me we should be grateful for Elsie's support. Without it, as they kept telling us, Mum would have to give up her job, and we'd never be able to afford nice things like the Hillman Avenger.

○ ○ ○

After Dad pulled into the filling station, he got out and chatted with Mr Graham. Having not seen any sign of Ollie on the way, I decided to go for it and opened my door. I stood for a while and looked over to Dad and Mr Graham. 'I'm off then, Dad. I'll see you later,' I shouted, as the petrol pump was quite noisy.

'See you later, James. Remember to try your best, and I'll tell Bill about your catch yesterday,' he replied and leaned towards Mr Graham to explain what was about to happen and to tell him about the three trout. As I walked away from them, I imagined myself as Gary Cooper walking through the middle of Hadleyville, alone and about to meet my nemesis, Potato Pete.

○ ○ ○

Mr Peter Crabtree lived in a detached house called Pomme de Terre that stood between the two halves of Valeview Terrace. The house looked wrong. It wasn't because it was detached; the house looked wrong because it stood a few feet shorter than the terraced houses on either side. It almost looked like a model house, painted white with the four front sash windows framed by decorous stones painted black. I knew these were sash windows because Dad had just replaced ours with casement windows despite me preferring the style of the older windows.

I knocked on the weathered door after I failed to locate any doorbell. Dad fitted one to our door, but it ran out of battery regularly, and visitors had to resort to using their knuckles when they failed to hear the chimes. The doorbell was funniest when the battery was about to run out, and it managed one last feeble out-of-tune ding-doooong.

I knocked again and waited. After a few seconds, I heard some scuffling, and Mr Crabtree soon opened the door. His appearance took me by surprise. He wore dark slacks, a white shirt, and what looked like a school-issue tie. He'd slicked his grey/white hair left to right, which appeared well moisturised. He looked formal, despite his rosy cheeks and lack of height.

'Come in, James, my boy; the board awaits in the parlour,' he enthused and stood to one side to allow me into the hall.

'Thank you, Mr Crabtree,' then, as I walked past, I remembered. 'Oh, how's the ingrowing toenail?' He seemed confused by the question, so I sought to explain. 'Yesterday, you said that you had an ingrowing toenail?'

The penny dropped immediately. 'Oh, that. I'm afraid I was teasing you, James, answering your charming felicitation with a rather sorry attempt at levity.' I suddenly had the feeling that this could be a long day.

'Keep going down the hallway; the battlefield is in the parlour opposite the kitchen, and you should remember where that is,' he instructed. I walked down the dark hallway and opened the parlour door. It was a dark room; it was Mr Crabtree's room. It may not have been to the scale or clutter that was Miss Havisham's, but the room gave me that same feeling of a black-and-white Dickensian film. Film noir would describe it nicely, with its dark wooden panelling propping up the ornate Dado rail that ran around the room, interrupted only by the door, window and unlit fireplace. The darkened yellow walls were perfect for the large sepia-toned family portraits housed in an eclectic collection of dark gothic frames. A long bookcase covered the wall behind the door, filled with all manner of books and magazines. Looking beyond the single armchair and coffee table positioned by the fireplace, I could see a dark table below the window. On either end of the oval table stood two high-backed wooden chairs, and in the middle of the table, silhouetted by light streaming through the dirty window and net curtains, stood Mr Crabtree's chessboard. Great Expectations. As I approached, I saw the turned and carved wooden playing pieces standing to attention like two opposing armies awaiting their generals to lead them to victory or defeat.

Behind me, Mr Crabtree switched on the light. The weak light gave the impression of making the room seem darker, even though that was impossible. 'Choose your station, young James.'

I turned and saw Mr Crabtree, palms open, giving me an option. 'I believe I shall opt for the chair to my left, if that's okay, Mr Crabtree.'

'That is perfectly fine, James. I have prepared some ham and tomato sandwiches, and I think it would be wise for us to consume the repast within the next hour, which will give us ample time and opportunity to reveal our opening gambits. Are you in agreement, or do you worry it might disturb your train of thought?'

'Firstly, I must thank you for preparing the meal; secondly, I don't believe a break, such as the one you suggest, will affect my game plan,' I smiled. Internally, however, I was cringing at the parodying nature of my words.

It was something I'd done all my life; I couldn't help myself. Whenever I was in the company of my cousins from Liverpool, I kept adding the phrase "you know like" into every sentence. I knew I was doing it, but my brain, or whatever controls that reaction, couldn't stop me. Apart from one instance in school where Mr Parkinson, our Physics teacher, asked if I was taking the mickey, I got away with it. Mr Crabtree, although he didn't mention it, did seem to notice because I saw a distinct raising of his eyebrows as I spoke.

'Very well then, James. Take up your chosen throne, and we shall commence,' Mr Crabtree sounded excited. I took my seat and looked down at the chessboard. It looked daunting, with the light from the window creating a sense of drama as it overpowered the weak room light. Mr Crabtree picked up two pawns and hid them behind his back. After a short while, he produced his two clenched hands and presented them to me. Again, I chose the left and saw the white pawn as he opened his fingers. 'Ah, so it will be you first to move, James,' the excitement seemed to be building up inside Mr Crabtree to the point that he seemed almost giddy. 'This is so exciting,' he said as he replaced his pawn and took his seat, or was it his throne?

As I looked down at the board, I became aware of a strange-looking pair of clocks housed in a single unit positioned between the chessboard and the window. 'Uh, I'm afraid I've never used one of those,' I said hesitantly, pointing at the timepiece as my confidence evaporated through the window.

"Worry not, dear James; it is simplicity itself. As you can see, I have set the two clocks to five thirty, indicating a thirty-minute contest. After you have completed the opening move, simply press the button nearest to you. This will activate my clock alone, initiating it to move inexorably towards six. When I complete my move, I will press my button, and it will then be the turn of your clock to start. This means that the longest possible game is?'

'It will be one hour plus the time I take to make the first move,' I offered.

'Precisely; so shall we commence?'

I nodded and, with my heart thumping and my head in a strange Dickensian parallel universe, I moved the King's pawn forward two steps.

'Press the button,' Mr Crabtree instructed, as I'd already forgotten the lecture about the clock.

'Sorry,' I blurted and pressed the button. Immediately our silence was broken by the rhythmic ticking of Mr Crabtree's clock.

Within a few seconds, he countered with his own King's Pawn and theatrically hit the button to start my clock. I had decided to open with the King's gambit and duly moved the Bishop's pawn two steps to stand alongside my first pawn. I hit the button.

'Oh, dear, I believe you have made your first mistake, James,' he said as he duly took my pawn with his. I only had a thin grasp of the intricacies of chess but had studied the King's gambit, so I moved the King side knight with the plan to develop the centre. Now my entire knowledge of chess had gone. All I knew was that position was more important than pieces, up to a point. Mr Crabtree, however, seemed not to understand this and very soon, I was able to develop the King's side attack even after sacrificing my knight, another move that Mr Crabtree thought was erroneous. With fourteen minutes left on my clock, Mr Crabtree was in a losing position, and I started feeling guilty. Where I had studied some aspects of chess, it was clear that Mr Crabtree only reacted to my moves rather than develop his position. As I studied his responses, he seemed to treat chess like draughts; Mr Crabtree only knew how the chess pieces moved. I decided to keep playing in the same manner, and three moves later, it was checkmate. As I moved the Queen to complete the game, I felt deeply uneasy, not knowing how Mr Crabtree would react. As I released my hold on the Queen and pressed the button to start his clock, I decided not to say that fateful word. Instead, I studied his face as he contemplated an escape that wasn't possible.

With his head supported by both hands, Mr Crabtree, having shaken his head each time an escape evaporated, eventually looked up at me. 'Well, James, you seem to have me soundly beaten, and I believe this to be checkmate. Do you agree?'

'Yes, Mr Crabtree, I do believe it to be so.'

'Excellent! That was most exciting, and I seem to have a very worthy adversary sitting opposite me. I suggest we take a break from our mental jousting and repair to the kitchen for sustenance.'

I had never heard the word repair used in that context and assumed it meant adjourn. 'Yes, Mr Crabtree, I think that is an excellent suggestion,' I answered, even though I sounded more like Oliver Twist than James Smith.

∘ ∘ ∘

After discussing some aspects of our first contest, Mr Crabtree fell silent, and an awkwardness descended around the kitchen table where we were seated. While I could respond to someone, I found it challenging to initiate a conversation and sat there finishing off the delicious sandwich and sipping my tea.

After the most protracted silence between us, Mr Crabtree looked up. 'I do hope you take this observation in the spirit in which it is intended,' he seemed to need a sign to carry on, so I nodded, despite being apprehensive about what he'd observed. 'I believe you to be an unusual boy, James,' he continued and watched for my reaction. 'Look, I do not wish to patronise you by calling you a boy, but it is the correct phrase, and I choose the word unusual because I've based my observation on boys of similar age that live and play in Ailsworth.'

I was feeling uncomfortable. 'I'm not sure I know what spirit you expect me to take, Mr Crabtree.'

'I'm not everyone's cup of tea, as I'm sure you know, James. In fact, many people find me tiresome and possibly pretentious. This is an unfortunate belief on their part because I speak in this manner deliberately in order to protect myself from being drowned in the colloquial tsunami of Ailsworth's language.'

'But speaking with a local dialect or vocabulary is what separates us from Liverpool or Manchester, for example. I can't see that as being a problem, Mr Crabtree.'

'Oh, no, you have mistaken my meaning, James. I have no issue with our local dialect; it is just that I do not wish to comply with the rigours of fitting in,' I must have looked blank. 'I'll attempt to elucidate. Not many people have time for me, which suits my needs perfectly. You see, I only wish to make acquaintances with people who see through my prose and can identify a kindred spirit. Your father is one such human being,' a surge of pride swept through me again. 'He knows I am a staunch socialist and share strong political ideals. He also knows I'm not a child molester, unlike many in Ailsworth who believe I am. He has taken the time to understand me rather than judge me on those wicked rumours he must have heard,' he fell silent.

'I'm a bit lost, Mr Crabtree. You said that I was unusual?'

'Sorry, James, I meandered. Yes, I wanted to explain that most children around Ailsworth will shout things at me, usually to my back, after I have walked past them; pervy Pete is their current favourite,' he looked at me to gauge my reaction. I'd also heard these nicknames, and for some reason, I felt guilty for having listened to them and said nothing in his defence. 'One of the worst offenders is your friend, Ollie Jenkins. He doesn't even wait for me to pass, preferring to say it to my face. I ignore it, of course, as one should do whenever someone vocalises ignorance, but this is the point I want to make. Firstly, I see you as having different sensibilities to the Ailsworth boys and would never expect you to utter such rubbish. Secondly, because of my first point, I fail to understand why you would befriend such a philistine.'

I felt ashamed. 'I'm sorry, Mr Crabtree. I have heard children say derogatory things about you, and I'm afraid I never stand up to defend you.'

'No, James! I could never expect a child, let alone an adult, to break ranks with their peers to defend me. I'm saying that you, James Smith, do not behave as they do. I remember you delivering my groceries, and it warmed my heart to meet a young person who behaved with such manners. You should be proud of yourself, James, but herein lies the conundrum; your friendship with the boorish Jenkins' boy,' he stared at me, and I knew I had to form an answer.

'It's complicated, Mr Crabtree. Ollie isn't all bad; he simply shows off in front of people. If you got to know him, you'd realise that he often puts up a false façade to fit in himself.' As I lied to Mr Crabtree, I felt nauseous. This was not the first time I'd defended Ollie in the face of similar questions, and at the end of a day where I'd defended him, I always analysed why I'd done so.

My justification for defending him came from picturing the opposite, where I'd agreed with the question and admitted that Ollie Jenkins was an evil human being. If I ever came out with the truth, I would also have to be evil because of our perceived friendship. I would either be evil or under his control, and my shame would not allow me to admit to being under his control. People would see the real me, a spineless excuse for a human being. At least by defending Ollie to inquisitive people, I hid the real me.

Mr Crabtree smiled. 'No, James. Ollie Jenkins is a malicious young man, and your defence of him raises worrying concerns in my silly head. Would you like another cup of tea?'

The statement surprised me. 'Yes, Mr Crabtree, that would be nice,' I answered quickly, but in reality, I wanted to return to the chess. Mr Crabtree got up and went over to the electric kettle. As I watched him fuss around the kitchen, I felt trapped and started to believe that the chess had been a simple ruse to get me into his house in order to interrogate me. I was losing control of my safe world, which I'd created to minimise the effects of Ollie's cruelty.

He returned to the kitchen table with a fresh teapot. 'We'll allow it to infuse for five minutes while I try to defend my insinuation that you are an unusual boy, shall we?'

'I'm rather uncomfortable with this, Mr Crabtree, and would welcome a change to some other subject if that's okay?'

He appeared to be concerned. 'No, James. This is your defence mechanism kicking in, and while I admire it, it will always prevent you from resolving things. You see, I admire how you have changed your conversation style and adapted to mine,' as he said these words, I felt sick, exposed as a sham. 'What this trait shows, however, is a severe lack of confidence in what *your* identity is. You are a chameleon, James, and chameleons only use their disguise as a defensive mechanism. Can I assume, should you find yourself in the company of young adults who constantly swore, that you would also swear in equal measure and adapt your grammar accordingly?'

He was so accurate that I smiled. 'Yes, Mr Crabtree, it's something I'm aware that I do, but, try as I might, I cannot break out of the habit.'

'Good, I'm pleased you said that, James. But what's strange is that, even though I've observed you with Ollie Jenkins, you never adopt *his* persona and mannerisms, and this is for a reason. A defence mechanism such as yours will not adapt to Ollie's environment because that environment lies outside your moral compass. So my question to you is, why on earth are you a friend to Ollie Jenkins? The answer to that is personal to you, James, and it would be unfair for me to push this further, but I would suggest that this friendship of yours is another form of your defence mechanism, and you use it to protect other people or other people's feelings.'

I couldn't speak. I wanted to, but I knew I would cry if I did. As it was, my eyes watered up beyond their capacity, and silent tears ran down my cheeks as I held Mr Crabtree's kind gaze. I sat there looking straight at him as he smiled, nodded, and poured the tea.

∘ ∘ ∘

Nothing further was said about Ollie Jenkins and my defence mechanisms. Instead, we returned to the chess and completed four more games before deciding we'd had enough. Mr Crabtree improved as the afternoon progressed, but with a final score of four matches to one, it was clear that the chess had been a ruse to talk to me.

As I shook Mr Crabtree's hand to thank him for a very interesting day, he said, 'I have lived in Ailsworth all my life, James, and I love the town and its populace, but I live here on my terms, not on anyone else's and this makes me content. I am sure you can also achieve a similar state of contentment and love for your town as you gain the self-confidence required by believing in yourself and trusting others.'

'Thank you, Mr Crabtree. I'm not sure what I'm feeling at this moment, and I am finding this difficult. Please believe me when I say I *am* trying to change my situation, so I was grateful to you for allowing me to wriggle free,' he nodded. 'Even though I didn't answer, I know I need to change to find my elusive self-confidence.'

'So I take it that will be the second thing you learned today?'

'What would have been the first?'

'That I can't play chess.'

I laughed and decided to ask a question, driven by a need to know. 'Mr Crabtree, I do not wish to appear rude or insensitive, but are you a homosexual?'

He placed his hands on his hips and gave the impression of being outraged. 'James Smith! You truly are a quick learner. I have given you the merest of nudges towards self-confidence, and you see fit to ask such a question? Truly remarkable.'

I blushed immediately and wanted to retract the question. 'I'm sorry, Mr Crabtree, that was rude of me.'

'No, James; that was brave of you, and the answer is complicated.'

'There's no need…' he ignored me.

'You see, I was married to Sally Draper for ten years before her tragic death at thirty-eight. We didn't have children, and since then, I have lived alone here in this house. Even before she died, I felt different to others in the town, but after she died, I took more of an interest in art in all its various forms. You see, young James, I believe I have always been a homosexual, but societal norms led me to believe that Sally was right for me. Don't get me wrong, I truly loved Sally and was bereft when the hospital gave us the news of her disease, but deep down, I knew,' he fell silent and lowered his head.

'Do you have a partner?' I asked.

He looked up, his eyes swimming in tears. 'No, James, I have never undertaken a homosexual act; I simply know I am so.'

'But that is so sad, Mr Crabtree. It is both sad and goes against the advice you have been trying to give me. You said that you didn't care about fitting in.'

The tears were running freely down his cheeks now. 'I still love Sally, James, and I know that if I did follow my natural path, people who remember Sally would dismiss our love and say it had all been a sham. It wasn't a sham, and I loved her very much.'

Looking at Mr Crabtree, I felt an extreme need to comfort him, so I stepped forward and hugged him. It was the right thing for me to do; it was the confident thing to do.

We stood there sharing each other's pain until he gently moved me away. 'Thank you, James Smith. You are indeed your father's son; he should be very proud of you. I will not tell him of my suspicions; that can only come from you, James. Take your time and take back your life when you are ready to do so. Until then, you are welcome here anytime to teach me more about chess.'

I nodded. 'Thank you, Mr Crabtree; I will bear that in mind,' I turned and made my way out.

∘ ∘ ∘

Once outside, I made my way down to the High Street. Despite being only five o'clock, I felt confident enough to navigate back home without bumping into Ollie and duly took the circuitous backstreet route.

Having covered over half the distance home, I turned a corner, and my heart almost stopped. As I rounded the corner, I saw Ollie's distinct shape. I immediately stopped and backed up out of sight. With my heart pounding harder than it had for days, I ventured a peek around the corner, and it confirmed my worst fear. Ollie was facing young Ernest Taynor, a boy who was two school years our junior and sneering into his face.

'I haven't seen him, Ollie, honest,' Ernie pleaded. I pulled back out of sight and listened.

'Somebody must have seen the little shit!' he snarled.

'I'll ask around, Ollie, and if anyone's seen him, I'll get back to you, okay?'

'Make sure you do, you little shit, or it'll be more than a slap next time, okay?'

'Okay, Ollie, I promise to get back to you, honest.'

'Fuck off out of my sight, or I'll hit you again, you little cunt.'

I knew that Ernie lived in the opposite direction to where I was hiding, but I had no idea which way Ollie would take, so I ran back until the backstreet emerged on Victoria Street. There, I took a sharp right and ran along Victoria Street until I could turn onto Jubilee Road. Even though I knew Ollie was as sporty as a three-toed sloth from Central America, adrenaline was fuelling my legs, and I didn't stop running until I came to our street. I bent over double and grabbed my thighs as I fought to suck air back into my burning lungs. As the haze of panic lifted and my breathing eased, I walked up the street towards our house.

9

'Hi, squirt, where've you been, then? Playing with lardarse Jenkins again?' Edward asked as he came out of our gate.

Seeing him lifted my spirits, but I had to joust. 'Well, hello, S.H; nice to see you awake. No, I've been playing chess, if you must know,' I knew he hated me calling him Ed Sleepy Head, but he did seem to spend an inordinately long time in his bedroom.

'Chess? With lardarse? Now I know you're lying.'

'No, I've been at Mr Crabtree's house, and we played five games.'

'Pervy Pete's? Jesus Christ, squirt, did Dad know you were going there?' he looked pretty concerned.

'No, Mr Crabtree saw me and asked if I wanted to see some pups, and when we were in there, we played this weird version of chess.'

'Fuck off, I know when you're pulling my plonker, you little shit,' he smiled broadly.

'Of course, Dad knew; he even drove me there. So don't worry about me; I'm more concerned about you.'

'What's that supposed to mean?'

'You calling Mr Crabtree pervy, it's not nice, and it's not justified.'

'Oo, listen to Mister Perfect here. It was only a joke; you know I don't believe those stories,' he sounded wounded.

'Yes, but by joking, you're normalising the untruth. It's not fair.'

'Jesus Christ, Jamie, get off that high horse of yours and come down to planet earth, why don't you?' Edward fell silent for a while as I kept looking at him. Eventually, he ruffled my hair. 'You're right, though; there are too many people around here, only too ready to besmirch people without actually knowing what they're like. Good on you, squirt; I like what you just said; it was sorta cool.' With that, he turned and started to walk up the hill.

I decided to push my luck, even though I knew it could end badly. 'Where are you off to anyway? Going to play with gay Graham?'

Edward turned around with a thunderous frown on his face. I'd gone too far, and as he marched back towards me, I almost ran into the house; instead, I stood my ground.

'Why the fuck did you say that?' he whisper-shouted after lowering his face to mine.

'It's what the kids at school call him, and I thought I'd let you know,' I answered nervously.

He stood straight with his hands on his hips and looked around before looking back at me. 'When was the first time you heard them call Graham that?'

'It was during the Easter holidays, and Ollie asked if you were still hanging around Graham. That's when he told me that some older kids called him gay.'

'Jesus Christ, James, you've known since then? And you didn't tell me?'

'Why would I say anything? You've been away at college, and I have no problems with anyone being gay. I only said it to show how hurtful rumours can be. I'm sorry, Edward; I can see I've upset you.'

He pulled me close and hugged me; it was a wonderful feeling, but for some reason, I began to cry. Edward hugged me tighter. 'I'm so sorry, James. I haven't been much of a big brother to you, have I? I'm sorry, mate, but I've been going through some stuff and needed to get my head straight.' He was struggling to explain, and I didn't want him to, so I pushed myself away and looked at him.

'I don't want to know, Ed; I honestly don't. I only want you to know that I understand stuff, and I'm not like the other kids. I'm only just learning I need to trust people and be honest because by doing that, I'll get through this phase of my life and come out of it a decent human being.'

Edward shook his head and smiled, 'Jesus Christ, Jamie, I've never heard you speak like this. All you usually do is play with your mate and then skulk around in silence until you get off to bed to read books,' he suddenly looked serious. 'You are okay, aren't you?'

'I'm fine, Ed; I'm okay,' I reassured him.

He seemed to consider something. 'You know that rumour about Graham.'

'Yes.'

'I'd appreciate it if you didn't say anything to Mum or Dad. You know how they might get the wrong end of the stick and stuff.'

I considered my answer and rubbed my chin for dramatic effect. 'I will never tell Mum or Dad anything that they should only hear from you. Is that good enough for you?'

Edward shook his head in disbelief. 'You're a clever little fucker, aren't you?' I shrugged.

'All I can tell you is that Dad understands stuff, and he might surprise you with his attitude towards that rumour about Graham.'

'Jesus Christ, I can't believe I'm having this conversation with my little brother. What the fuck's happening?' I assumed it was rhetorical. 'Right,' he continued, 'I've got to go; see you soon. Oh, and by the way, Uncle Harry's staying over for a couple of nights.' With that, he bounded away, leaving me alone in the street. As he disappeared over the hill, I turned and walked into the house, preparing myself to face Uncle Harry.

10

Harry Smith is bombastic (I think it's the right word) compared to Dad, his older brother. Where Dad digests information carefully before assuming he understands stuff well enough to express an opinion, Uncle Harry vocalises his views at every opportunity, with little or no in-depth understanding.

'You must take Uncle Harry with a sizeable pinch of salt, preferably a handful,' Dad would always say after a whirlwind visit from his kid brother. There was a six-year gap between the two, which meant that Dad was too old for National Service in the nineteen-fifties, but Uncle Harry wasn't and duly spent two years preparing to fight for Queen and Country. He still did a lot for the Legion in his home town of Longridge, north of Preston, where he was their treasurer.

After understanding his ways, I now get along with Uncle Harry, but it wasn't always like that. He didn't have a filter on his mouth, which could catch you unaware if you were of a sensitive disposition. One day, Uncle Harry, Dad and I were driving up Catfish pass, just outside of Ailsworth, to visit a beautiful spot to take in the view. Mum and Auntie Harriet had gone shopping. For some reason, I forget why; I was sitting in the front passenger seat when Harry turned to me. 'Would you say I was a better driver than your Dad, James?' He asked seriously.

That's one of those awkward moments, like Mr Crabtree's ingrowing toenail, where I had to assess what answer to provide. I decided to be honest. 'No, I'm afraid not; Dad's much better, uncle Harry.'

Barely had I finished saying his name when he slammed on the brakes, bringing his beloved Maxi to a brutal stop. 'Get out! Get out this instant!' Harry leant across me and opened the passenger door, pushing it wide. I panicked; Catfish pass isn't a place to be wandering about on foot. I turned to look at Dad; he simply shrugged as if to say I deserved it. I was close to tears as I undid my seat belt, hoping this was a cruel joke. I looked back at Dad once more, but he was looking out the window. I then realised this was a joke because Dad couldn't keep a straight face. I slowly moved off my seat onto the grass verge, expecting Harry or Dad to start laughing, but they didn't. Once I was out of the car, Harry leant across, pulled shut the car door and drove off. I was initially shocked and even considered how best to get home. I was twelve years old, and I knew that this must be some sort of joke, but the car moving off did make me question my assessment.

The car stopped about twenty yards further up the pass, so I walked casually towards it, taking time to analyse stuff. Harry's action was cruel, but it was Harry; it's what he did. As a twelve-year-old, I was learning about the male tendency to not take things seriously. Dad was a case in point, having a reputation for being a practical joker, and I think uncle Harry was trying to out-dad Dad. The problem was that Harry couldn't get it right because he always looked up to Dad, and if you do that, you can't be original, despite trying hard to come up with something. As I approached the car, Harry jumped out of the car and leaned against the roof; the traffic was light.

'Well, are you happy to come back into the car?' Harry asked.

'Yes, I am,' I answered.

'Even though I'm the driver?'

'It would be better if Dad drove, but you'll do, uncle Harry.'

He smiled, shook his head and indicated with his eyes for me to get back in.

'Didn't think we'd leave you, eh?' Harry said as we drove on.

'I was worried when you drove off,' I pretended to admit.

'You, okay?' Dad asked from the back.

'Yes, of course I am, Dad,' I answered dryly, and we continued up the pass. The silence that followed demonstrated what happens when an intended practical joke backfires. I imagined uncle Harry feeling wretched because he took it too far, and Dad felt awkward because he'd witnessed a poor attempt at a joke. As we drove on, it was me, the victim of the prank, who sat there feeling smug and superior.

○ ○ ○

Back when I was twelve, I never analysed stuff as I do now. As a twelve-year-old, life washed over me like waves covering footprints on a beach and erasing them to await a fresh set. I never analysed stuff like Uncle Harry's prank, but I do now.

I believe it is a side-effect of Ollie's dominance over my life.

Before Ollie, I used to mix with different sets of kids as I grew up, but not after that first punch damaged me. After that punch, whenever I wasn't in Ollie's presence, I was physically and metaphorically alone, and during these lonely hours, I began to analyse what I had experienced. I stopped taking things for granted. It wasn't like a eureka moment when I suddenly began looking at stuff; it was gradual and started when I tried to assess why Ollie bullied me and why James Smith allowed himself to be bullied.

Obviously, I looked at the here and now as my life careered into despair, but I also began to look back on my life to search for any instance that may have made me more susceptible to bullying. That is why I now have a different past life from the one I experienced living through it. I'm now the hindsight champion of Ailsworth, if not the world.

○ ○ ○

As I walked past the kitchen window towards the back door, I knew Mum was cooking because of the steamed-up pane; clearly, or opaquely, the open casement window couldn't cope with Mum's cooking.

Mum was on her own, feverishly preparing our dinner.

'Hi, baby; sorry I can't talk; I'm just preparing dinner,' she said, surrounded by the chaos. It was wise not to disturb her.

'It's okay, Mum; I'll just go upstairs for a wash.'

'Oh, Uncle Harry's with your Dad; they're having a cuppa in the parlour,' she informed.

'I'll just pop my head in to say hello, on the way,' I said as I moved out of the kitchen.

The living room had been transformed. The dining table, usually employed to support our two fruit bowls, had been moved away from the wall, covered with a cream-cloured tablecloth, and set for four places; I guessed Edward would eat later.

The living room door opened onto the relatively short front hallway, with the parlour door on the right as I left the living room. I knocked and poked my head around the door.

'Hello, Uncle Harry,' I said to the back of my uncle's head. He was sitting in the small armchair facing Dad. Although he seemed humourless when I entered, Dad smiled and winked at me. Harry stood up, holding a cup and saucer.

I was pleased for the Royal Albert tea set; it didn't get used very often. I always felt sorry for the pristine Old Country Rose set, which stayed hidden in the parlour, gathering dust in the display cabinet. Those striking red, yellow, and pink roses below the gold rim of the cups were desperate to fulfil their intended function. I only hoped that Mum employed a rotation system to ensure all six cups had a chance to feel needed. I'd given up any hope for the plates.

Uncle Harry placed his saucer on the coffee table and stood to shake my hand. 'James,' he began, and this is where he should have said, *my, how you've grown,* but he couldn't, 'you look very smart; where have you been?' I walked over to shake his hand. I looked at Harry smiling at me, but I'd noticed earlier that his face was etched with worry when he stood up to greet me. He immediately replaced it with smiley Harry, but I'd seen the concern behind his eyes when he first looked at me, and I had a horrible feeling they'd been talking about me.

I pulled my hand away. 'I've been playing chess with Mr Crabtree.' I answered politely, now standing beside Harry's chair.

'What, Pete? The, the,' Harry looked worried and couldn't say the word that had entered his head.

'Yes, Mr Crabtree, the potato wholesaler who lives between the two halves of Valeview Terrace. He's a lovely man,' it was a stuffy answer, but I had to set the record straight.

'Yes, Peter asked me if it was okay; he was desperate for someone to challenge him, and I said James would play him,' Dad chipped in.

'Oh,' Harry sat down again.

'Well? How did you do?' Dad asked.

'It was a lovely day, and I managed to come out on top,' I answered, not wanting to expand further. Dad gave me a nod and a thumbs up.

'I'm just going up to get washed, so I'll see you later, Uncle Harry,' I said. I left and closed the door. I stood in the hallway for a few seconds, any longer would have been noticeable, but I heard nothing to support my suspicion. As I began up the stairs, I shook my head and hummed, "You're so Vain".

∘ ∘ ∘

Dinner – lamb chops, chips (the source of the humidity on the window), and peas, followed by treacle sponge and custard – was lovely. Throughout the meal, the adults talked about family, friends and work, sometimes dragging me in by asking about school, and Mum didn't disappoint me when she heard the result of the chess game.

'Oh, well done, my little Bobby Fischer,' she beamed.

I smiled, impressed with Mum's new comparison but not wanting to tell her that Fischer was the US champion by the time he was fourteen. The meal fizzled out, and I volunteered to help Dad wash and dry the dishes in the kitchen, where we chatted about chess and fishing. It was all fine and dandy, but the chatting felt different, and I couldn't put my finger on what it was.

'Did Ollie call by when I was at Mr Crabtree's?' I asked innocently.

'No, he didn't, son, unless he called when I was at the garage,' he shrugged.

'Oh, that's strange. I hope he isn't ill or something,' I added, glancing at Dad to gauge his reaction.

'I'm sure he's fine, James. Probably decided to play with someone else.'

'Yeah, probably.'

∘ ∘ ∘

That night lying in bed, I reflected on a terrible evening spent with Dad and Uncle Harry. I tried to process everything that had happened and concluded that it would only be me that saw it for what it was.

If things are bad, they're bad. They will remain bad because bad things are what they are, like a headache. Knowledge has taught parents that "Anadin" will improve headaches, showing them that their understanding influences bad things to improve them. However, if I complained of a gnawing pain in my abdomen or came down with a fever, my parents would immediately seek medical advice to improve that bad thing. They wouldn't guess for fear of making it worse. I only wished they'd done the same this evening.

∘ ∘ ∘

It was getting close to nine when Mum emerged from the parlour, carrying her empty sherry glass.

I know about glassware. I could easily recognise a pint glass, a wine glass, a whisky glass, and a sherry glass. I did, however, get confused when it came to flutes and small glasses that I'd seen at Christmas parties where the adults remained a safe distance away from the grotto, leaving the kids to stare admiringly at Mr

Edward Pearson, town councillor, AKA Santa. Mum was carrying a sherry glass and a peculiar smile.

'Are you okay, Mum?' I asked, alarmed at the length of time her smile remained fixed.

'James! Come and give me a hug!' She'd opened her arms wide, and I got off the sofa to comply; my TV show had finished anyway. I leaned into her, and she closed her arms tightly, pulling me close. I could smell the cigarettes she'd been smoking outside with Uncle Harry.

'I had a little drink with Harry and Dad, you know, but I remembered I needed to catch a TV show, so I left them chatting away about boring politics.' Smiling, she pushed me away but kept hold of my arms. 'Boring!' She shouted animatedly, eyes wide.

I smiled. 'I'll pop in to say goodnight because I'm thinking of going fishing again tomorrow.'

Mum had moved past me, plopped herself on the left side of the sofa, and raised her feet, so they were under her bottom.

'Yes, that's a good idea, James,' she seemed to remember something. 'Oh, can you be a love and switch the TV to BBC 2? I've just got myself comfy,' she explained unnecessarily. I did what she asked, and she settled back to watch the travel show.

'Night,' I said on my way out, but she was already in Italy or Greece and didn't reply.

I could hear the voices as I stood outside the parlour. I don't yet personally know what beer and sherry do to people; all I can say is that I have witnessed the effects of beer and sherry. People change. Mum becomes smilier, softer, and sleepier. Dad becomes chattier, tearier, and more opinionated. Edward, who is probably still an apprentice, becomes slurrier, incoherent, and aggressive. Tonight, I can hear that Uncle Harry and Dad have become chattier and more opinionated; I only hope they don't become teary.

I pop my head around the door. 'Hi, just want to say goodnight,' I said.

'James! Come in, come in.' Harry shouted. 'We were just talking about you,'.

My heart sank, dreading joining them, concerned about why they'd been talking about me. I crept in timidly and closed the door. I sat on a stool to face the two brothers leaning back in their respective armchairs with a whisky tumbler in their right hands. They looked relaxed.

'Why were you talking about me, Uncle Harry?' I asked, wanting to cut to the chase.

It was Dad who started talking. 'Harry is driving around Anglesey tomorrow and thought it might be a good idea if you joined him for the day; give him company, sort to speak.'

Uncle Harry is a travelling salesman for a sweet manufacturer, but their name escaped me sitting there in the parlour. When Dad mentioned the idea, it sounded awful; sitting in a car all day, going from sweetshop to sweetshop in the wilds of North Wales; but, because my plan was in full flow, it did qualify as another day spent fishing.

'That would be great, Uncle Harry. Would you mind?' I asked, perhaps too enthusiastically.

'Not at all, James; it would be great to have some company.' Harry said.

'I'll go and get an early night then, shall I?' I suggested.

'No need, no need,' Harry assured, 'you can nap in the car. Look, James, I haven't seen you for such a long while, so why don't you tell your Uncle Harry about school and stuff,' he sat feigning interest.

One of the other things that getting drunk does is reduce a person's ability to carry out subterfuge convincingly. It may work on another person who was drinking, but it didn't work on someone whose senses were abnormally heightened because of the situation's awkwardness. I looked across at Dad and saw the same fake look on his face. They *had* been talking about me but not as a passenger to keep Uncle Harry company. I played along to see what would become of this falsehood.

After listening to me gush about History as a subject, the pair digressed onto politics and argued about the recent vote to stay in Europe. Despite the large majority for staying in, it was apparent that Uncle Harry was part of the minority and tried to explain his fears about European confectioners taking over the homegrown products. Now, I would be the first to welcome an opportunity to discuss politics, but not with two men who had been drinking; it would end in an argument, so I let it fizzle out.

On returning to the subject of James Smith, Uncle Harry somehow brought up size or the lack of it, that I was experiencing. He sought to reassure me by saying that he and Dad were short for their age, and apparently, it wasn't until after they left school that they both sprouted to the giddy height of five foot eight (Harry was probably half an inch taller). Suddenly the chat moved on to its inevitable purpose; physicality and fighting.

Over the next hour or so – it felt much longer – Uncle Harry and Dad proceeded to describe in self-promoting and gratuitous detail how they'd beaten the living shit out of every other boy in their neighbourhood, even incurring the wrath of their local bobby. Uncle Harry even described how he sorted out some lads from Manchester conscripted to the Army at the same time as he was. They smiled at each other's memories and had a wonderful time bigging themselves up as being hard men.

I knew Dad's family were hard, and he often told me about the legend that was his father, Jack, the grandfather I never had. I have seen black-and-white pictures of Jack - in the football team - in the silver band - at work in the mine - with other men, but never with Grandma Joanna, and never with his children. He was taller than everyone else in every picture, hence why he was a goalie, and he never smiled. He was gaunt and dark-haired, looking every inch like a historical version of Dracula, and the dark eyes *did* make him appear formidable.

I was not Jack Smith.

I was not John Smith.

I was not Harry Smith.

I was James Smith, the smallest boy in my class who had self-diagnosed psychological issues and whose attempt to dig himself out of his own mess had taken a mental pounding from two well-meaning but ill-equipped hard men.

11

I slept most of the way to Anglesey.

○ ○ ○

Mum woke me up at six thirty. I was shattered, and she was no longer smiling. Uncle Harry and I ate our porridge in silence but had perked up slightly for the toast and marmalade.

'Thanks, Martha; you're a lifesaver,' Harry said, taking a generous mouthful of his coffee.

Mum, hands on hips, looked as if she was about to tell him off; she was pretending again. 'I don't know, Harry Smith! Keeping my poor husband up until god knows when, drinking whisky and arguing about stupid politics; I don't know, I really don't.'

'John got to work on time, didn't he?' Harry asked timidly.

'Oh, worry about his work, why don't you? Don't worry about me having to put up with that awful snoring of his, oh no, don't worry about that.'

'Sorry, Martha, we just got carried away, I suppose.'

Hearing the remorseful voice, Mum smiled; objective achieved.

○ ○ ○

I woke up when Harry informed me we were crossing the Menai Suspension Bridge. It linked Anglesey to the rest of Wales and was built in 1826 (We didn't cover it in any great detail during History; politics was more important, I guess.) to carry the A5 road. It was pretty short but quite spectacular.

'Well, sleepy head, caught up with your beauty sleep?' Harry asked.

'Yeah, sorry, Uncle Harry, I couldn't stay awake,' I answered, pushing myself up to see better.

'Our first stop is Llanfair PG, followed by villages on the island's southwest side to reach Rhosneigr. From there, we'll move inland, pick up the A5 and travel back towards Menai Bridge, with stops at Gwalchmai and Llangefni. We'll then travel up the northeast coast and end up in Cemaes. How's that sound?' Harri asked excitedly.

'I'm not sure, Uncle Harry; all those places sounded pretty foreign to me.'

'They're the Welsh place names. They're pretty proud of their language, so it's important to show respect, even though some words are difficult for us to pronounce.'

I started to panic. 'So the people here speak a different language to English?'

'Yes, James; so I've picked up some useful phrases like, "bore da".'

'What's that mean?' I asked.

'Good morning. Bore da means the same as good morning,' Harry explained.

'Bore da,' I tried.

'That was good, James. Good is da.'

'So, they say morning good rather than good morning?' I surmised, genuinely fascinated.

'I guess so,' Harry added, pulling over opposite a small sweetshop in Llanfair PG. 'Right,' Harry picked up a clipboard with a long list clipped to the front, 'I won't be long.' Harry then opened the rear doors and picked up two boxes of sweets. Before closing the door, he said, 'there's an open box back here of samples. Help yourself while I'm away.' Harry threw the clipboard onto his seat, closed the door and walked into the shop that wasn't dissimilar to Gordon's in Ailsworth.

A car is a very quiet place to sit, like an isolation booth, cut off from the noisy world. I looked around and saw that the sweetshop was semi-detached, with a laundrette next door. It was fascinating looking at an alien town, or was it a village?

There were no pit head winches, their associated slag heaps, and no one walking around with NCB written on their backs. What did these people do?

I twisted and reached to pick up the box of sweets. Jamesons. The sweets were all Jameson sweets. Looking into the box, I realised I'd never seen this brand before; they were alien to me. I knew about Cadbury, Mars, Trebor, Terrys and Rowntree, but never Jameson.

I looked at the alien offerings and saw that most were sweets called Raspberry Ruffle; I guessed at least thirty per cent. I unwrapped one and was immediately horrified to see plain chocolate lurking underneath. Plain chocolate! What on earth was Uncle Harry playing at? I looked at the evil black layer I assumed held raspberry and a ruffle within. I was torn; every child likes a sweet, but plain chocolate? I also felt my parents sitting behind me, telling me not to waste food, even plain chocolate. I closed my eyes and put it into my mouth. I had decided to bite through the evil layer, hoping the raspberry and ruffle would save me; it almost did. The ruffle was a raspberry-flavoured coconut filling that was sweet and dry and overcame the plain chocolate without giving me the mellow finish that milk chocolate provided.

I studied the rest of the box, and, to be fair, the sweets did resemble Quality Streets in the shape and colour of wrappers. I saw a suspicious-looking Peppermint Ruffle I assumed would also house plain chocolate, so I opted for a sweet wrapped in the replica of a strawberry, complete with green stalk. It tasted okay but seemed one of the rarer sweets; I'd have to be judicious in my consumption, and luckily wasn't in full sweet-eating mode yet, so I put the box back.

I looked around the car. Compared to our Avenger, the Maxi was very spacious, ideal for Uncle Harry's work, and comfortable. I did the boy thing of looking at the controls on the dashboard, rocked the steering wheel back and forth, and quickly became bored. I then noticed Uncle Harry's clipboard and picked it up to study the list. In the left-hand column were the names of shops, and number one on the list corresponded to the shop Harry had just entered, 'Llysiau Llanfair". I looked down the left-hand column and turned over the page after reaching number fifteen and saw that six more shops were listed on the second page. Twenty-one shops! My heart sank, and I slid down the seat, realising it would be a very, very long day.

○ ○ ○

It was a long, slow day, and luckily I'd brought a book along for company. I picked it up from Edward's collection and chose it because it reminded me of the seaside. Brighton Rock may have been set in a seaside resort, but it didn't remind me of *my* experiences in coastal towns like Blackpool; it was dark and unsettling. I also found it challenging to read because it tended to cram a lot of description into some paragraphs, forcing me to re-read them for fear of missing something important. It felt fast, frenzied and surreal. Breathless. It used words I didn't understand or, rather, didn't understand their context. "Buer" and "polony" were terms for women, "vitriol" was used as some form of weapon (I always thought it meant hatred), and terms like "Belisha Beacon" were totally alien to me. I made a point of looking them up when I got home.

As I read the book, two things began to upset me. Firstly, Rose is depicted as being uncomfortable with anything Pinkie introduces her to, unable to escape her impoverished upbringing. We're not impoverished, but I've seen my parents change whenever Mum drags Dad into a restaurant. Mum becomes posh and sits more upright, while Dad becomes tense and nervous. For some reason, Mum believes she should be there, but Dad is more concerned with protocols he's unused to following. I think most working people are like my parents. They work, can manage a house, raise a family, have a minor holiday, and maybe buy an old car. They don't go out to restaurants and the like; they don't have the money. So, when, perhaps, for a family get-together, Mum's sister takes us somewhere that involves formality, I can see the uncomfortableness Rose experiences in the book reflected in my parents. I also didn't like the author's jibe in referring to Rose's "Woolworth compact". It was *her* compact, like it was *my* chess set; to note where it came from defines the narrator, not the subject.

Secondly, Pinkie scared me. I kept substituting Ollie for the little gangster, and it scared me. The way Mr Greene described the heartless eyes was vivid, and a simple phrase – "*anger like a live coal in his belly*" – shocked me. Did Ollie carry anger like that in his body? All in all, I found the book disturbing and regretted picking it from Edward's collection to while away the long day.

When Uncle Harry disappeared into Mr Jones' Sweet Heaven in a town called Amlwch, I busied myself in the book and the tense scene at the racecourse, where Pinkie had set up poor old Spicer. Suddenly, a loud knock on my window made me jump, almost making me scream in panic. I looked out and saw a large ruddy-faced policeman telling me to wind down my window; I did as he'd indicated.

'A be wyt ti'n ei wneud yn fama?' he said. I heard the words but hadn't a clue what they meant.

'I'm sorry, but I don't speak Welsh,' I answered, assuming the policeman had addressed me in his own language.

'Sorry, young man. I asked you what you were doing here?'

'Oh, I'm waiting for my uncle. He's a travelling salesman, and he's gone into that shop,' I answered. I'm not sure why, but even if you're the most innocent person in the world, being questioned by a policeman makes you feel guilty.

'Harry? I know Harry, but I've never seen anyone sitting in his car before. So you see why I had to check now, can't you?'

'Yes, officer. He's brought me along because our school's on summer holidays,' I explained.

'Oh, so where do *you* live then?'

'I live in a town called Ailsworth.'

The policeman shook his head. 'Never heard of it,' he lowered his head to my level. 'Are you on the run for anything I should know of?'

Now, for some reason, I knew he was teasing me. I didn't feel like I did when Mr Crabtree told me about his ingrowing toenail; I felt calmer. 'Yes, I'm afraid I've kidnapped Uncle Harry and sent him into Mr Jones' shop to steal all his Mars bars.'

'Mars bars! So you're the evil mastermind we've been looking for behind the latest spate of confectionery-related heists!' The policeman smiled. 'Nice to meet you, Mr?'

'James Smith, my Dad's Uncle Harry's elder brother.'

'Nice to meet you, James Smith. My name's Arwel, but you should call me Officer Hughes,' Arwel said.

'It's nice to meet you too, Officer Hughes,' I didn't know what else to say.

'I'll just pop into the shop to have a quick chat with Harry, but it was nice to meet you, James.'

'You too, Officer Hughes,' I said as the policeman turned and sauntered to the shop, tipping his helmet to a woman who walked past pushing a pram. I picked up my book again and watched the Officer disappear into the shop. I suddenly thought about Ida, the big-breasted heroine of the book. The big breasts are referred to frequently throughout the book and initially created a strange feeling within me as I read the words. However, as she and her breasts were re-introduced in part four of the book, I wasn't sure how I felt or what I should think. This is where I get worried about clever books; they make me feel inadequate and thick. When I watched Officer Hughes walking into the shop, it wasn't Ida's large breasts I was thinking about; I was thinking about her acting as a policeman to make sense of the murder of the man she'd befriended. Clearly, she was behaving as a detective, but I saw her as a Priest for the guilt that the young catholic couple carried around Brighton. I was confusing myself because I didn't know what else to read into the story. I'd gone past halfway and decided to stop reading further because I wasn't equipped to enjoy it as I believed the author wanted it to be appreciated.

I threw the book onto the floor by my feet and thought about my lack of engagement during English Lit lessons. I enjoy books, and I've seen our teacher provide insights into the subtler or more profound meanings of books whenever one of her favourites asks. The favourites are the cleverest in the class and appear to operate at a different level from the rest of us. I close my eyes and think about how I'm allowing Ollie to ruin my life. It isn't the bullying itself; it's more to do with me making adaptations to mollify Ollie. I knew that if I were to ask Mrs Meeking about Ralph's capitulation or Roger's innate evilness, Ollie would pull me up afterwards and belittle my attempt at furthering my understanding. "Who the fuck do you think you are, Smithy?" or "What the fuck was that about?" followed by lessons in discipline and knowing my rightful place in the world.

Stupidly I began to cry.

o o o

When Uncle Harry returned, he was too distracted to notice my reddened eyes and lifted my spirits by saying that the next stop at Cemaes would be his last. As we drove, he told me the story that PC Arwel Hughes had recounted, which he thought was hilarious.

The local police had managed to apprehend a suspected house thief they'd been after for some time after three people came forward saying they'd seen the thief during his getaway. Even though they had the thief bang to rights for the robbery, PC Hughes asked friends from the local darts team, of which he was a member, to make up the identity parade. Imagine the shock during the parade when Mrs Nesta Davies picked out John Elvis Williams, a member of the darts team, as the person she'd seen running away with silverware from the vicar's house. Despite being with the darts team, eight miles away at the Ship

Inn in Cemaes, Elvis couldn't contain his nerves. He had to be given a chair because he almost fainted and kept mumbling, "It wasn't me, it wasn't me," while trying to drink from a glass of water without his shaking hand spilling its contents. Uncle Harry laughed as he told me the story, but all I could do was force a smile; I couldn't quite see the comedy gold that Harry was seeing.

Cemaes is a pretty seaside town or village on the north of Anglesey, and the sweetshop was in its centre. 'Why don't you go along this road to the beach to stretch your legs while I'm here, James. It's only around that bend, and I'll pick you up from the beach car park. We'll be going home after this, so you may as well get the old circulation going, eh?' Harry said as he gathered his gear for another foray into the confectionery war.

I walked up Bridge Street as Harry'd directed and crossed the street's eponymous bridge. I saw the short road down to the beach and strolled towards the car park and the crashing waves. It was very picturesque, and I was glad Harry had suggested the short break. I felt good, happier and back in control. Beyond the car park, a promenade of sorts followed the curve of the beach, so I started along it with my hands in my pockets. As I strolled, I saw two cyclists approaching me from the far end, and they soon went past. It was a boy and a girl about my age, and my vanity believed they studied me as they flashed by.

Suddenly I heard a girl's voice from behind. 'O lle ti'n dod?'

I turned and saw that the two cyclists had dismounted and were standing close to me. 'I'm sorry, but I don't speak Welsh,' I said again.

'Tyrd o'ma, mae hyn yn boring,' the boy said, then remounted and cycled away, leaving the girl studying me.

'I asked you where you were from,' she said.

'I'm from a town called Ailsworth, not far from Wigan. My name's James.'

She smiled, leaned her bike against the prom wall and leaned back, standing next to me. 'My name's Rhian, and I live here in Cemaes.' She was pretty, about the same height as me and had a kind face.

'Hello, Rian; you live in a lovely place,' I replied.

She shook her head. 'I'm not called Rian; I'm called Rhian,' she said, emphasising the start of her name. I became embarrassed. 'Sorry, I didn't want to embarrass you, James,' she said, 'it's just that I'm trying to teach you how to say my name properly.'

I returned the smile. 'I'm sorry, but I'm not used to saying R that way.'

It was clear that she found this funny. 'Right, let's think about this.' She did just that, and after a while, she gave a single nod and looked at me. I felt strange. 'Okay. Can you say, huh?'

'Yes, of course I can. Huh.'

'And I know you can say R,' she said phonetically, 'so all you have to do is say the R and add the huh, before finally adding the ian. Try it.'

I looked to the tarmac to gather my thoughts and remember the instructions before looking into her face again. 'Hello, R huh ian,' I tried.

Her face lit up. 'That was good! Now all you need to do is shorten the, huh, and you'll know my name.'

'Hello, Rhhian.'

'James!' Uncle Harry was shouting from the car park.

Rhian had turned to see the source of the voice. 'Who's that? Is that the sweets salesman?'

'Yes, that's my Uncle Harry; he's been delivering sweets to the sweetshop in town,' I answered sadly. 'This was our last stop, and we're leaving for home now. How do you know him?' I asked.

Rhian pressed her index finger against the side of her nose and smiled. 'At least you've learnt how to say my name properly.'

I decided not to follow up on the Harry issue. 'I have, Rhian. It was nice to meet you,' I said, suddenly feeling awkward, unsure what to do next. I offered her my hand to shake, but she laughed loudly, leaned across and kissed me on my cheek.

'That's for trying to learn how to say my name correctly. It was nice to meet you as well, James, and I hope you come back again sometime, so I can teach you some more words.'

'James!' The unwelcomed Harry repeated.

'Will you walk with me to the car?' I asked, amazed at my newfound confidence.

'It's best that I go home. Tea's ready, and I don't think we'd be able to talk about anything significant between here and the car park, so take care, James,' she said, mounted her bike and rode away, waving as she left the far end of the car park. I made my way back to Uncle Harry, and despite my disappointment at leaving Rhian, I felt pretty positive as we began the journey home.

'I see you met Rhian,' Harry said, her name pronounced perfectly

'Yes, she stopped and taught me how to say her name correctly. Do you know her?' I asked.

'Yeah. She's Mrs Thomas' daughter, and Mrs Thomas runs the sweetshop. She has a brother called Bryn. and I've known them for a few years. I think Bryn's older than you, and Rhian's about the same age.'

I looked across at Uncle Harry. 'How come you know so many people, Uncle Harry?' I asked.

'It's just part of my job, James. Listening and remembering people is an important attribute, I think.'

'For a travelling salesman, you mean?' I suggested.

'No, I don't mean that, James. It's an essential human trait that you need to work at,' Harry said. 'Everyone has a story, a life, a problem, or a solution; you only need to talk to people to find it out.'

I could now see Harry in a different light. He was in his own environment, not his brother's. 'Oh,' was all I could muster.

Uncle Harry looked at me and seemed satisfied that the chat had run its course as we headed out of Cemaes towards the A5. As we came out of the town, I was astounded to see a strange-looking building away to our right.

'Is that the nuclear power station?' I asked in wonderment. I knew one existed on Anglesey from news reports or science programmes.

'It certainly is, James. Impressive, eh?'

'Uh huh,' I nodded. The sleek grey building dominated the surrounding countryside and coastline. The enormous central grey structure had two cylinders at both ends, surrounded by smaller cream-coloured square-shaped buildings. It was impressive and seemed a generation removed from the coal mines dying around Ailsworth. It was also very close to Cemaes.

○ ○ ○

During the journey home, Harry asked if I'd tried the sweets and what I thought of them. After I told him about my disgust at seeing dark chocolate, he laughed and said I should try the chocolate caramel. It was called "Merry Maid", and he had a separate small jar of these in the glove compartment. They were lovely and helped pass the time from Anglesey to Ailsworth.

As we drove in silence, I thought back to Rhian and how good I'd felt. She didn't know I was a failure; she took me at face value as an equal, and it felt good. It didn't *need* to feel good; it should have been an everyday occurrence and not built up by me to mean something else. It should have been a typical interaction between a boy and a girl, but it wasn't; I wasn't typical. Rhian was probably doing okay at school, got on with her friends, and was accepted by everyone else. I was a stupid freak that allowed himself to be humiliated. How could anyone be friends with someone as worthless as me? I had no one, and meeting Rhian reminded me that when I returned to Ailsworth, all I'd have would be my family, Mr Crabtree, Maude, and Doris.

I thought back to when I bumped into Brenda, Maureen and Sally in that back alley. Instead of being on equal terms, they'd all seen me being stripped of my personality at school and that I had nothing to interest them as an equal. It was natural for them to treat me in the same way they'd seen me treated by Ollie. No one who knew me at school would want to do anything with me for fear of being contaminated by my patheticness.

Meeting Rhian today made me feel warm inside and gave me confidence that I didn't know existed, but the truth was that meeting Rhian today made me realise there was a serious flaw in my plan. I was lonely.

12

Despite staying up late drinking with Mum and Dad, Uncle Harry left early on Tuesday; he was going to the Blackpool area, and I made an effort to get up early to see him off. 'Thanks for yesterday, Uncle Harry; I really enjoyed it.'

'I was glad to have you with me, James, and remember, you can come with me any time if you want,' he said.

I remembered all the tedious waiting around and shrugged. 'I think I'd need some pretty good books if I was to do it again; some of it was quite boring,' I ventured.

Instead of pretending to be offended, he leaned towards my ear. 'Even if I was going to Cemaes?' Harry whispered.

I must have blushed. 'What did you just say to him, Harry?' Dad asked.

'Nothing, John, mate, nothing at all, eh James?'

'Yeah, it was nothing, Dad; just a funny story a policeman told us.'

Harry winked, jumped into his Maxi, and soon disappeared from my life until his next visit, which would probably be around Christmas, accompanied by Aunt Harriet.

Dad and I returned to the house - Mum was having a well-deserved lie-in to compensate for the sherry - and sat for a mug of tea. 'Was it really boring?' Dad asked.

'Yeah, it was pretty dull, but I got to read and see parts of Britain I don't usually see. It was pretty weird, to be honest.'

'What do you mean, weird?' Dad asked.

'Well, I slept most of the way, and when I woke up, we were crossing this big bridge into Anglesey. After that, it was like towns, houses, shops, and small buildings. There weren't any mines or big factories and stuff, but people were there walking and going into shops. I suppose I could never imagine a world without big industry, that's all.' I looked at Dad, hoping I'd made sense.

'But there *is* industry on Anglesey, James. There's a big nuclear power station and an Aluminium Works, and I'm sure there used to be a Copper mine. So there is industry; it was just that you never saw them,' he explained.

'I did see the nuclear station; it was near Cemaes in the north, but it looked so clean compared to our mines,' I said excitedly.

Dad made one of his funny facial expressions, rolling his lower lip over the upper and tilting his head to the side. I know this usually means, "yes, but".

'I'm sure it looked clean, but nuclear energy does have a huge problem associated with it. You see, the fuel they use, I think it's Uranium, becomes more radioactive and causes radiation. This radiation is very dangerous to human health and causes cancers if people become contaminated.'

I started to panic, thinking about Rhian. 'But it must be safe, or they wouldn't build it near people,' I said.

'Oh no, it's safe in the power station. That's why the buildings are so big. It's the waste that's the problem. After they've used up all its power, the old Uranium has to be removed and transported to the North West of England to a place called Windscale, where it's stored. The problem is that waste Uranium remains radioactive for hundreds of thousands of years.'

'That doesn't make sense, Dad. So that power station near Cemaes will remain operating for hundreds of years?' I asked.

'Oh, no, it can't run for that long. Something happens to the reactor after a while, and it must stop. Sorry, James, but I don't know much about it; I'm just telling you what I read once in an edition of National Geographic.'

I could see that he was being stretched. 'Sorry, Dad, it just seems like a short-sighted way of producing electricity, that's all.' I thought we best end the chat because I sensed Dad had reached the edge of his comfort zone. I was feeling nauseous.

I get like that when my brain can't absorb something, like looking up at the sky on a clear night when Dad, Edward and I went night fishing. I'd given up on God a few years ago; I can't blame Ollie for that, so looking at the stars made me ill. I know people talk about the Big Bang and other concepts I don't understand, but what was before that? And what was before the thing before the Big Bang and so on? Looking at the stars and knowing space was infinite made me feel physically sick, and I had to change the subject in my head. Now that Dad had told me that radiation lasts hundreds of thousands of years, I felt physically sick again.

Dad looked at me quizzically. 'How did we get to talking about nuclear power anyway?'

'We were talking about places that don't look like here,' I reminded him.

'Yes, so they have the power station, and the Aluminium Works, oh, and a Port in Holyhead. So, they may not have mines on Anglesey, but there is work there.'

'It was just odd to see, that's all, Dad,' I said, slowly feeling better.

'It's good that you take in things the way you do, James; it's good,' he stopped, seemingly thinking about something. 'I tell you what, I'm going to a meeting of the Labour Party this evening in Wigan, and I'll ask Arthur Clarke if there's any work at the Party Offices.'

'I don't know. What would I be doing?' I asked, knowing even the Labour Party didn't require a grocery delivery boy.

'I don't know; I'll ask. There may be nothing, but you never know; there may be some office work, like filing minutes from meetings,' Dad suggested.

Again! Another word I didn't understand. 'What are minutes? I thought they were sixty seconds.'

'No, minutes are the notes that are kept to record the key points of a meeting. They have nothing to do with time.'

'So, why don't they call them notes? Minutes is a confusing word.'

Dad smiled. 'Bloody hell, James, give me a break. Look, I think the word minutes comes from Latin and means a concise note or something like that. It's like break and break. James, don't break the glass and, James, take a break from hassling your Dad,' we both smiled. 'Anyway, what are your plans today?' Dad asked.

'I feel a bit tired and fancy finishing that stupid book, Brighton Rock.'

'That's fine, but don't isolate yourself too much; it's not good for you,' Dad said.

I wondered if he was fishing again. 'Look, Dad, it may seem strange, but I think it's time for me to take a break from Ollie. If I'm being honest,' which I wasn't, 'I'd rather read a book than play with him, if you don't mind.'

'No, of course, I don't mind. Have you two fallen out or something?' Dad was still fishing.

'No, we haven't fallen out. It's just that I find him boring, but I don't want to hurt his feelings. This way, I hope he'll find new friends and get used to being without me.'

'That's kind of you, James, but it doesn't mean *you* can't find new friends, does it?' He was still pushing.

I looked into Dad's eyes. 'I'm working on it, Dad,' I didn't or couldn't say any more. He seemed to accept this, shrugged and picked up his paper.

∘ ∘ ∘

It was only Tuesday of the first week, and I felt lousy. I stayed in my room in the morning and heard Ollie arriving at the door again. Dad, who'd started his Nine Five shift, must have told Mum about me not wanting to play with Ollie because she lied pretty naturally when she told him I'd gone fishing. I love my parents.

I finished Brighton Rock. I enjoyed it as an adventure but not as a book, if that makes sense. That Pinkie boy was dressed up as evil incarnate, brought about by his upbringing, but as far as I was concerned, all Pinkie Brown did was feel obliged to fill Kite's boots, a role he was ill-equipped to fulfil. Our Oxford English Dictionary told me what "Buer", "Polony", and "Vitriol" meant, and Mum told me what a "Belisha Beacon" was. Vitriol was the word that upset me the most. Knowing that Pinkie always carried a bottle of Sulphuric Acid in his pocket made him even more of a pathetic character. I threw the book onto the dresser and dug out my dictionary.

LONELY: Adj

- *My life now – brought about by my association with Ollie.*
- *James was lonely; he had no friends.*
- *A realisation that I'm alone*

Although surrounded by kind people, a friendless James realised he was lonely.

∘ ∘ ∘

Lying on my bed, I thought about what Dad had said. It was easy for him to say that I should go out and make new friends, but how would I do that?

How did I do that?

When I was younger, I did have friends, and it was great to belong. I used to play with a large group of friends, mainly football, but we hung out and spent hours in summer simply hanging around talking. Those were my Primary years, but I lost those connections at Secondary because I struggled with meeting new children that came to the Secondary from the eight Primary feeder schools. I remember maintaining my friendship with some children from our Primary school, but as the second year progressed, it became apparent that I was a slower developer than the other boys. While they grew and got stronger, I was dropped from the football team, and the boys also started to focus on the girls. I kept my distance because I was shy and conscious of my childlike appearance. Then came the third year and Ollie.

I was crying. Again! I was crying again, unsure how to dig myself out of my mess. My mess, not Ollie's. Ollie is simply a cruel human being who triggered a psychological capitulation in a vulnerable individual. I contrasted my life as an eleven-year-old to my life now and realised that I'd gone from having a large pool of friends to a situation where I had none. Since Ollie took command of my life, I hadn't exchanged a normal conversation with anyone my age.

Rhian!

I did talk with *her*. I spoke with Rhian without once thinking about Ollie. Perhaps the three days without Ollie had an unexpected effect on me, but Cemaes was another world away. If I were to walk around Ailsworth hoping to bump into a classmate, Ollie would find me. I was trapped. I closed my eyes and tried to remember my meeting with Rhian. I saw the bike, her voice, her eyes and her smile, but I then heard the conversation. It was all about her name. It wasn't a brilliant conversation that two friends shared; it was a chat between two strangers. But that was Uncle Harry's fault for disturbing us, so what would we have talked about if we'd had the chance?

A letter! I could write a letter. If she doesn't like the idea, then all she has to do is not reply. I'd understand that. I jumped up, made sure the dictionary was safe and ran downstairs. Mum had moved all the living room furniture to hoover every last square inch of the floor and skirtings.

Mum doesn't drink much. Where Dad regularly goes out twice a week to the Railway or the Club, Mum restricts her drinking to Christmas, rare restaurant visits, and family. As I mentioned, Mum becomes extremely happy when she drinks, but I forgot to mention that after every night of drinking, Mum undertakes extreme housekeeping. I'm unsure if that's because she feels guilty, but it happened too regularly for it to be a coincidence.

'Mum!' I shouted, but she couldn't hear me above the noise of the pink and white ball-shaped hoover. I reached across and touched her left shoulder.

'Aaaaa,' she screamed and turned around, her eyes wild with panic. She kicked the off switch, and the hoover quietened. 'Don't scare me like that, James! You shouldn't creep up on me when I'm hoovering,' she took a couple of deep breaths. 'Anyway, what is it you want?' Mum asked.

'Sorry, Mum, but I just wanted to know if we had some writing paper and envelopes; that's all.'

'The Basildon Bond's over there in the top drawer of the sideboard. I think there's a pretty fresh pad.'

'Thanks, Mum,' I said and turned to the sideboard.

'Who are you writing to?' Mum asked, her head tilted like an amateur detective.

'Oh, not sure yet; I just wanted to see how the letter shapes up first. It's part of the English coursework,' I lied. I couldn't tell her the truth, or I'd be interrogated for days.

'Oh,' she said disappointedly and kicked the hoover's switch to finish her guilt-cleaning.

o o o

On the previous Sunday, I'd arranged a return match to play chess with Mr Crabtree on Saturday. I just needed to fill in the rest of the week.

Writing the letter to Rhian took care of what was left of Tuesday, and I asked Edward to post the letter for me. It felt good to share a secret with him.

On Wednesday, I went to Maiden's Lake but didn't catch anything. I still enjoyed the day out, and between the bouts of fishing and reading, I'd lay back and think about the plan's progress, how long it still had to go, and what Rhian would write in her reply. Maiden's is where we get our drinking water and has a reputation for good fish. Despite my poor performance, I doubt its reputation has been tarnished unduly. It's a sizeable oval-shaped lake, a bit characterless, and I spent most of the day reading Great Expectations by Charles Dickens. I wouldn't usually read such a serious book, but as it is part of my GCSE English syllabus, I thought I'd kill two fish with one stone. As it turned out, the fish remained quite safe. I remained at the lake until five; I no longer saw the need to stay there all day, knowing that my parents were adept at lying to Ollie. I spent the evening reading and thinking about what Rhian thought of my letter.

On Thursday, I visited Bracken Water, a small lake above North Ailsworth. Bracken Water is much smaller and far more interesting. Although it had been dammed by the old coal works outside North Ailsworth, a natural lake has been there since the Ice Age. All the dam did was raise the level by around ten feet, enough for the NCB's needs. It's an interesting lake because its three small lagoons offer the angler various options. The two on the west shore are deep enough for spinning, and the almost flat land around the shallow lagoon on the south shore allowed me to practice fly-fishing.

Dad's fly rod is made of three split cane lengths that fit together to create a twelve-foot fly rod. The rod had a hexagonal cross-section and was a beautiful thing to behold but a nightmare to use. I wasn't strong enough, and despite knowing the technique, I didn't have the strength to cast the line far enough out. I persisted for about forty minutes, but by then, as I'd lost all ability to lift my right arm to wipe the sweat from my brow, I knew it was time to give it a rest. I resumed my bubble-and-fly method and caught two fish that were not long enough to keep. I noted where I caught them to avoid that spot when I returned to fish another day. I preferred my alien analogy to the perceived wisdom of other fishermen.

On Friday, I stayed at home to read Great Expectations. My own expectations of an instant reply from Rhian vanished when the postman didn't deliver it.

○ ○ ○

So on Saturday, Dad dropped me off at Lower Valeview, and Mr Crabtree and I played chess for a few hours. We spend a similar length of time talking about various subjects. Eventually, politics reared its ugly head when Mr Crabtree told me he'd shared a car with Dad to Wigan on Tuesday evening for a meeting of the Labour Party.

'I know; Dad asked Mr Clarke if I could help around the office. He wants me to go there next week to help clear up some stuff before he takes a break.' I explained.

'I'm afraid I'm not acquainted with this Mr Clarke you refer to, young James,' replied Mr Crabtree.

'The MP. The MP you went to see on Tuesday?'

'But you're mistaken; that was Doctor Clarke, not Mr Clarke,' Mr Crabtree corrected me.

I smiled. 'Is pedantic a word you recognise, Mr Crabtree, or did you simply invent it?' I asked, and Mr Crabtree burst out laughing at this.

'Well done, James, excellent. You see, others would say nothing like that. They'd keep the bile I'd raised hidden within, souring their opinion of me. That was precisely the correct reply to such a churlish comment.'

I smiled and tilted my head. 'You have a question for me?' Mr Crabtree asked.

'Yes, I do. Why are you a Labour party supporter? I know I should never make assumptions, but I always thought you were a Tory, Mr Crabtree.'

'Me, a Tory? Good grief, James; whatever gave you that idea? Despite my misgivings about recent developments, I have always been a staunch supporter of the Labour Party.'

'I don't know; I suppose I always associated working families with the Labour Party, and because you were a businessman, I thought you may have been a Tory.' I said.

Mr Crabtree shook his head. 'You see? There you go again, young James. The easy answer was to say that I was posh, but no, you used worker and businessman as your source of wonderment about my politics. Well, I do see the side of business and commerce, but I see the effects of government policies on working people first-hand, and it has been a natural progression for me to move away from the Conservatives to Labour.'

The conversation felt natural, unforced and enjoyable. 'What were the misgivings you mentioned?' I asked.

'Ah, now we come down to political detail, a dull and very subjective subject. You see, James, I will perceive things a certain way, and others will see the opposite viewpoint. Neither can be proven correct; therefore, such viewpoints should only be discussed with people that you know can see both sides without violent objection to either. Your father is one such person,' Mr Crabtree tried to explain.

'That was a very political answer, in that you didn't, Mr Crabtree. Dad always tells us politicians go around the houses to avoid answering questions. To my inexperienced ears, you did precisely the same thing. If you believe I'm too immature to understand your misgivings, I would have no issue with you saying so. However, if you believe that a political viewpoint is so deeply ingrained within me, then, although I'm flattered, you are mistaken.' I struggled to formulate my chameleonic response.

Mr Crabtree got up and turned on the kettle. He kept his back to me, waiting for it to boil before making a fresh pot of tea and bringing it to the table.

'We'll allow it to settle for a few minutes, shall we?' I nodded. 'Vey well, James Smith. What do you know about the current state of British politics? This answer will assist me in designing my reply.'

God, he called my bluff, and I had nothing to give him. I only knew the basics. 'Well, Harold Wilson is the Prime Minister after Labour won the last election last year, beating Edward Heath again. There's also been a recent vote about our membership of the Common Market. Apart from a couple of Scottish Islands, everywhere else voted to stay,' I answered unconvincingly.

'That is a very rudimentary understanding, if I may say. Right, James; do you know why Edward Heath called a snap Election last year?' Mr Crabtree asked. I'd made a colossal mistake, and I wanted it to stop.

'I'm not sure unless it was something to do with strikes by the miners,' I suggested.

'Yes, well, inflation at the time was very high, and the Tory Government introduced an income policy to control this inflation. The NUM, led by Lawrence Daly and Joe Gormley, who'd had success after their strike in 1972, decided to strike again in 1974. Mr Heath was aware that an anti-union sentiment was building up among the British people, so he called the election to ask the British people, "Who governs Britain?". It was a mistake, and Labour became a minority Government. The second election in October gave Labour a slim majority, and the mine workers got a 35% pay rise.'

'But that's good, isn't it?' I offered.

'Yes, for the miners, and it is what they deserve. To sacrifice your body in the thankless task of dragging coal out of the earth for the country to function is something I could never imagine. My problem is this nagging fear that the long-term consequences of the strikes could harm most of Britain. This is where I fall foul of others within the party. I worry that the unions have overstepped their intended purpose in the manner by which they achieved their goals.'

'But aren't the unions *supposed* to look after workers' rights, including pay?' I asked, concerned I was becoming a violent objector.

'Yes, but it has to be proportional to the current financial status of the Country and what others are being paid. I would rather our government commit to tackling corruption and

Britain's grossly unfair balance of wealth. I also fear that picketing other places, such as gas works in the Midlands, Power Stations, and docks, has created anti-union sentiments that may remain within people's thoughts for decades.'

Mr Crabtree appeared to be very sad as he gave me this information. 'But it will be okay under a Labour Government, won't it?' I asked, trying to look at the bright side.

'Alas, I fear for us because, at this year's special conference, the Labour Party came out in favour of voting against continued membership of the EEC by two to one. That no-vote was union-driven, but many Labour cabinet ministers wished to stay in Europe. The British people voted by over two to one in favour of staying in Europe! Over sixty-seven per cent of us voted to remain in the EEC. So my concern is that the Labour Party has been dragged away from the people by the unions, and we will pay the consequences at the next election. The sad thing about all this is how disrespectful some unions are towards Harold Wilson. I'm afraid he is the glue holding the Party together, and I would hate to see him forced out by the Party's extremes.'

'The Tories have a woman leader now, don't they?' I asked, changing the subject.

'Yes, they do, James,' my diversionary tactics didn't work, 'and I'm afraid the unions will eventually erode Labour's ability to run the Country for everyone's benefit. We could see the first-ever female Prime Minister at the next election, and I fear that if the Conservatives return to power, they will have learnt stark lessons from these strikes. The consequences of that don't bear thinking about.'

'Has the tea brewed?' I asked.

Mr Crabtree smiled. 'I'll make a fresh pot.'

13

On Thursday morning, Bryn and Rhian Thomas sat in their tiny kitchen eating breakfast. After hearing the postman delivering the mail, their mother had just walked to the front door. Sifting through the half dozen envelopes, Eirlys Thomas stopped and glanced over to her children. 'Dyw, mae'na lythyr yn fama I ti, Rhian. Wel dwi'n meddwl I ti mae o.' She walked to the kitchen and handed over the envelope.

Rhian finished her bowl of Weetabix and looked at the envelope. Rhian blushed immediately and ran to her bedroom but only after suffering various taunts from her brother. She slammed the door shut, sat on her bed, and looked at the envelope.

Miss R huh ian Thomas,
c/o Mrs Thomas' Sweetshop
Cemaes,
Anglesey.

Rhian smiled, remembering the quiet boy she met on their promenade, but then hesitated. Did she really want to know what a boy had written to her? He'd never know if she threw it into the waste basket, and he could carry on with his life in blissful ignorance in that place near Wigan.

A gentle knock on her door disturbed her thoughts. Her mother peered in and asked if she was okay. Rhian said she was fine and went on to describe the sender and the circumstances by which they briefly met. Her mother told her there was no pressure on her to open the letter, but equally, there would be no pressure on her if she did read its contents. Rhian's mother went on to say that if anything within any letter was upsetting or seemed untoward, she would be happy to discuss it with her daughter. Rhian thanked her mother and gently placed the letter into the waste bin.

○ ○ ○

Edward was sitting with his friend Graham. They were sitting on adjacent rocks below the Secondary school at a spot called Mill Bank. It was a grassy outcrop with a scattering of boulders sloping down from the school towards the oak woodland that covered the slopes of the shallow vale below. Ailsworth Secondary school stood on a promontory at the highest point of Ailsworth and towered over Mill Bank like a modern version of a Transylvanian castle.

'I hated that place,' Graham said, looking back at Edward after studying their old school behind them.

'Snap,' Edward added, 'best years of your life, my arse.'

'Are you okay?' Graham asked, 'because you don't seem like your usual happy self. Is there anything bothering you?'

'It's nothing,' he said dismissively before reconsidering. 'It's my kid brother; I'm worried about him.'

'What, James? What's wrong with him?' Graham asked, seeing the concern on his friend's face.

'I can't put my finger on it, exactly. I sense that Jamie's going through something in his life, but I don't think it's the same as we had to hide. Remember?' Edward asked.

Graham smiled and nodded. 'You carried off that hard bastard routine with aplomb, though, and no one in their right mind dared to challenge you. I can still remember that day when you beat the shit out of the O'Rourke twins; it was brilliant.'

'Got me suspended for a week, though, despite them starting it, wankers.'

'Patrick's become a real bastard since he left school. The story is he's heavily into the supply of dope around the council estates. I spoke with Liam the other week, and he's really pissed off with him.'

Edward nodded. 'I felt sorry for Liam; he was always getting dragged in by that idiot brother of his, but I had no option once he swung at me after I'd decked Patrick.'

Graham seemed to behold Edward with renewed adoration. 'No one dared cross you after that, and if it wasn't for your flamboyant dress sense, none of them would ever think you were anything but a rampant heterosexual.'

'Yeah, that and my girlfriends,' Edward recounted, smiling.

'God, yes. You had a posse of about six, didn't you?' Graham said, and Edward nodded.

Suddenly Edward remembered James. 'God, talk about going off on a tangent,' he said. 'I don't think Jamie's gay; I just don't see any of the signs, but there's something wrong.' The pair stayed silent for a while. 'I think he believes we are; he practically said so last week,' Edward paused, trying to recall James's actual words. 'No, he only said that your nickname was Gay Graham,' Edward continued. 'Yes, that's what he told me out of the blue the other evening.'

'Does what your kid brother thinks worry you?' Graham asked, worried that Edward was overreacting.

'No, it's not that; it's a lot of things. He quite rightly defended Pervy Pete and made me feel ashamed of myself. He even told me that, despite knowing about your secret, he told me I had the right to choose the right time and place to let Mum and Dad know. I actually felt like *his* kid brother; it shocked me.'

'He's a bright kid, no question, but that shouldn't shock you. Christ, you've been away in college all last year, so maybe you've missed seeing him grow.' Graham suggested.

'No, it's more than that, Gray. I was never that perceptive at his age. He's picking up stuff he shouldn't be, and that's a symptom of someone who's become introspective.'

'So?' Graham couldn't see the problem.

'Something is making him like that. He's grown a bit since last year, but he's still small for his age, and I haven't seen any other signs, either. A couple of weeks ago, I walked into the toilet, and he was in his kecks, and there was hardly any hair, Gray. He looked like a tall Primary kid. Something is worrying him, and I don't think being with that pudgy shitbag is helping.'

'Ollie Jenkins, you mean? Never liked that lad; I saw him kill a small bird once; it had a broken wing. Just stamped on it and walked away as if nothing had happened, cruel bastard.'

'I don't like him either, but Jamie's always with him for some reason. And I don't like it much; they don't look like a natural pairing.'

'Why don't you have a word with your Mum or Dad about him? Maybe they know something.'

'I might just do that, Gray; sorry for unburdening myself, so thanks for listening,' Edward sounded lighter.

'Anytime, mate, anytime.'

○ ○ ○

After spending the day at her friend's farm, where she helped clear out the cow shed and feed the two pet ponies, Rhian was back in her bedroom above the sweetshop. Despite having a lovely time with Anna on the farm, Rhian kept thinking about the unopened envelope she knew awaited her return. Consequently, she was back sitting on her bed with the letter in her hand. Taking a deep breath, Rhian opened it.

Rhian,

She smiled at the fact that he hadn't written *dear.*

Bore da – Uncle Harry taught me that.

I got home and realised I was thinking about you. I know that's stupid since we only had a brief chat, which was mostly about your name, but I realised that I'd enjoyed myself and felt good in your company.

I haven't written to anyone before, and it feels strange. It also feels safe.

I'm not a cool person, as you could probably tell, and I don't have many friends. In fact, I don't have any friends. I used to, but not any longer.

I could say I'm mates with Edward, Peter, Maude and Doris, but Edward's my older brother, and the other three are over seventy. Maude and Doris run a fruit and veg shop, and I was their delivery boy until I was almost fourteen. You see, my Dad said I should make new friends, but I can't; I'm sort of contaminated here in my own Town.

I've been bullied by this one boy, and since it started fifteen or so months ago, he's the only person I'm allowed to mix with. I hope you or your brother have never been bullied – it didn't look that way because you had the confidence to come to talk with me – it is horrible. You are the first person I've ever told. That's crazy. I met you for ten minutes, and I'm telling you something that I can't tell my family because of the shame I feel for letting it happen.

So when Dad suggested I make new friends, I thought of you, but you don't have to be my friend – that's just presumptuous – I just thought I could tell you this.

You see, I'm in the middle of a plan. School broke up last Friday, and I decided to avoid my bully for the whole summer holidays by going fishing, reading books, playing chess with Peter, and accompanying my Uncle Harry around Anglesey. My hope is that the bully will have forgotten about me by the end of the holidays. I realise that this could be wishful thinking on my part, but I had to try something.

Your island (obviously, I don't think the whole of it) is beautiful, but I expressed my concern to Dad about you living so close to a nuclear power station, but he told me it was safe.

I plan to go fishing tomorrow and Thursday and maybe play chess with Peter on Friday or Saturday. I hope you're having a lovely break from school; I got the feeling that you and your brother don't have stupid self-induced problems that I've created for myself.

Letters are funny things to write. This looks like a continuation from the last paragraph, but there's been a long break where I've re-read my words multiple times. It's embarrassing, and it's been in the bin twice, but I thought that if I could start with you, I might eventually be able to tell other people.

Sorry for being a self-obsessed freak, but even if you throw this into the bin or fire, I think it's an important start for me and part of my plan for the summer holiday. I hope you don't mind.
Yours – James.

Rhian re-read it a couple more times before putting it back in the envelope and placing it in her drawer. She shook her head; James had forgotten to include his return address.

○ ○ ○

On Saturday evening, after returning from the cinema, where he and a gang of four had been to watch "Jaws", Edward walked into the sitting room. 'Hi, Dad, can I have a quick word?' Edward asked. John Smith was reading the Daily Mirror in the living room while Martha was preparing a sponge cake in the kitchen.

'Of course you can, Ed. What's bothering you?' John put his paper down, and Edward sat on their sofa to face his father.

Edward glanced around. 'Is Jamie in his room?'

'Yeah, he's resting after narrowly beating Peter at chess; why?'

'Because I'm worried about him, that's why,' Edward whispered.

John Smith looked at the kitchen door and decided Martha had a fair bit left to do. 'In what way are you worried, Ed?'

'I don't like it that he's only playing with that weird Ollie Jenkins; that's what's bothering me, Dad.' John Smith remained silent; then, to Edward's horror, tears streamed down his father's cheeks as if a tap had been opened. 'Dad, are you okay?' Edward asked.

John Smith composed himself. 'Look, Ed, don't say anything of this to your mother, okay?'

'Okay, but you're scaring me, Dad.'

John Smith shook his head. 'It's nothing to be worried about, but I've found out that Ollie's been bullying James for over a year.'

'What? That pudgy fucker?' Edward's eyes were wild.

'Ed, listen, listen. I found a dictionary that James has been keeping, and it almost broke me when I read what's in it. It's horrible.'

'Have you been to sort the fat fuck out?'

'No, listen. Look, it would help if you calmed down, Ed,' he paused. 'I've seen Ollie since and acted as if I knew nothing. It wasn't easy to not wring the cruel bastard's neck, but I didn't because I owed it to James, because he's been trying. Without me saying anything to him, so far, he's spent all the summer holidays without seeing Ollie. He's been fishing, playing chess, reading, and selling sweets with Harry. He's trying to fight back in his own way, which will be the best thing for him.'

'I could stop it right now, Dad. All I'd need would be two minutes with that coward, and he wouldn't dare look at Jamie again.' Edward was still seething.

'I know, son, but it wouldn't help James develop. He needs to sort this out himself, but in saying that, I'm keeping an eye on him, and I know it's early days, but I am seeing signs that he's sorting himself out.'

Edward held his head in his hands. 'I can't believe I didn't see it, Dad. I'm so sorry, so sorry.'

'It isn't your fault, son; you were busy growing up yourself,' he looked at his son. 'Do you think you can keep this secret, even if you see Ollie? For James' sake?'

Edward raised his head and stared at his father through tear-filled eyes. 'Yes, Dad, I can keep that secret for James' sake, even if I see that sad excuse for a human being.'

'Thanks, mate, it will be the best thing for him. But if I see it happening again, I'll sort it out once and for all, okay?'

'Promise?'

'I don't need to answer that, do I, Ed?'

'Sorry, Dad. And thanks for telling me.'

14

Sunday was an absolute washout. It poured all day, so it was a perfect book day, and I persevered with Great Expectations, Pip's life, and the striking differences that a century has instilled in society. It was a fantastic book for me at this time because it provided a romantic depiction of life in the period covered by my History syllabus. As I read the book, I was aware that British society at that time was governed by the newly formed Liberal party under Palmerston, but despite being pleased that they won in 1859, I knew they had no right to do so. They had no mandate (Dad taught me that word) because the industrial working classes were not eligible to vote, and not a single woman was eligible to vote. It was crazy.

The only significant development happened at the end of Sunday lunch.

'Dad tells me you don't want to play with Ollie anymore,' Mum said. Dad and Edward immediately looked up. I don't know if they were surprised by Mum's question, but it certainly got their attention.

'Yeah,' I answered nonchalantly, 'he's a bit boring, and I didn't want to say that to his face and hurt his feelings. This way, Ollie can find new friends and learn to be without me,' I looked down and concentrated on chasing the last few peas around the plate.

'Well! I never had Ollie down as boring, did you, John?'

'I don't really know the lad, Ma, so if James says he's boring, then that should be good enough for us, don't you think?' Dad answered, and Edward nodded.

'That's why I'd appreciate you telling him I've gone fishing if he calls.'

Mum shrugged. 'If that's what you want, then I will lie for you, James,' she said, 'but I'll tell you now, young man: I'm not comfortable lying like this, and I felt awkward the other day when the poor boy called by.'

I took that as a telling-off. 'I'm sorry, Mum, but it is for the best.'

The remainder of the day was spent asking Dad unanswerable questions about what to expect from my three days at Dr Arthur Clarke's office in Wigan. Finally, with me on the sofa, Ed at the dining table reading the paper, Dad in his armchair, and Mum sorting out the kitchen, Dad gave his final thought on the matter.

'I honestly don't know, James; you'll have to find out for yourself when you get there. All I know is that it's nothing to be worried about.'

'Yeah, just try it and see how it goes,' Ed added. 'The only thing I'd be worried about is the rumour that someone died in the waiting room once, and they say his ghost keeps returning on Monday mornings.' He followed this by making weird eyes at me.

I smiled at his attempt at levity. 'That doesn't worry me much because I've just seen a ghost float out of your body that used to be your sense of humour that's just died.'

Ed jumped up, grabbed me around the midriff, lifted me up with his left hand and scrunched my hair with his right. 'You cheeky little sod, you're going to pay for that.'

We fell onto the sofa and started laughing. Dad laughed from his armchair, and, after running into the room, Mum joined in when she realised the wrestling was a play fight and no more than that.

○ ○ ○

In bed that evening, I looked back at the day and realised I'd enjoyed it. I was still lonely, but my family was cool, and I liked that feeling. I then laid back and decided to perform a battlefield assessment of my plan's progress. Of the nine days completed, the breakdown was as follows: Fishing 3; Chess 2; Reading 2; Letter writing 1; Travelling sales assistant 1. The plan was going well, but then I added the following breakdown to the assessment: Lonely days 7 (I removed the chess days); Days waiting for a reply 4.

I decided to ignore the bare facts and decided to assess the overall effect of the campaign.

I was:

Happier.

More confident.

More engaged.

Feeling less worried about Ollie.

In control of my life.

I could only have dreamt of these feelings nine days earlier as Ollie pressed my head into the dust; the plan was working. Even after these nine days, I felt I would fight back if Ollie confronted me again.

Other aspects of my life were also changing. Today, when I was talking with Mum and Dad and playing about with Ed, I felt far less shame than I usually felt, the shame that held me back from fully committing to my family.

I turned on my side and pulled the sheets over my shoulders. I felt safe. I felt lonely.

○ ○ ○

On Monday morning, I took the nine-thirty bus into Wigan, making sure to get on at the Commercial square stop instead of the Town centre. Dr Arthur Clarke's constituency office was opposite the Prudential Building on Library Street. Although on a long street, the office stood on the corner where a road off Library Street led to Barracks square. I felt nervous as I walked down from Westgate towards the office. Beyond the office, I could see the gothic red-brick building that was Wigan college.

Looking down this street gave me an insight into what Wigan looked like in the past.

I knocked on the door and waited. A young man looked in my direction but seemed to ignore me. I knocked again, and eventually, a middle-aged woman came to the door.

'Hello, my name's James Smith, and I'm here to help.' I felt like a character out of Dickens. If I had a hat, I would surely have doffed it and held it to my breast.

'Well, come in, James; I'm sure we could do with your help.' The woman held the door open. I walked in and stood to await further instruction. 'My name's Anita, and over there's my son, Alan. We're the only two who usually work here.'

It was such a pokey room that I couldn't believe it needed as many as two people to man it. The room was partitioned with the doctor's private office hiding behind frosted glass. The front area looked like a medical doctor's waiting room, with a small desk at the front that was probably manned by Anita acting as a receptionist whenever Doctor Clarke was in residence. Today the front desk was being manned by Alan, a long-haired youth, who appeared to be reading New Musical Express, with the option to read an Autocar magazine, should his interest in the music industry begin to wane.

'If you come through here with me, James, I'm sure we can find something useful for you to do,' said Anita in a bright and cheery voice. There was no doubt in my mind that her glass was always half-full. As I walked toward Alan, his head was forced down in his paper. There was no way he was going to say anything.

'Good morning, Alan, nice to meet you,' I said brightly, but the reader said nothing, not even a grunt. Anita and I walked past him to Dr Clarke's office.

After closing the door, Anita whispered, 'don't mind Alan, he'd in a bit of a mood after his girlfriend left him over the weekend.'

'I don't mind at all, Anita; I hope he gets over her quickly,' I said, thinking it to be the right thing to say. 'Are you sure you don't mind me calling you by your first name? I usually call adults Mr or Mrs.'

She smiled. 'My, but you're an old-fashioned soul, aren't you, James. No, I'm happy for you to call me Anita; I prefer being called Anita to Mrs Sidebotham.' I then wondered, probably unfairly, if Alan's mood was more to do with his surname than his recent split. Anita then showed me a pile of documents; these were notes of various surgeries the doctor had held here since 1974.

'Right, James; these are A4 suspension files, and I'd like you to create a file for each surgery by placing a plastic tab on the top, like these.' Anita then showed me a rack of suspension files with the aforementioned tabs. 'You then, for each surgery, need to sort the records into alphabetical order based on the attendee's surname. Right, see those metal filing strips,' I nodded that I had seen them, 'well, you need to poke these through the suspension files like this.' Anita then showed me how to push them through to create two metal prongs inside the suspension file. 'So now, all you have to do is to use that large paper punch to make two holes in the records for that day's surgery.' I nodded again, but the amount of detail was creating a sense of panic. 'Right, now turn the day's pile of records over and pick the records for the person with the surname closest to zed.' She demonstrated all this and picked up the uppermost record from a pile she had prepared earlier. 'Ah, on this day, that person was Mrs Katherine Yates. I now place this record over the two prongs and place a tabbed spacer card over it. I write her name on the tab, proceed to the next record, and so on. Any questions, James?'

'Not really, Anita. I'll start with this pile you've prepared, and if I feel I'm not doing it correctly, I'll ask you or Alan for guidance,' I answered.

'I'd rather you ask me, James, if that's okay?' I nodded, happy with her suggestion.

○ ○ ○

The day was dull and monotonous, giving me a newfound respect for administrative staff. Still, I managed to file away about a third of the documents and enjoyed the packed lunch Mum had prepared. I felt a warm glow when I opened the blue Tupperware box and saw the tidy triangles of bread holding the prized salmon paste and cucumber filling. As I bit into the first sandwich, it was as if I was sitting in our kitchen, with Mum asking me if they were okay, and not sitting on my own listening to Anita and Alan talk in the front office about their domestic arrangements. That was the best memory of the day.

As I saw Ailsworth coming into view, I was at the front of the upper deck of the bus, and having been in Wigan and walked its majestic historic streets, I realised how small it was in the world, despite it being my entire life. Would it be here forever? Is there a place in the world for towns that no longer serve their intended purpose? I knew unemployment was high, as was the number of houses for sale. Still, it plodded on, building new units to house new businesses with grants to lure companies that had never heard of Ailsworth before filling in their application.

As I stepped off the bus at the Town centre stop, I'd totally forgotten I was mid-plan and casually walked down the street. Luckily, something caught my left eye, and instinctively I turned to see what it was. Running towards me with a look of thunder on his face was Ollie Jenkins. His face was contorted with rage, and my stomach filled with fear.

Once he saw I'd spotted him, there was little need for his stealthiness. 'Oi, come here, you little cunt,' he bellowed and sped up towards me. I turned and ran in the opposite direction, hoping my acceleration would be adequate enough to keep us apart. It was. Ollie Came to within five yards of me, but by then, I was up to speed, and I knew that my intrinsic fitness and speed were superior to his. Gradually, we pulled apart, and I heard him stop. I turned around and stared at him. He was bent double with his hands holding onto his knees as he gulped in the air he so desperately needed. I wanted to say something to him. That I wasn't afraid anymore, but I couldn't because I was. I was still scared, despite my feelings to the contrary last night. Ollie straightened up, placed his hands on his hips briefly, and then pointed at me.

'One of these days, I'll catch you unawares, and the fucking pain you'll experience will be like nothing you've experienced in your pathetic life so far,' Ollie snarled breathlessly.

I saw no traffic coming, so I sprinted across the High Street and jogged in my original direction towards home. I looked behind and saw Ollie walking dejectedly home. Despite knowing that Ollie hadn't the fitness to restart after me, I kept glancing back to make sure.

COMPLACENT - COMPLACENCY: N, Adj

- *Something I must avoid at all costs.*
- *It was the one thing that could undo all my hard work.*

Ollie was busy beating the living shit out of James because James had been Complacent.

James was at risk of being ambushed by Ollie because he'd allowed Complacency to creep in.

Once I knew I was safe, I stopped to catch my breath. What the hell was I thinking? Strolling around Ailsworth Town centre without a care in the world? I had no right to do such a thing. I closed my eyes and tried to imagine what Ollie would have done had he the speed or stamina to outrun me or if I hadn't glimpsed his movement. For a brief moment, I felt thankful that it was Ollie who had chosen to bully me; most other lads I knew would have had me in their grasp. I wasn't grateful for long because I knew most other lads were not evil. Having evaded Ollie for almost ten days, I realised that when I came face to face with him, I was never going to stand up, take a beating and then tell him to fuck off; that it was over. I saw his eyes, and the dread flooded back into my heart. I started back home.

During the walk home, despite my pounding heart, I did consider, in hindsight, that the level of dread and panic I experienced may not have been as high as the level of terror I usually experienced during the school year. I thought back and realised that I *had* run away. Even when he was snarling at me, I remember feeling a level of control I'd never felt before, making it possible for me to assess the situation and run across the road. So, despite my earlier conviction that I was still under his control, my reaction convinced me it was worth persevering with my plan, although I'd have to change my bus stop tomorrow.

◦ ◦ ◦

Tuesday and Wednesday were again uneventful and tedious, the highlight being Alan spilling his mug of tea over his car magazine.

'What are you looking at, you little shit?' Alan turned on me because he needed someone to blame. I didn't answer, and he ran into the back kitchen for paper towels. It was pointless; the magazine was beyond saving.

'Never mind, dear, there'll be another out in a couple of weeks,' his mother reassured him after hearing his little rant.

'Why does he have to be here, anyway? He's a total waste of time,' he nodded towards me.

'I may well be a waste of time, but at least I'm not being paid to be one,' I said, much to my own amazement.

Alan took a few seconds to digest what I'd said. 'You cheeky little….'

'Now, boys, stop this nonsense. It was clearly an accident, and no one here is a waste of time, okay?' Anita spoke authoritatively to quell Alan's temper and satisfy me that I'd be safe. I returned to finish my work, leaving mother and son to chat about more family arrangements or whatever else they discussed. By the end of Wednesday, I'd completed the task given to me, so I thought that would be the end of my time there. But, as I was picking up my little bag, Anita told me to come back tomorrow because Dr Clarke would be conducting his surgery tomorrow, and since Alan wasn't available, it would help her greatly if I attended. I said I'd be happy to help out.

Before I left, I went over to Alan to offer my hand. 'Since you're not here tomorrow, Alan, I thought I'd say goodbye. Sorry for being cheeky and all that,' I said.

Alan looked at me, gave a shrug, and shook my hand. 'No problem, squirt; you did okay to stand up for yourself. Sorry I was arsey, it's been a bad week, that's all. Nothing personal.' I nodded and knew that would be the last I'd ever see of him.

I've noticed that this happens throughout someone's life. It has undoubtedly happened in mine. You meet someone, and then they disappear, never to be seen again. In primary school, one of our "gang" was a boy called Tony Hazzard. He played football and made us laugh with his impersonations of TV stars Johnny Ball and John Noakes. He was a part of my life but disappeared towards the end of our final year in primary. Mum told me that his Dad had been offered a new job and had moved to Newcastle. Unlike Alan, I missed Tony, but only in passing. He simply wasn't there anymore, and no one felt any sadness despite him being a small part of our lives at the time.

As I sat to ride home, I reflected that the one brief meeting I had in Cemaes would be the first and last time I'd ever see Rhian. She hadn't bothered to reply, so my first stab at making some sort of friend had ended in failure. I wondered if you became more aware of these losses the older you get. Do people become more important in our lives as we depend on them to fill a void that our solitary existence creates? Despite that setback with Rhian, I still felt the plan was working and thought about tomorrow and meeting the good doctor; I desperately wanted to meet my first-ever MP.

○ ○ ○

As I walked down Library Street on Thursday morning, people would notice a distinct bounce in my step, a happy air about my persona, and a contented smile on my face. We were going on holiday! Dad told us last night that he'd booked a B&B in Blackpool for a whole week. A full week! I skipped into the Labour office and saw that Anita was already there.

'Right, no time to dilly-dally this morning, James,' she said, confusing me because I never thought for one moment that I'd dilly-dallied. 'Arthur will be here shortly, and he'll take his place through there. You need to be ready with appointment forms,' I nodded, looking at the blank form she held. 'When someone comes in, hand them this form, clipboard and pen and ask them to fill in their details. Once they've finished, return the form clipboard and pen to me, and I'll pass them on to Arthur. He will then see the first five sequentially before taking a ten-minute break.' I nodded.

At around ten to ten, Dr Arthur Clarke and his secretary, an efficient prim-looking woman, the likes I'd seen throughout my school life, entered the building. He seemed like a lovely man and thanked me for helping out this week. To be fair to Anita, she took time to show Dr Clarke the filing I'd done, and I heard her tell him how well I'd stuck to the task.

The day was probably more boring than the others because I had less to do, the compensation being the varied types of attendees I came face to face with. Naturally, there were men and women, but the sub-categories were varied. There were black and white, young and old, and smart and casual attendees. The casual category could, unfortunately, be broken down further into the poor and hippy (although hippy is a rather generic description, on my part, of young people who had long hair, wore jeans, strangely patterned tee shirts, and sported weak beards). The one I liked least was a shaven-headed young man wearing jeans and a similar jacket who sat with his arms folded as he waited, sporting a ridiculously animated frown. He certainly wasn't happy, and I felt sorry for Dr Clarke because I doubted anything he'd say would cheer up that young man.

Apart from a few raised voices, unsurprisingly, the frowning bedenimed man was the most vociferous; the day was relatively uneventful. At half past three, Anita gave me the good news that everyone had been seen and asked if I could look around the room for any discarded litter. To give people their due, considering how many people had attended the surgery, the room was reasonably tidy, and the worst job was emptying the cigarette butts into the dustbin outside. When I told Anita I'd finished, she gave me an awkward hug.

'You've been such a help for us this week, James. Thank you so much,' she said. She held me at arm's length, smiled, and tilted her head. I'd seen this expression before, which usually happened when my parents were about to reveal a gift. 'James,' she spoke slowly, raising my expectations, 'Dr Clarke would like to see you in his office; he'd like to thank you personally.' Her eyes were as wide open as I'd ever seen them when she finished.

'Oh,' I said, hiding my disappointment at the news, 'that's great, Anita. Now?' I asked.

'Yes, yes; in you go, James,' she knocked and held open the door for me.

The doctor was behind his desk, signing some forms that his secretary then placed in a briefcase before walking out to talk to Anita. I patiently watched the doctor put his impressive-looking pen to one side as he asked me to sit.

'James Smith! Your Dad was right when he said you were a good 'un. Anita has said how good you've been, and I thought I'd take this opportunity to thank you myself. But before I do that, I wondered how you found this week? Did you get anything out of it, sort to speak?'

Doctor Arthur Clarke was thin and tall and didn't conform to my stereotypical image of a northern Labour MP. He was young compared to the Wilsons and Callaghans of the Labour Party, and he spoke clearly with only a slight accent to indicate his northernicity. His thin, tanned face gave an intelligent allusion that his calm manner and smooth movements supported. But what had I got out of helping this man out?

I could have mentioned how lazy Alan Sidebotham was and that I must be an ist of some kind because I'd instantly categorised the frowner as being trouble. I know that doesn't make me a racist, but it does make me something; I'll check when I get home. I played it safe.

'I found that I could cope with new tasks and, more importantly, finish them. I also met different types of people I don't usually see around Ailsworth,' I said.

'Good, excellent. I'm glad you enjoyed yourself,' said the doctor, and I didn't want to disappoint him by saying, "I wouldn't go so far as to say that", but I didn't. 'Is there anything you'd like to ask me, James?' Dr Clarke asked.

That took me by surprise, but I immediately decided that rather than ask about the purpose of an MP's surgery, I thought back to the conversation I'd shared with Mr Peter Crabtree. Yes, my question will be political, a veritable grenade that will make the MP quiver at its controversial implications and subtle nuances.

It's incredible how quickly your mind works, (I obviously couldn't know how fast other people's minds operate – I use it as a medical term to describe the marvel we contain within our skulls. In saying that, do I consider the mind of Ollie Jenkins and others of his ilk marvellous? I'd dug myself into a quandary that would require careful consideration at a later date. But that digression does show the speed with which thoughts flash through one's mind), and I scanned through the new political knowledge I picked up last Saturday.

Will I ask him if the miners' 35% pay rise would alienate the unions from people who received far less? Will I ask him if the Labour Party should stick to serving the Unions and allow the

Liberal Party to represent our social conscience? Will I ask him if it was okay for the Unions to drag the Labour Party into being the only political party to oppose the continued membership of the EEC? No! I had my question, and it came from a combination of my History lessons and my newfound political expertise.

'Why are the Conservatives always the baddies?' I asked, cringingly realising that I'd used a Western film analogy.

The doctor smiled. I deemed that a reasonable response to my childlike question, and I could see him placing James Smith into the pigeon-hole reserved for Primary school children. 'Www, now,' he said patronisingly. 'I didn't expect that kind of question, James. Right, I'll try my best to give you an answer,' he paused for a few seconds. 'To start with, not all Conservatives are bad, and I'm on friendly terms with several of their backbench MPs. So, why do you believe that they are the baddies?' He asked and seemed to emphasise the last word.

'Well, in the nineteenth century, for example, it was the Whiggs who seemed to care about social justice, then the Liberals and now the Labour party. Why is it that the Conservatives are always the anti-party and unwilling to support fair play?' I asked.

That response seemed to take him aback. 'That puts a different slant on your first question, so now, the answer you're looking for is hidden deep in the old values of the Conservative party. They are historically the party that supports landowners and businesses, and to support those, they are happy to sacrifice the rights of working people. That is to say, they try to remove any barriers that prevent businesses from making more money. Does that make sense?'

'Not really, Dr Clarke. If that were the case, I could not imagine the Conservative party getting even ten per cent of the votes at an Election. Surely, some working people must also vote for them?'

Dr Clarke folded his arms. 'You bring up an important point, James,' he said, seeming to ponder his reply. 'There is an unfortunate trait that many people possess. It is a trait that has fed the Conservative Party for decades. You see, most young people are socially sensitive. It is an intrinsic belief that comes from sharing experiences with classmates and friends from different social classes. When you play football, do you refuse to play against Fred because his father's unemployed?'

I didn't know a Fred, but I could see where he was going with this. 'No, of course I wouldn't refuse.'

'Similarly, when you talk with someone, do you base your liking of them on their social status or on the similarities of your beliefs or shared sense of humour?'

'Social status is never a consideration, as far as I know,' I offered. In thinking about what the doctor was saying, I could picture groups in school with something in common, but I didn't know a group that only comprised rich children. 'However, I don't know what goes on in Grammar schools, sir,' I cringed as I said the word. Thankfully, the doctor ignored the metaphorical doffing of my cap.

'In theory, Grammar schools should be no different to state schools. But Grammar schools are perceived to be of a higher grade. That is not true. The difference between the two types is the eleven-plus test that children have to sit in order to qualify for Grammar school. Since 1965 many grammar schools have converted to be comprehensive. The Labour government will force those remaining direct grant grammar schools wishing to remain as grammar schools to either convert or become fee-paying. Did you sit your eleven-plus, James?' he asked.

I was still reeling from his last answer. 'Uh, no, Dad thinks eleven is too young an age for children to be categorised,' I managed to dig out.

'So, are you happy with the standard of education you're receiving at your state school? Is it challenging you?'

'Yes, most subjects push me in some way or another. I think a lot of the quality of education is linked to the teacher's ability. For example, we all hated our RE teacher because he was a psychopath.'

The doctor smiled at this. 'Apart from psychopathic teachers, we must defend the universal right for all children to receive the best possible education. In doing so, we ensure that everyone, irrespective of social status, competes intellectually and not based on privilege and class.'

'You're talking about private schools, aren't you, Dr Clarke?'

'Yes, James, I am. Entry into these schools is based on satisfying financial and academic criteria, making it difficult for children like you to compete. These private schools also create networks that protect their privileged society. I think it is regrettable that Britain still has private schools.'

I was beginning to lose the thread of our original debate and saw that the doctor sounded more depressed. 'But this doesn't explain why so many people vote for Conservatives, does it?'

'Ah, yes,' he seemed to remember the original question, 'the problem with society is this trait within people to move away from seeing the importance of social justice to where they wish to preserve the status they reach, perhaps through hard work. I know many people who, during their youth, were very vocal in their support of socialist ideals, but after working for a while, buying a house, and maybe gaining a promotion, they suddenly change and fear losing what they've worked for. They become Conservatives with a small c. I've seen it happen throughout my adult life. I studied at Bath university, and of that year's intake, I know that fifteen of them vote conservative, only Terry Price from South Wales, and I vote Labour. The scary thing is that Terry and I were probably the most moderate when we were studying; the others espoused radical socialist doctrines that seemed to come from the USSR.'

I genuinely found that interesting and thought I'd cheer up the doctor. 'Don't worry, Dr Clarke, I won't change.'

He chortled. 'Thank you, James; I'm glad to hear that. Tell me, do you like to read?'

'Oh yes, I love reading. I'm currently reading Great Expectations and need to re-read Lord of the Flies for my 'O' levels.' I'd suddenly forgotten about politics.

'Good, what do you make of Pip, then?' Dr Clarke asked, and I went into a sudden panic. 'Do you like him as a character?' he asked, seeing my reluctance or inability to answer.

'Since it is written through his voice, disliking Pip would be counterproductive. I will need to understand Pip rather than like or dislike him,' I answered.

'That is a politician's answer if ever I've heard one, James. Excellent. Anyway, read it through and see what becomes of him and what drives him to strive for what he thinks he wants. It is a fascinating book, and I have two more books I'd like you to read if you have the time.' The doctor began to scribble on a blank sheet of paper, like a proper doctor writing out a prescription, only legibly. 'Check your local Library and see if they have these books available. They will be an excellent way to combine History, Politics and English.'

He handed me the sheet of paper for me to study. I knew about "Animal Farm" by George Orwell, but I'd never read it because I believed the title was too childish for my discerning tastes. 'The Ragged Trousered Philanthropists? By Robert Tressell?' I read aloud. I'd never heard of the book or author.

'Yes, James Smith. That is a book I'm sure you'll understand and appreciate,' he said. It sounded as if the chat was winding down.

'Thank you, Dr Clarke; I'll look them up. So thank you for this week and for the opportunity to help out. It was interesting,' I stepped towards him and offered my hand.

Dr Clarke stood up, and we shook across the desk. 'Thank you, James; I've really enjoyed this chat and hope you continue to take an interest in politics because it affects everyone.' We released our hands, and the doctor smiled. 'Here, this envelope is for you. I hope it demonstrates my appreciation for what you did this week,' he handed over the envelope with "To James Smith", beautifully written using that impressive pen.

I looked at the envelope and then back at the doctor. 'Thank you,' I said, meaning every word of it. The fact that it was only two words may make me sound ungrateful; I wasn't.

∘ ∘ ∘

On the way home on the bus, I opened the envelope and was overjoyed to see two five-pound notes depicting the Queen and the Duke of Wellington in all their pomp. I imagined the fun I would have in Blackpool next week with this newfound wealth.

Blackpool. It was great to be going on holiday, but something about it was off. I had a sense of unease about the speed with which the holiday had been announced. I wasn't sure what I was uncomfortable with, but the initial joy had slowly evaporated to be replaced by an itch that required more and more scratching.

I replaced the money and looked at Dr Clarke's envelope with my name written in his immaculate handwriting. Unbeknown to me, this wouldn't be the only envelope I'd see addressed to me today.

15

When I arrived home, I'd alighted at the Commercial Square stop and made sure there was no sign of Ollie, I began to tell Mum about my day and the chat I'd had with Dr Clarke, but she seemed to ignore me.

'There's a letter for you,' she said, and my heart began to pound joyously. 'It's from Uncle Harry,' she added, and my disappointment quickly dampened my previous reaction.

'Oh, that's weird,' I said, having never previously received a letter from Uncle Harry. I opened it and saw that Uncle Harry's envelope housed another, like a Russian doll. I looked at the second envelope and, despite my excitement, smiled.

To James
The boy who forgot to include his address.
A Town near Wigan – I forgot what it was called.
England, as in not in Wales.

'Is that another envelope? Hidden inside Harry's?' Mum asked.

'Yes, last week I wrote a letter to a girl I met in Anglesey, and she's sent me a reply. It came from Uncle Harry because I'd forgotten to include my address, and this girl's mother runs one of the sweetshops that Uncle Harry delivers to.' I was surprised that I used girl instead of Rhian. It was probably an unconscious protective measure, and I was also surprised I'd told Mum the truth. It felt good, natural, and shame-free.

'That's nice, son. What were you saying about Dr Clarke?' I found it remarkable how Mum appeared to lose track of a conversation only to rejoin it later as if nothing had been said in the intervening period.

'Oh, I was just saying we had a lovely chat, and he gave me ten pounds for my efforts,' as I spoke, I was studying the writing on the envelope.

'That's good of him. Means you'll have some pocket money for next week. On that subject, can you decide what you want me to pack for you? Remember, we're going for a week.'

'Okay, Mum, I'll have a look through my stuff,' I said and walked off to my room with the sole intention of reading Rhian's reply.

∘ ∘ ∘

Dear James,

Why didn't *I* start with dear?

Thank you for your letter. I threw it into the bin initially because I couldn't see the point in it. Since I'm replying, you know it didn't stay there.

Don't worry about the power station. My Dad works there as a health physics monitor, and he's more than happy working there (I think it also pays well).

It was sad reading about your bully, but I can't say much to help you. As you say, it's something for you to sort out yourself; anything I say here will be pointless.

It's so sad that, as a result of the bullying, you have no friends. I have two friends, Gwen and Megan, whom I've known most of my life. I mix with others, but they're my two true friends. So, even though I only met you briefly, I couldn't imagine the boy I met being friendless. You came across as being confident, James.

Bryn and I have never experienced bullying as such, but I have had cause to adjust and pretend to like someone because I knew that if I didn't, then there would be a fair chance that she and her friends would target me. As you know, a community exists within schools that has as much impact on your life as the community we know outside.

I'm saying this because I don't think it's healthy for you to have seventy-year-old friends without having friends of a similar age to yourself. I think you need to trust Edward. I'm sure he'd understand because he's already negotiated school.

It's funny what you wrote in your letter about time. I stopped writing after that first section, and now that I've re-read it, I can see that after I said it would be pointless for me to say anything about bullying, I then went on and on about how you could adapt. Please ignore it, but I've left it in to show how difficult it is for me to understand.

I don't know what else to say, James, except - carry on with your plan.

I probably won't see you again, and I don't think you sending me letters will help you in your quest (it's not a plan, it's a quest to rid yourself of a monster), but if something interesting happens, then I promise not to throw your letters into the bin – just remember to include your address next time.

Yours Sincerely

Rhian

I read the entire letter three times but re-read the last paragraph six more times. Initially, I thought that was the end of it, that she didn't want any more letters, but the last part suggested she did. From this, I deduced that she didn't want to be inundated with pathetic "help, I'm being bullied" letters and only wanted occasional letters when I had something positive to say. I smiled and felt happy with her sensible approach.

I looked up Quest in the dictionary and loved the description – "A long search for something, especially for some quality such as happiness".

QUEST noun

- *My desperate search to find James Smith.*
- *My search for an escape from my current life.*

In his quest to find happiness, James Smith devised a plan.
In order to rid himself of the monster, James set out on an arduous quest that would test his self-belief.

∘ ∘ ∘

After Mum left for the Bingo at nine, Dad and I sat watching TV together. During the first ad break, Dad asked how I'd gotten on with Dr Clarke.

'He seemed quite nice, but still a politician and not talking like a free man,' I said, deliberately trying to get Dad engaged.

'I'm afraid they're all like that, son,' he wasn't taking the bait. 'It's one of life's great disappointments that people who should look after you and your interests are usually too afraid to voice their honest opinions about matters. A Labour MP, especially a backbench MP is guided by their National Executive Committee, and it takes a brave MP to stand up against their directives,' he said, with more than a hint of sadness in his voice.

Since I'd failed to wind up Dad, hoping he'd defend Dr Clarke, I changed tack. 'He gave me ten pounds for my work this week,' I said.

'That's not much money for four days' work, is it? I'll have a word with him next time I see the old miser,' Dad joked, but again not engaging.

'Why are we going on holiday next week?' I asked. Despite my joy hearing about the Blackpool break, it had come out of the blue, and something had been niggling me. Usually, Mum and Dad would tell us about a holiday, weeks, if not months, in advance.

'What do you mean?' Dad asked, and I noted his tone had changed.

'You never mentioned we were going on a holiday this year,' I answered. 'You've told us we needed to look after our money because of the inflation.

'Well, this B&B became available when Arthur from the sorting office told me they'd had to pull out because his mother-in-law had been taken ill. I'm simply paying Arthur what he paid for the holiday, and that way, no one is out of pocket because he won't lose his deposit.' Dad pointed out that the programme was about to restart.

I stared into his smiling face and concentrated on his eyes. I nodded and turned to watch whatever it was we were watching, and my senses bristled as I tried to control my nausea.

Dad had just lied to my face.

○ ○ ○

Dad's lie resurfaced as I lay trying to sleep, making me anxious. I sat up and tried to work out why he would do such a thing. After considering every possible angle, it was apparent he knew about me being bullied by Ollie; nothing else made sense, and he thought a week away would help me. I knew he hadn't seen my dictionary, or he would have said something earlier, so how on earth did he find out?

Mr Peter Crabtree!

16

On Friday morning, I felt ill at ease, with questions flying through my mind, making me rather tetchy. Mum, unaware I was struggling with my inner thoughts, kept trying to glean some information about the contents of the letter I'd received. Initially, I answered her questions in good humour, always returning to my inner turmoil when I believed I'd satisfied her curiosity. But when Mum persisted in prodding me further, I screamed at her and stormed out of the house.

Outside, I felt wretched and cursed myself for being so insensitive. I couldn't leave Mum like that; it wasn't fair, and I had nowhere safe to go. I knew she wanted me to be a daughter, and now I could see why. I looked at our terraced house from the gate, the only home I'd known and Mum's entire world, her dreams. I returned to the house to face her.

When I got back in, Mum was in the living room, drinking tea. She'd been crying. As she sipped, I saw her bottom lip quiver. 'I'm sorry, Mum, I shouldn't have done that. It was pathetic.' Mum shrugged, holding her mug in both hands and stared at the dark screen of the unplugged TV, probably staring at her sorrowful reflection and life. I felt awful. I knelt in front of her, blocking out the TV.

'You've no idea, James; no idea at all what I go through every day,' she managed to say before taking another sip to hide her emotion.

'I know you wanted me to be a girl, and I can imagine how hard it is for you to live with three males. I also know I've been a disappointment to you.' I lowered my head, thinking of the times I'd lied or hidden my bruises from her.

'Oh no, James, love. You're not a disappointment, God, no! It's just John, Edward and you, plus one other. I feel I'm always in your shadows, unable to shine in my own right.'

'God, Mum, don't be daft. Without you, we'd be lost. It's just, well, I can't speak for Dad or Ed, but I find it difficult to share things with people. I don't know if I would be able to if I were a girl; that's impossible for me to say, but I honestly don't deliberately exclude you, Mum. I'd never do that; I love you too much to do that.' I bowed my head in shame.

Mum must have put her mug down because she leaned forward, held, and kissed the top of my head. 'You're a silly sausage, James Smith. I love you, too,' she squeezed her head against mine. 'Look at the two of us, sad and despondent on a Friday with a holiday to look forward to.' She sounded happier as she pulled away to sit back.

'I know, Mum. It will be great in Blackpool, but it's a shame Ed's not coming.' I tried to sound upbeat and decided to share a fragment of my story. 'That letter was from a girl called Rhian. While Uncle Harry was in the sweetshop, I went for a walk, and this girl stopped to talk. She was friendly, and I thought I'd send her a letter saying I liked talking to her.'

'So it's nothing serious?' she asked, smiling now.

'No, I just,' I didn't know what to say next. 'I've been stupid, Mum. I've relied on Ollie for too long as a friend, and now that I want to wean myself off him, I find that I don't have any friends left. So, after I met Rhian, it was natural for me to send her a letter. So it's nothing serious, but it shows that I'm struggling a bit here in Ailsworth. It's hopefully a phase in my life that will soon pass,' I said, knowing it was a half-truth at best.

'Oh, James! You shouldn't have cut yourself off from other children like that. I know you were true to Ollie, but you should have mixed with others. It's not good for you to not have friends.' She sounded totally engaged in my woes, forgetting her own.

'I know that now, Mum, but I was just thinking, are *you* okay?'

Her eyes opened wide in shock. 'Whatever do you mean?'

'I know you go to Bingo on Tuesdays and Thursdays, but I never see other women here chatting.'

(I'm only fifteen, and many things will probably haunt me for some time, but what happened next was one of the worst things I've ever experienced.)

Mum sat stock-still for a few seconds before starting to tremble as tears ran down her cheeks. She dropped her head into her hands and bawled uncontrollably. I didn't know what to do; I'd broken my mother!

'Mum, Mum, I didn't mean anything by that; I'm just worried about *you*. Sorry, sorry; Mum, are you okay?' I was desperate to know.

She continued to cry uncontrollably, but slowly, gradually, she began to calm herself. She pulled a handkerchief from her left sleeve and blew her nose, wiping it side to side. When she raised her face to look at me, the carefully applied eyeliner ran freely like a black wave down her reddened cheeks (I didn't appreciate that Mum wore make-up, but that was another example of me selfishly taking her for granted). Her upper lip and nose seemed red raw, and her cheeks appeared puffy. Her face looked like a grotesque mask, and then she smiled. From behind her pain and misery, she smiled. That's what hurt most. Her smile.

'I'm okay, James, love; I'm just being silly.'

'No, you're not. You're hurt, and I made it worse. Instead of helping you, I said a horrible thing, I….' I couldn't finish my apology as I felt the tears well up. 'I'm sorry, Mum,' I eventually managed.

Mum took two deep sniffs and pushed herself upright, regal. 'James, I'm forty-four years of age, and I struggle to make friends. It's my fault; I know that and am trying to improve the situation.'

'I don't understand,' I said, genuinely confused why Mum would struggle to make new friends.

'Do you remember Aunt June?'

'Yes, I think I do. She lived three doors away, and I played with her son, Chris,' I answered, remembering being close to Chris in Primary school. 'Yes! She used to come here for chats, didn't she?'

''Yes. June and I were very close and used to visit each other's homes when you were in school.' Mum's eyes suddenly brightened up. 'We used to share everything, talk about everything and laugh about everything. It was great having a friend like that, but then her husband got a promotion to Birmingham somewhere, and she left.' A dark shadow descended over her face again.

'Yes, I remember feeling sad when Chris left, but I had school, didn't I? You had nothing.' I immediately regretted saying it. I was stating the obvious and hurting Mum like Ollie would hurt me, prodding and punching a defenceless target. I wasn't handling this at all well.

'No, I had nothing. Dad knew something was wrong and began taking me out for dinner more often; it was Dad who told me about the job at the Post Office. I think he hoped it would help me. It did sort of help, but there's a glass barrier between the customers and me at the Post Office counter where I work, and because of that, I suppose I feel different about them.' Mum was keeping it together, but I still didn't quite understand. I decided not to say anything for fear of upsetting her further.

Mum seemed to sense that I still had questions, and we both fell silent. As I studied her face, I knew she was thinking of how best to explain something else. I held her hand and waited. 'I find this difficult to admit, James, because, by recognising it, I should be able to sort it out.' I was unsure what she meant, and my confusion was probably apparent. 'You see, I'm a bit of a snob, and I keep thinking my current state of affairs is temporary, and I'll soon be whisked away by your dad to live in a beautiful palatial house to live happily ever after.' She looked at me, knowing it was a silly thing to say.

'There's nothing wrong with wanting more out of life, Mum, but everyone wants that. Aunt June left to find that, but she was happy here, from what I remember. She was always smiling and content and certainly not a snob. Do you think she's happier now?' I asked.

'I'm not saying that, James; I'm just saying that I find it difficult to mix with people. They all seem to have established friendships, and because I'm afraid of letting my guard down, I don't see a way to make new friends.' She sounded lost.

'I know we're not snobs. We're Ailsworth people, and our families come from around this area. I'm sure that, either through work, or the Bingo, or whatever, you will have friends again, and I know you'll be happy,' I looked at her intently as if forcing my words to penetrate her sadness. 'You deserve to be happy, Mum, and I'm sure you'll make friends in no time.' I remembered something. 'What about that family who've just moved into number nine? Have you been to talk to them yet?'

'Number nine? They're in their early thirties. Why would they want to be friends with a forty-four-year-old snob?' She smiled as she said this.

'Because I've seen her walking her son to school, and she seemed nice whenever I said good morning to them. They've only been here for six weeks, and I'm sure she also feels lonely.'

Mum smiled and pulled me close. 'I love you, son, my little Sigmund Freud. I've always wanted a chat like this, and I should have encouraged you to share more of your life instead of letting you fend for yourself. Well, at least you're in charge of *your* life, and I'm so happy about that, but it's not fair that you should worry about me. That's not fair at all.'

'Mum! I'm not worried about you. You're fine. You've just allowed yourself to lose confidence, and confidence is like riding a bike after falling off,' I suggested.

'What, you just need to jump back on and away you go?'

'No, you need to ensure everything is okay *before* jumping back on. Check the tyres, the brakes, the chain and the bell. If the bike's ready, *then* you jump back on it. You need to make sure that *you're* ready, Mum, and from what I can see – you are, you really are.'

'I've never been compared to a bike before, but I sort of understand what you're trying to say. Bloody hell, James, I was only joking when I called you Sigmund Freud, you know!' We both laughed and held each other tightly. At least Mum hadn't lied to me.

17

After Mum and I shared a mug of tea and a slice of her victoria sponge, I decided to visit the Library in Ailsworth to search for the two books suggested by Dr Clarke. I carefully mapped out my route to minimise potential spots for an ambush and set off, feeling happier after my long overdue chat with Mum. The only sour note was hearing Mum bravely admit her shortcomings while I said nothing about mine.

My route worked well, and soon I was busily searching for the books. "Animal Farm" was there, but there was no copy of "The Ragged Trousered Philanthropists". I decided not to take out "Animal Farm"; instead, I caught the bus for Wigan. This was all spur-of-the-moment stuff, but I was now far more confident in avoiding Ollie.

Wigan library wasn't far from the Labour Party offices, just further down Library Street. As I walked past the empty office, I wondered what Dr Clarke was doing now. He was probably packing his suitcase for a well-deserved holiday, and I doubted it would be in Blackpool. After walking past, I could see that Library Street was quite grand, with beautiful gothic red-brick buildings on the left as I walked down the street. I passed The Royal London Friendly Society building, totally unaware of what went on there, which was quite grand, but the next building was really splendid. I stopped on the pavement on the opposite side of the road and studied the steps leading to the darkened cave-like entrance of the technical college.

A lady pushing a shopping trolley bumped into me. 'Stop hogging the pavement!' her voice was shrill and angry. I apologised and walked further down until I came to the public library. That was also red-bricked and grand, with a shield that said "Loyal Au Mort" below the carved words of "Free Library".

I went in, filled out the registration form and strolled around the shelves to look for my books.

I could have asked the librarian where the two books were, but instead, I decided to carry out a leisurely wander and enjoyed a lovely experience. Seeing so many books in so many different sizes, written by so many authors, on so many subjects, and in so many genres filled me with wonderment. In addition to housing books, magazines, newspapers, and quiet people, a library also contains a particular smell. I can't explain what it smells like because it simply smells of a library.

After thirty minutes or so of taking in the delightful atmosphere, my senses were satiated, and I focused on the task. I soon found both books, took them to the desk to be stamped and thanked the librarian. As I left, I smiled; it had taken quite a bit of effort, the bus and so on, to finally take so little time to complete. It didn't feel proportional, but I suppose life is like that sometimes. A lot of effort for such a tiny return, like when Mum and Dad decide to decorate a room. They huff and puff and argue, and the room hardly looks any different when it's all done. I'm probably too young to understand effort and reward where decorating's concerned, but I know that the effort I'm making this summer will be worth it. The reward is enormous.

○ ○ ○

Before Dad set out for his usual trip to the Railway Inn, I asked him if he'd ask Mr Crabtree if it would be okay for another game of chess tomorrow. When I got up on Saturday morning, there was a note on the kitchen table. "Peter okay for chess – 11.00hrs – but needs to finish by 13:00hrs". That would do me fine.

○ ○ ○

After finishing my breakfast, I washed my bowl and spoon in the still-warm water and dried them. As I was putting them away, I heard someone behind me. It was Mum, and she was standing close to me.

'Bloody hell, Mum, you almost gave me a heart attack!'

'Sorry, love, I just wanted to hug you, that's all,' she said. 'I know that sounds creepy, but I wanted to say thanks, that's all.'

'It's nothing, Mum; I always wash my dishes when I'm finished,' I said, knowing it wasn't what she meant.

'I don't mean the dishes, you fool; I mean yesterday's chat. It did me good.'

I sat back down at the table, and she sat opposite me. 'I was afraid I'd touched a few raw nerves and made things worse,' I offered.

'God, no; it did me good, and I think the old bike's ready,' she said, immediately putting her hand to her lips. 'Oh, that sounded wrong, didn't it?' I nodded, and the two of us laughed. 'I took your advice and went to see Patricia at number nine yesterday. She was lovely and was so happy that I'd gone there with a cake as a welcoming gift. We had a mug of tea, and she told me they were from Burnley. Her husband's a police sergeant, recently promoted, and he's been posted to Wigan,' Mum enthused.

'Weren't you a bit too old for her, then?' I asked.

'Ha bloody ha, James Smith! No, I wasn't; she was lovely,' Mum smiled, 'but if it wasn't for you, I'd never have known that, so that's why I wanted to thank you, my little Marge Proops.'

I knew who she was referring to, but I didn't much care for that comparison. 'Mum, I much preferred Sigmund Freud,' I said.

She reached across the table, held my hand and said, 'thank you, James, my son.'

○ ○ ○

As I emerged from the backstreet onto the High Street just up from Lower Valeview Terrace, I saw a boy walking towards me down Lord Street. It was Ernie Taynor.

'Hi, Ernie; you okay?' I asked.

The nervous-looking boy looked up. 'Oh, hi James, I'm fine, thanks. Are you okay?'

'Yeah, I'm good,' I answered. It was clear that Ernie wanted to move on. 'Uhm, can I ask you something, Ernie?'

'Uh, what's that then, James?' Ernie looked nervous.

'It's more like advice, really, because I saw Ollie Jenkins shouting at you the other day. Well, he's been bullying me for a long time, and I should have done something about it, but I didn't,' I waited for a reaction. There wasn't one; Ernie kept dumbly looking at me. 'It's just that I should have told someone older about it before it became too late. I don't want that to happen to you, that's all, Ernie.' I looked at him, and he nodded.

'Thanks, James. I'm okay; he only did it that one time. I've had nothing else to do with him apart from that.'

'Good, I'm glad. Anyway, where are you off to now?' I asked.

'Oh, just popping to the bakery; Mum wants a couple of cakes for lunch,' Ernie said, looking happier.

'Cakes for lunch?' I gasped. 'That sounds brilliant!'

Ernie smiled. 'They're for after the mixed grill; we always have iced buns for Saturday lunch.'

'God, I'm so jealous,' I said.

'Anyway, where are you going?' Ernie asked.

'I'm going to Peter Crabtree's house to play chess; I'm due there for eleven,' I said.

'What, Pervy Pete's?' He naturally asked.

'He's not pervy; he's a lovely man, and we share an interest in chess. It's a good way to pass a couple of hours,' I smiled. 'So, I should get on, but it's been nice talking to you, Ernie,' I said and moved off.

'And you, James, and thanks,' Ernie added before moving off, no doubt lured by the sweet aroma of the iced buns.

As I strolled up from Lower Valeview towards Mr Crabtree's house, I was aware of a gnawing feeling that seemed to be getting worse. I think I was feeling stressed with everything that was happening. The letter from Rhian suggesting I ease off from my planned letter-writing outlet, Dad lying to my face, and Mum revealing her sadness had accumulated my stress to such an extent that I felt nauseous. I'd stored Rhian's letters to one side, and I'd address that if and when I have something to write about. My worry about Mum might be resolved if Pat at nine was a suitable replacement for June. Even if she were, I'd still encourage Mum to engage more openly with people she meets in the future. I think she'd enjoy the chats. My main issue was Dad's lie and the fact I believed Mr Crabtree to be the source of the leak of a secret. I felt our trust had been compromised and needed to sort it out before going on holiday.

○ ○ ○

'I do believe that to be checkmate, James, making it one game apiece,' Mr Crabtree was a gracious winner.

'Well played, Mr Crabtree; I didn't see your move with the Bishop until it was too late,' I said, hoping we'd have a break. I wasn't disappointed.

'I think this calls for a short interlude whereby tea and cake will refresh us in preparation for the final game.' Mr Crabtree rubbed his hands together theatrically, then stood and moved off to the kitchen. I followed.

The cake was a coffee sponge, one of my favourites. 'I met Dr Arthur Clarke on Thursday,' I mentioned.

'Mmm, interesting, and what did the good doctor have to say?' Mr Crabtree seemed intrigued.

'Not much, to be honest. He defended the Labour Party and its role in looking after the rights of the working people. We even discussed how people change, becoming more conservative as they grow older,' I explained.

'Good, I'm pleased you met him and got something out of it. Did he perchance pay you for your hard work?'

'Yes, he paid me ten pounds and recommended two books I should read.'

'No doubt that "The Ragged Trousered Philanthropists" would be one of the choices, and possibly "The Road to Wigan Pier" the second?'

I smiled. 'You're correct about the first, but the second was "Animal Farm".

'Yes, "Animal Farm" is an excellent choice, and you can always rely on the good doctor to recommend the "Philanthropists"; it's a socialist staple.'

'I did feel as if I could *trust* him, Mr Crabtree; that was reassuring,' I said, trying to set up my question.

'Yes, Arthur does come over as very trustworthy; I'd have to agree.'

'You, see, I believe that *trust* is an essential trait in a person, don't you, Mr Crabtree?'

Mr Crabtree remained silent for a while. 'Have you lost your confidence, James?' he asked.

'Why do you ask that, Mr Crabtree?' I asked.

'I ask because you clearly wish to broach a subject causing you some concern, which revolves around trust. So come! Say what is on your mind, James Smith.'

I was shocked by his sudden change of mood, but I was the injured party and persisted. 'On Thursday night, I chatted with my father about our forthcoming holiday to Blackpool. While a holiday is not unusual, the fact that he'd arranged it at such short notice was,' I explained.

'I'm sorry, James, but what point are you trying to make here?' Mr Crabtree asked, his temper now in abeyance.

'Well, in trying to explain the sudden decision by roping in a colleague from the Post Office, my father lied to my face. To my knowledge, he has never done that before and always encourages us to be honest and truthful.'

'Of which you are neither, James. Yet you suppose your father is lying to you, so I wonder why he would do that?'

'He's lied because he's using the holiday to remove me from Ailsworth and to protect me.'

'And what on earth could be negative in this approach, if I could ask?' Mr Crabtree was getting frustrated.

'There's nothing wrong with his approach, Mr Crabtree. The problem is the decision supposes he knows about my trouble. So, my concern is not about the holiday but understanding how my father found out about my problem.' When I finished my accusatory statement, I saw Mr Crabtree's face change as the penny dropped.

Mr Crabtree stood up from the table and went to stand at the kitchen sink. He stared out the window, holding the edge of the stainless sink and lowered his head. It was clear I'd upset him, and I realised, looking at him, that I'd accused an innocent man. He nodded twice and returned to the table.

'You thought your trust in me had been compromised by my earnest wish to save you from your troubles, that I'd cast adrift what I cherish most, and for what? To be popular with your father? Is that what you think, James?'

'No, not now. I can see in your demeanour that I reached a terrible conclusion. One that was incorrect,' I lowered my head in shame. 'When I saw my father lying to my face, my heart broke, and I was desperate to know how he found out. I'm ashamed to say that I pictured you and my father conversing in the Railway Inn, with my feebleness your chosen subject. I'm sorry, Mr Crabtree. I can see now, talking with you, how strong my trust should have been in your confidence.'

I expected and deserved a tongue-lashing. 'James, when you seek to better yourself and do it on your own, you will still need certainties that remain solid, steadfast. Your trust in me must be total, or I have failed you as a friend. It is as simple as that, and to hear that you did doubt me fills me with a terrible crushing sadness.'

It was too much for me, and I began to cry. My rescue mission was proving too much for my feeble mind to cope with. My head began to spin as my tears came, and I found breathing hard. Ollie's evil, Dad's lying, Mum's loneliness, the letter, and challenging Edward, even a politician. I was drowning and was shocked that I even considered my life might be better if I was still with Ollie. At least I knew what to expect despite my life having to live a wretched existence. Now I had hope, and the fear of losing it was the most frightening thing I could imagine. I wanted to scream.

To be fair to Mr Crabtree, he allowed my emotions to settle without intervening. Eventually, he saw that I'd gathered my thoughts and offered me another slice of cake. I declined.

'I'm so sorry to have doubted you, Mr Crabtree. It was unforgivable of me and makes me unworthy of your confidence.'

'James, my boy, you need to learn from this and trust people again. It will serve as a valuable lesson for your future,' he smiled.

'Thank you, Mr Crabtree; I do appreciate your support and guidance. They are an essential component of my current state of affairs,' I said, finding it difficult to fully colour the last sentence. We didn't have enough time for a final game of chess, so we chatted about the two books until it was time to leave.

I offered my hand at the door, and Mr Crabtree shook it enthusiastically. 'Take care, James Smith and enjoy your holiday. I would suggest "Animal Farm" over the other as your starting point.'

'Thank you, Mr Crabtree, and I again apologise.'

'Away with you, James,' he smiled and closed the door.

Despite the emotional rollercoaster I'd experienced, I felt good as I walked away. It was good to have support such as Mr Crabtree's. As I started down the steep road towards the High Street, a strong arm grabbed me around my throat from behind.

18

You hear a phrase in the movies or read it in a book, and you think nothing of it, but in that split-second, as I felt that arm across my throat, many things flashed through my mind. Considering the many things that appeared, either time stood still or slowed down considerably. What I saw so much more vividly than everything else was the first fish I caught at the Great Black lake and how I snapped its neck. The other memories of Chess, MPs, Maude, Doris, Peter, and Rhian flashed through like frames of a film that ran faster and faster until the movie faded to black. All that work! I wasn't going to let this go; I couldn't. I squirmed and struggled, but Ollie clenched my head tightly in his arm, and he wasn't about to let go.

'Think you could stay away from me all summer, did you, you little wanker?' Ollie snarled. I couldn't speak as I struggled, but at least I *was* struggling, leaping out of the water and trying to dislodge Ollie's barbed hook. 'Keep still, or I'll crush your puny little….'

Suddenly his arm disappeared, and I was free from him. The hook had worked free from my mouth, and I could swim away! Trying to understand what had happened, I turned around and saw Mr Crabtree with his arm around Ollie's neck. I was terrified, worried that Mr Crabtree couldn't hold on and Ollie would turn on him.

'Was this little turd mistreating you, James?' A flushed Mr Crabtree asked.

I'm not sure I'll ever understand how or from where my reply came, but out it came anyway. 'He was being quite disagreeable, Mr Crabtree and I'm glad you intervened.'

'Could I suggest you return to my house,' Mr Crabtree said, but his breathing was becoming laboured with the effort, 'and I'll get word to your father to pick you up?'

I was pleased with the suggestion because I could keep an eye on how Mr Crabtree handled Ollie once he's released him. 'I'll do that now, thank you.'

I stood at the door and watched as Mr Crabtree released his arm and pushed Ollie away. 'Now fuck off and return home,' Mr Crabtree said and stood his ground.

Ollie turned to face him with his fists clenched, and I dreaded the worst. His face looked like thunder, and I thought violence was imminent. But, seeing Mr Crabtree standing his ground with his fists clenched, Ollie just stood there. 'You fucking bent bastard. I'm going to report you to the fucking police for what you've just done. Attack a child, you fucking pervert?'

Mr Crabtree shrugged. 'Prove it, you pathetic loser, because I had a witness, didn't I, James?' He shouted the last part

'Oh yes, Mr Crabtree, you certainly had a witness, and I'll testify that you were a victim of a vicious verbal attack that you fended off with a verbal barrage of your own that made likkle Ollie cry like a baby,' I shouted.

Without turning away from Ollie, Mr Crabtree said, 'thank you, James. I knew you witnessed everything.'

Ollie looked at me and pointed. 'Be careful to check behind every wall, you little shit, because I'll get you someday, and when I do, I'll fucking kill you!' With that, Ollie turned on his heels and stormed off.

Mr Crabtree didn't move until Ollie had disappeared down the road; even then, he waited another thirty seconds. Only after satisfying himself that Ollie had gone did he return to his house, and the two of us returned to the kitchen.

'Thank you, Mr Crabtree; I was very careless,' I said, knowing that poor Ernie had told Ollie of my whereabouts.

Mr Crabtree's colour and breathing were returning to normal, and he turned to me, looking quizzical. 'Now, James, what possible reason would I have for asking your father to come here to pick you up without arousing suspicion?'

With renewed admiration, I looked at this man, so cruelly labelled by the community and who I'd so spinelessly doubted. 'Didn't you see?' I asked rhetorically, 'I twisted my ankle as I stepped off the pavement and came back here for help.'

'Excellent, James; very believable. Far more believable than an ingrowing toenail, eh?' He smiled, picked up his phone and dialled.

19

Rhian Thomas was smiling as she looked at the letter addressed to her.

The Waste Bin
c/o Rhian Thomas,
Mrs Thomas' Sweetshop,
Cemaes, Anglesey.

She decided against the waste bin and opened the letter.

Dear Rhian, (or do you prefer Annwyl Rhian?)

I've just returned home after a week's holiday in Blackpool. It was terrific to have a break, which meant another whole week had gone by without seeing my bully.

However, unfortunately, he did manage to get a grip around my neck on the Saturday before the holiday. My bully lay in hiding outside my friend Peter Crabtree's (aged 72) house. I had trustingly told Ernie Taynor (aged 13) of my plans to play chess with Peter and felt I could trust Ernie. I was mistaken, and poor Ernie (also being bullied) told my bully where I was.

Anyway, he grabbed me around my neck and was in the process of detailing my punishment when he stopped abruptly. Peter (aged 72) had seen him jump me, so he sneaked up behind the bully and grabbed the bully around the neck until he let me go. Imagine being rescued by a 72-year-old! It was brilliant, but a reminder to keep my wits about me.

Last Sunday, we drove to Blackpool and stayed in Mr & Mrs Preston's B&B for seven nights. Blackpool is what Blackpool is, and I had a couple of swims in the sea as well as enjoying the Golden Mile and all it had to offer. Strangely, I got hooked on playing Bingo, you know, the one where you slide the plastic doors to hide your numbers. You might be impressed if I said I won three full houses, but considering that I played at least five games a day, that's a pretty poor rate of return. Don't worry, I didn't get you a present.

My worry about the holiday was the suddenness of it all. I got the distinct feeling that Dad knew about my ~~plan~~ quest; I even accused Peter of revealing our secret. He didn't, and I know you said it isn't healthy to have seventy-year-old friends, but I trust him completely and have a newfound love for him. (I can see you shaking your head, but you need to meet him; he's a bonafide eccentric and has such a flowery vocabulary; it's like being in a room with a character from Charles Dickens.)

It was good to have some chats with Mum and Dad, and I had a couple of heavy sessions with the old man (nothing about the bully) after he came home from the pub and Mum went to bed early. The last chat I had with him was borderline surreal, and he told me something I don't think I'll ever forget.

Anyway, I'm sure I'm boring you by now, and I will stop going on about me.

Right! I've told you my news (boring as it was). I now would like to know a bit about you. I'll be honest, your last letter didn't exactly flood my senses with anything about your life, despite you demanding interesting news from me. So you know, Mum called me her little Sigmund Freud the other day after we'd shared a lovely mother/son kind of chat, so if you want to share anything, please unload them onto me.

Yours Sincerely

James Smith – No5 Cromwell Street, Ailsworth, WIGAN.

Rhian reread the letter and smiled. She liked this; it intrigued her and made her feel happy to know about someone else's life that had nothing to do with hers.

20

On Sunday, after returning home from Blackpool, I composed a new letter to Rhian. In the evening, after handing the letter to Edward to post, I returned to my bedroom and lay on my bed to reflect on our holiday before picking up my next book. I did enjoy the holiday, but the fact that Bingo was my highlight says a lot about what kind of week it was. Come to think of it, Bingo wasn't my actual favourite. It was my favourite shared activity, and I loved sharing the experience with Mum. My favourite activity was reserved for when I was alone and able to read "Animal Farm". Oh my god, what a brilliant little book. It blew my mind, and I ended up reading it twice, something I rarely do.

I'd always put it off because I thought it would be childish, but it wasn't; it was heavy, sad, and thought-provoking. How can a human being like Mr Orwell depict political life in such a perfect allegorical form? It must have been borne out of his frustration that something as pure as communism could be highjacked from within and turned into something that is probably just as bad as capitalism. After reading it, I had a chat with Dad and suggested to him that it was anti-union. It wasn't our only chat that week, and now I've reminded myself, one of those chats with Dad *was* a memorable shared experience.

○ ○ ○

The week in Blackpool followed a fairly routine schedule. We'd get up, wash, and get ready, then wait for Mum and go downstairs for our full English, which was always lovely. Mr & Mrs Preston, who owned the B&B, were a lovely couple and had another three families staying with them. We were usually last for breakfast, mainly due to Dad recovering from the night before and Mum putting on her make-up. Having seen it running down her face previously, a sight I never wish to see again, I fully appreciated the effort Mum took to apply the various liquids, powders, and pencil lines. Because effort equated to time, Dad wasn't as appreciative as I was. Despite getting up late, Dad would pace around the room studying his watch, possibly thinking that his irritating actions would get Mum to hurry up. He had no chance.

Apart from one-offs where we'd visit Blackpool zoo, go up the Tower, see Louis Tussaud's waxworks, walk along the piers, and visit the enormous fun fair, we'd regularly visit the arcades dotted along the Golden Mile. When I say we, I mean Mum and me because Dad would go off alone. I don't know if it was our heart-to-heart chat, but I suspect it was; Mum and I had grown closer. I loved spending time with her playing Bingo in those arcades, and I soon became hooked sitting on the high round stools waiting for the games to start. It was addictive, staring at the red, blue, yellow, green, and white columns of numbers waiting for the caller to reveal the number, accompanied by a colour. It was exhilarating when I only had one or two numbers left for a prize; the excitement was difficult to contain. It was also fun hearing "On the Red Line; Harold's Den, one oh, number ten", or "Blue this time; two little ducks, all the twos, number twenty-two", or "on the yellow line; Heinz Varieties, five and seven, number fifty-seven". I inwardly chuckled at some of these calls but was confused by a couple and later had to ask Mum their meaning. How was I meant to know that "Was she worth it? Five and six, number fifty-six", referred to the historic cost of a marriage license? Once Mum explained this to me, I then understood why the audience shouted back, "of course she was".

Often, after the Bingo had finished, or we'd had enough, Mum and I would sit in a café and look out the window while discussing different things. While Mum had her coffee, I'd either have a coke or a glass of cold milk, but choosing the latter depended wholly on the establishment having the proper cold milk dispenser. Mum and I would talk about silly things like TV programmes, Movies (Mum *did* have a thing about Tyrone

Power that I thought bordered on fanaticism), and Bingo. Mum explained that the arcade version differed from *actual* Bingo because it went up to 100. Real bingo, she stated, only went up to ninety. When I asked why she said, 'because that was the way it was.' I don't usually allow answers like that to pass, but seeing we were on holiday, I did.

Mum deliberately avoided talking about her life, but I wanted to learn more. So, one day, sitting in a café, I eventually asked her about Edward.

'Did you and Ed ever have chats about stuff.?' I asked, and when I didn't get an immediate answer, I tried to expand it. 'You know, like discussing important stuff that I'm sure you'd expect from a daughter?'

Sipping her coffee, Mum turned to stare out the window, looking at nothing in particular. Eventually, she looked at me and smiled. 'Yes, Edward and I were very close before he left for college, but since coming back, he seems to have changed and doesn't have as much time for me as he did. He seems preoccupied.'

'I know, Mum, but I think that's because he's going through some important stuff and is finding it difficult to come to terms with college and a new way of life. I don't think it's anything personal.'

'Oh, I know that, James. I don't expect him to be the same as he used to be; I just miss talking with him, that's all.'

We both took a sip as an awkward silence descended. 'I'm sorry, Mum,' I eventually said, feeling guilty again.

Mum looked at me quizzically. 'Whatever for?' She asked, putting her coffee down.

'It's just that I realise how distant I've been for the past few years and how rubbish it's been for you since Ed left for college.' I said, and frightened myself with how serious I sounded. I continued in the same vein, 'I can sort of remember you and Ed having chats after I'd gone to bed, but I didn't pay them much attention; I certainly didn't realise how vital those chats were to you. If I had, I would like to think that I'd have tried to take Ed's place,' I said, knowing that it wasn't true because of my impossible life with Ollie at the time, but I wanted to reassure Mum that I'd be there from now on,

Mum reached across the table and held my hand; she was smiling. 'You're taking this far too seriously, James, love,' she said, studying my reaction. I kept her gaze, nodded and gave a weak smile. 'Mind you, I have noticed a big change in you this summer, I really have. It's as if you're catching up on growing up, and you seem so much happier. Well, apart from screaming at me last week, that is,' she said, tilting her head in mock rebuke. That seemed to lift our mood, and we both laughed.

We had a few chats after that, and although they were about run-of-the-mill stuff, they always gave me a warm feeling. It genuinely felt like a curtain had been raised, and I could now see Mum centre-stage for the first time. While Mum and I did the Bingo and visited most of the cafes on the seafront, Dad was absent. Although he joined us for the one-offs, he never came to the arcades or cafes.

On Tuesday that week, while Mum and I were sitting at a café's window, I saw Dad across the road, walking along the Promenade with his two hands in his pockets. He was quietly strolling along contentedly, looking out unfocusedly to the sea or across in our direction at the shops, cafes and arcades. When I asked Mum why Dad did this, she said it made him happy and would do this whenever they visited a seaside resort. It was what he liked doing at the seaside. As I watched him slowly walk out of sight, I realised that Dad was in his garden shed, and he wasn't the only one. Yes, there were couples and families walking, but many men were walking alone, and they'd brought their garden shed on holiday. Dad was in his own little world, and in seeing him, I saw the difference between men and women. Where Mum felt lonely and craved companionship, Dad, although he worked and went to the pub, was more than happy spending time alone. I concluded that it was probably due to him always being with others at work, in the pub, or even with us. So while Mum craved companionship, Dad craved solitude.

○ ○ ○

In the evenings, we'd visit a restaurant or fish and chip cafe before returning to the B&B, and Dad would pop out to one of the local pubs for a couple of drinks but was usually back with us within the hour. The three of us would then play various card games, like "rummy" or "thirty-one", and Mum and Dad allowed me to gamble five pennies instead of the matches we'd normally use as lives. Over the week, I think I made a slight profit on the cards, but I probably lost all of it, plus a lot more in the arcades or playing Bingo with Mum. Even though Dad would drink cans of beer during the card games, Mum wouldn't drink any alcohol, and consequently, I think she won far more than Dad. If Dad had any chance of winning, he'd have to do so on the first or second hand. I don't know how much Dad drank, but he seemed to have an endless supply of beer cans. I can remember the name because I saw the empty white cans with Double Diamond encircled by gold, red and yellow rings in the bin the following morning. When Dad made a stupid mistake at cards, Mum would shake her head, smile and say, 'I don't think that beer is helping you, love,' and Dad would smile weirdly, shrug and say, 'it works wonders, don't you know.' Looking back, I don't think Dad realised how wrong he was.

As I mentioned, Mum and I regularly chatted throughout the week, but the most memorable chat happened on the last night when Dad stayed out a bit longer at the pub and came back a bit merry. After playing one hand, Mum said she was off to bed because she had a lot of packing to do and needed to get up early tomorrow. Even though their bed was in the same room, Mum fell quickly to sleep, and her gentle snoring gave us the giggles as we tried to play another hand, but Dad gave up and went over to sit on the small sofa.

'I'll go off to bed, then,' I said, disappointed that the game had concluded so abruptly.

'No, James, come here for a chat with your old man,' he said.

I shrugged and turned my chair to face him, not fancying sitting on the sofa next to him. I waited. It's always awkward for a conversation to start after someone explicitly said we were to have a chat, and Dad was obviously finding it so.

He took a swig from his can. 'Well, possibly your last year at school coming up,' he said, which, as an opening gambit, was a bit of a grenade.

'Yeah,' I said, unsure what to add.

'Well? Any idea what you're going to do? College like your brother or an apprenticeship?'

Because of my love for History and English, I always thought I'd study in college, but being faced with a question like this, made me worry that I hadn't considered my future beyond these six weeks.

'Well, I love History in school, and I'm also interested in politics, but I haven't a clue what sort of jobs they would open up for me,' I said, hoping it was enough to satisfy his first attempt at fishing.

Despite the beer, Dad seemed to become more engaged. 'Well, what are you like in maths and science, then? Any good?'

I shrugged. 'Yeah, I'm okay on both subjects, but not brilliant, if you know what I mean. I just don't see myself doing engineering, that's all.'

'But why not? Inflation is high, and there are signs that unemployment is getting worse, so,' he opened his arms in a grand gesture, 'I think the country will always need engineers, and if you get an apprenticeship, you'll get your training paid for, see? That's all I'm saying; I don't want you to struggle; I want you to be okay. *You* deserve that,' said Dad, pointing and staring at me.

I knew Dad had drunk too much, but the conversation seemed sensible aside from the exaggerated gestures. I also noticed his emphasis on me deserving not to struggle, as if I'd struggled enough. 'I'm not so sure, Dad. I'm not the most practical person I know; many of the boys are far better than me at Metalwork, for example,' I replied, trying to dampen his enthusiasm for the subject.

'No, no,' he said immediately, 'I don't mean that you should undertake manual engineering work! I want you to *be* an engineer, to understand how things work. I *know* you can do that!' The drink made him deliver his words more forcibly than he usually did. He sounded passionate. He rested his two elbows on his knees, raised his head, and pointed at me. 'I would be so proud of you,' he said, and that short sentence cut through me like a cold wind.

I didn't know how to respond and sat there digesting his words. I always wanted to make my parents proud, but the thought of being an engineer and telling people what to do scared me. 'I don't think I'm cut out for leading other people, Dad; I don't think it's part of my make-up,' I finally managed to say.

'Of course you are, but you need to learn the theory first and then explain it to your team. You'd be great at it; I've seen how you're changing and how you've begun to analyse things. Honestly, James, it will suit you perfectly.' He seemed to think of another angle. 'It's like being a teacher! That's what you'd have to do with History and English, isn't it? So do it with engineering and teach your team.' He sat up and opened his arms as if the case had been proven.

I hadn't thought of teaching with my knowledge of History, but I wasn't going to argue. All I saw was a class full of my year's lower stream, throwing engineering items at my head and ignoring my guidance. 'Bloody hell, Dad, some of those lads are as basic as cavemen; I wouldn't stand a chance! At least I know that using History would mean I mix with similar people.'

'Ww, so you think that you're better than some others, do you?' Dad mocked, making me angry.

'Come off it, Dad; you only need to look at how they treat the teachers and are always fighting. That's why we have different streams for each year, and anyway, what's this got to do with my future?' I asked.

'What? Oh, yes, sorry, got a bit carried away,' he thought for a few moments. 'Yeah, sorry, I used teaching as an example, didn't I?'

I nodded.

'Well, work isn't like school; it has strict rules of behaviour. You see, in our sorting office, I'm in charge and, using my knowledge, I set the team up to provide the best service for the people of Ailsworth and the surrounding villages. Do you understand that?'

I nodded.

'Right, I'm not a huge bloke, but Stuart Rowley is massive and has a reputation around town for being handy with his head and fists, and he's disagreed with my decisions from time to time, to the point of us having nose-to-nose disagreements about things like the rota. We both know he can't take it further, or he'll lose his job, and if I explain why I did what I did and that it was based on practical objective reasoning, then he will accept my decision, and no more will come of it. I will never say to anyone, do what I do because I'm the boss! If I did that, I'd lose all respect from everyone else.' Dad was using his hands and shrugging to convey the message, but I was still losing the thread. 'So, can you see why Stuart would listen to my explanation and abide by my decision?' Dad asked.

It was one of those awkward questions again, and as I was already losing the thread, I was sure I'd get it wrong. 'Uh, because you were his boss, and he knew he couldn't take it further?' I suggested.

'No, no, don't be stupid, James,' Dad said. I realised the drink had removed his filter, but his response still riled me. 'No, Stuart didn't care that I was his boss; what Stuart knew was that I had more practical knowledge than him because I'd done and seen it all over the years. That's what I mean when I talk about Engineering.' He opened his arms; the case proved again.

I seemed to grasp what he was saying but needed to point out the shortcomings. 'So, on the one hand, you're asking me to become an engineer, but on the other hand, you're asking me to know about the practical side of the job. Is that what you're saying?'

'Yes, that's exactly what I'm saying,' he said and immediately saw I was confused. 'Last week, I popped into the Club and chatted with Dick Mason. He told me his son Bernard is starting with the CEGB in September as a Technician apprentice and will attend Salford Tech and Agecroft Training Centre. He'll get his engineering theory at college and his practical training at Agecroft, where he'll learn about welding, machining, electrical wiring, etc. On top of this, he'll be paid, and as the course progresses, he'll spend time at Westwood power station in Wigan to put his training into practice. It's a win-win scenario, and Dick tells me that he had to teach his son how to wire a plug before the assessment panel, and he still got in.' The arms came out again.

As I listened to Dad, I had to admit that this sounded feasible and working for the CEGB could mean that I ended up working at the nuclear power station in Anglesey. I nodded. 'That sounds good, Dad. I know Bernard by sight, and he never struck me as being any better than I am, so I'll give this careful consideration; thanks.'

Dad smiled, happy that he'd convinced me to think about it. 'Good, good,' he said. The silence returned and felt even more awkward than before. It was time for me to adjourn to bed.

'Thanks for the chat, Dad. I'm a bit tired, so I'll turn in if that's okay.' I stood and looked at Dad. He seemed more drunk now, with his head drooping slightly.

He looked up. 'You're lucky, you know.'

I didn't know what he meant, but I said, 'yeah, I think I am lucky.'

'No! You don't know how lucky you are,' he said. I shrugged, unsure how else to react. I moved towards the bed, not wishing to extend this chat further. Dad held my arm, and he stared into my face. 'I think you are a special person, James. You've been born into this world and are healthy and intelligent. Never forget where you're from because it will be so easy for you to believe you are better than others and that you may look down your nose on other people trying their best to make their way in the world without your attributes.'

I was getting angry with Dad. The drink had loosened his tongue, and I wasn't enjoying the consequence. 'I don't look down my nose at anyone. That's not who I am, and I never will be like that!'

'I've seen people. I've seen people change, forgetting their upbringing and moving on to another form of society, where they join the Tories and look down their noses at people who once were their friends.'

The politics had arrived at last. 'Dad, I know you're a Labour supporter, and I will also be Labour, but I sometimes think that the Liberals may also be okay because Labour is controlled too closely by the unions. I will never ever be a Tory; that would be unthinkable.'

'I'm glad to hear it, son, but I've seen well-meaning people change to defend privilege as if it was a right given to them by their industry, good fortune, or a combination of both.' Dad had released my arm and bowed his head to drunkenly contemplate something. He looked up, a sad expression on his face. 'I'm not a Labour party supporter, but Labour is the closest thing to my beliefs where they can make a difference to help people.'

I looked puzzled. 'But if you're not Labour, what are you?' I asked.

'I, I don't know, James, I just don't know. I have no problem with Labour representing the Unions, but I can see that the unions are becoming too focused on their own concerns instead of looking at society as a whole. You see, I think I'm simply a socialist who wants the Labour Party to look after everyone.'

My head was buzzing now, so I sat back down to look at Dad, who continued to look sad. 'Dad, I think the drink is making you unhappy, and it may be a good idea for us both to go to bed.'

Dad looked up at me and gave a silly little shrug as if he had nothing else to lose. He gave a smile that seemed to indicate what he said next would be stupid. 'You see, if I didn't believe that the whole world would become one nation during my lifetime, then I would find it difficult to carry on.'

I was shocked. Vietnam had just finished: the IRA was fighting the UK: America hated the USSR: the UK hated Iceland, and everyone was afraid of communism. I couldn't see Dad's dream being realised anytime soon.

Dad saw my bewilderment. 'I know it's a dream, but it's my dream, and it sustains me,' he smiled. 'I know you think I'm stupid for saying what I did, but when you go to bed tonight, do me a favour, okay?'

'Sure, Dad,' I said, not daring to disagree with someone who may have been on the brink of having a breakdown.

'Try to imagine being born and opening your eyes for the first time. But instead of seeing your mother's eyes looking at you, try to imagine the eyes of an African woman close to starvation looking at you.' He stared at me, and I sat there dumbfounded. 'When you opened your eyes as a newborn baby, you could have been anywhere in the world. You had no choice in the matter, and at that very instant you took your first breath, safe in your mother's arms, a hundred other babies also took theirs. Those babies from around the world, who had no choice where they were to be born, were your brothers and sisters, and you all had an equal share in the world. Unfortunately, as the way of the world now is, five of that hundred will possess ninety per cent of the world's resources, and the other ninety-five have to find their way from what remains.' Dad stared at me, unblinking. His voice had become more and more passionate as he spoke, and I was breathing hard, mesmerised by his words and fire. Dad pointed at my face. *'That's* why I vote Labour,' he said and collapsed back into the sofa, looking exhausted.

I stood up and stared at my father. He was sitting back, eyes closed, with his arms folded over his head. 'Dad,' I whispered. 'Dad, I'm going to bed now; it's getting late.'

He opened his eyes, lowered his arms and smiled. 'Sorry about that; I've had too much to drink, and you should never pay any heed to anyone who's had too much; they always say stupid things.'

I nodded and helped Dad to stand up, and out of the blue, he pulled me close for a hug. 'I love you, and you must never ever forget that, okay?' He pushed me off to look at my face.

I nodded and smiled. 'I know that, Dad. And I love you and Mum as well,' I answered, but I didn't try to break his hold, knowing it had to be his move to do so. I didn't have to wait long.

He smiled, released my shoulders and ruffled my hair. 'Right, off to bed with you; I'll just tidy around here first, so I won't be much longer.'

'Night, Dad,' I said as I walked to my single bed positioned at the far corner of the large room, beyond their bed, where Mum was still snoring away, oblivious to the surreal chat I'd just shared with John Smith, socialist, a citizen of planet Earth, and my Dad.

21

I tried to make a start reading "The Ragged Trousered Philanthropists" but soon began to struggle with the details it contained. After completing the first few chapters, I put the book down, and even after such a brief section, I understood why Dr Clarke had recommended it; the book was both political and anti-Conservative. The passage that struck me most was part of a speech from Frank Owen, who referred to "children born into the world". It immediately took me back to Blackpool and Dad's speech about uniting the world. I came to the conclusion that Dad must also have read the book.

I closed my eyes and listened to the sound of my family downstairs. It's great going on holiday, but it's equally great coming back home to a place of sanctuary where you can rely on things to be your constant. It was reassuring hearing Ed burst out with laughter after being told a story from our adventures (I, however, couldn't actually think of anything that happened to induce such a reaction) and Mum joining in, albeit at a much higher pitch.

Suddenly it dawned on me that it was Sunday evening, and three weeks of the summer holidays had passed. I was halfway to completing my quest. Even the one time Ollie had me in his grasp gave me a sense of resistance I didn't possess previously. I was winning and suddenly felt I owed something to my family. I sat up and listened to the voices from downstairs. A warm feeling swept over me, and I knew what to do. I got up, put on my dressing gown, and descended the creaking stairs.

Edward was the first to see me walk in. 'What's the matter, Jamie, can't sleep without Mummy and Daddy being in your bedroom?' He looked around to see if the others thought the joke worthy of utterance. They didn't; they stared at me. Even

Bambi the cat, who'd been spoiled rotten by Mum since we returned, stared.

'Can I talk to you about something?' I asked.

Mum looked to Dad, who took his cue, stood up and switched off the TV, much to Edward's annoyance.

'What is it, James?' Mum asked as Dad returned to his seat.

I made my way to the TV and turned to face them. I was immediately aware this was theatrical, with me on stage and my family the expectant audience. Dad was back in his armchair, and Ed and Mum were sharing the sofa. 'I want to tell you something,' I began, 'but I'd prefer if you didn't get angry with me and ask too many questions.' My heart was pounding, but my mind was focused.

'No, we won't get angry at all, James, and we promise to listen calmly,' Dad said, and I saw him glance quickly at Ed.

My heart beat faster when I saw this, but I didn't allow it to deflect me. After a brief pause, I looked at their faces, satisfying myself they were ready. 'I'm being bullied at school,' I said, and my heart calmed instantly. It's not much of a statement when you assess its contents, nothing like the "one small step for man" thingy that Armstrong voiced, but it was a hugely important statement for me.

'What?' Mum almost screamed.

Dad leaned forward and touched her knee. 'Ma, let James finish.'

Happily, Mum took Dad's advice, and I could continue. 'I've been bullied since May last year,' I stated. 'I don't know how or why it happened, but happen it did. You see, I've allowed Ollie Jenkins to dominate my life for almost fifteen months, and I've been ashamed of myself every day since the bullying began.'

Mum's eyes were tear-filled; Ed looked like he'd explode, and Dad smiled. I felt remarkably in control of things and decided it was okay to proceed. 'I think bullying is a psychological thing, more than a physical thing, and it was the psychological thing that stopped me from telling you. I'm so sorry to have let you down like this, and I'm trying to sort it out myself,' I paused. 'I created this mess and need to sort it out myself.'

'Good on you, son,' Dad said.

'So, what I'm doing is making sure I don't see Ollie at all during the summer holidays, and that's why I've started fishing, playing chess, reading, helping uncle Harry, and working at the Labour offices. I've managed three weeks so far, and I'm halfway there. I feel positive about myself and more confident I can face up to him when school restarts,' I took a breath and scanned their faces. 'I only hope you'll forgive me for always lying to you because that has been one of the worst things about this.'

'It wasn't your fault, James, and you don't need to apologise,' Dad said and stared at me intently. 'I am so proud of you for standing before us and telling us this. It can't have been easy.'

'It wasn't, Dad. I've waited until now because I needed to feel confident enough to reassure you that I'll be fine,' I suddenly felt confident. 'Oh, and by the way, Dad.'

'What's that, son?'

'I forgive you for lying to me,' I said and watched him for a reaction.

'Whatever do you mean?' Mum asked.

'Dad lied to my face about getting the B&B after a colleague pulled out because a mother-in-law was ill.' I paused, and something else dawned on me. 'Is that why you arranged for me to go to the Labour offices?'

Dad shook his head and smiled. 'I'm sorry, James, but I've known about Ollie since you first went to the Black Lakes.'

'What!' Mum screamed. 'What the hell do you mean you knew?'

'I read James' diary..'

'Dictionary,' I corrected.

'Yes, sorry, dictionary, and I kept it a secret because I believed it was up to James to sort this out himself.'

'But he was being bullied! My son . . . *our* son was being bullied by that monster, and I didn't know about it, so I couldn't protect him.'

'You did, Mum. The Black lakes was the first day of my quest to rid myself of Ollie, and you set me off and told Ollie where I'd gone; it would have confused him. But, if you knew about this, I don't think you would keep it to yourself, and at that time, I don't think I could have coped with the shame I was feeling. I'm far more robust than I was, and you can now tell Ollie anything you want if he comes here again.'

'Believe me, that will not be a problem,' Mum said, her arms folded tightly across her bosom.

I smiled and looked at Ed. 'I'd also appreciate it if you didn't mete out any punishment, Ed.'

'I know, squirt. Dad and I have talked about this, and I've agreed to keep my fists to myself.'

'What! You knew about it as well?' Mum screamed again. 'Why am I the last to find out?'

'Ed asked me, just before the holidays, if everything was okay with James, and I told him about what I'd found,' Dad said.

'What? You could trust Ed, but you couldn't trust his mother, your wife?'

'Mum,' I said. She turned her angry face to look at me. 'Dad was right. You're too honest, and I think you love me so much that you'd find it impossible to keep it inside and wait for me to be ready.' Mum seemed to relax, so I looked around once more before continuing. 'What you all did was perfect. If it had played out any differently, I don't think we'd have arrived where we are today,' I could still see that Mum was irked. 'Mum, this has been perfect, but if you continue questioning Dad and Ed after I've gone back to bed, you'll undermine my effort, and I'll feel regret.' They remained silent. ' Look, Ollie may be nasty, but it was my fault for allowing him to dominate me so totally and almost ruin my life. So, please, no incriminations. I'm going back to bed.'

Mum jumped up and squeezed me tightly. 'I love you so much, and I'm sorry for not seeing what you were going through.'

I pushed myself free and looked into her face. 'You can call me your little Tyrone Power now for acting as if nothing was wrong.'

She smiled at me. 'I love you, James, I really do, but nobody compares to Tyrone Power.'

I laughed, and Mum joined in with me, but somehow my laugh seemed to morph into a sob. Suddenly I was bawling my eyes out, pulling Mum tightly to me until I felt safe and warm. Mum held me as my crying subsided, and when I was ready, I pushed myself away and walked to the door.

'Goodnight,' I said and walked up the creaky stairs.

○ ○ ○

Back in bed, I pulled the sheets over my head and vainly tried to sleep. Dad knew! He'd known since the first day of the holidays, yet he managed to stay civil with Ollie when my tormentor came to see me on that first Sunday. What sort of man would do that? I asked myself, but I didn't have to wait long for the answer. I pulled the sheets over my head and fell into a contented sleep with the answer swimming happily around my head - my father would do that.

22

I woke up on Monday morning; Dad had already gone to work, and I saw through the window that the torrential rain meant it would be another reading day. This filled me with a sense of unease because I hadn't really enjoyed the first few chapters served up by the "Philanthropists"; it was tilted by the author's politics. I was shocked at how it used blatant derogatory names for the bosses and the town. This is what I mean when I say books are clever.

I dressed and ran downstairs for breakfast. Mum was busy dusting down and polishing the living room furniture before setting the formidable Hoover to finish the job. As I passed through to the kitchen, I bade a breezy 'good morning' and dug out the cornflakes and milk from the cupboard and fridge, respectively. As I sat with the bowl in front of me at the small Formica table, Mum stopped what she was doing and sat opposite. I smiled and started to eat.

'Are you okay, James?' Mum asked, her voice serious.

I looked at her as I finished my mouthful and thought of saying everything was fine, but that was too easy. 'No, Mum, I'm not okay, but I am better now.'

'I can't believe it!. All those times I've spoken so nicely to that brute! I can't understand why someone would want to treat you in such a way; it's so horrible.'

As she spoke, I'd managed another spoonful, but I immediately realised that this method of consumption was both unsatisfactory and unsustainable in light of the inevitable barrage of questions I'd have to answer. I resigned myself to soggy cornflakes.

'Mum, kids are horrible,' I said and immediately regretted using a universal categorisation. 'Sorry, that's not fair; some kids are horrible, and they latch on to the weaknesses of others for no good reason than to hide their own deficiencies.'

'But Ollie behaved with such manners when he came here,' she said. 'I would never have thought him capable of hurting you like that. Why did he do it, James? I don't understand.'

With the cornflakes congealing, I dug out an answer I hoped satisfied her mystification. 'As I freed myself from him, I did ask myself why he did what he did because, in reality, he was as tied to me as I was bound to him. I can only assume that his life was empty, and Ollie needed to control me to have something in his life,' I paused to develop my thesis further. 'Ollie isn't good at sports and struggles academically, but he manages to stay within our stream even though he's regularly near the relegation zone. I think he needs this control over me to compensate for what's lacking in his life.'

'Don't you dare feel sorry for him!' Mum said sternly. 'You can't destroy someone else's life to support your own; it's disgusting!'

I smiled, admiring Mum's reaction. 'I know, Mum, but it's over now,' I said. 'I simply need some time to rebuild my life and allow the real James Smith to stand up.'

'Good . . . I'm so proud of you for telling us; it's made the horrible news easier to absorb because I can see how determined you are,' Mum smiled.

'Did Dad tell you about the dictionary?' I asked.

Mum nodded, reached across the table, unable to speak as tears flooded her eyes, smiled, squeezed my hand, and then got up to carry on in the living room.

I waited for her to go out of sight before taking a deep breath and debating whether I could slurp the soggified mess floating in my bowl.

○ ○ ○

As he left to see Graham, I reminded Ed to post my letter, and I spent the remainder of the morning on the sofa reading. The

"Philanthropists" required a great deal of attention on my part, and, despite not truly enjoying the book, the hours flew by to lunch. It was shocking that such working conditions existed in Britain seventy years earlier and that those working men would still vote for the Conservatives. It was very depressing to read about the hopelessness they were experiencing and the cruelty of the church-abiding foremen who would sack workmen on the spot because they could replace them with someone at a cheaper rate. It made me feel sick and angry. As I walked into the kitchen for lunch, sausage, egg and chips, I decided to not allow the book to upset me any further; after all, we had moved on so much since then. We! Before I'd even started work, I considered myself part of the working class; Mr Tressell would have been disgusted.

After lunch, I took a break from Tressell's book and picked up "Lord of the Flies". It was the second book I needed to study for my GCSEs and, having read it once before, I knew it would be a far more engaging read.

Mid-afternoon, after returning from Graham's, Ed parked himself next to me on the sofa. It felt awkward, and we were both self-conscious, unsure of what to say and how to say it.

It was Edward who broke the silence. 'Are you as strong as you say you are, Jamie, or are you pretending to be to allay their fears?'

It was a good question, but I wasn't afraid to answer it as I usually was when confronted with a question. 'Of course I'm not, Ed. You know that!' he nodded to indicate he did. 'I *am* stronger, and even though I'll probably get a beating, I won't be bullied again. There's a difference.'

'I know, Jamie. A beating is totally different, but I hate thinking about that happening to you, despite you becoming free as a consequence.'

I could see he wanted to say more, and I knew what he wanted to say. 'No, I don't want you to beat him up, Ed; please don't,' I pleaded.

He bowed his head. 'I know what a beating means, Jamie, but I also know not to cross the line. Does that pudgy bastard know?' Ed asked fiercely.

'I don't really know how to answer that. I know he's stronger than me, but I've never fought back in the past, and I think that will reduce the risk of him inflicting anything serious,' I answered.

'Fuck's sake, Jamie, listen to us! Sitting here knowing that you'll have to face this shit and accept it as if it's inevitable. Sorry mate, but it's making me angrier and angrier.'

I smiled at Ed. 'I can see in your eyes that you'll probably confront him when you see him next, but that will just make me seem weaker. You know how kids think, Ed. Look, I have no problem with you, Mum or Dad telling Ollie you know what's been going on, but please leave it at that. For my sake.'

Ed bowed his head again and stayed silent. When he raised his head, he smiled. 'You're the boss, Jamie; you're the boss.' He ruffled my hair and got up to make a cup of tea. Just as he entered the kitchen, there was a hard knock on the door. I stood up to look through the window and saw what looked like a boy in a hooded jacket facing the door. I sat back down, and panic set in as I heard the door open and Edward's voice offering a greeting. I imagined Edward inviting Ollie into the house and standing us face to face, with him forcing Ollie to apologise.

It was Mum who walked into the living room. 'James, there's someone here to see you,' she said, flicking her head for me to attend the kitchen.

I walked over to the door, dreading what would be there to confront me. Edward was talking to the figure, who was in the process of taking off his dripping-wet jacket. Even with his back to me, I knew it wasn't Ollie. Edward took the jacket, and Nigel Mannion turned to face me.

'Nigel!' I exclaimed too enthusiastically as the adrenaline replaced the dread. 'What a brilliant surprise, but you picked a really lousy day to come here,' I said, indicating the weather.

Mum was beaming. 'Nigel, love, would you like a cup of tea?'

'Yes, please, Mrs Smith, if that's okay?'

'Milk and sugar?'

'Yes, milk and two sugars, please,' Nigel answered.

I felt giddy seeing a boy other than Ollie in our house. It was brilliant, confusing and awkward.

Edward came to the rescue of the situation. 'Jamie, why don't you take Nigel through to the parlour because I want to watch something on the TV.'

'And I'll bring your teas through,' Mum added.

I flicked my head and led Nigel to the parlour. 'Take a seat,' I said, indicating where uncle Harry last sat while I took Dad's seat. 'Bloody hell' Nige, it's great seeing you,' I beamed.

'It's good to see you as well, mate,' he said but seemed anxious to say more.

'Is something wrong?' I asked.

'God, no, why the hell would you think that?' Nigel asked.

'Because you've braved the shittiest day of the summer to come see me, that's why I ask.'

He smiled. 'Okay, Columbo, you've caught me out,' he said, and I immediately feared he suffered from the same ailment afflicting Mum. I tilted my head, and he took the hint to explain. 'What it is is the Inter-Colliery tournament, and our school's under-sixteen team's been given a wildcard entry because we're doing well in the inter-school championships.'

'Bloody hell, that's awesome,' I exclaimed. I knew Brinsley Grammar School's football team did well last season, especially compared to Ailsworth Comp, but I never knew that under-sixteen teams could compete in the infamous Inter-Colls.

○ ○ ○

Every summer, Ailsworth held a football tournament. It originated in the late 1950s and began as a competition between the various collieries in the area. It was initially called the Inter-Colliery Tournament, but over time it became known as the Inter-Colls. Most collieries fielded at least two teams. As the pits began to close, the organisers opened up the entry criteria to include any local businesses. Today, in addition to the colliery teams, the Inter-Colls also comprises teams from the Post Office, Norweb, Local Pubs, young farmers, and any other group that could put eleven players out onto a football pitch. The one rule they were keen on was that a team could only have two signed players in their squad. A signed player was anyone who played in a team affiliated with a recognised league.

Before the Ollie days, I watched the games from the sidelines with Ed because Dad, despite his age, used to play goalie for the Post Office. I remember Dad hating it when the ground was dry because it meant that any bouncing ball coming towards him would go over his head. They did, and he conceded many goals in this manner. To be fair, I also recall Dad saving a penalty which meant the Post Office progressed to the second round for the first time ever. They never made it any further. Dad always seemed to relish being on display for the town to laugh at his antics, and one of his most famous was when he faced a penalty awarded late in the game to the British Legion Club, who were already winning seven to nil. As their prolific centre forward placed the ball onto the spot, Dad walked up to him, whispered into his ear, nodded, walked back to his goal, and stood with his back against his left post facing the open goal. The centre-forward looked to the referee for advice, but the official just shrugged, indicating it was within the rules; the striker shrugged and shook his head. The crowd were in stitches by now (it didn't take much), but Ed and I were mortified. As the striker waited for the referee to blow his whistle, Dad took the sporting pose of a sprinter, poised to sprint across with his bottom touching the post. The striker saw this, and everyone knew he had two options. The referee blew, and the striker decided to aim for the corner furthest away from Dad instead of wrong-footing him by going right. As the striker made contact, Dad was in full sprint mode, dashing across the goal. Dad had no hope of covering the distance in time, but luckily he didn't need to because the striker pulled his shot wide of Dad's right post. The crowd cheered wildly, the striker turned away laughing, and Dad ended up on the floor screaming after he pulled a muscle.

Unfortunately, another thing about the matches that stuck vividly in my mind was the brutality of some tackles and the ensuing fights. They may have called it football, but it didn't look anything like the sport I watched on Match of the Day.

I recall one match between the Cooperative and the Fox and Hounds. Ed and I were standing on the touchline, and the play was about thirty yards further away in the Cooperative's penalty box. As the Cooperative's centre forward tracked back along our touchline, he approached the Hounds' centre half from behind and threw such a hard punch that the centre half just fell motionless onto the grass like a bag of spuds. None of the other players saw the incident because the Fox and Hounds were in the process of scoring. Even their goalie, who was concentrating on their striker's magnificent volley, missed it. Since the gasps and shouts of derision from the crowd who witnessed the assault were swallowed up when the goal was scored, the first anyone on the field knew of the incident was when they ran back to celebrate and saw the comatose player. By then, the centre forward was twenty yards away, shaking his head at the poor defending after doing his utmost to give his team a numeric advantage. According to folklore, the centre half was taken off and only recovered consciousness in the pub afterwards, after he was carried into the Fox and Hounds still wearing his kit. Legend has it he enjoyed a great evening celebrating their win at the pub before visiting Wigan Infirmary the next day to reset his dislocated jaw.

These types of tales seem to surround the mystical Inter-Colls tournaments, and I always took them with a large pinch of salt. I know I saw the punch, but I also saw the centre half being supported by two of his teammates as he groggily walked off the pitch. I suppose the tales are funnier than real life, but even the most imaginative spinner of yarns found it challenging to repeat the whimsical story the following year. That was when that same centre half launched his studded boot through the shin guard and tibia of the centre forward in an act of revenge that had been twelve months in the planning.

∘ ∘ ∘

'God, but aren't you worried?' I asked, thinking back to the past.

'I know what you mean, Smithy, but I've trained with some of the blokes from the local league side, and they're not that much bigger than us. In fact, Eric "Man-Mountain" Woolfall, our centre half, is taller than anyone in their first team,' he answered.

I knew who he meant. 'Isn't Eric a year older and off to college or whatever?' I asked.

'Yeah, at least five of the under-sixteen team are sixteen, but that's okay according to the rules; they just had to be under-sixteen at the start of the last season.'

I wasn't sure why exactly we were talking about this. 'Are you and Thomas in the team?' I asked excitedly, thinking this was why Nigel had come around.

Before Nigel could answer, a knock on the door announced the arrival of the expected cups of tea and unexpected slices of Mum's post-holiday victoria sponge.

'Wow, thanks, Mrs Smith; this looks awesome,' Nigel enthused.

I merely gave a curt, 'thanks, Mum.'

As my flushed mother walked out, Nigel smiling at her as she left, I saw a dramatic difference between him and me. He exuded charm, charisma and confidence. I realised as time progressed, I had grown confident enough to converse with Mr Crabtree, but Nigel hadn't seen my mother in years, unless he was already taking his Giro out under false pretences, and he was making Mum blush with his charm as if he'd suddenly turned into Tyrone Power. I had a long way to go.

Nigel took a bite from the cake and looked over. 'God, this is lovely, Smithy. Your Mum's a proper Delia Smith,' he said, taking a sip of tea to complete the perfect combination and producing another comparison. I was glad he chose the new TV chef over the old one because I never took to Fanny Craddock.

We devoured the cake and continued sipping our tea.

'I was asking if you and Thomas had made the team?' I prodded.

'Oh, yeah, we've been in since after Easter,' he answered as if it was a silly question.

'Wow, that's so cool, but I'm not a hundred per cent sure if you won the league this year or not?'

'Oh, God, yes. We won the league on goal difference with a six-nil win away to Mearston on the final day of the season. It was incredible; both Thomas and I managed to get on the scoresheet,' he said, his eyes shining excitedly as he seemed to picture the match.

'Bloody hell, Mearston must be pretty rubbish if you two managed to score,' I said, hoping to bring him back down to planet Ailsworth.

'Ha fucking ha, Smithy,' he replied, smiling. 'Oh, and who the hell was that fat load of uselessness you were messing around with the other week? He was embarrassing! And you were patronising the poor idiot by pretending you couldn't play. What was all that about?'

The banter suddenly turned sour as I again faced the issue of Ollie and what I should tell people. Despite telling my family, I wasn't sure I should make my patheticness public knowledge outside our school. I weighed up my options and quickly realised there was only one. 'The lad Ollie I was playing with?' Nigel nodded. 'He's been bullying me for the past fifteen months, and I wasn't patronising him; I was pretending he was better than me to avoid retribution,' I said and looked at my old friend for his reaction.

'What? That lardarse?' He paused, thinking back. 'But you nutmegged him and scored that lovely goal,' he recounted.

'Yeah,' I said sadly, 'but luckily, you didn't hang around to see the punishment I suffered as a consequence.'

'Fuck's sake, Smithy, that's one thing I can't stand. It really gets under my skin... So, what's happening now?' Nigel asked.

'That was the last time I saw him because I decided enough was enough, and I've managed to get my life back, so all's good at the moment,' I said, not wishing to elaborate.

'That's brilliant, Smithy. I know what you did is not easy because we had to intervene last year when it became apparent that Spencer Lewis was making a younger lad's life a misery. We cornered him in the bogs, and six of us pushed him around throughout our lunch hour. He was seething by the end. The next day, we asked his victim if he'd laid off. He hadn't, so we dragged Spencer back and took turns punching his arms; we made sure our punches landed in the same places where his punches had bruised his victim. We left him crying,' he paused. I must have seemed unengaged. 'Sorry, Smithy, what am I thinking! I know from talking with the victim that the worst thing you can do is crow about standing up to someone. I realise that I've just done that with you. Sorry, mate.'

I smiled, warmed by his unnecessary apology. '*You* don't need to apologise! I'm glad the victim had someone looking after him;

I'm afraid I was alone, but I took advantage of the summer break, and now I should be okay.'

'I'm glad,' he said, 'because it's taken us away from the point of my visit.'

'Which was?' I asked, unsure where he was going.

'What it is, Smithy, is we're short of a substitute fullback,' he began.

'And?' I interrupted.

'Well, I was hoping you'd sign up for us,' he said sheepishly.

'What? Me?' I looked at him, but he kept my bewildered stare. 'Are you crazy? Just look at me, Nige; I'm tiny!'

'But you've so much skill, Smithy. It would be stupid not to ask you,' he said, noticing I wasn't responding as I digested his request. 'Look, I know you're smaller than most, but size isn't everything. Think about what a fullback does,' he prompted. 'Have speed to keep up with the winger: check. Tackle: check. Pass: check. Overlap to drag their fullback: check. You'd only struggle with the heading, and we have man-mountain Woolfall for that,' he said, looking like I imagined a car salesman looking after his well-rehearsed pitch.

I wasn't convinced. 'I'm not sure it's as simple as that, Nige.'

'What have you got to lose? The first game doesn't start until a week next Saturday, and we've got five training sessions and a warm-up match before then,' he encouraged.

Fishing! I *was* getting bored with reading, and while I liked fishing and chess, I knew I couldn't do it every day until school restarted; the previous three weeks had shown me that. 'Okay,' I began.

'Yes!' Nigel said, clenching his right hand into a victorious fist.

'Hold on,' I cautioned. I held out my clenched right hand and raised my thumb. 'One: I can't play for you if Ailsworth school is playing.'

'They're not.'

I raised my index finger. 'Two: I need to ask the old man.'

'Agreed.' He wasn't wavering.

I raised my middle finger. 'Three: do you have a kit small enough to stop me from looking stupid?'

He started to laugh. 'Yes.'

Since I always struggled to raise my ring finger independently of my pinkie, I dropped the thumb and raised all four fingers. 'Four: I require a minimum payment of £25 per game.'

Nigel smiled. 'Agreed, but you can either have twenty-five quid per game or a kit that fits; you can have one or the other.'

'Bloody hell, it's got to be the kit then; no question,' I blurted out in mock panic, and we both shared a gentle laugh.

○ ○ ○

I waited for Dad to finish his tea before broaching the subject. To say he was shocked was a massive understatement.

'There's no way you can play the Inter-Colls! You're too small!'

'Thanks for that vote of confidence, Dad,' I said.

It was clear he regretted his choice of words. 'You've seen those games, son. They can be brutal!'

'I probably won't even play, Dad, and if I did, I know what not to do,' I said.

'Like what?' He asked.

'Like being alone with an opponent when the ref isn't looking and always looking all around for a sneaky punch,' I explained, trying to demonstrate I knew what to expect.

Dad stared at me, saying nothing for what felt like ages. He shrugged. 'If you're happy to do it on your terms and conditions and not being forced into anything, then I'm happy for you to do it,' he said, the words clearly spoken. Despite their clarity, I could sense they'd been forced through a dark cloud of apprehension.

'Thanks, Dad, it's going to make the last three weeks fly by,' I added to show there was another reason why I wanted to take part. Dad nodded his understanding, and I hugged him before he got up to get himself ready for a couple at the Railway Inn. Despite Dad's defence that he only went out twice a week, it was also customary for Dad to frequent the Railway immediately after a holiday. I assumed the locals were desperate to hear what he'd been up to. Before he left, I asked if he'd clear it with Peter for me to attend his house for another bout of chess.

In my bedroom, I wasn't sure if I should file the new entry under admit or confess. Had I admitted to a shameful secret or confessed that I had a secret? In the end, neither found their way into the dictionary.

DISCLOSE: Verb
DISCLOSURE: noun
- *To reveal my shame to my family.*
- *To share my pain with my family.*
- *Lifting the veil or opening the curtains to show what I'd hidden for so long.*

I disclosed my secret to Mum, Dad, and Ed; it was painful.
The disclosure of my secret caused a great deal of pain and anguish for my family.
The disclosure of my secret lifted a great weight from my shoulders.

Instead of replacing the dictionary in its customary spot, I placed it in my small rucksack, ready for tomorrow. I then picked up my book.

Later, as I pulled my sheets over my shoulders to sleep, I heard a couple of short, gentle knocks on my door, followed by Dad's voice. 'James,' he whispered.

'What?' I responded.

'Peter wasn't at the Railway tonight, so I couldn't pass on your request, sorry.'

'No problem, thanks anyway, Dad.'

'Night, son.'

'Night, Dad.' The door closed, and I drifted to sleep after noting the reverential treatment I was getting as a result of my disclosure.

23

Despite the lack of forewarning, I decided that Peter wouldn't kick me out if I turned up at a reasonable time. Football practice was not scheduled until six this evening, and I felt I owed my friend some concrete explanation about my behaviour. That was why I'd brought my precious dictionary along.

At half-past-ten, I knocked at his door; the weather was cloudy but dry. In due course, the door was opened by a rather flustered-looking Peter Crabtree.

'Oh, it's you, James, why, oh, come in, come in, why don't you.'

We ended up in the kitchen, where Peter had an almost drained mug of tea. He picked it up and studied me as he finished it off.

'Is everything okay, Mr Crabtree? Only you appear to be somewhat flustered, if I may say.'

'No, no, everything is fine, James. I'm just aware of the time, that's all,' he said hurriedly.

'That's okay, Mr Crabtree. It's nothing urgent on my part, so I'll come back at a later date if that's okay.'

'No, no,' he said. 'Now that you're here, you can accompany me to the High Street if you don't mind. You see, I need to visit Maude at her establishment because I've promised to help her today,' he explained. as he put on his coat.

'That's not a problem, Mr Crabtree; I'd be happy to keep you company.'

'Despite walking boldly through the High Street? Because I will not skulk around the back alleys as I'm sure you've been doing.' He stared down at me.

'With you by my side, I'd be happy to walk anywhere,' I assured him.

'Then off we go, my little Sancho Panza,' Peter announced as he swept out of the kitchen towards the door. I stood my ground. Seeing I hadn't moved, Peter returned, looking perplexed. 'But whatever is the matter, James? Have I not emphasised the importance of being prompt at Maude's?'

'You may well have, sire, but you have hurt me with the vilest of insults. It is one I cannot tolerate and insist it is withdrawn immediately, or I fear our friendship is finished,' I said haughtily, with my arms folded across my chest, offering only my left cheek to the bewildered Peter.

Peter studied me for a few seconds until the penny dropped. 'Oh, my goodness, I do apologise, James. That was inexcusable and, as you say, the vilest of insults. Therefore, please accept my humblest apologies, and I withdraw your comparison to the pot-bellied, flatulent, garrulous buffoon, Sancho Panza.'

I smiled. 'Apology accepted, Mr Crabtree,' I replied, and we set out together for the High Street. I realised the mock outrage delayed him, but I was equally sure he enjoyed our little verbal joust.

We walked briskly; maybe the delaying tactics may not have been such a good idea after all, and I tried to tell Peter as much as I could about Blackpool while trying to inhale sufficient Oxygen to maintain my pace. By the time we approached Jenkins' Tool & Hardware store, I think he had the gist.

We were walking on the opposite side of the High Street, and as we drew level with the Hardware store, Ollie inevitably stepped out of their door and saw us. I felt no panic and watched him as he pondered what to say.

'Where's pervy Pete taking you now, you little shit?' He shouted. I kept looking at him but chose not to reply. 'I'm talking to you, you worthless piece of crap.'

I stopped and turned to face him; Peter stopped a couple of steps ahead of me. 'No, you're not talking to me; you're shouting *at* me, and it means nothing to me anymore, Ollie. I've told my family about what you've been doing, and as far as I'm concerned, you and I are finished.'

'You can think what you want, but school will be here soon, and that bent bastard won't be there to save you when you and I are sitting next to one another,' he snarled, and I think I saw a blob of white spittle eject from the side of his mouth. I shrugged and walked on with Peter to Maude's.

'Good on you, James; I'm proud of you,' Peter said as we walked on.

Maude's shop was down New Street, just off the High Street. The door was open, but Maude was nowhere to be seen, and neither was Doris. I knew there was a backroom, and it was from there that Maude appeared wearing an elegant coat and hat.

'Oh, Peter, thank you for coming . . . and you too, James? How wonderful.' She spoke at a higher pitch than usual and seemed fragile and flustered.

''You're okay for the bus, dear,' Peter reassured her.

'Am I, am I?'

'Yes, Maude, I believe there are another ten minutes before it is due at the Town Centre stop,' he detailed.

That calmed her down immediately. She then took a look at me. 'My goodness, James, you've sprung up so much since I last saw you,' she said, quickly pulling me close for a hug. My eyes watered immediately as they again experienced the undiluted pungent smell of the earthy green-moss notes of 'Moonwind'. 'Don't cry, James,' she said, mistaking the tears for sadness. 'She'll be fine, and I'll pass on your regards.' She kissed the top of my confused head. 'I best be going, and thank you once again, dear Peter.' With that, Maude practically ran out with her shiny black handbag on her left arm.

Peter and I just stood there in silence. It was only natural for this silence to be profound because of the overwhelming whirlwind which preceded it. 'What did she mean by she'll be okay?' I asked.

Peter moved behind the counter and put on a brown shopkeeper's overall. 'It's Doris. She suffered quite a bad stroke last night, and Maude's on the way to see her at Wigan Infirmary.'

I was taken aback. 'Is Aunt Doris okay?' I asked, embarrassed I'd brought the dictionary.

Peter shrugged and remained sombre. 'I'm not sure, James, but I think it was quite a bad stroke, from how Maude described her condition.'

'I don't really know what a stroke is, Mr Crabtree, but I know it's not good for you.'

Peter thought for a few seconds. As he was about to answer an elderly couple, I recognised their faces, but I wasn't sure of their names, came into the shop.

'Hello, Mr & Mrs Hollins, how can I help you today,' Peter asked.

'Oh, are Maude and Doris not around?' The woman asked anxiously, unsure what to make of Peter's presence.

'No, I'm afraid Doris has been taken poorly, and Maude is en route to see her at Wigan Hospital. Is there anything I can help you with?'

I then witnessed the transaction for the purchase of half a dozen apples, four oranges, and a grapefruit, take at least thirty minutes as Peter, in addition to bagging and taking payment for the produce, provided the couple with the details of what he knew of Doris' condition. God knows how he'd cope if the shop got busier.

After they'd left, Peter turned to me. 'A stroke is when the brain is starved of its normal supply of blood,' he explained, and I found it remarkable how he picked up where we'd stopped earlier. 'In poor Doris' case, we believe the cause was a blood clot that blocked the usual supply.'

I studied the ground for a while before having the courage to speak again. 'Could Aunt Doris die?' I asked quietly.

'Yes, there is a distinct possibility that that could happen, James,' he said thoughtfully.

'Oh.'

'Are you okay with that?' Peter asked.

'I know what you're asking, Mr Crabtree, and to be honest, I don't quite know what I think about the subject. I've been lucky in some ways that my grandparents died when I wasn't yet born or too young to be affected negatively.'

'That was a pleasant answer, James, and I think this subject should be brought up with your family when you next share a conversation.'

'I'll do that, Mr Crabtree, but first, we need to be more efficient around the shop, or Maude's profits will suffer a calamitous plunge, and we cannot be responsible for that, can we?'

Peter smiled. 'No, we cannot; after all, we are a nation of shopkeepers,' and as he said this, he puffed out his chest. 'So, James, what do you suggest we do to negate such a possibility?'

'Could I suggest we practice a concise summation of Doris' condition and deflect additional questions with ignorance?' I suggested.

'Yes, of course, we can, and your excellent suggestion will enable us to process customers both speedily and courteously.'

'Precisely,' I added, and we warmly shook hands on our proposed action plan.

○ ○ ○

It was almost four thirty by the time Maude reappeared, changed to her overalls and took over from us. The news on Doris wasn't so good, but she was stable and as comfortable as possible. As Maude explained, the effects of the stroke were pronounced and unflattering, and it filled my being with a strange feeling of loss, despite Doris being alive. I waited until a distinct lull to explain I had football practice to attend and asked if it was insensitive of me to participate in light of the sad news we'd been discussing.

Maude, who had been magnificently robust throughout her recollection of the hospital visit, suddenly burst into tears as I finished my silly question. 'Oh, James, you are such a sweetheart,' she managed amidst the tears. 'Doris and I love you to bits, and I'm so happy to see you looking so strong and healthy.'

I smiled, and we shared a fresh hug. It was crass of me to worry, but 'Moonwind' had diluted to a safe level, and my eyes watered up this time for the right reason. I repeated the hug with Peter and admired how this fish out of water had coped admirably with running the shop in Maude's absence; he even offered to stay on to help into the evening. I said goodbye to my lovely friends and headed cautiously back home.

∘ ∘ ∘

Brinsley is a town comparable in size to Ailsworth, lying about four miles west. Although similar in size, Brinsley is a market town rather than a town born out of any industry. It still qualified for the Inter-Colls tournament because of Ailsworth secondary school's catchment area, which included Brinsley, but the four miles meant I required a lift for the first training. As Nigel and Thomas could not be sure of my attendance, I hoped after tonight, we could either share the lift duties or arrange for the training to align with the bus timetable. After dropping Elsie back home, Dad drove in silence as I told him about poor Doris and the symptoms reported back to us by Maude.

'That's so horrible to hear, James. I like Doris very much, and she's worked tirelessly with Maude at that lovely shop of theirs.'

'I know, Dad,' I said, knowing that we rarely used them nowadays, opting instead for the Co-op. 'I hope she'll pull through it; as you say, she is a tough lady.'

Dad nodded and drove on; clearly, he was thinking about past encounters he'd shared with Doris.

∘ ∘ ∘

Nigel and Thomas were pleased to see me arrive and made a big fuss about handing me the kit. The small kit. They then introduced me to the rest of the team, and I instantly recognised man-mountain Woolfall; he was huge!

'Nice to meet you,' Woolfall grunted.

'Likewise,' I said. 'And can I thank you, Eric, for your old kit?' I added, showing him the shirt.

Eric burst out laughing and held the shirt against his naked stomach. The difference was surreal. The tiny shirt held against his wobbling body was like a school badge on a blazer, but it did the trick and was a quick and easy way to break the ice. Nigel appreciated the gesture.

The training was brilliant, and I immediately felt at ease amid these strangers; football did that; it seamlessly unified. I was also pleased to see their fullbacks were excellent athletes, which meant I'd need a warm coat for sitting on the bench, something I honestly didn't mind.

After that first session, the team agreed to reschedule the training for a quarter to six, which meant Nigel, Thomas and I could catch the bus there and back.

○ ○ ○

After giving Mum and Dad the rundown of how the training had gone, Mum called me her little Kevin Keegan; I think based more on size than position, I decided to change the tone of the evening.

'What does death mean?' I asked. The question made Mum freeze on the spot, still holding a cup in her hand, but Dad just put his down as if clearing a desk before doing a job. Mum managed to flick her eyes between Dad and me, but her body remained rigid.

'That's a question with a simple answer but a difficult explanation,' Dad said. I nodded, wishing him to continue.

'Death simply means that your body can no longer sustain your life. This can be for many reasons, but ultimately your heart fails, which starves your brain and organs of the blood they need. I've known people whose hearts stopped but were resuscitated in time by a first aider or doctor, so it's too simplistic to say that you die when your heart stops. Your brain also has to show no signs of activity. So it's simple in one way and complicated in another. I'm not helping you, am I?'

Mum and Dad looked at me in silence as I digested his explanation.

'Is this because of Doris?' Mum asked.

'Uh huh,' I grunted, staring at my feet. The room was aptly deathly silent.

'I didn't mean that at all, Dad,' I managed to say. I knew I was treading on fragile ground, but I couldn't shake it out of my head.

'I was worried you were searching for something else, and I'm not sure I'm ready to talk to you about it,' Dad answered.

'No, James, that's far too much for you at this age,' Mum added and turned to me. 'You've been through a lot already this week.'

I couldn't answer immediately; I was scared. I was back in the countryside, lying on my back in the middle of the night, staring at a cloudless sky and feeling nauseous. This was beyond my mind's capacity to understand, yet I was desperate to do just that. The silence hung around as I tried to compose myself.

'Shall we leave it? For now?' Mum suggested.

I shook my head. 'It's exactly because of this week and what I've been through that I need to ask you this. I'm trying to understand stuff, like Ollie, my patheticness, hope, and my relationship with you three. This is probably the ultimate question I could ever ask you, and if *you're* not ready to trust me with the answer, I'm happy to postpone it.'

Dad gave a wry smile. 'You've spent far too long with the MP, James, or else Peter Crabtree's opened his box of secrets on the art of subtle persuasion.'

I returned the smile. 'Wasn't that subtle though, was it?' I answered.

'Death is a fact,' Dad began, his face serious. 'What happens after death is a matter of belief because no one has ever returned to tell us,' he said, staring at me to reinforce his difficulty. 'People would love for there to be something beyond death; believe me, they have spent trillions to support this love they hold. These trillions are usually cruelly dragged out of the hands of the poorest in society to support belief systems based on a promise that there may be a better life should you choose a particular path.'

'John, this is too much,' Mum interrupted. 'We were in our mid-twenties when we sorted this out to our satisfaction; he's only fifteen,' she said, and I noticed tears running down her cheeks.

My left leg started to bounce, a sure sign I was tense. 'I can cope, Mum. I know I'm pushing my limits, but with Doris taking ill, I've thought about my family that are no longer here. Dad, your parents Jack and Joanna have gone, and Mum, your Dad has. How do you cope with that?'

'They haven't gone, James; don't be stupid,' Mum said, and Dad smiled at her words.

'But you hinted there's no afterlife,' I replied angrily.

'There isn't,' Dad intervened. 'As Mum said, they're in this room right now.'

'What? Are you talking about ghosts?' I was getting confused, and they were making me angry.

Dad suddenly became stern. 'I told you this wasn't going to be easy, so consider what we say carefully before becoming riled.'

'Okay, sorry,' I replied sheepishly.

'Right, my father died, which was the end of his mortality. Where Jack lives is in here,' Dad pointed to his head.

'And here,' Mum pointed to her heart. They were answering in unison.

Dad continued. 'You will have *some* feelings about Jack from the stories we've told you and the photos you've seen. That means he may live beyond my life through Ed's and your memories and emotions.'

It was then Mum's turn. 'You may remember something about Grandad Ted because you were six when he died.'

I smiled, glad to remember something lighter. 'Yeah, I can still remember Gramps pushing me along in the carnival; it was a beautiful summer's day, and Ailsworth was rammed with people.'

'Yes, I remember that one,' Mum joined in. 'I was for ages making your costumes.'

'And I made up the pram,' Dad butted in proudly as the atmosphere lifted.

'Yeah, I remember the pram and feeling like a stupid baby,' I joined in.

'I'd taken it apart to make it sit much lower, and Mum covered it in that silver grey satin cloth to resemble that stupid floating chair of that character,' Dad explained.

'You were Commander Shore, and Ed was Troy Tempest.' Mum was now smiling broadly. 'You were as grumpy as hell, and Ted couldn't stop laughing the whole route. It's one of my loveliest memories of him,' she added, and tears replaced the smiles.

'So can you see what we mean when we say they are still here? We know they're not somewhere else; there is nowhere else. This is it! This is your life, and memories are what's left after death.'

As answers go, I'd grade this inconclusive, but it was sufficient to satisfy my current needs. I also understood the subject to be very emotive, and with Mum alternating between tears and smiling, I thought it best to leave it at that. 'Thanks,' I said. 'I know that wasn't easy for you, and you've allowed me options to shape my own route around this challenging maze we call life.'

Dad shook his head. 'You have definitely spent too much time with Peter,' he smiled broadly. 'But you're right, Mum and I cannot and shouldn't be too prescriptive on matters like this one because these are issues you will delve into as you assimilate knowledge and experience.'

'Now, who sounds like Peter Crabtree?' Mum asked. 'Assimilate knowledge and experience? It's as if someone's taken over your body!' Mum nodded curtly at Dad. It was lovely that, even now, she chose to defend me, probably because she didn't appreciate Dad's retort to my Crabtrinian metaphor.

'Thanks for tonight; I'm glad you kept it vague, and I'd also like to thank you for introducing me to Peter Crabtree. I believe it's been through talking with him that I got the confidence to face my problems and share them with you three,' I smiled. 'Goodnight, it's been a funny old day, and I'm physically and emotionally exhausted,' I stood up and hugged them before going to my bedroom. I opened my rucksack and pulled out the dictionary.

DEATH: noun

- *End of life – generic def.*
- *Its meaning is yet to be analysed.*

James Smith didn't fully know what death meant.

James Smith understood that the loss of someone through death was something he had yet to experience within his current level of consciousness.

I placed the dictionary back in the rucksack and laid back to consider what I'd heard. Of all the things swimming around my head, the thing that flashed brightest was finding out that Mum and Dad had shared ideologies. I felt ashamed that I'd only thought of Dad as the keeper of such things, but it was clear that

Mum was his equal but that she'd rather keep it hidden behind her façade of being just Mum, comparator extraordinaire.

24

The following day, I was pleased to find the sun shining and to celebrate, I considered a fishing trip to the Black Lakes. As I hurried to finish my cornflakes, aware that Mum could descend any moment rendering them mush again, I felt uneasy about my proposed adventure to the lakes.

I read the "Flies" until ten and asked Mum if I could use the phone.

'Of course you can, dear,' she affirmed as she sorted out the washing.

I didn't use the phone regularly, and each time I did, I felt a twinge of anxiety as it rang at the other end, worrying that I'd somehow misdialed.

'Hello,' a strong voice answered. 'Peter Crabtree at your service for whatever it is you need to speak to me about.' I was not disappointed.

'Good morning, Mr Crabtree; it's James Smith,' I explained nervously.

'Ah, good morning, young James. What can I help you with this fine summer's morn?'

'I was wondering, Mr Crabtree, if you may have heard any further news about Aunt Doris' condition?'

'Oh, yes James, unfortunately, I have. Maude is not opening the shop today because she's been told that Doris' condition has worsened. I myself intend to catch the eleven o'clock bus in order to go see Doris and to provide some relief to poor Maude, who must be emotionally drained.'

I was pleased I'd rung. 'Oh, that's terrible news, Mr Crabtree, but I was thinking that maybe I could come with you?'

Mr Crabtree paused before continuing. When he next spoke, his voice was softer. 'That would be lovely, James. I shall see you at the town centre bus stop.' He hung up immediately.

I held the receiver to my ear for a further half a minute in case Peter returned. He didn't, and I carefully set down the brown receiver with its coiled cable onto its cradle, reuniting it with its mushroom-coloured body.

o o o

I was slightly nervous waiting for Mr Crabtree to arrive, carrying my library books; the bus stop is only fifty yards from Ollie's den, but its resident bully never made an appearance, and soon, Peter turned up to stand next to me. While I wore my anorak, noticing that the sleeves *did* look a bit shorter, Peter wore a striped Harris tweed jacket with alternating dark, mid and mustard brown stripes over a pale yellow shirt and a dark blue paisley patterned cravat. He contrasted the jacket with dark navy Oxford twill trousers and tanned brogues. With his grey-white hair slicked down, he looked the part of an elderly gentleman going on a first date. The small bouquet of roses was the icing on the cake.

'Do you think she'll mind that I haven't brought her anything?' I asked after the bus set off, and we were seated together, Peter next to the window.

'No, James, I think Doris will simply be glad to see you. Despite Doris' poor health, these ostentations are merely a habit I find difficult to break. I mean, it is unlikely the poor dear will even notice the flowers.'

I nodded and stared ahead along the aisle, focusing on the elbows jutting out from the seats in front. A gnawing dread gripped my stomach as the bus took us toward our destination. Every reference to Doris sounded dire and hopeless, and I didn't know what to expect when we saw her for the first time.

o o o

I asked Mum if she was happy for me to go with Peter, and she was. She did, however, offer me some advice. 'Please be careful with this kind of thing, James. It is very easy to become too involved, which could leave you vulnerable,' she said.

'But vulnerable to what?' I asked, unsure what she meant.

'Grief and sadness can make you vulnerable because you've opened yourself up and have exposed a side of your emotions that normally lie dormant.'

'I don't care if other people see my emotions, Mum. I don't want to hide anything again.'

Mum smiled and tilted her head into the "yes but" pose. 'I don't mean other people, silly. Grief will open you up to yourself, and this is when you may question your own reaction to the grief. You may find that you're cold-hearted or soft-hearted, and you'll have to accept that this may be your natural emotional setup,' she smiled. 'If you can prepare yourself for all outcomes, you'll be far stronger.'

'Thanks, Mum. Growing up is quite tricky, isn't it?'

'Yes, James, very tricky indeed.' he kissed the top of my head and went upstairs to get herself ready; she was setting off to Glad's Caff for elevenses with Patricia from number nine.

○ ○ ○

Although we didn't have far to walk along Wigan Lane to the Infirmary, there was adequate time for Peter to be verbally accosted by two youths bearing an uncanny resemblance to the bedenimed skinhead from Dr Clarke's surgery. They even had the same furrowed brows, which only levelled out after they vented their vitriol at Peter. Peter, for his part, ignored them with good grace, and in no time, we were approaching the medical ward where Doris was a patient.

Peter stopped at the double doors. 'James, could I ask you to wait here while I try to find Maude so she can enlighten me on Doris' progress?'

Where we'd stopped in the corridor was adjacent to a waiting area. 'No, certainly I don't mind, Mr Crabtree. I'll wait in there until you return.'

'Thank you, James. I'm sure I won't be long,' said Peter; he turned and pushed open the doors. I entered the empty waiting room and took a plastic seat facing the corridor I'd just left. Despite carrying my two library books, which Peter agreed I could return later, I looked down at the small table and flicked through the various magazines until I came across a Reader's Digest. It was from April, and I was amazed at how many stories they'd crammed into such a thin volume - and all for thirty-five pence! After reading a short two-page effort on Life, I turned to the supplement where the subject was Ulster and the violence the people had suffered. Luckily, I didn't have to delve deeply into what could have been a sad revelation about something I knew very little about because Peter emerged into the corridor with a sad-looking Maude by his side.

I threw the Digest onto the pile and walked over to them. 'Are you okay, Aunt Maude?' I asked, fearing the worst.

Maude bravely wiped her nose with her hankie and smiled at me through reddened eyes. 'I'm fine, James, my love. It's lovely to see you here; I can't tell you how lovely it is.'

'Uh, how's Aunt Doris?' I asked.

Peter took the lead as he helped Maude take a seat. 'Doris is as good as can be expected, James. I've insisted Maude take five minutes to rebuild her fortitude. I will pop down to the RVS for some coffee and sustenance if you could wait here with Maude in the meantime.'

'Certainly, Mr Crabtree, I'll sit here with Aunt Maude,' I answered, and Peter left.

I was unsure where to sit but decided that proximity was preferable to distance and sat in the chair next to Maude. As Maude continued to chase the sadness from her reddened nose, I felt awkward, unsure how to start a conversation with someone so plainly hurting.

'I'm in training to play in the Inter-Colls tournament,' I said. Even though I said those words, I cannot believe I did. They were my opening words to a kind woman grieving her closest friend's serious medical condition. It was a bizarre thing to say, but it seemed to shock Maude out of her dolefulness.

'What? The Inter-Collieries? Oh no, James, it won't be safe for you,' she answered, her eyes focused on mine, her distress replaced by panic.

I smiled. 'It's okay, Aunt Maude, Nigel Mannion's invited me to play as a substitute for Brinsley Grammar's under-sixteen team. I probably won't get a chance to play, but I'm meeting some new boys who seem nice,' I spoke quickly, minimising the chances for any interruption.

'Even so, James, I've heard terrible stories about fights and broken legs about that competition, so be careful,' she warned. She seemed to think of something. 'Is that Ollie Jenkins playing with you on the team?' Maude asked.

'No, I haven't seen Ollie since the Friday evening school broke up for the holidays. I remember you saying that six weeks was a long time, and I took your advice and steered clear of him since.'

'Oh, how wonderful,' she enthused and clapped her hands, the hankie muting the noise. 'I never liked that boy, never did. He had a look about him.'

I bowed my head. 'He was bullying me,' I admitted.

'Oh, James, my poor boy.'

'That was why I stopped working for you,' I shamefully admitted. 'I'm sorry, you deserved better.'

Maude smiled. 'Growing up is very difficult, James, and Doris and I both suspected he was doing something nasty to you. It is us who should say sorry to you, perhaps?'

That made me feel hot, and I became teary. 'No, Aunt Maude, don't be silly and don't worry about me now; I'm fine. I've told my family, and Nigel and Peter know, and now you know. I've also let Ollie know that my family know. I should have done it ages ago, but your reminder that six weeks is a long time was the trigger, and I'll never forget that.'

Maude stood up. 'Come here, James Smith,' she commanded, and I stood up to be enveloped by her arms and 'Moonwind'.

We were still hugging when Peter returned with the coffee, sandwiches, and a bar of chocolate for me.

'Here we go,' he said. 'If you could place the reading material onto a vacant chair, James, and then move the table so it is within our easy reach, then we shall be fine.'

I quickly did the required, and soon we were sitting as a trio enjoying the fine lunch. I finished my chocolate long before Peter and Maude had eaten half their first sandwich. Taking a sip of her coffee to clear her mouth, Maude turned to me. 'Why don't you pop in to see Dor, James, while we finish here. She's in the 'C' bay, the second bed on the right.

I heard her words but sat rigid and unsure how to react. Peter noticed my response. 'It will be fine, James,' he said calmly.

I rose shakily and made my way from the waiting area to the foreboding double doors leading to the medical ward. I pushed the left leaf open, having to use a fair amount of strength to overcome its resistance, and walked past some closed doors to a chaotic central area where nurses and doctors buzzed around in various coloured garments. While most colours moved around in quick-step, I noticed that two ladies wearing navy uniforms appeared calmer. The others, in light-blue, green and yellow uniforms, seemed very busy indeed. I walked numbly through the chaos and saw the entrance to 'A' ward; this made me refocus. As I reached 'B' ward's open entrance, a gaggle of white lab-jacket-wearing people walked briskly out. The large swan at the front carried an air of superiority as the flapping members of its retinue jostled for the prime spot in its wake. This extraordinary movement of people reminded me of ballet, but I think that was more to do with my current state of befuddlement than the reality I was passing through. I kept walking but slowed as I approached the entrance to 'C' ward.

Ignoring the other beds, I focused on the one that was my target. The screen curtains were open, and I saw Peter's roses on the bedside locker. I crept forward, hoping to see Doris sitting up, packing her suitcase in the inimitable way she packed the fruit and veg into those boxes at Maude's. She wasn't. Doris was lying down under a crisp white sheet and a light-blue blanket. She looked so small; her hair was not as tightly curled as usual and instead seemed full of ringlets.

The two steel side rails of the bed were up, and I went over to the left rail to look down at her calm face. Her pale pallor was almost opaque, and I saw the unmistakable droop along the left side of her face, her mouth the most pronounced as she took short, shallow breaths. I closed my eyes, leaned down as far as possible, and filled my lungs to their capacity. I repeated the act and again the same result: there wasn't any trace of "Lily of the Valley". Of all the things I wanted from today, the one thing was to know she smelt like Doris. She didn't; she smelt of Grandma Elsie when we visited her and hadn't spruced herself up.

'Hello, Aunt Doris,' I whispered, not wanting to wake her. 'It's me, James Smith, and I'm just here to tell you that I hope you get better soon.' It felt foolish, me talking to someone fast asleep. 'I just want to let you know I'm okay; I've rid myself of Ollie Jenkins forever. I know you were worried about me, but you no longer have to worry. I'm fine, and the only thing I want now is for you to get better.'

'That's very nice of you, James,' Peter said, standing with Maude at the foot of the bed. I stood up immediately, embarrassed I'd been so close to Doris when I spoke to her.

'There's no need to be embarrassed, James,' Maude added. 'The doctors have said that hearing familiar voices is good for her, even if she doesn't respond.'

'It's okay, Aunt Maude; I just wanted to tell her she didn't have to worry anymore.'

Maude smiled. 'I know, James, and look, she's given us a smile.'

I turned to look at the still-sleeping Doris, and although difficult to be sure, I had to agree her face did seem to have brightened.

I looked at Maude. 'She does indeed appear happier, Aunt Maude,' I paused. 'Could I ask you a silly favour that I'm not sure is possible?'

'Of course, James; what is it?' Maude asked kindly.

'If you have packed it for her, could you please spray a little "Lily of the Valley" onto her gown?'

Despite tears welling in her eyes, Maude answered. 'Of course I will, James; it will be lovely for me to do that for her.'

I looked down at Doris. 'Thank you, she'll like that.'

o o o

Peter and I hardly spoke on the bus ride home. We'd returned the books recommended by Dr Clarke to the Wigan library (I'd decided to give up on the "Philanthropists"), and I felt odd without them. It was as if I'd left my own books somewhere.

As we entered Ailsworth, Peter turned to me. 'Will you be okay from here?' He asked, telling me his intent to stay for a further stop.

'I'll be fine, Peter …. Sorry, Mr Crabtree,' I answered, flustered at my overly personal reference.

'I prefer you call me Peter, James. I have been meaning to ask you to do just that, and it appears the transition happened naturally. So, goodnight, James.'

'Goodnight, Peter, and thank you for today.'

I jumped off the bus and took my bearings. It was six o'clock, and a fair bet that most people were at tea, including Ollie. I crossed the road and started down New Road. I stopped outside Maude's shop and looked in.

It was dark inside; the sun had sailed past its windows and was settling in at the back somewhere. I could still make out the vivid oranges, my favourite of the whole shop, standing out proudly from the slatted wooden boxes. Doris would have emptied them from their Outspan or Jaffa delivery boxes and kept those for the delivery boy. I looked beyond and saw the apples, bananas, pears, and dull vegetables, sitting sadly in the darkness. It was as if the whole shop was in a deeper shadow than was usual for this time of day.

∘ ∘ ∘

I was starving when I got back home; I realised I could never live on chocolate alone. Mum had made shepherd's pie, and it was lovely; I even enjoyed the veg. I decided to skirt the day's events and asked Mum if she thought I'd grown.

'Why do you ask?'

'It was something Aunt Maude said, and my anorak felt shorter than usual,' I explained.

Mum's eyes lit up, and she transformed into a game-show host. 'Well, James, my lad, just take your shoes off and step right over here!' Mum had jumped up and stood at the door frame between the kitchen and living room. I took off my shoes and walked obediently towards the host. 'Here, stand upright with your heels, bottom, shoulders, and back of your head touching the frame.' I adjusted myself accordingly. 'Now, look straight ahead,' and again I complied. Magically, Mum produced a Biro; I don't think Biros are ever far away from bingo players, and she made a mark in the white gloss. I knew she would then scribble a tiny J next to the line.

I turned and tried to find the new mark.

'Goodness,' Mum said, 'you have grown since May.'

I finally saw the new mark, and it was clear that I had grown over an inch since that previous mark. It wasn't much, but it was a wonderful achievement for me. All I had to do now was wait for the comparison.

'Look at you,' she said, and I knew I would not be disappointed, 'you're going to be a proper John Cleese, aren't you?'

○ ○ ○

I was almost asleep when I heard a soft knock on my door.

'Are you awake?' Dad whispered.

'Yes,' I answered.

'That was Peter on the phone just now; he wanted me to tell you that Doris passed away in her sleep at around nine o'clock. He and Maude were with her, but according to Peter, the poor dear never woke up after you left.'

'Thanks, Dad. Goodnight.'

'Goodnight, son.'

I leaned over the edge of the bed, picked up a handkerchief from my trouser pocket, and squeezed it tightly into my face. Instead of experiencing the grief I expected, I smiled and fell quietly to sleep with "Lily of the Valley", soothing my aching heart.

25

'Oh no, James. It's little wonder you can't cast with that heavy old thing,' Tom Renshaw explained. 'Here, try this,' he encouraged, handing over his sleek black rod while taking the golden split cane antique from me. 'It's graphite and relatively new to the market, but they are making a massive difference to fly-fishing.'

We were up at Small Black lake, and Tom had been trying to teach me how to cast with Dad's old fly rod. Despite being slightly irked by his disparaging remarks about our rod, the difference in weight between the two was remarkable. I tried it out and surprised myself with the distance I managed. The drag of the line was familiar, but the graphite rod was a joy to handle, allowing me to pull and flick it to pay out enough length of the line, and I could lay it gently onto the lake's surface.

'Wow, that's good, James; now remember what I told you about collecting the line in your hand in a figure of eight,' I nodded and did as I was told. I didn't catch anything, but I enjoyed proper fly-fishing for the first time, and I was grateful to Tom for taking the time to show me.

∘ ∘ ∘

Before Tom arrived, I'd stuck to the bubble-and-fly method and, after four hours, had caught two sizeable brownies from the Great Black. Because of this evening's football training, I'd set out early and spent most of my time thinking about Doris and Maude. I felt sad that Doris had died, but somehow I felt worse for Maude as she adjusted to being alone. Like Maude, Elsie had been left behind after Ted died nine years earlier. I found it difficult to remember Ted and Elsie together; the memories appeared fragmented and incohesive. The only thing I've detected with Elsie, I think, is that she's less confident than I remember. It's as if she feels guilty because she sees herself as burdensome. Thinking of Elsie made me embarrassed as I realised how obnoxious I behave when she's covering for Mum. I ended up worrying about Dad without Mum or Mum without Dad. How would they cope? If Mum was left alone, how would I feel if my children began to denigrate my mother if she came to help?

Catching the fish made me forget for a while, but as soon as the excitement of the moment had passed, I quickly allowed my mind to wander back to the dark shadows. When Tom Renshaw appeared, I made my way over to him and thus began the fly-fishing masterclass.

o o o

I left Tom and the lakes at around three; I wanted to be back home in plenty of time for the football training. I popped into Peter's house on the way back and shared a cup of tea as he updated me about Maude, and I explained what I'd been doing and planned for the evening. Peter ushered me out of the house at around four to ensure I fuelled up adequately before I undertook the physically punishing endeavour. I bade him goodbye and made my way safely back home; I began to think that Ollie had left the country. I knew that that thought was wishful thinking on my part, but that was how it felt. I knew I had to be careful, but the unfounded fear that Ollie was bound to catch me, no matter what route I'd take, was gone.

When I got back, Elsie was setting out the table for tea. After showing Elsie the fish, I placed them on a plate in the fridge and went over to my grandmother for a warmer-than-usual hug.

'What's come over *you*?' Elsie asked, taken aback by the unexpected warmth of the greeting.

'Nothing, just glad to see you, that's all. Can't a grandson be happy to see his grandmother?' I asked, feigning hurt.

'Of course he can, but since he hasn't appeared glad to see me for the past fifteen years, it's only natural for the grandparent to question his motive,' she said. What is it about my family and friends? Why do they make everything so bloody difficult? The amount of time my mind spent on secondary answers was ridiculous!.

'Mum and I had a chat about Ted the other evening, and although I'm sorry he's not here, I'm happy you are,' I answered.

'I'm glad I'm still here, as well, lad,' she smiled and placed the liver and onions, peas, mash, and gravy in front of me. Before eating, I went to the sink and filled a large glass with water; this would be a struggle.

The food was better than usual, and I washed and dried the plates and cutlery while Elsie caught up with the TV. It was quarter past five when I'd finished, and I just had time to prepare for the footy. As I passed through the living room, I told Elsie my plans.

'That's good, lad,' she said, not looking away from the TV for a second. As I turned to go, she added, 'oh, there's a letter for you; it's on the table in the hall.'

My heart bounded and sped to the "hall" to pick up my letter. It was from Rhian, but I didn't have time to read it and give it the attention I was sure it warranted. As I changed for footy, I painfully left the letter on my pillow. At least there would be something to cheer me up if the footy practice went badly.

○ ○ ○

I picked up the bus at Commercial square and watched passengers change at two further stops until Nigel and Thomas entered. They saw me and sat in the two seats opposite.

'Ready for this, Smithy?' Nigel enthused.

'Been looking forward to it, Nige,' I answered.

'I was talking to Mr Brightwell, and he reckoned that he might play two teams against each other after we complete the boring training,' Nigel added.

I suddenly flipped from being quite relaxed to being excited, perhaps anxious. To play an actual football match! It was one of the side effects of Ollie that I never took football seriously, but it was also because I lost confidence when I moved to secondary school. As trivial as it may have seemed at the time, that stupid knockabout with Ollie on that Friday managed to reawaken my love for the sport. The sport I used to obsess about when I was younger. 'That's going to be brilliant, Nige,' I responded.

I knew I was a very last throw of the dice for Nigel, but to be fair, he tried to explain further. 'The coach will probably pick his strongest nine players and play them against the subs; it will mean two from the first team will play with the subs.'

'So that will be the goalie and one other?' I suggested.

'No, I think "the cat" will play with the first team to ensure the communications work,' Thomas added.

'Oh, I thought he'd get more practice playing for us,' I said, knowing we'd be defending most of the match.

'Fair point, Smithy; I might suggest that to him,' Nigel smiled, and the bus trundled soothingly towards Brinsley.

As I looked out the dirty bus window, I thought back to school and me dreaming of escaping on the school bus every day, but here I was, James Smith, sitting on a public bus sharing a ride with two friends who were going to do something totally natural; we were going to play footy. It was surreal because I couldn't believe my optimism for the future. I knew that Ollie would physically assault me when we returned to school, but I promised myself that whatever he did, I'd fight back; I had too much to lose.

Despite growing taller, I was still the smallest of the boys getting ready in the changing room. I also had the least amount of body hair but knew it would only be a matter of time, and in the big scheme of life, this was something I had to endure for a relatively short time. As I finished tying up my laces, I looked around at the strangers with whom I was sharing the cold changing room and again felt detached. It was as if my whole head was numb, existing in a different time and place from where my head had existed for almost two years. As I stood, I shook my head to see if this dreamlike state would come into clearer focus. It didn't; I was still in this beautiful world that three weeks earlier seemed as far off as Tralfamadore, Brighton, Kent, a farm run by animals, Mugsborough, or a deserted island. Where I was now had to be fiction; it just couldn't be real, but I wasn't going to stop living in it because I was afraid I'd never find it again.

The first part of practice went well, despite my left foot feeling pinched in my ageing boots; I even surprised myself with my fitness level. The coach, Mr Brightwell, then split us into two teams, with the goalie and a midfielder reluctantly joining our side. We then played forty minutes of actual football, and it was brilliant! Despite being overrun in midfield, we kept them to only two goals in the first half, and Paul Parker, their left winger I was marking, saw little of the ball. After the break, the coach must have told the 'A' team to make more use of the flanks; consequently, Paul saw more of the ball, which gave me plenty to think about. I could just about match him for pace, and, frustratingly for him, I could also time my tackle unnervingly accurately, so he never once got past to create an opportunity in our box. This game of cat and mouse played out for the first fifteen minutes of that second half, and then, during another attack down my wing, I slid in to tackle, kept the ball at my feet, as Paul continued sans ball for a further five yards, stood up and started a counter-attack down their right flank. I fed Mark, our right-wing and kept running beyond their full-back to provide an overlap. Mark fed the ball past the onrushing full-back, and I picked it up on the edge of the box. I waited for Eric "Man-Mountain" Woolfall to commit and squared it to our centre forward, who got underneath it, and the ball flew harmlessly over the bar. I didn't care; that one joyous minute was pure exhilaration.

As I began to jog back to position, Eric stood in front of me and smiled. 'Do me like that again, squirt, and I'll break your fucking leg, understood?' I ignored him and took up my defensive position. Unfortunately for me, the 'A' team were hell-bent on supplying Paul, their winger, until the very last minute; consequently, when I saw a pass being under hit, I intercepted it and rushed forward, cutting more inside and coming face-to-face with Eric again. As he approached, I opened my body to pass out to Mark on the wing, but, at the last second, I pulled the ball left and left Eric stranded. Once past him, I waited for his centre-back partner to dive in before using the outside of my boot to set up Mark, who had read the move and he side-footed it beautifully for a consolation goal. As I considered jogging back, the coach blew for full time, and I turned for the changing rooms. As I walked, a shadow descended, and man-mountain Woolfall stood in front of me; he had no intention of moving.

I looked up at his scowling face. 'You were saying, Eric?' I said and stood my ground, not even trying to get past him.

Suddenly his face transformed, and he beamed. 'You are, without doubt, one of the cheekiest little fuckers I've seen on a football pitch.'

'So, we're okay then?' I asked.

'Course we are squirt. I only said that to see if you'd back out next time. You didn't, and I'm happier now because of it.' Eric said.

We'd started walking off the pitch together. 'What do you mean happier?' I asked.

'Don't get me wrong, I liked you straight off when we met, but you *are* small, and the Inters can get quite nasty. If you do manage to come on, I just don't want some bastard breaking you in half, that's all.'

I nodded, appreciating the concern. 'Thanks, Eric, I am a bit worried about that, but I hope I've got enough nous to see trouble when it's headed my way.'

He smiled. 'Just promise you'll be careful, okay?'

'Okay, I promise, but I'm not likely to tell you to piss off, am I?'

Eric shook his head, smiled and pushed me over.

○ ○ ○

After telling everyone about the football training, I excused myself and went to my bedroom. I stared at the envelope for some time. For it to arrive today, Rhian must have replied immediately. What did that mean? I was there staring at an envelope and reading something into it with the letter safely tucked inside. Eventually, I grabbed the envelope and carefully opened it.

Annwyl James,

Thank you for your letter and for not sending it too soon.

I was shocked to read about you being strangled by the bully and then felt guilty for telling you that having old friends was not good for you. That Peter guy sounds like a real hero, and I'm glad he was there for you. The sad thing about it was that the poor boy, Ernie, has to bear the brunt of your bully's frustration. That's so sad.

I've never been to Blackpool, but it sounds brilliant. We have something similar, I think, in a town called Rhyl, and we've been there a few times. I did play bingo there but didn't get as addicted as you seemed to have been. I'm also glad you didn't get me a present – that would have been awkward. I'm intrigued about your chats with your parents, but I'll leave that as personal for you because talking will eventually break down barriers, and maybe then you could tell them about your bully.

It must have been horrible to wrongly accuse someone; I only hope it hasn't soured your relationship forever because, at this moment, you seem to need Peter in your life. That's the other trouble with keeping secrets from your family; you become suspicious.

You embarrassed me with your last letter when you said I hadn't told you anything interesting about what I've been doing. Right; during that week you went to Blackpool, we stayed in a caravan in a town called Cricieth. If you look at a map, you'll see that it's a small town on the south coast of the Llyn Peninsula (the long thin arm of Wales). We went there for the National Eisteddfod, but you won't have a clue what that is, so I'll try to explain.

Every year, in the first week of August, welsh speakers gather to celebrate our shared culture. This includes: art, singing, poetry, literature, dancing, acting, brass bands, choirs, and music. We've always done it as a family, and my mother plays the piano to accompany our local choir, which was competing (but didn't win). We also spent time driving to some beaches and just having a really relaxing time of it. Okay, there was no bingo, but we met up with old friends and family and had a lovely time.

God, I've just read that last bit again, and it sounds boring, but it wasn't; it's something you must experience. So that's what I've been doing. Oh, I've also started work as a waitress. It's in a small café in Cemaes, which will be for the last three weeks of the holidays. At least it will stop me from being bored.

Anyway, continue your quest – and let me know if anything interesting happens.

Yours Sincerely

Rhian x

○ ○ ○

As letters went, that was quite disappointing, but what did I expect? I only met Rhian for two minutes, and I'm hoping for what exactly? That she thinks that this thing I'm doing is incredible, heroic? That I'm trying to do what most other fifteen-year-old boys do daily, without referring to it as a quest? No, I'd been using Rhian as my first friend of the summer, and now that I'd admitted to my shameful secret, I no longer needed a confidante. I re-read the letter a couple more times but found no alternative conclusion. I'd probably send her a letter after school re-starts, but there was no pressing need for me to compose another.

As I lay thinking back on a busy day, I began to feel a deep sense of unease. I knew something was wrong but didn't want to face it; it was ridiculous that I felt like this. I had football, Peter, Rhian, books, and fishing; my secret was public knowledge, and my fear had gone. Despite all these positives, positives I could only have dreamed of last month, I was lost.

Of all the things I dreamed of during my dark days with Ollie, the one thing I didn't consider was James Smith. *Who is James Smith?* I asked myself. When Ollie was bullying me, everyone knew who James Smith was; even I knew. But now, as the fetters of my former "life" loosen, I realise I no longer know who James Smith is or what he wants to be.

26

On Friday morning, I woke up in agony! My thighs *burned* with pain, the likes of which I'd never experienced before, toothache excepted. It felt as if the front of my thighs were on fire, and I struggled to get myself changed for going down for breakfast. I was like a doddery old man clinging to the balustrade and using my arms to take the weight off my legs. Once downstairs, I robotically walked to the kitchen with my knees locked, unable to trust myself to bend them for fear I'd collapse.

Ed was already in the kitchen. 'What the hell's wrong with you? Shat in your pants or something?'

I was worried, so I didn't find it funny. 'I dunno, I think I've pulled some muscles after last night's footy training; I can hardly move,' I said, sounding panicky.

'Don't be soft,' Ed laughed, 'you've probably not stretched properly after running about.' He was enjoying this. 'Right, sit down nice and gently on that chair, lift yourself up, and repeat.'

'I can't,' I said in a pathetic voice.

Ed shook his head, stood before me and took my hands. 'Now back up to the chair.' I did as he said. 'Now, slowly lower yourself down while I take your weight,' he said. Slowly, I bent my legs and felt my thighs take the strain. I held on to Ed's hands for dear life, and slowly my bottom reached the seat. Instead of releasing me, Ed started to pull me up. 'Get back up,' he commanded, and reluctantly, I complied.

'It hurts!' I screamed.

'Keep coming, keep coming,' Ed urged, and, despite the pain, I slowly got to my feet. 'Now, back down,' Ed said, and, throughout the painful repeats of this agonising exercise, he never stopped smiling once. After five repetitions, I felt better but couldn't face doing any more.

'Thanks, Ed, I think,' I said.

'No, problem, Jamie. Just get some breakfast down you; you'll feel better after you start walking about and stretching those muscles.' He picked up the Daily Mirror and read as I prepared my cornflakes.

As I ate, I looked across at Ed's hands holding the paper, wondering what he'd been doing through the summer. I knew he had some shifts at a local restaurant on some evenings, but he had whole days to himself; he even had a week with a free run of the house while we were in Blackpool. Even though I loved him, Ed was always a mystery to me. To be honest, the person who was the world's most open book, who wore his heart on his sleeve, would have been a mystery to me if I'd met him during the last sixteen months. Why did I think that person would be a man? I needed to stop this narrow-minded business from floating through my head. But irrespective of my attitudes, Ed remained a mystery.

'Why are you being so nice?' I asked after trying to scrape the pattern off the bowl. The cornflakes were lovely.

Ed pulled the paper down. 'What do you mean?' he asked.

'I mean, the Ed I thought I knew would have let go of my hands when I was halfway down to the chair and that Ed would have laughed his arse off watching me suffer.' I dared him to contradict me.

Ed shrugged. 'Fair comment. Guilty as charged.' He smiled, clearly not wishing to add any more.

'So, what is it you want, exactly?' I asked.

'I don't really want anything,' Ed began. 'I only wanted to soften you up so that when Mum asks, you'd be happy to sleep on the camp bed in my bedroom next Tuesday and Wednesday night.'

'What? Why the hell would I want to do that?' I asked, panic streaming through me as I worried about the dictionary.

'Don't get yourself wound up. My mate Doug is coming to stay for a couple of nights; that's all,' Ed explained and opened his arms, á la John Smith, as if it was obvious to everyone.

'That's all?' I shouted as I pushed my chair back and stood up to confront Ed.

Ed didn't stir. 'Don't mention it, Jamie,' he said, which threw me into a state of confusion.

'What?'

'For curing your pulled muscles,' he said, smirking.

I looked down at my thighs and realised I'd practically jumped up without a single groan. 'Oh,' was all I managed.

'Don't worry; Doug is from college and wants to visit the local colliery because he's writing an article he hopes to get accepted by the Socialist Worker newspaper,' Ed said.

'That's crazy, Ed,' I said, forgetting the disquiet about my bedroom.

'Why? It's what he does; he's the editor of the college mag, and he fancies doing this for a living.'

'No, it's crazy because what the fuck does a college boy know about work?' I asked.

Ed's eyes were wide open. 'Did you just swear at breakfast, Jamie?' I must have blushed instantly

∘ ∘ ∘

I spent the remainder of the day reading because I didn't wish to risk my thighs by going up to any of the lakes surrounding Ailsworth. Luckily, despite being my 'O' level book, Lord of the Flies was a joy to read, and the day slipped by painlessly.

As I was helping Mum dry the dishes, Dad suggested we visit Maude to pay our respects and for him to apologise for being unable to attend the funeral.

'I know Ed is working late, but I think it right that we go to see how she is,' Dad said. Mum and I had no objections, and after washing and changing our clothes, we set off.

Because the shop was a single-storey building, I knew Maude lived at another address. However, I didn't realise, until Dad explained on our walk there, that Maude and Doris lived together in the same house on Springwell Terrace, and they'd done so since Charles, Maude's husband, died eight years ago; Doris had never married. As we approached, knowing this new fact, I felt a new kind of pain and dreaded seeing Maude.

Beatrice, Maude's sister, let us in and guided us through the small kitchen to the living room, where Maude was sitting opposite Mr Jim Gibson, leader of Ailsworth's Chamber of Commerce. He sat on the right side of a sofa as Maude sat regally in a floral-patterned armchair. The room stood centrally within the house, and I could imagine a smaller but more ornate parlour beyond the door standing behind Maude. The living room was nice and bright, with a central circular fluorescent light illuminating every corner. The wallpaper was light and floral, making the large dark wood sideboard stand out. If the polished sideboard dominated the room physically, there was no question that the collection of photographs living on its surface dominated emotionally.

As I heard Maude welcome Mum and Dad and introduce them to good old Jim, I broke away and looked at the photographs. Two rows of three were fitted into different types and sizes of frames, separated by a large fruit bowl positioned centrally. I could see Maude's wedding day, a family I assumed was Beatrice's, and a couple of Maude and Doris together. One showed the two standing outside the shop in their wonderful housecoats, and I could almost smell their perfume. Another of a single child had been taken in a studio, and I assumed this was Doris. It was a brown-and-white photograph and looked ancient. Interesting as all these were, my eyes were drawn to another brown-and-white photograph housed in the largest and most ornate frame. It showed a family.

Positioned front left, a small, sad girl stood with a small basket in her hands, a white band prominent in her dark ringletted hair. She was leaning slightly against the right leg of her seated mother, who was holding a much younger girl, possibly a baby, on her left knee. The mother's dark hair was swept on either side and tight against the top of her head, and I wondered if that was why she looked so stern. The baby didn't look as sad as the other two, but that was because she seemed transfixed by the photographic apparatus set up before her. All three wore light, possibly white, dresses, but to the left of the woman, with a grey hand on the baby's shoulder, wearing a dark grey suit, waistcoat, watch chain, white shirt and black tie, stood the proud father. His slick dark hair was split into two perfect halves, and his face was dominated by the bushiest moustache I'd ever seen.

A hand touched my shoulder; it was Maude. 'That's me sitting on mama's knee,' she said, pointing to the baby.

'Is that Beatrice?' I asked, pointing to the sad girl.

'Yes, that's Beatrice,' she answered softly.

I turned and hugged Maude, pulling her as close as I could. After a while, I pushed myself back and looked into her face. 'They did a good job raising you,' I said.

27

'That's two-nil to me,' Peter said thoughtfully. I didn't respond and began to reposition my pieces. 'I think,' Peter said, 'we should adjourn to the kitchen.'

I nodded and followed him. As he switched on the kettle, he turned. 'You're not concentrating on the chess, James. Is something the matter?'

That sort of shook me out of my stupor. I looked at Peter and shrugged. 'I don't know what it is, Peter; I'm confused about things and can't seem to focus.'

He poured the boiling water onto the tea leaves, stirred the contents (three gentle stirs – no more, no less), and replaced the ceramic lid. 'Oh, and why is that then?' He asked, tea brewing.

I watched him sit down opposite me and saw he was genuinely interested in my forthcoming answer. 'This will sound really strange, Peter, but . . .'

'You miss being bullied?' he asked.

I nodded. 'I don't miss being bullied as such; that's stupid, but I seemed to have lost the nervousness I had at the start of the holidays. I feel blasé about the whole thing,' I said, attempting to explain.

'But surely, my dear boy, that's a good thing, isn't it?'

'I suppose it is, but I don't know what to do with myself. It's as if I'm in limbo.'

Peter thought for a few moments. 'The problem, as I see it, is that you are no longer being bullied, and you've achieved this through your actions. The issue remains that Ollie Jenkins *will* try to bully you again, but that deluded fool is unaware that you have already broken the vicious circle.'

I agreed and nodded. 'Yes, that's exactly it.'

'So,' Peter continued, 'it also means that you can't live a normal life in Ailsworth, and by normal, I mean the everyday life of a fifteen-year-old boy because you know that carelessness could mean you having to defend yourself against that thug.'

I nodded. 'It's as if I've trapped myself within a hybrid life,' I said.

It was true; by ridding myself of Ollie, I'd had to face what was left of me, a friendless, worthless shadow that drifted in and out of classes, whose only redeeming feature was that everyone who knew me in school was glad they were not me.

Peter gave a strange, resigned smile. 'Like befriending septuagenarians and playing chess with them?' he suggested.

I bowed my head; the act was more to give myself time to find an answer than a sign of remorse. I looked up. 'I could remonstrate that your suggestion was untrue, but that would be disingenuous. All I know is that I desperately needed to fill my days throughout the summer holidays, and fishing was the first thing that sprang to mind. On that first day, we met as I made my way up to the Black lakes, and subsequently, we started playing chess, another way for me to spend my days hiding from Ollie. These are the bare facts of what I did physically,' I paused to see if Peter wanted to say anything.

Peter nodded his understanding. 'Pray proceed, James, as I await your next utterance with bated breath.'

'Before I proceed, can I ask if the tea has over brewed or is it still quaffable?' I asked.

Peter smiled. 'Despite using the incorrect term, palatable or drinkable would have been better, I believe your timely intervention has saved it.'

I watched Peter hurriedly fill the mugs through his ornate strainer before adding the milk and handing me the mug. As I picked it up, I could see it would be too strong but perhaps ideal for what I needed.

'You were saying,' Peter prompted.

'As a normal fifteen year-old-boy, it *should* be strange for me to have someone such as yourself as a friend. You are from a different generation and *should* be of no value to me as I develop. Do you agree?' I asked.

'Yes, I do agree with that blunt analysis,' he answered bluntly.

This was scary because I knew what I wanted to say, but being able to say it correctly made me anxious. 'The issue here is the word *should*. In this case, the word *should* refers to *normal* septuagenarians, but you are hardly one of those,' I paused. 'I have sat here with you as you informed me, in no uncertain terms, that I am unusual for my age. Well, for your information, Peter, you are also unusual for *your* age, and I find the manner in which we unusual pair interact to be challenging, informative, beneficial, and stimulating. What I know for certain, as I grow older, find myself and hopefully become "normal", is that I will invariably see less of you. But I also know I will consider you a close friend until mortality brings our unique friendship to a close.'

Peter picked up his mug and took a leisurely sip. He placed the mug on the table and, still holding it, stared at me for what felt like ages. Imperceptibly his round ruddy cheeks became more flushed, and tears rose in his eyes which seemed to close in an attempt to hold them back. Dramatically, Peter bowed his head, and I watched as his tears dripped to the table on either side of the mug. I allowed the situation to play out but still allowed myself a sip of the strong tea.

Raising his head, Peter stared at me through his red-rimmed eyes. 'What a silly fool I am,' he said, a smile appearing at the sides of his mouth. 'What sort of friend is this that bawls at the mere mention of mortality when he would best be employed positively supporting the stated goal of his friend?'

'That would be a close friend, Peter,' I said. 'One who has had to change his outlook on life since that first meeting. It's not only me who has to face up to my newfound life, my rebirth. You, the man who, more than anyone else, supported and lit the fire within me to forge my new self, may well regret your involvement and feel a sense of betrayal; you should never allow yourself to think this. I will still need your advice, guidance and opinion because they will enhance my understanding of the world. If I don't get these, I'm afraid I may indeed turn into a very ordinary person.'

'Thank you, James, but fear not; you will never become an ordinary person. I am certain of that because I will make it my life's mission to prevent it from ever happening.' Peter said triumphantly. I smiled. 'What I find astonishing,' Peter continued, 'is how much you have developed over a relatively short period. I remember the uncertain fisherman worried about the severity of my ingrowing toenail, and now hearing this confident young man who is able to analyse the future of our relationship in such a mature manner. I could not be prouder of you if you were my own son, and I look forward to watching you develop further.'

I smiled at hearing this. 'If you believe I have developed, then I can safely say that you have been the vehicle in . . .'

'James!' Peter interrupted. 'Don't you dare!' he commanded. I was taken aback, unsure of what had happened. 'You should never have considered using that metaphor. The forge metaphor was barely acceptable, but me being the vehicle? Please, James, our conversation deserved far better than that. As a rule, you should never use multiple metaphors within any conversation.'

I smiled broadly. 'Q.E.D, Peter. Who else would provide such valuable feedback during such an intense discussion?' I asked rhetorically. 'And, while we are discussing important issues, Peter,' I continued, 'I do need to make one important observation.' Peter raised his eyebrows. 'You do need to improve your tea-making skills.'

Peter laughed. 'It's awful, isn't it?' I nodded, and we shared that precious moment when tension is multilaterally released.

○ ○ ○

We agreed it was too late for any more chess, so Peter disappeared for a few seconds only to reappear with newspapers. He placed them on the table, our mugs had been refilled previously, and turned them around to face me. 'These two editions are from the twelfth and nineteenth of July just gone. There's an article about the miners on the back page here and an article about them within this one from the nineteenth,' he paused, and as I studied the papers, I felt him staring. 'Tell me, James, why would you want to read anything from these?'

I explained about Ed's friend coming to stay and his wish to write an article for inclusion in the Socialist Workers Newspaper. Peter was not impressed. 'While I welcome any form of the written word, I do, however, feel that the author should have experience of what he or she writes about. Edward's friend cannot believe a flying visit can adequately describe the conditions the miners experience throughout their lives! Frankly, it is patronising.'

'I'll tell him about your concerns, Peter, but in the meantime, I thought I'd get a feel for the newspaper he's striving to populate.'

'An excellent idea, my friend, an excellent idea.'

∘ ∘ ∘

After an early tea, I was ready to leave for the bus when Dad turned to me, 'Going for another practice?' He asked.

'Yeah, but I'm not sure my thighs will cope with too much punishment if the aftermath of the last practice is anything to go on.'

'God, you should have seen him yesterday; the Cybermen are more flexible!' Ed chimed in.

'You'll be alright, son,' Dad said. 'I just noticed that your football shoes are a full size smaller than your everyday shoes, and I took the liberty of buying you these.' Dad then produced an orange box from beside the sofa and made to hand it to me. I almost snatched it in my excitement but managed to control myself. I opened it and saw a beautiful pair of black Gola Speedster shoes with their distinctive yellow stripes. They took my breath away.

'Dad, they're absolutely brilliant, but why?' I asked.

'Well, I assumed, should you have known about the Inter-Colls *before* going to Blackpool, you would have saved your money for these,' Dad suggested.

'Spoiled brat,' Ed added. 'I've got to work in that poxy restaurant for *my* money.'

As I sat to lace up my new boots, I sought to lighten the mood. 'Ed, next Tuesday, I think you need to bring this most grievous of injustices to the attention of the supremely able Doug, who will undoubtedly bring Dad's heinous crime to the attention of the distinguished Socialist Workers Newspaper. I'm confident it will adorn their front page and garner many letters of support.'

I looked up and was surprised to see Ed and Dad staring at me with their mouths agape. Mum, who was standing at the door, winked at me. 'That's my little Tony Benn,' she said, smiling at the dumbfounded pair.

∘ ∘ ∘

Despite the new boots, the practice didn't go as well as the previous session. Before we started, I asked coach Brightwell about the possible cause of the soreness in my thighs. He explained that the thigh muscles are underused in everyday activities and that the soreness was a sign that I hadn't played much football. He suggested I stretch more often and put aside time to kick my football against a suitable wall, alternating with knee over the ball and then full extension. It seemed to make sense, and I continued the rest of the practice but didn't commit myself as much as I did last time.

When I got back home, I went to bed early so I could read the newspapers given to me by Peter. As I read the twelfth of July issue, I was amazed at how many articles it contained. I was also shocked at how much the Socialists hated the Labour Party; it confused me totally because I thought they were on the same side. The tone of words made for uncomfortable reading and confirmed just how little I knew of real-world politics. I even found an article about the dangers associated with producing carbon fibre for those working at the chemical plants, so that's me not buying a new fishing rod, simply on principle. Not only did the newspaper cover UK politics, but it also covered socialist issues in Portugal, Argentina, Dublin and New York. It even had an article on how badly the right-wing media treated General Idi Amin of Uganda. It compared his racist treatment to that doled out to the Irish through Punch magazine. The whole tone of the newspaper made me tense and somewhat disheartened. It cast doubt on what I was learning through History at school and knocked my belief that the things I'll learn through my lessons would be factual rather than written by people who may have pre-judged the issues and conveyed them using their preferred political slant.

I decided to skip much of the stuff and go straight to the article about the miners on the back page. It wasn't about the miners. It was about the NUM, how they disagreed about their pay, and how people stabbed each other in the back. After reading it, I felt a deep sense of unease and couldn't face reading the next edition.

As I lay on my back, thinking about the article and the general tone of the newspaper, I felt my heart booming and had to sit up from feeling nauseous. I saw the trade union movement revering the conch with its rules and a new tribe saying it was meaningless. I saw two tribes, and as the members left the conch to side with Jack, I saw how Jack's tribe descended into an utter hatred for those that remained with the conch. Didn't the deaths of Simon and Piggy count for anything? I began to cry like a littlun, turned to my side, pulled the sheets over, and knew there was a good chance I'd see the beast in my dreams.

28

I felt numb on Sunday morning, and my head pounded. I got out of bed but lay back down as I started to feel queasy; at least my thighs didn't ache. I looked at the newspaper on the floor and decided I wasn't ready to face Ed's friend with anything close to a balanced point of view should Doug choose to express any political opinion. After all, I was still a littlun.

I may have developed in some ways throughout the holidays, but I was still a fifteen-year-old boy who hadn't experienced real life. I contented myself with that thought and successfully left my bed on the second attempt. As I dressed, I felt I needed a refresh, a reset, so I decided to revisit the Black Lakes and take a new book from Ed's collection to accompany me.

○ ○ ○

The walk to the lakes was calming and much-needed after cramming my head with so much stuff. I considered that Doris' death had somehow contributed to this profound state of analysis I was constantly entering. It wasn't. As I walked up those glorious slopes with the sun on my back, I realised it was the letter from Rhian.

Reading that reply made me realise I had to grow up, that I wasn't a victim any longer and didn't need the assent of others to live this new life. I needed to satisfy myself, no one else, that my actions were what I wanted to do and that I wasn't doing them to gain favour. Yes, the catalyst for my sudden outpouring of opinions was my attempt to be me, but, like those political journalists, my thoughts had been coloured by experience. The reality was that my experience had been gained rapidly through my decision at the start of the holiday to avoid Ollie. I shrugged and decided the best course of action would be to leave myself open to accepting and analysing information with an open mind.

I caught two good trout and started to read a new book. It was called Heart of Darkness, but I don't think I'll continue with it. I'd asked Ed to recommend a light-hearted book to lift my spirits, but, having read the title, I should have known it would be anything but. It was difficult for me to understand the author's use of language, and in my current state of confusion, I didn't have the energy to continue with it when I got back home.

Even though I will postpone further reading of this book, I did stumble across a phrase that shook me to the core. After reading this devastating phrase, I knew I would have to return to the Heart of Darkness, but not until I was ready. I read the phrase repeatedly, and it seemed to encapsulate everything about my relationship with Ollie and what made him what he was. I transposed the quote to fit us – *Ollie was a conqueror, and for that, he required only brute force--nothing to boast of when you have it, since his strength is just an accident arising from the weakness of others, the others being people like James Smith and Ernie Taynor.*

When I arrived home, I threw the book back to Ed, who laughed, thinking I was upset. 'Thanks, Ed,' I said, 'I can't wait to read it through, it sounds brilliant, but I can't face reading any more of it in my current fragile state of mind.'

Ed stopped laughing immediately, and I managed to keep a straight face before turning away from him to place the trout in the fridge.

∘ ∘ ∘

Monday passed without incident, apart from the team enjoying their most cohesive training session. On the way home, Nigel and Thomas suggested we may do quite well in the forthcoming tournament, something we'd never previously considered. The first round started on Friday evening, but we weren't due to play until Saturday afternoon.

After returning home, I didn't think about the football. Doris had gone, and I began looking for her face, voice and hugs in my memories. They were still there, and in a way, my decision to change my route on that last Friday rekindled those memories. It was weird. What would I have felt had I not seen them? Would the memories be as fresh as they are now? I had no answers to my questions, but I still had the memories. Tomorrow may well create new ones.

On Tuesday morning, Mum and Dad came home at around ten. Mum had her colleague, Ken, come in to cover her for a couple of hours, and Dad had also managed to get cover, and he was going to drive Peter and us to Doris' funeral. I was glad to see him come home, but seeing him in his funereal outfit made me worry that I appeared disrespectful. I satisfied myself that it couldn't be helped because fifteen-year-olds couldn't be expected to have clothes for such an occasion. I ended up practically wearing my school uniform.

'The trousers, shirt and shoes will be fine,' Mum said as she busied herself with her outfit. After I put them on and faced her, she closed her eyes in despair; the trousers were over an inch too short. 'It can't be helped,' she assured me. 'Just wear your black socks; it won't look so bad.' She then proceeded to throttle me with one of Dad's spare black ties until I looked halfway respectable, apart from my half-mast trousers and anorak with its go-faster yellow stripes along the sleeves that were also shrinking away from my hands. I wondered if I should wear navy gloves so it didn't look so bad!

I knew I looked terrible when Elsie waved us goodbye. 'Remember to give my regards to Maude. And James! You look very smart indeed,' she shouted before turning to the kitchen to search for those pesky sausages and carry out her diabolical method of making them inedible.

○ ○ ○

Dad picked Peter up from the garage; he was far more sombrely dressed in a dark grey overcoat, black trousers and polished black shoes. I had to smile, however, when I noticed the tie that accessorised his white shirt. It was dark blue adorned with oranges, and Doris would have loved him for wearing it; I certainly did, pulling my sleeves down as far as they would.

The service was boring, full of religious references that meant nothing to me and songs I hadn't a clue about their words or tune. Still, I mumbled magnificently, ignoring the superficial sounds and thinking about Doris' body lying cold in the coffin. The coffin appeared dimensionally standard; I'd seen others on TV programmes and wondered if Doris would have been happy with it only being half full. I imagined Doris would have been far happier if they'd carefully arranged the bright fruit around her head and shoulders and the dull veg around her legs and feet.

'Sit down!' Mum whisper-shouted as the hymn ended, and I remained the only person standing.

∘ ∘ ∘

After the coffin was lowered and people filtered out of the cemetery, we filed past Maude and her sister to formally say sorry for your loss and deposit an envelope into a tin box. I felt awkward and only shook Maude's gloved hand. We then drove to the Women's Institute, where tea, coffee, sandwiches and cakes awaited the hungry mourners. We don't usually eat sandwiches for lunch, but I guessed that funerals were the exception to that rule; we certainly didn't eat cake at lunch. As Mum and Dad mingled, Peter and I sat at a linen-covered table, drinking tea and eating a slice of coffee and walnut sponge. I was glad to sit down because it hid my stupid trousers from any fashion experts that may have attended.

'Are you okay, James?' Peter asked.

I was worried about how I was reacting. 'No, Peter, I'm struggling to engage in the sombreness I believe the occasion warrants. I'm feeling childlike and giddy, if that makes any sense?'

Peter nodded. 'Yes, it makes perfect sense, James. After all, how could you possibly have, within your arsenal, a means of categorising the collective grief of people and the sudden transformation when they then try to lift the spirits of the bereaved. It must appear to you that they're saying, "okay now, Doris has gone, and we can move on", but it isn't quite like that. If you listen to their conversations, they will be talking of episodes in their lives where they've interacted with Doris, and memories such as these will help Maude, in the short term, come to terms with her loss,' he smiled.

'Thank you, Peter, that did help,' I said and took another bite of the cake; Mum had competition!

Eventually, the mourners began to thin out, and Maude was increasingly left alone. I decided it was time for me to see her on my own. I left my dishes with the three enthusiastic ladies, working like a well-oiled machine, who manned the large Belfast sink armed with dishcloths and drying towels.

Maude was sitting at a table with her chair pointing along its length. A cold cup of tea and an uneaten slice of cake sat on the table beside her; she appeared to be somewhere else.

'Hi, Aunt Maude,' I said, and she looked up. I smiled. 'Would it be okay if I gave you a hug?' I asked. 'Because I didn't really enjoy shaking your hand; it didn't feel like you, and I didn't feel like me.'

Maude pushed back her chair and stood in front of me. It was only then that I felt anything of what I thought I should feel. 'Of course, we can hug, James, dear. I would like that very much indeed.'

Awkwardly at first, I placed my arms around Maude, she did the same, and suddenly the strange ceremony disappeared. I hoped Maude understood my hug was my collective memory of Doris and the times she teased me for being slow, asking about someone's address again, and being too fast and not allowing her time to prepare the next delivery box. I hugged Maude tighter when I saw Doris getting frustrated with me for calling her "my little Amy Turtle" but ended up smiling as she acknowledged the striking similarities between her and the star of Crossroads.

We pulled apart. 'Thank you, Aunt Maude; I enjoyed that hug more than I enjoyed the coffee sponge cake, and that was the best coffee cake I've ever tasted,' I said.

'I also needed that hug,' Maude replied, and I was pleased to see she was smiling rather than crying.

'Can I also say, Aunt Maude, that I particularly loved your perfume today. It was a lovely thing to do.'

This time tears did well up in her eyes, but she still managed to smile. 'You're the first to notice, James; thank you.' I nodded and gradually released her hand to back off to find my parents. I saw Mum raise her hand, and I walked over to where they were talking with Peter, taking an opportunity to smell my hand and the lingering aroma of "Lily of the Valley", Maude's touching tribute to the fabulous Doris.

○ ○ ○

When we dropped Peter off, I also left the car, asking Dad to wait. 'Well, James, I suppose it may be some time until we next meet,' Peter said as we stood awkwardly facing each other.

I nodded. 'I will need to concentrate on the football this weekend, but perhaps, we could meet for a catch-up between matches?' I suggested.

'Are you presuming that your passage to further rounds is definite?' Peter mocked.

'Not at all, Peter, but it would be foolish to arrange a meeting if there was a possibility of our team preparing to play, wouldn't it?'

'Touche, young James. So, I will see you sometime next week, and you can inform me of your glorious advancement or valiant failure.'

'I will do just that, Peter,' I confirmed, leaned to him, and shared a warm embrace. As we parted, a sense of change hung in the air, and we knew things would never be quite the same again.

Back in the car, Dad turned to me. 'Are you okay, James?' He asked.

'Yeah, I'm fine, Dad,' I replied, and we drove the five minutes home to face Elsie's sausage and mash.

∘ ∘ ∘

We survived the sausage and mash; Elsie's cooking was improving as the holidays ended, and I hung around the house after changing into casual clothes that fit me a bit better than my uniform. As Elsie was relaxing watching the TV and I was reading a new book entitled "The Spy Who Came In From The Cold", I felt confident it would be a lighter read than "Heart of Darkness", a loud knock disturbed our peace.

'Whoever can that be?' Elsie asked, but her eyes remained locked on the TV screen. I took that as a cue, put the spy novel down and answered the door. It was a stranger; it was Doug. I held the door.

'Uh, hi, is this Edward Smith's home?' He asked. He was pale, thin and tall, taller than Ed, and had curly dark shoulder-length hair with the base of his face supported by a darker chin-strap beard. His thinness and gaunt cheeks made his face appear to be very long. He carried a blue rucksack over his right shoulder, and, under its strap, I could see a black donkey jacket. This had no discernible company logo to indicate where he'd worked or *if* he'd worked to get his hands on the industrial garment. The jacket was covered with small circular badges: Socialists against Racialism, CND, but most bore N.U.S followed by a slogan like NUS No to the Milk Snatcher. Under the jacket, he wore a dark brown jumper broken up with cream horizontal rings at the crew neck collar and around the midriff. Doug was undoubtedly a student.

'Are you, Doug?' I asked pointlessly.

'Yeah, I'm in the same college as Ed,' he expanded.

'Come in, I'll shout for him; he's up in his room,' I said, allowing him into the kitchen.

After shouting for him, Ed came bounding down the stairs and greeted Doug in the kitchen. I explained to Elsie who the stranger was, but she couldn't care less. After a while, Ed brought Doug through.

'Uh, Doug, that's Jamie, my kid brother, and that's our grandmother Elsie; she comes here whenever Mum works at the Post Office, usually Tuesday and Thursday,' Ed said to Doug.

'Hi,' Doug said, and I acknowledged him with a nod.

'Jamie, this is Doug Molyneaux from college. I'm just going to show him where he's sleeping, okay?'

From his tone, Ed must have thought I'd be arsey about the whole business, but I'd accepted the situation and moved my essential stuff in my rucksack to Ed's attic bedroom. 'That's fine, Ed. I hope you'll be comfortable, Doug.' Ed then led his visitor upstairs to *my* bedroom.

Elsie turned to me. 'He was a bit shabby, wasn't he, James? You'd think he'd have made an effort,' Elsie tutted. I smiled and read on.

29

'Tosser!' Ed hissed as he walked past my camp bed on Thursday morning, nudging it with his leg to indicate his frustration level. I pulled the sheet over my shoulders and, although I knew I wouldn't get back to sleep, decided to stay there until I heard the door close to indicate our visitor had left.

○ ○ ○

Wednesday was, for the most part, very unremarkable. Doug and Ed hung around until eleven, when it was time for the visitor to go to the larger Ailsworth 'A' Pit. It was a forty-minute walk, and Ed acted as guide for the intrepid journalist. I just hung around and cleaned up my new boots, ready for that evening's final practice. I then cautiously walked to Maude's shop to see what was happening.

I was shocked to find Maude actually working, thinking she'd take a few days off at least. 'Nature waits for no grocer, James,' she said. 'If I left the produce you see here for too long, they'd end up in the river.' Maude was referring to the small river that crossed underneath the High Street and flowed directly beneath her shop. At the back of Maude's store, there was a three-foot by-two trapdoor, and it was through this aperture that Maude's unsellable products were dumped. This action, and that of other shops, gave Mill River a distinct and unique smell.

I nodded and asked if there was anything I could help with. Reluctantly Maude said there was, and I spent the afternoon moving stuff around, checking what was sellable, dumping the perished items and preparing the first three boxes for Eric to deliver this evening. Maude had to make emergency arrangements to supply her customers tonight after the non-delivery of their usual goods last Friday evening and Saturday morning because Maude was mourning for Doris.

I followed each list carefully and tried to imagine how Doris would pack them and in what order. "It isn't just about packing," Doris once explained. "You must also consider the customer's unpacking and how they'd move our products into storage." I smiled as I remembered and could almost see her doing the packing as I stood at the door, watching her.

When I finished the work, I turned to Maude. 'Do you want me to come in every day to help?' I asked.

'No, James, once I get this backlog sorted, I should be okay,' she assured me.

'What if I came in on Friday afternoon and Saturday morning to help with the packing? It would free you to look after the shop.'

Maude thought about this. 'That would be helpful, James. Could you do it?' She asked.

I knew the Inter-Colls was starting on Friday evening, but I'd be finished before five, and I also knew that the work on Saturday morning would be completed before ten. 'Yeah, of course I can, Aunt Maude; I could even carry on helping you after school restarts,' I said enthusiastically.

'Okay then, James, consider yourself hired,' she said and held out her hand, which I shook to cement our deal.

As I left the shop, I glanced over to the High Street and caught a glimpse of a familiar shape. It was Ollie, and Ernie Taynor was walking beside him, probably nursing a sore arm. I waited for them to walk past and circled around the back alleys until I emerged about fifty yards behind them. I watched with a sinking feeling as Ollie parked his arse on that same small wall and saw Ernie walk across to Gordon's shop. This vantage point allowed me to observe Ollie to see what he did when I was in the shop. He did nothing apart from looking up and down the High Street, picking his nose, stretching, and yawning. The only time I saw him stir was when poor Ernie emerged from the shop carrying Ollie's reward for being such a splendid master. I felt sick, unable to understand Ollie's evil, twisted mind. Still, I did nothing and trudged home despondently to prepare for the final practice.

○ ○ ○

The practice went well, and there was a feeling of optimism that we could win a couple of matches, so long as we avoided the favourites, such as Pit A's first team. When I got home, Dad had popped to the Railway with Ed and Doug, so I sat and watched a bit of TV with Mum, and I told her about me working with Maude on Fridays and Saturday mornings, but she didn't say much, she was transfixed to the TV, it was like watching Elsie, but thirty years younger.

Sitting there, taking everything in, I couldn't help reflecting on Dad's sociable side. Despite not knowing Doug, it was still a good enough excuse to accompany Ed and his pal because he said it was good manners. I concluded that adults liked breaking the rules to suit their personal agendas. Tonight was another example of Dad needing only the slightest excuse to go out; tonight, it was to entertain Doug. Eventually, the trio returned and retired to the parlour for more drinks, but I stayed with Mum. As the News at Ten finished, I pecked Mum goodnight and popped my head into the parlour to say goodnight. Dad, who seemed to be in an ebullient mood, ushered me in. After a bit of chit-chat about everyone in the pub talking about the upcoming Inter-Colls tournament, I thought I'd ask something. 'How did it go at the Pit today, Doug?' I asked, honestly interested.

'It was an eye-opener, for sure,' he said but didn't seem to want to expand.

'Oh, in what way was that then?'

'God, they work so hard, man,' he said, 'and the conditions are so shit.'

'Is that what you'll say in your article – that they work hard and in shit conditions?' I asked, bristling after hearing Doug use "man".

'Jamie!' Ed interrupted. 'Chill out, for fuck's sake.'

Dad didn't correct Ed's use of the expletive but sat there happy for us to carry on. 'I was only asking, Ed, because I've read the Socialist Worker newspaper, and it doesn't usually carry articles about the day in the life of,' I explained.

'Yeah, but you've got to experience the shit they go through if you want to understand why they're the leading opposition to this fascist government,' Doug said.

'But it's a Labour Government, the party democratically elected and formed originally to represent the unions,' I said.

'Doesn't stop them being fascists, though, with their social contract bullshit, does it?' Doug was warming up, challenging me by making the last statement a question.

'So why did the NUM, in their own conference, agree to uphold the social contract, much in the same way as the TUC have done?' I was now glad to have read Peter's newspaper.

'What? They didn't do that! That's just the fascist media spreading lies to prop up this government of bullshit traitors,' Doug said.

'They *did* do that, Doug. At their conference in Scarborough, everyone failed to support the Yorkshire miners' demands for the £100 wage target. The majority spoke, and therefore democracy won. The fact you keep calling people fascists doesn't actually mean that they are fascists; that's just childish,' My cheeks were burning.

'What the fuck?' Doug asked and seemed to implore Ed to step in.

'Jamie!' Ed barked. 'You need to stop talking about stuff you know nothing about right now.' He looked at Dad.

'Don't you dare stop, James,' Dad said. 'No one should ask that of anyone. You have the right to your opinion, as does Doug, and I'm enjoying this immensely,' he smiled.

'But to be fair, dude, you don't really know what's going on, do you?' Doug asked patronisingly.

'I know more than you, for a start, and that means my opinion counts just as much, if not more,' I said and loved Ed looking really uncomfortable, or was it a look of someone controlling a wave of seething anger.

'How the hell do you work that out, then?' Doug asked.

This was the question I'd been trying to get him to ask. I'd picked this manoeuvring tactic from jousting with Peter, where I'd pick up on something and then test it with a statement I'd assessed to be true. 'Because *my* family has experienced mining life. My grandfather was a miner, my grandfather died a miner's death, my grandmother lived the life of a miner's wife, my father was a miner's son, and we've lived in a mining town, sharing our lives alongside miners. Do you think popping into a pit for a couple of hours like a tourist gives you the right to represent them?' I asked, hoping his family hadn't all died from "black lung". He remained silent, taking gulps from the beer can he held. 'What does your father do?' I asked calmly.

'What my father does has nothing to do with this. I don't need to justify my upbringing to a snot-nosed kid like you,' Doug answered.

'His parents are both teachers,' Dad said.

'That's nice,' I said. 'So I'm assuming that your grandparents had something to do with mining, then?'

Doug became sheepish. 'No, Dad's lot were farmers, and Mum's lot were like preachers and stuff,' Doug added, probably because he'd already told Dad at the pub and feared being exposed again.

'You see, I don't mind you highlighting the shit miners have to endure for an unfair wage; what I don't like is that you're trying to get an article into the Socialist Worker when you'd be equally happy getting an article into The Spectator. You don't care about politics; you only care about your own brand. Consequently,' I continued, 'I don't mind being called a snot-nosed kid by someone like you; the only thing that surprised me with that description of me was that you didn't call me a fascist snot-nosed kid.'

Dad laughed, almost choking on a mouthful of Double Diamond, but Doug and Ed were silent, giving me hateful looks. I decided I'd said enough. 'I'm going to turn in,' I said. 'Night all.'

○ ○ ○

When I eventually got up, Dad, who had popped home for a quick coffee, was in the kitchen. 'Ed not here then?' I asked.

Dad looked up from his paper. 'No, he's taking that prick to the bus station,' he said.

I smiled. 'He was a prick, wasn't he?'

'One hundred per cent, twenty-four-carat prick, and I was proud of you last night for showing him for what he was. Ed was embarrassed because I think Mr Molyneaux is highly regarded in the Student Union at their college.'

'Still doesn't stop him from being a dick, does it?' I stated, starting to remember why I didn't like the bloke.

Dad indicated for me to sit, and I assented after making myself a mug of tea. 'What is it?' I asked.

Dad had put his paper down and pushed it aside. 'It's you. It's as if you've suddenly become a different person, or else I'm guilty of not watching you properly.'

I thought about what he'd said for a few seconds. 'I've had a shitty time, Dad, and there were times I hoped you could see that something was wrong. You didn't. Mum didn't, and I couldn't expect Ed to. I was alone, Dad, in that stupid world I'd created, and I did a lot of thinking. Since I've broken out of my foolish world, I can see that honesty is more important than appearances, and I think admitting my weakness to you three was the catalyst I needed. Knowing that you knew about my dictionary, I'm so glad you allowed me to sort it out myself; the problem with that is that it's created a gobby little git like me.'

Dad laughed. 'We had a chat during the holiday, didn't we?' He asked.

'Yeah, we had a long chat,' I confirmed.

'Well, can you please ignore everything I said about your future then?'

'I can. But why should I?' I asked.

'Because I'll be happy with whatever course you take in your life, and it wasn't fair for me to try to influence you,' he said.

I smiled. 'No, I won't ignore it, Dad,' I said, 'because it showed you cared.'

○ ○ ○

'Hello,' I said to one of the salespeople in the Co-op store, 'where can I find Mr Taynor?' I asked.

'Uh, Mr Taynor is in the office back there,' she indicated, pointing to a grey door marked "Staff Only". 'But you can't go in.'

'That's okay; I just wanted to know when he finishes work,' I explained.

'Oh, I think he knocks off at four-thirty,' she confirmed.

'Thank you,' I said and walked out. The Co-op had been in Ailsworth since I could remember and existed harmoniously alongside all our other high street stores. The problem was that they were building a new, much larger Co-op supermarket on waste ground near the Grady council estate, and people were predicting it would severely affect the viability of shops like Maude's. I wasn't sure it would because Gordon's sweetshop still seemed to thrive, despite Woolworths and their pic'n'mix.

○ ○ ○

Having spent the afternoon kicking my football against our garden wall, I told Elsie I'd be late for tea and set off for Lord Street. I was focused on what I was going to do, but as I walked along the back alleys, I felt numb and anything but focused. Lord street was attractive, rising steeply from the High Street, comprising five blocks of four houses. I knew the Taynors lived in the semi-detached number eight because I'd delivered there once, although I was never sure why they'd be buying from Maude's. Now, as I walked up the street, I wondered if Mr Taynor had been acting as a spy and checking out the competition's produce; I dismissed the thought and stood looking at the door. I stared unfocusedly and began to doubt my chosen plan of action. Could I make things worse? I doubted that. Could I change the family dynamic? I didn't know; they were not my family.

I took a deep breath and knocked. As I waited for the door to be answered, doubts began to resurface, and I felt like running away, pretending it was "knock-doors". The door swung open.

'Hello?' Mrs Taynor asked as she held the front door open. 'It's James, isn't it?'

'Yes, Mrs Taynor,' I said, unsure how to continue. 'I was wondering if I could have a word with you and Mr Taynor.'

'Oh, well, yes,' she said, unsure how to respond. 'Is there anything wrong?' she asked.

'Yes, Mrs Taynor, I think there is, but I don't want to speak out here,' I said, glancing up and down the street furtively.

'Oh, you best come in then,' she said, leading me into their well-appointed living room where Mr Taynor was sat in his armchair reading the Daily Mail.

'Michael,' she announced, 'James here would like a word with us about something. He says there's something wrong.'

'Oh?' he said, closing his paper. 'This sounds very mysterious. Are you looking for a job at the co-op, by any chance?' Mr

Taynor asked, trying to lighten the solemn atmosphere I'd brought into their lovely home.

I steeled myself to carry out my intended course of action. 'No, Mr and Mrs Taynor: I want to talk to you about Ernie,' I said, and Mr Taynor's posture stiffened immediately. Mrs Taynor left me to sit on the armrest of Mr Taynor's chair; they were both now looking at me.

'Ernest's okay, isn't he? He hasn't done anything wrong, has he?' Mr Taynor asked in a slightly louder voice.

'No, Ernie's done nothing wrong, and I don't want you to think that anything's happened to him, but,' I paused and saw the anxiety build in their eyes. 'Ernie's being bullied,' I said.

'What do you mean?' Mrs Taynor demanded.

'Ernie's being bullied by a boy called Ollie Jenkins,' I explained.

'No. Ernest would have told us if anything was wrong,' Mr Taynor said. His voice was calmer and seemed to dismiss my accusation as a foolish piece of imagination.

I shook my head. 'No, Mr Taynor, Ernie will never tell you because I never told my family when I suffered bullying from the same boy.'

'I know Mr Jenkins quite well from the Rotary Club, and I can't imagine his son to be a bully. He was here the other day, wasn't he, Mary?' He turned to his wife for confirmation, but Mrs Taynor was quiet and didn't respond; she just stared at me. 'Mary?' Mr Taynor repeated.

'You're serious, aren't you?' Mrs Taynor asked, still staring fixedly at me.

I didn't flinch and stared back with what I hoped were sympathetic eyes. 'Yes, Mrs Taynor, I'm very serious,' I said. I watched as Mrs Taynor squeezed her husband's hand after it had sought hers. 'I didn't tell my family and suffered for fifteen months as a consequence. I think Ollie has only just started to bully Ernie, and I'm telling you because I would have welcomed someone telling my parents about it, even as ashamed as I was.'

Mr Taynor was not a big man, and I doubted he'd ever beaten anyone up during his childhood, so he looked unsure of what to do next. Mrs Taynor, however, knew what to ask. 'What should we do, James?' She asked in a clear cold voice.

'You need to get Ernie to tell you he's being bullied. That in itself takes most of the shame away. You then need to support him in whatever way he wants, and because Ernie's younger than I am, you need to go to Mr Jenkins' house and tell him what's been happening. It won't be easy for Ern . . .' I stopped as I heard the door opening.

'It's only me,' I heard Ernie shout.

'We're in here, Ernest, love,' Mrs Taynor answered. 'We have a visitor.'

As Ernie walked in and saw the unusual seating arrangements taken up by his parents, I saw the confusion across his face and watched as it turned to panic when he saw that I was the visitor.

'Hi, Ernie,' I said.

'Uh, hi, James. You okay?' Ernie asked, but I had no time to answer.

'Is that boy, Ollie Jenkins, bullying you, Ernest?' His mother asked kindly.

'Ollie? No, of course he isn't bullying me. We're just mates; that's all,' Ernie assured them, and as he did, I could see myself standing there.

'I was telling your parents that Ollie bullied me for fifteen months, and I thought I'd warn them before he ruins *your* life.' I said.

'No, James, I can't believe Ollie would do that,' Ernie said. 'He's as nice as pie when *we* play.' A quiver in his voice betrayed his inner turmoil.

I felt uneasy as I looked at Ernie. I was now doing the bullying, and although I wasn't punching him, *I was* hurting him.

'Mr and Mrs Taynor, I have no reason to disbelieve Ernie, but I know the truth, and to show you the truth, I'd like you to ask Ernie to take off his shirt.'

'What? Don't be stupid,' Ernie protested.

'Please, Ernest,' his mother asked kindly, 'for me.'

Ernie looked at me, and I nodded. Despite tears falling, Ernie gave a slight smile and turned to face his parents as he undid the buttons of his shirt. As Ernie allowed the shirt to drop to the floor, I saw the tears flood his loving parents' eyes. From my position, I saw that his puny right arm was heavily bruised from halfway up his upper arm. I assumed the left arm would sport similar marks. As if standing there in his vest was not enough, Ernie decided that that garment should also be removed. As his back was revealed to me, I saw the familiar shapes on his flanks that I'd seen in our bathroom mirror.

'Sorry, Ernie,' I said.

Ernie turned to me, and I saw he'd stopped crying. 'No need to say sorry, James,' he began. 'I'm glad that Mum and Dad know, but I couldn't . . . you know?'

'Yeah, I know you couldn't tell them, and you may feel shitty now, but tomorrow and the next day and the next day, you'll feel better and better. It's like a great weight lifted.' Ernie nodded.

Mrs Taynor stood and hugged Ernie in silence, making me feel awkward. Mr Taynor continued to sit, but his head was in his hand as he tried to digest what he'd seen on his son's body and what he should or could do about the matter.

'I best be going,' I said, edging past mother and son to let myself out.

I closed their front door behind me and breathed in the air that felt so fresh after leaving that oppressive room. I'd gone ten yards when I heard a door opening behind me. I turned and saw Mrs Taynor standing there. 'Thank you, James,' she said. I smiled, but I could see on her face that I'd brought a great deal of pain into her life.

'It *will* become less painful the more you talk, Mrs Taynor; I promise.'

Nothing more was said, and I turned away, nauseous as the memory of Ernie's bruises returned to pollute my senses again.

As I walked home, I couldn't stop thinking about the cruelty living within Ollie Jenkins and the world surrounding him.

His father was in the Rotary Club!

So bloody what.

Was his father abusive? Is that why he is like he is? His parents *look* nice, but I know that looks can be deceiving. Is there a secret room inside their house where they train Ollie to be the freak he is?

Or was it simply that Ollie Jenkins was born evil?

As I walked home, I decided I favoured nature over nurture, which meant he was unlikely to change, and I *would* have to face him when I returned to school. Having seen the cowardly way he'd beaten a younger child, there was anger within me, and I felt like charging over to his house to confront him now and get it over with. I didn't. Instead, I walked down the High Street knowing that if he did face me, I'd stand my ground so that there would be witnesses when I fought back against him.

By the time I'd arrived home, the adrenaline, or whatever it was that had fuelled my wish to face him, had dissipated, and a cold sweat swept over me as I realised how stupid that course of action would have been. I sat on the sofa, glad to be home, and when I thought back on the day, I was happy that I'd helped Ernie despite knowing many tears would be shed as the family came to terms with knowing that someone had been brutalising their precious son.

∘ ∘ ∘

'Here he is! The cheeky little git who's embarrassed me to hell,' Ed spat as he walked into the living room. Mum and I were on the sofa watching TV, and Dad was reading in his armchair. Ed had been working, but I could tell he'd had a drink or two.

Dad looked up and decided not to say anything. Unaware of last night's chat, Mum didn't like the tone. 'Edward!' she said. 'That's not a nice way to start any conversation.'

'A nice way to start a conversation?' Ed began. 'Tell that to that little shit-stirrer sitting next to you! I couldn't believe you said what you did, James; it was bloody rude.' I liked how Ed, despite his temper, still managed to not swear in front of Mum.

I wanted to shrug, but knew that the gesture might antagonise Ed even more. 'I'm sorry you thought I was rude, Ed, but Doug Molyneaux is a fake, hiding in plain sight and using the Student Union to pull the wool over your eyes. If he can't win a political argument with a snot-nosed kid like me, you need to call an extraordinary meeting of the NUS to chuck him out when you return to college.'

Ed shook his head. 'You won't say sorry, will you?'

'I just did,' I explained. 'I'm sorry if you thought I was rude, but I'm certainly not sorry for facing up to an imposter like that. I never will be.'

Ed was clearly unhappy. 'You're becoming far too cocky for someone who actually knows nothing,' Ed said and pointed at me. 'Do you know what? I preferred you...'

'Don't you fucking dare say that!' I screamed, jumping up to square up with Ed.

Ed stood his ground, fists clenched. Dad had sat up but still wasn't going to say anything.

I stared at Ed and suddenly realised my sight was deteriorating as my eyes welled up. 'Don't you dare say that you preferred me when I was being bullied.'

'But,'

'But nothing, Ed. And to think you said it to defend a pretentious piece of shit like Molyneaux!' I was seething, and Ed kept silent. 'I've just been to Ernie Taynor's house and told them that he was being bullied by Ollie. He denied it, and I made that poor boy take his shirt off!' I said, my tremulous voice cracking as I tried to string the sentences. 'In front of his Mum and Dad, Ed; in front of his Mum and Dad, I watched Ernie . . . take off his shirt, and there . . . .' I pointed to my upper arms. 'There . . . bruises, both arms black, blue, purple, pink . . . even brown where they'd faded. I . . . he then took his little vest off . . . and I saw . . . here,' I placed my hands on my back. 'Bruises . . . my bruises. . . bruises I hid from you for all that time. . .' I stopped, unable to carry on, and took slow deep breaths to control my crying. Ed made to step towards me, but I lifted my left hand and shook my head. I wasn't interested in sorry; he should have known how hurtful his words would have been; he's my big brother.

30

Saturday morning just flew by. I hadn't been as excited about something for ages. I breezed through my work with Maude and thought I'd done a reasonably good job packing the produce using the Doris method. After Maude's, the earlier excitement flooded back. We were due to play our first match in the Inter-Colls and would be the third and final match this afternoon, kicking off at four-thirty. Dad was playing in goal for the post office in the preceding game.

The first two matches of the tournament were played on Friday evening, and Ed and I went to spectate after I'd finished at Maude's. It was brutal, almost gladiatorial, and as I watched the games, I thought about how our side would fare against the four on show. The teams from the pits played to a high standard, but their opponents were a ragged group of hackers from a social club and a pub. Both pit teams won by more than six goals and made sure that they beat their opponents on the score sheet and in the number of punches thrown once it became clear that the social teams fancied themselves as amateur boxers. They were no match to the hardened miners, and the pits' two signed players had a vastly superior skill level. It was like watching primary school football, where a skilful player would dribble the entire length of the pitch and score with strewn tacklers all over the place. The matches are only thirty minutes per half, but even the shortened games left the pub teams struggling; two of their "midfielders" threw up on the pitch due to over-exertion.

○ ○ ○

After my outburst on Thursday evening, Ed came into my bedroom on Friday morning, and we had a long chat about stuff. I was sat up, still in bed in my pyjamas, and Ed sat on the edge. I explained that the euphoria I felt after admitting to being bullied made me look for ways to replicate it, hence my visit to the Taynors. I then did something stupid.

'Ed, I knew I was belittling Doug the other night, but I thought it important to show you that I crave the truth despite knowing I'd be a little shit.'

'You weren't such a little shit; it just made me feel bad for someone I knew, that's all,' Ed said.

I looked at Ed intently. 'You see, this craving I have,' I said, 'makes me want to ask you if you're gay, but I know that when I ask you that question, you'll hate me all over again.' I held my breath. After remaining silent for a few seconds, Ed lurched forward, grabbed my pyjama collar with both hands and pulled me towards him. His strength shocked me. In that split second, all I could think of was how stupid I'd been to confront Ed last night.

With my face close to his, he snarled through his bared teeth. 'Don't you fucking well dream of asking that question to me, you pompous little shit,' he spat. I said nothing as I fought to calm my senses. It was a surreal experience being gripped by someone as strong as Ed while also remaining calm. I realised I no longer feared being hit; my weakness no longer existed. I reflected on that wonderful phrase from "Heart of Darkness" I'd memorised and smiled. 'Don't you fucking smirk at me, you arrogant little shit; this is my life you're ruining.'

I shrugged myself free from his hands. 'I'm not smirking at you; I'm smirking that you think violence will make me not ask you that question. You or Ollie can beat me up as much as you like, but the truth, for people like you, is I will still have that question, and that question needs answering,' I said. 'Okay, I don't need you to answer me now, but someday I need you to answer that question,' I stared at him.

'Fucking hell, Jamie, what's with all this truth stuff? You're doing my head in; you're seriously doing my head in,' Ed said, sounding desperate.

I leaned forward and placed my arms around Ed's shoulders, pulling him close. 'I love you, Ed, and you're better than people like Molyneaux, but keeping secrets makes you vulnerable. I just need to know, and I want you to know that I know because we're brothers, and that should mean something. If anything happens to me again, I'll tell you straight off because I've opened myself up. I opened a metaphorical door by telling you about Ollie, and I've let Mum, Dad, and you into my life. I don't intend to close it because I can see, looking at you, that being afraid to open that door makes you incomplete.' I knew it was very Crabtree-esque, but I was in the flow.

Ed pushed me away, but he was smiling. 'I am gay,' he said.

'Thanks,' I replied.

'I've always known it, I suppose, even growing up. If I said anything now, people might say that college made me change, but I have never changed; I've always been Edward Smith, gay.'

As Ed said that simple phrase, the emotion of it all became unbearable. I started to cry uncontrollably and saw Ed looking mortified. 'No, no,' I said, desperate to explain. 'I'm being stupid, Ed.'

'Fucking hell, Jamie, I didn't expect that!' Ed sounded dismayed.

'Don't be soft,' I said. 'I'm crying because I saw myself sitting there and telling *my* secret. I just . . .' I couldn't explain it adequately. 'It's just that I saw you change, Ed. The moment you said Edward Smith, gay, I saw you change. You knew in that instant that someone else knew you, and whenever the four of us are at dinner, from now, you will know that you're not alone hiding another life from us.'

Ed's face became serious. 'I'm not sure I'm ready for Mum and Dad yet, Jamie,' he cautioned.

I shook my head. 'You don't need to, Ed. I *was* ready for you to tell me. The only thing you need to do is maybe test the water occasionally.'

'What does that mean?' Ed asked.

'If you see things on TV or in the paper that could start a discussion, and you're in their company, just try to gauge their response. I'll tell you something,' I said, remembering my chat with them about death. 'Mum is way more cool than I gave her credit for. It's clear that she and Dad were more rebellious than I ever thought parents could or should be. After all, what gives our generation the right to think we invented cool?' I asked.

'Don't know, Jamie. It's just that they keep it hidden, don't they? They don't scream from the top of every building about this or that, do they? They just hide in the kitchen or behind a newspaper.' Ed said thoughtfully.

'Dad hated Doug, but he never let it show, did he? He wanted you to suss him out yourself; that's what he does. Like seeing my dictionary, reading it, but doing nothing about it; he allowed me space to sort out my own mess.'

'Can I read it?' Ed asked, taking me by surprise.

'What?'

'Your dictionary,' he said. 'Can I read your dictionary?'

I looked into his face. 'You want to read about my weakness?' I asked.

'No,' he said, 'I want to see what you went through when we were blind to it.'

I dragged myself out of bed and went over to my rucksack. I pulled out the book and studied my handwriting on its frayed cover.

I looked at Ed and held out the book. 'It will be my pleasure to share my pathetic dictionary with my brilliant gay brother,' I said and handed it over. Ed smiled, and I knew we'd be okay. 'Do you fancy coming to watch the opening matches tonight?' I asked.

'What, with my little kid brother?' Ed asked mockingly; I nodded. 'I'd be proud to, Jamie, I'd be proud to.'

○ ○ ○

In the second match on Saturday, Dad's team were beaten eight-two, and Mum accompanied Ed and me to watch. The football ground at Ailsworth is at the south end and almost on the way out of town. It has a row of corrugated shelters along the West touchline, and the two breeze block dugouts are on the East touchline. Behind the North goal, the ground slopes away, and many families park themselves there, lying on various blankets and sitting on deck chairs. It's a great carnival atmosphere, and I love seeing the contrast between the grunt and aggression on the pitch and the frivolity of the small kids running around the North slope playing tag or having play fights.

As we watched Dad's team, we did have a fright when, following a melee in their goalmouth, Dad ended up screaming in agony on the ground, holding his right knee. Suddenly, from behind the dugout, two men wearing nurses' uniforms ran onto the pitch carrying a stretcher. I recognised them as postmen and joined in as the crowd burst out laughing, watching them comedically placing an unconscious Dad onto the stretcher and carrying him off. When they got to the touchline, they lowered the stretcher onto the grass, and one of the "nurses" gave Dad the kiss of life. Dad then sprung to his feet and jogged majestically back to his goal.

A few locals came by Mum and said how much they'd enjoyed the sketch, but looking at Mum, I don't think she knew anything about it and must have been horrified when it was enacted.

'Don't worry, Mum,' I said. 'He'll soon grow out of it.'

Mum gave a shake of the head and a wry smile. 'James, I don't think he ever will. I'm afraid I'll have to suffer this for as long as your Dad's working. I think that's the only time he's ever likely to grow up,' she said, smiling.

After the post office match finished, I gathered with the under-sixteens and listened as the coach delivered his pre-match speech. We had to wait for the last two teams to leave the changing rooms before being allowed in to change. I knew from the teamsheet that I was a substitute and wore my anorak over my kit to keep warm.

The Inter-Colls tournament allows teams from Ailsworth, North Ailsworth, Brinsley, Garstford and Flinsby to compete. This means any town or village within five miles of Ailsworth Town centre. We were drawn against a team from a pub called "The Lion" from Gartsford. They called themselves "The Stout Lions", and a couple of them made our "Man Mountain" look more like a hillock.

'Jesus Christ,' Eric said, looking across as we warmed up. 'I hope to god those bigguns are in defence.'

'You'll be okay, Eric,' I said. 'Big fuckers like that are easy to get around.'

He smiled. 'You are a cheeky beggar, squirt, and for that, I'll do by damnest to give you a hospital pass. If you come on, that is,' he said, smiling.

The game went well for us, scoring three first-half goals once the "bigguns" stopped moving after ten minutes. They were clearly struggling with our team's pace, and we scored a further three goals after fifteen minutes of the second-half.

After Nigel scored our sixth, the coach turned to us and told all six outfield players to prepare. Waiting on the touchline for Andrew Scott, the first-choice right-back, to reach me and shake hands was exciting. I kept thinking how I'd been a no-one in Ailsworth for sixteen months, and here I was, running onto the pitch to play football in front of the town. Once we'd handed over, I dashed onto the pitch and took up my position. It felt fantastic playing in front of my Town, participating as an equal within a team of talented players. Once I began playing, I forgot everything about analysing my life and concentrated on the task at hand. The Stout Lions had run their race and didn't have the energy to commit a dirty tackle, let alone mount any significant challenge. Tackling was easy due to their lack of pace, and I spent most of my time on the pitch, charging down the wing on overlaps and supporting Damon John, our right wing. By the end of the match, we'd added a further two goals.

In the changing room, coach Brightwell seemed more than happy with our overall performance but said our next match on Wednesday would be far more challenging despite not yet knowing our opponents. 'We're facing the winner of the first match to be played tomorrow,' he explained. 'They'll have a win under their belt, like us, but if we play like we did today, I think we can give anyone a game.'

After he said this I looked at the programme and the draw. We were in the lower half of the draw, and our opponents would either be the Cooperative or Ailsworth Sports and Social Club team. I gulped, remembering the Co-op's obsessed centre-half smashing through that cowardly striker's leg.

On the way home, rucksack on my shoulder, I saw that a few people were still milling around. My eyes darted around to see if I could see Ollie. I couldn't, and I felt I wouldn't care if I did.

'James!' Someone shouted. I turned around and felt slightly confused. 'James!' The voice repeated, and this time I saw a man with his arm raised; it was Mr James Edmonson, the PE teacher from school.

Confused, I made my way over to Jim Gym (he didn't know his nickname, but even if he did, it wasn't bad as nicknames go). 'Uh, hello, sir, didn't see you there,' I said, embarrassed to be talking with a teacher.

'Playing for our rivals, eh?' He mocked, arms on hips.

I became flustered. 'Uh, yeah, well, uh . . . I did check that our school didn't have a team in the comp, sir. Before agreeing, that is.'

He smiled. 'No need to apologise, James. You were good. I was impressed but surprised at the same time,' he said, and I understood where he was going with this.

'I'm sorry I didn't play for our school team, sir, but . . .' I began. Suddenly, I faced a dilemma but knew how to address it.

'I didn't try at school, sir. I was in a bad place and couldn't be myself. I'll be okay next year,'

He looked earnestly at me. 'What do you mean, in a bad place?' He asked.

I know what snitches are. As children, we hate a snitch, telltale, squealer, grass, or rat, and there, standing in front of Jim Gym, I was happy to become one. 'Oh, I've been bullied at school for the past fifteen months by Ollie Jenkins, and me being good at sports was not something he'd countenance. I thought you knew, sir.'

'No, James, I didn't. That's terrible,' he said, thinking back to our lessons. 'I'm sorry to hear that and embarrassed I wasn't more perceptive,' he said and did seem genuinely concerned.

'It's okay, sir,' I said breezily. 'I've spent the summer holidays sorting it out, and I'll be okay next year, and as I said, I'll be happy to help out our school team if there's a place for me.'

He smiled. 'I'm glad for you, James, and looking at you this afternoon, I'm sure you'll be an asset to our team.'

'That's great, sir, but I would ask you one favour,' I said, thinking, "in for a penny, in for a pound".

'Oh, what's that then, James?'

'If you ever see Ollie Jenkins with another boy, usually a smaller boy, please assume that that boy is also being bullied. Ollie Jenkins is not a nice human being, sir.'

He nodded. 'Now you've brought it to my attention, I will make it my duty to be as observant as possible regarding that individual.'

'Thank you, sir.' I said.

'Would you mind if I passed this information to different teachers, including the headmistress?' Jim asked.

'Oh no, sir, I think you must, but please remember that it is only my word against his. Unfortunately, or fortunately from my point of view, since the evidential bruises have disappeared from my body, that is all I have.'

Jim shook his head and offered me his hand to shake; I complied. 'Thank you for speaking so honestly, James. I only wish you'd told me when this first began; it would have eased your pain and prevented me from feeling this terrible.'

We completed the handshake. 'It's honestly okay, sir. You can't imagine how much I'm looking forward to next year and what it holds for me.'

I headed home, running along the back alleys to get home as quickly as possible. Running along the maze of alleys was terrific, knowing I wasn't doing it this time to avoid Ollie.

○ ○ ○

The football almost made me forget that the summer holidays were drawing to a close. Our school would restart on the first Tuesday in September, six days after our next match against the Co-op.

I'd made it. As I gambolled lightly to Peter's, I looked forward to stretching my language to its floweriest extreme and began philosophising.

Not only had I dragged myself away from Ollie and forced open his evil hand, but I had also weakened him. A bully can only exist on the blindside of society's blinkers. I know some people are reticent to see beyond theirs and feel comfortable within the narrow life they choose, but these are the cowards. The truth will remove or widen the blinkers of the courageous, leaving the bully less room to grow his evil as those blinkerless braves give confidence to the cowards to remove theirs.

I had just beaten Peter to put me one up after playing our third game. 'Time for tea,' Peter said, and once again, I made my way to the kitchen. This time, Peter wasted no time preparing the tea, and, with the mugs steaming in front of us, he stood to seemingly make an announcement. 'Today, to commemorate the excellent chess and to celebrate your football team's glory, I have prepared a special surprise.' Peter opened a pale green door of the green and cream pantry cupboard and reached for something. He stood, kicked closed the door and turned to the table carrying a beautiful glass cloche and associated glass stand. He carefully placed it on the table. 'James, I present to you the world's best coffee and walnut sponge cake,' he announced.

I looked through the glass, and it did look lovely. 'It absolutely does look like the best coffee cake in the world, Peter, but unfortunately, that prestigious accolade cannot rightfully be awarded until the judge has tasted the said cake.'

'So speaks a very wise judge indeed,' Peter agreed and proceeded to slice up the cake and presented me with an octant that looked far too big for me to attempt to eat.

After enjoying the wonderful cake (it *was* fantastic), Peter raised his mug. 'Here's to James Smith, vanquisher of the dreaded Ollie Jenkins, whose name we may never again utter within these four walls.'

I smiled and raised my mug. 'Here's to Peter Crabtree, a true friend and champion of the lost, whose support, company and guidance will never be forgotten.'

We clinked the mugs and fell silent as we finished what tea was left. After a while, Peter asked about Ed's visitor and agreed that he was indeed an imposter, and I'd done right to show him up. As we discussed things that orbited my planet, I realised we never talked about his world or life.

'What have you been doing since Doris' day?' I asked.

'Very clever, James,' he swerved, but I wasn't going to be deflected, and sat looking at him expectantly. 'Well, I have been engaged in various enterprises,' he began, 'that took up most of my time until I found time for today's match.'

'That's good to hear, Peter, that you're keeping yourself occupied,' I said. 'But what exactly were these enterprises that occupied the time of a man whose mind I'd imagine requires constant watering for fear of it withering.'

'Well, James, my cruel inquisitor,' he said. 'You are assuming that I have been idle, that I have not put to use my faculties that you seem so happy to place on an idealistic pedestal.'

'I don't much care for that title you bestowed upon me, Peter. My question was asked simply to highlight your preoccupation with my life while cleverly managing to avoid discussing any aspect of your own. It's as if your life has been in abeyance since the funeral, yet I cannot believe that to be true,' I said, trying my utmost to use the floweriest words I could without sounding like a Shakespearean play and careful not to use a metaphor.

Peter nodded, seeming to accept my statement. 'I am glad to report that your hypothesis was only partially correct,' Peter paused. 'Following dear Doris' funeral, I did fall into a self-centred spiral of moroseness that persisted until Saturday. On that day, I, the accused, decided to snap myself out of this dark spiral and enrolled on the Open University to study something called A100,' he said.

'That's brilliant, Peter,' I said. 'But A100 doesn't mean much to my ears; unless it is one of our major highways.'

'Uh-hum,' Peter began, as if preparing to start a speech. 'The A100 is an undergraduate foundation course on the subject of Humanities. It will start next February, but I have safeguarded my place and will begin to prepare for my venture in January.' He smiled smugly.

I was so happy to hear about this wonderful development and bizarrely felt some weight of responsibility disappear. I must have been worried about him. 'I should think so too. It wouldn't be healthy for an articulate person like your good self to not be motivated or look beyond the next horizon. For beyond each horizon, new worlds await.'

'James Smith, can we park the Dickens for a while and get back to the chess?'

'Very well, Beadle of the Parish, lead on, and I, your urchin, will follow.'

Peter stood and started for the living room; we'd have time for one more match. As we walked through, Peter leading, I saw him shake his head. 'I now know how the unfortunate Professor Frankenstein felt.'

I smiled.

31

I was beginning to feel agitated. I could only see as far as the next match, but football couldn't possibly be my main priority. I still needed to face Ollie. If it wasn't to happen during the holidays, it would have to be on that first day back in school. I tried to imagine how either encounter would go and began to think that the school encounter was preferable, especially after grassing Ollie to Jim Gym.

After watching the two second-round matches with Ed and his mate Graham on Tuesday evening, a trip to Wigan's Marks and Spencer store for a new school uniform filled up Wednesday morning and early afternoon. Mum bought me two pairs of grey trousers and socks, two white shirts, and a pair of navy jumpers. Reluctantly, because the last one was purchased when I was thirteen, Mum had to buy me a new blazer, and, as a growth spurt was underway, she made sure I could grow into it. She would transfer the school badge from the old blazer when she had time in the evening. It was funny comparing this year to last. I can hardly remember last year's visit for new trousers and shirts; I must have been in a trance. This year, however, I asked Mum for a more stylish cut of trousers because I felt this year I needed to stamp my identity on the shadow that had been representing me for sixteen months.

I spent the rest of the afternoon thinking about facing other kids in my class. During the past fifteen months, they'd colluded with Ollie, ignoring my misery and spectating as Ollie meted out various punishments; pinch, punch, or ruler. That wasn't fair; they may have been secretly urging me to do something about it. Why should they do anything if I wasn't willing to do something first? My only conclusion was that it would take time for me to settle and for my classmates to accept me as James Smith, the person, instead of James, Ollie's slave.

I suddenly remembered that Maude was due to receive a fresh delivery and rushed to help her move the various sacks and boxes ready to be redistributed to the display boxes later. It didn't take long, but it made me feel good, and I hoped it helped Maude in some small way. I knew that Maude would have managed by herself, but even the tiniest amount of help lightens someone else's burden, and if I could do that, then where was the harm? Despite being there to lighten Maude's workload, I couldn't help but think about the football, and I'm sure Maude could see my mind was elsewhere.

'You're thinking about the game, aren't you, James,' Maude observed.

'Uh, yes, Aunt Maude. I think it's going to be quite a tough match.'

'I think you'll be okay, James,' she said. 'They're a good side, no question, but I think your midfield trio are probably the best I've seen in the tournament. If they spread the play like they did in the last match, you'll beat them comfortably.'

I stood, mouth open, unable to reply to Aunt Maude, who Mum would have described as her little David Coleman or Jimmy Hill.

○ ○ ○

Unfortunately, the match didn't quite follow Aunt Maude's prediction. The game against the Co-op was very tight. Our youthful midfield did have a lot of possession, but we couldn't break through their stubborn defence. The first half ended without any side scoring, and our changing room felt extremely tense as coach Brightwell suggested slight changes to our attacking formation, substituting one of the midfielders with an additional striker.

'Right, lads, were changing to a four-four-two formation because we easily controlled the midfield. Get the ball forward to Eddie or Chris as soon as possible, and move up to support them. That's the best way to break down this lot.' Many heads nodded, and grunts of acceptance rolled around the breeze block room. I could sense the team was worried. Even though substitutes may not have been on the field, they still feel a sense of camaraderie with those representing the team. I never once wanted Andrew to be taken off; he was the best right-back for the team, and I was happy with that.

The second half started disastrously for us when they managed to take the lead from a messy corner. As I watched from the touchline, I could see the leadership qualities of lads like Nigel and Eric shine through as they urged the team to respond. Luckily, we were far-fitter and scored two quick goals halfway through the half. To be fair to the Co-op's team, they never gave in and managed to put us under pressure by using long balls to bypass our midfield. Because of the tightness of the game, coach Brightwell couldn't risk changing the team, so I spent the entire match on the touchline, shouting encouragement as the team held out for a great win. I genuinely felt like a part of the team, and when the final whistle blew, I congratulated my teammates as they came off.

It was euphoric in the changing room as we realised we'd reached the semi-finals. 'A great performance,' coach Brightwell kept saying, but we weren't so sure as Nigel, Thomas, and I walked to the bus. Nigel and Thomas are midfielders and were worried that the Co-op's long ball had exposed us. 'It's not fair on Eric to deal with everything,' Nigel said. 'He was dragged from pillar to post because Malc doesn't like the high ball.'

Unsure what possible remedy we had in our locker, I agreed because I remember seeing Eric slumped on the bench in the changing room. I greatly admired Eric because he gave everything for the team and, for such a big lad, he was extremely fit. When, for the umpteenth time, I watched him shouting "Eric's ball", I kept thinking back to Boxer and his willingness to do everything for the farm, his team.

When I got home, I had to listen to more analysis of what went wrong as Dad and Ed gave me their expert opinions. To be fair, they sort of made sense, but we were not United or Liverpool; we were Brinsley Grammar under sixteens'. Dad naturally couldn't understand why the coach didn't bring me on instead of Andrew Scott, but Andy's size was invaluable against a physical side like the Co-op.

'You know who you're facing in the Semis, don't you?' Ed asked.

'It's Ailsworth Pit B team,' I answered, having seen them win their match by four goals to one.

Ed stared at me with a look that suggested he knew something significant about the pit's 'B' team. 'What? What's this mystery you seem to be keeping from me?' I asked, getting frustrated.

'The O'Rourke twins?'

Liam and Patrick O'Rourke, wingers for Pit B's team and Ed's sworn enemies after he'd beat them up. I shook my head. 'Ed, on the pitch, they're just football players, and tonight I saw that they're pretty dirty but no dirtier than some Co-op players. We coped okay against them, didn't we?'!' I suggested, not sure why Ed was being so dramatic.

'Nah,' Ed began, 'tonight was different; they were always in the lead. You just watch that team when they're not winning,' Ed pointed his finger. 'I'm just warning you, okay?'

I could see that Ed was really concerned. 'Okay, Ed, I'll warn the lads before Friday's kick-off.' That seemed to satisfy him, and we chilled for the rest of the evening.

○ ○ ○

I spent Thursday morning kicking the football against our garden wall and could feel my legs had strengthened since our first practice. I kept pretending to pass the ball down the line and found different ways to use my chest and thigh to accept a hard pass. By the time I'd exhausted myself, I was sweating and decided to go for a quick wash.

When I arrived downstairs, Elsie was busy dishing out the liver mash and gravy. It looked okay, but I still used one of Dad's pint glasses to hold my water; appearances could be deceptive. Ed appeared from his bedroom to join us but disappeared straight after lunch to see his mates.

I told Elsie to sit down as I cleared the table and washed and dried the plates and cutlery. It didn't take long, and I decided to make a brew. Elsie deserved it because the liver was perfect.

'You've changed,' Elsie said as she accepted one of the mugs of tea I'd made for us.

'Not sure what to say about that, gran,' I replied.

'You've growed up,' she added.

I ignored her lax use of language. 'It's what we do as kids, I suppose. It isn't anything deliberate on my part.'

She smiled. 'I like this new you; it's a better version, but I suppose you'll change again next year and go back to skulking in your bedroom and not spending the time of day with us.'

I was taken aback. I never considered my interactions with my family during the Ollie era. 'Is that what I was like?' I asked.

Elsie sipped her tea. 'Nice tea,' she said. 'Yeah, I suppose you were a bit of a recluse, but we all thought it was your teenage anti-oldies period like Edward's.'

They all thought? They could see I was acting differently but chose to categorise me as a stroppy teenager because of Ed. Now, thinking back, Ed *was* an arsehole, flying off on one if you even dared say something about his behaviour. It was as if he was the perfect embodiment of man, and everyone else was too thick to understand him. 'I was never as stroppy as Ed, was I, gran?' I asked, hoping for confirmation.

'Oh no, never as stroppy, I suppose, but we thought you hid yours, and that was why you'd spend so much time alone,' Elsie explained.

I didn't know if Mum had explained the Ollie situation to her, but I knew it had to come from her rather than from me. 'You're right, gran,' I said. 'I was just coping with it my way rather than taking it out on you lot,' I said, thinking that would be the end of our chat.

Elsie glanced across and cocked her head. 'Didn't stop you slagging off my Crossroads, though, did it?'

32

Ours was the second of the two semi-finals. In the first, Ailsworth Pit 'A' team beat the team from Flinsby pit by three goals to nil. It was sad to see the Flinsby team lose because there wasn't a working pit in Flinsby; the team just adopted the name in its memory.

I'd spent the morning reading - flicking would have been more apt - through last week's "Shoot" football magazine. Dad bought it for me for inspiration. He only needed to look at the front cover of Joe Jordan of Leeds having an aerial battle with Liverpool's Phil Thompson and Emlyn Hughes to know it was more likely to fill me with dread than inspire me.

I decided to switch off and picked up my spy novel. Books were great for transporting you away from your own worries, only for you to start worrying about others' chances of living through certain chapters. What was worse, these people were fictional, and the author made me care for them! Whatever it made me do, it passed the afternoon until I was due at Maude's; job done. I don't know why I was so tense; I guessed it had something to do with Ed's impersonation of Private Frazer and his "we're doomed, we're doomed" mantra.

I rushed through my work at Maude's and had time to explain where we were up to in the tournament. At the time, I thought it was nice to see her pretend to be interested, but as we prepared for our match, I saw her standing with Peter a few yards away from my family.

In the changing room, coach Brightwell went through the final pep talk and decided to go with the same formation we'd used successfully in the second half of the last match. I felt awkward as I listened because I couldn't find an appropriate place to stand up to warn the team about the O'Rourkes. I left that until we were out on the pitch warming up. I asked Eric to gather the defence together, and as we huddled, I told them about the physical dangers that the O'Rourkes, and Patrick in particular, could pose. They all nodded their understanding, and I felt much better getting it off my chest.

I took my position on the sideline and felt a buzz of excitement as the referee blew to start the match, even though I wasn't playing.

Both teams played good football during the early exchanges, and the O'Rourkes seemed to be decent players, carrying the ball well. After about ten minutes, our midfield seemed to get the upper hand, and Nigel managed to slip a perfect pass into the path of Eddie, who swept the ball past their stranded goalie. We were playing well and continued to dominate the midfield, and that was when some of their tackling became more physical. It seemed they didn't care much for our quick give-and-go method and ensured that the player who played the give pass would be taken out, leaving the go pass being intercepted by their midfield. For the first time in the tournament, Coach Brightwell started to berate the referee, telling him in no uncertain terms to look after our team's well-being.

Despite the physicality of our opponents, Nigel and Dave managed to carve them open again before passing to Chris, who hammered it home to double our lead. As the scoring party jogged back, I watched Patrick O'Rourke give Thomas a subtle but solid shoulder charge and pretend our team had run into him. As I watched everyone square up, the referee trying his utmost to calm things down, I felt a tap on my shoulder. I turned around.

'Told you,' Ed said before walking back to Mum and Dad.

I turned back to watch the match, and any subtlety the pit team may have had before disappeared. The sad thing about that was their own football seemed to deteriorate, and they resorted to hitting aimless long balls for their forwards and wingers to charge after. On the whole, our defence handled these with little bother, and as the half drew to a close, we seemed to have dampened down their anger. Then, as Andrew, our right-back, picked up one of these long passes, Patrick O'Rourke arrived a fraction of a second later and smashed into Andrew's knee. The scream was instant and horrible, and I seethed inside as I saw Patrick raise his hands in mock repentance and go over to the prone Andrew to tap his head to feign an apology. Our entire team jostled and pushed Patrick as he made his way from Andrew before the referee dragged Patrick to one side and recorded his name in his little black book. The game had to be stopped as a gaggle of St John's Ambulance personnel ran to Andrew's aid. After treating him on the ground for around five minutes, they decided that Andrew could only be removed by stretcher. This took another five minutes as coach Brightwell protested with the referee that Patrick should have been sent off and possibly jailed for such a cowardly tackle.

'It's a man's game, coach. You knew that when you registered your team. The tackle was slightly late, and I took the appropriate action. If you wish to remove your team from the tournament, then please consider this option during halftime,' said the referee, a local builder and ex-miner.

As it was so close to halftime, coach Brightwell didn't bother with a substitution and waited until we were back in the changing room before addressing our problems.

'Look, lads, I've talked to the St John's staff, and they don't think Andrew's broken his leg. They believe he's damaged the ligaments around the knee quite badly, and there's no way he'll play in the second half.'

Eric looked up. 'Smithy warned us about that psycho, coach, but we never believed he'd do that,' Eric said, his voice flat.

Despite leading, the whole team was flat. 'I'm not sure we should take the field for the second half,' coach Brightwell said, causing every player to look up. Amidst various lads shouting, coach was clear-headed. 'I don't want any more of you to be hurt like that; football isn't worth it. Even if he wants to, Andy probably won't play again for another three months, and I can't expose you to that kind of brutality; I just can't.'

The changing room fell into a sombre silence, the earlier objections not repeated. I stood up. 'Coach, I don't want anyone else to be hurt either, but look, I've been the victim of bullying for the past fifteen months, and I've decided to face up to it. Being with you lot has helped me on my journey. That team out there is bullying us because we're better than them, and I don't think we should let a bully win,' I said and immediately lost my confidence. 'Uh, that's all I have to say.'

'I agree with Smithy, coach,' Eric said, followed by others saying we were here to play football, not give in to bullies like these.

The coach smiled, probably seeing his team in a new light. 'If I see this deteriorate, then I will withdraw you; is that clear?'

'Whatever, coach,' said Eric and everyone burst out laughing.

As we took to the field, coach took me to one side and said I'd be on instead of Andrew. I nodded to indicate I was happy, and he warned me to be careful. So, with a sense of excitement and trepidation, I took up my position, deliberately ignoring the crowd; the last thing I wanted was to see the faces of my worried family.

The game restarted, and I soon faced Patrick as they pushed forward. As the ball was rolled up to him, I closed the gap, and as he tried to turn, I dived in to put the ball out for a throw. The tackle also meant he fell over, and I ignored him as I ran past him to take my position.

With his back to me, Patrick glanced back, smirking. He studied me. 'You're gay Eddie's kid brother, aren't you?' He said.

A split-second! The things that flash through my head in a split-second!

I shrugged at Patrick, smiled and puckered my lips, sending him a kiss. The change was instantaneous, and a dark shadow swept over him. Their throw-in went to his feet. I approached, but not as tight as previously because I sensed a tension in his arms. This forced him to turn to face me, and that was when I went in and took the ball cleanly before going through him. I picked myself up and ran down the wing, feeding Damon, before running on to accept the return and then square it to Eddie, who lashed it in for our third.

As we jogged back, I kept an eye on Patrick, but he was otherwise occupied, remonstrating with the referee about my tackle. As we lined up again, I saw Patrick was focusing on me, but rather than feeling worried, I felt good and in control. It was as if everything that had happened during the holidays was now within me, and it felt wonderful.

After the kick-off, they failed to mount much of an attack, and Nigel intercepted the ball. He looked for support and passed it back to me as he had no other option.

I knew what was coming.

I didn't need to see him.

I knew what was coming alright, and as the ball reached me and I saw that Damon was free, I passed the ball forward and immediately jumped as high as possible. Normally, that would be a bizarre thing to do on a football pitch, but I knew what would happen. As I jumped up, I saw Patrick's sliding body beneath me, but I hadn't reckoned on the height of his intended assault. With me at the zenith of my leap, Patrick's boot caught on the front of my right foot's Gola Speedster, causing my body to spin uncontrollably. The combination of the speed at which Patrick was travelling and the height I reached resulted in me flipping over, landing on the front of my feet, and the momentum making me roll forward onto my face in the grass unhurt. I screamed! I grasped a fictitious injury on my right knee and screamed.

In no time at all, I was surrounded by my teammates. 'Smithy! Are you okay?' Eric shouted. I looked at his worried face, winked and carried on screaming. He contained his smile before standing to allow the St John's staff to inspect my broken body. As I got to my feet and said I was okay, I saw Patrick screaming at the referee before being dragged away by his brother Liam and other teammates. He'd been sent off.

As he trudged off, kicking at the turf every five yards, he turned. I felt like waving my hand to bid him goodbye, but I didn't; that would have been bullying.

○ ○ ○

We went on to win by six goals to nil and, despite our concern about Andrew's injury, managed to enjoy the subdued post-match celebrations. Eric kept saying he couldn't get over what I'd done. 'You knew he was coming for you, didn't you?' He asked, and I shrugged. 'You got him sent off!' Eric stated the obvious, and the others smiled. I was feeling uncomfortably sweaty.

After the euphoria had died down, Nigel came over. 'You did really well out there, Smithy, but I almost gave you a real hospital pass, didn't I?' He paused as I shook my head.

'It wasn't that bad a pass,' I reassured him, feeling awkward.

It looked like he was thinking about something else to say, and he eventually looked directly at me. 'It's just that I'm so sorry Thomas and I weren't there for you when that lardarse bullied you,' Nigel said. 'But if he tries anything again, don't you dare keep it to yourself, okay?'

I smiled but was embarrassed he was feeling guilty. There was no need; it was mainly my fault, but to explain that would take too long. 'It won't happen again, Nige, but I know who to call if it does. I can't explain to you how this feels, but it means a lot to me to know I have friends, a hell of a lot.'

'Come on, let's get back home,' Nigel said, and Thomas joined us as we left the happy changing room.

○ ○ ○

On the way home with Nigel and Thomas, I decided to disembark at their stop, undaunted by the long walk home. As we walked from the bus, we encountered a gang of Ailsworth lads. They were all from my year at school, and three were from my class.

'Hey, Smithy, how's it feel to be known as a traitor?' A boy called Glen asked. He was from my class, was a good all-rounder, and played for Ailsworth's under-sixteens. The three of us stopped.

'To be honest, I never considered myself a traitor, Glen. But if that's what you're calling me, then I guess I prefer it to being called Ollie's punchbag,' I said and saw him thinking about what to say next, so I spared him the ordeal. 'Did you see the match?' I asked.

'Yeah, too right we did. You've got a good team there, lads,' he said, and the chat descended into a general synopsis of the game and how the final would pan out.

As we walked away, Nigel turned to me. 'You're not comfortable with them, are you, Smithy?'

I shook my head. 'Not really, Nige,' I answered, not wanting to discuss it.

'Bloody hell,' Thomas said. 'If that had been our classmates, they'd have been all over us, paying us compliments and boosting our morale by saying we'd have a good chance in the final.'

'Is all that because you've been bullied, and they did nothing to help?' Nigel asked thoughtfully.

I shrugged. 'Don't know, really, but I don't think they feel guilty or anything; I just think they saw me as subhuman, contaminated, and someone they didn't want to be associated with.' I answered.

'I hate fucking bullies,' Nigel said as we walked along, and Thomas nodded in agreement.

'Not half as much as I do,' I said, raising a smile on our faces as we marched on like victorious soldiers.

○ ○ ○

After surviving Mum's inquisition about the game and that "horrid boy" (Dad and Ed had gone out), I relaxed, watching TV with Mum and then going to my bedroom to read.

I put the spy book down and thought back about the events of the evening.

Not the match.

Not Patrick O'Rourke.

Not Andrew's injury.

I thought back on how I'd reached this point. It was as if I'd arrived in Ailsworth from another town. I could have been Patricia from number nine's eldest son, who had just come here looking to make new friends. I shook my head; no, he would have been normal before he came here. I was me; if I went to another town, I would know I'd been bullied.

∘ ∘ ∘

Meeting those lads from Ailsworth was significant. I know they called me a traitor, but that was tongue-in-cheek and could be seen as some form of recognition. One thing was for certain, it was more attention than Glen and Co had paid me for over a year. That is progress. James Smith is now somebody, and people have begun to notice him. All that remains for me to do is confront Ollie so that this recognition will remain and allow me to form normal relationships with people.

Having satisfied my inner turmoil, I was about to fall asleep when my bedroom door burst open, and two drunk family members invaded my bed, insisting I gave them a blow-by-blow account of the game. It took me an hour to satisfy their repeated questions, and I was glad when Mum came in and told them to leave her little Kevin Keegan alone.

I love Mum.

33

Shrugging off my tiredness, I forced myself out of bed to have breakfast with Mum. It was nice to chat about something other than football as Mum explained she was going to Wigan with Patricia and her boy, Gavin, who was three. She asked me if I wanted anything.

'I wouldn't mind a new anorak or jacket,' I said. 'My old one's getting a bit short.'

Strangely, an excited look swept over Mum's face. 'Ooh,' she began, 'do you want the same one in a bigger size, or would you like a change?' Mum asked.

I almost screamed "no", but controlled myself. 'I wouldn't mind a change if that's okay, Mum.'

'Leave it with me, love; I'm sure we'll be able to find something; after all, Patricia will be with me, and she can help,' Mum said.

My heart sank, but I thought it would be ungrateful to say anything negative. 'Thanks, Mum,' I said, hoping I sounded sincere.

After breakfast, the phone rang, and Mum, putting on her coat, shouted me over, 'It's for you,' she whispered, with her hand over the mouthpiece.

'Hello?' I asked nervously.

'Hi, Smithy,' a breezy voice answered, 'it's me, Nige.'

'Hi, Nige, you okay?'

'Yeah, good, mate. Uh, I was ringing because Thomas and I are going to Wigan this affers to go see Andrew, and I wondered if you'd like to come with us?'

'Hell, yes,' I said, suddenly remembering about Maude. 'Uh, what time are you planning to go?' I asked.

'We're catching the one o'clock bus from our end; I think it will be with you five pastish.'

'That's great, Nige; see you at oneish, then.'

'Brill, Smithy; see you at one, bye,' he hung off before I had the chance to reciprocate.

When she came over to peck me on the head, Mum was wearing a different coat. 'See you later, love,' she said and turned to go.

'I'm going to Wigan on the one o'clock bus to see Andrew Scott in the hospital, ' I shouted after her.

She turned, looking serious. 'Is that the boy that was hurt last night?' She asked, and I nodded. 'That could have been you,' she said, paused to make sure I'd heard and walked out after I nodded. Alone in the house, I realised how worried Mum must have been throughout that second half, even after Patrick left the field, because, unless you play football, it can look quite intimidating.

○ ○ ○

There were quite a few orders to pack for delivery this morning, and it seemed that Maude's slump in sales during Doris' short illness was over. Rubbing my hands after helping Eric with the last box, I turned to Maude. 'Well, that's that, Aunt Maude. I'll see you next Friday evening,' I said.

'No, James. I don't want you,' she said.

'What?' I asked, taken aback.

'I don't want you to come here next Friday or anytime after today,' Maude clarified.

'It's no bother, Aunt Maude, no bother at all,' I said, trying to allay the concern I thought she may have harboured.

'No, James,' she said kindly, 'I know it's no bother, but I'm going to close the shop,' she explained.

'Why,' I asked. 'Is it because of the new Co-op being built?'

Maude smiled at my assumption. 'No, no, James. The co-op will never be able to provide fruit and veg of *our* quality! I'm selling up because I'm moving to the same town as Beatrice, my sister. I need to spend time around family,' Maude said.

I smiled broadly, happy with the reasons behind her decision. 'That's great, Aunt Maude, but I'll never forget what you did for me, and *you* must never forget that you can come back here to visit your second family anytime,' I said.

'I'll never forget that, James, never.' We shared a lovely hug in the middle of Maude's small shop, and I went home knowing Maude would be okay.

Walking briskly home, I wondered if I carried some kind of responsibility gene. That I had to make sure everyone was okay before feeling relaxed? Had this gene been lying dormant, unable to flower until I was free of Ollie? Walking, I wondered if other genes were lurking in my body.

An artistic gene?

An engineering gene?

A gregarious gene?

A garden shed gene?

A drinking gene?

A clown gene?

I'm sure there were other genes, but my train of thought was broken when I arrived home and had to prepare myself for the trip to Wigan.

○ ○ ○

I was glad it was sunny; I didn't have to wear my anorak, and it was great sharing the bus ride with Nigel and Thomas down to Wigan. I did get a bit uncomfortable when they started to talk about girls, but the fact they referred to girls from their school meant I wasn't dragged in. They also knew my bullying meant I'd have little or no experience.

I did ask them about Brinsley Grammar, though, because I was under the impression they had to convert to be Comprehensive or become fee-paying before the end of the year. According to Thomas, their school would be converting to a comprehensive, and plans to that effect were almost complete. It wouldn't affect them this year, but it would if they decided to stay for their 'A' levels. I didn't push it much further, but I did ask them what they intended to do after their 'O' levels. I was pleased to hear they had as much idea as I did and decided to broach the subject of apprenticeships, and they saw them as a good compromise so long as you got in with a decent company. Despite the whole conversation sounding like it was being conducted by old men, I loved it for its beautiful banality.

○ ○ ○

Andrew was glad to see us; I'd daringly picked up a Milk Tray bar from Gordon's before catching the bus. This chocolate bar may not seem like much, but to us kids, it was the Ferrari of chocolate bars; nothing else came close. Andrew's parents had stepped outside the ward to the waiting room to give us ten minutes with him.

'That fucking psycho could have crippled me for life,' he snarled, starting with the Turkish delight.

'They couldn't cope with us taking the lead,' Thomas said. 'They just thought they could just mow us down one by one.'

I looked down at his heavily strapped leg. 'What did the doctors say?' I asked.

Next, Andrew picked out the Almond Swirl. He seemed to have a consumption strategy already worked out. 'They reckon,' he mumbled, chewing, 'the hit to the knee has caused a bad tear to the MCL,' he explained.

'MCL?' I asked.

'It's the Medial Cruciate Ligament on the inside of the knee. When that psycho's boot connected, it forced the knee to bend sideways, and that's what tore the MCL,' Andrew said, placing a chunk of Orange Crème into his momentarily empty mouth. He was making me feel both hungry and regretful. 'I had to have an X-ray to check there's no fracture.'

'Fucking hell, Andy. I know this sounds daft, but when I saw that tackle, I thought he'd smashed your leg, so I kinda think you've been lucky,' Nigel said.

'I know what you mean, Nige, but I'm not feeling lucky right now,' he said as the Crème Strawberry followed the Orange Crème. He thought for a moment. 'Were you okay, going on afterwards, Smithy?' he asked.

'Not really, Andy,' I said. 'I knew that Ed, my brother, had some history with that lad, and it made me nervous, especially after watching *that* tackle.'

'I'm glad we went on to beat those fuckers, though,' Andrew paused for the fudge. 'It shows people that thuggery doesn't pay.'

'Too right,' Nigel said. 'And you need to get back on your feet to remind everyone that it doesn't pay.'

Andrew nodded. 'The doctors reckon I can leave on Monday with a brace, but it will be a while until I can walk without it,' Andrew said and must have expended too much energy because he needed the Coconut Ice.

'Physio?' Thomas asked.

'Mmm huh,' he Mumbled, and as he did, the ward doors swung open, and his parents reappeared.

'Anyway, Andy, hope you get better soon and look forward to seeing you in school,' Nigel said, and Thomas and I nodded.

'Oh, and thanks for the chocolate, Smithy,' Andrew shouted as I heard him snap another piece off the remaining three centres.

I turned. 'No problem, Andy. See you soon.' I said.

'Here,' Andrew said, and the three of us turned around. 'I don't like the coffee crème. Any of you want it?' He asked.

'God, no,' the three of us said almost simultaneously.

'I'll take it,' Andrew's father said, and we turned to leave, with me knowing he still had the Caramel and Lime Barrel to finish off. As we walked through the corridors and down different stairs, I realised that that bar was probably the most luxurious chocolate bar I'd ever bought. I just wondered if Andrew really needed it because I'd noticed at least four other chocolate boxes on his locker by the bed.

o o o

The journey home was relatively uneventful, but we all had something to say about Andrew's injury and how well he seemed to be coping. I asked them how keen Andrew was when it came to schoolwork, and Thomas and Nigel both reckoned he wouldn't be off for too long because of the importance of this school year.

I left them on the bus and ran straight home, using the back alleys from Commercial Square. As I rounded a corner, past a wall, I bumped into someone and saw it was Brenda Johnson with three other girls, including Sally and Maureen. This time it wasn't a lighter I dislodged; this time, I dislodged a bottle. It crashed to the floor but somehow remained intact despite its contents beginning to trickle onto the concrete.

'What the fuck?' She screamed.

I looked at the bottle. 'Sorry, Brenda, I didn't see you there,' I said and walked on.

'Where yous goin?' She asked.

'Home,' I said, stopping a few yards beyond them.

'What about my bottle?' She asked.

'It's a nice-looking bottle, Brenda, I'll give you that, but if I were you, I'd pick it up quick before it empties,' I said and turned to resume my journey.

I heard footsteps behind me, and a hand grabbed my shoulder to pull me back. I turned.

'Pick it up!' Brenda screamed.

Instantly, I was raging inside and felt my eyes burn with hatred. I pushed Brenda's shoulders with my palms, making her step back. 'Pick it up yourself, you stupid bitch,' I shouted into her face and stood my ground, face burning.

Brenda stood there, mouth open, before looking back at the other girls. 'We've got enough to share, Bren; leave it be,' Maureen said, and the others nodded.

Brenda turned to me. 'Lucky for yous,' she said, returning to her posse. She grabbed a bottle and took a swig while staring back at me. I just shook my head and walked home, angry with myself that I'd reacted as I had and feeling ashamed I'd pushed her away. That burst of anger had frightened me, but what was I supposed to do? Stand there and be humiliated again? As I walked on, I concluded that my reaction was acceptable and probably a natural development after the six weeks without Ollie.

∘ ∘ ∘

Back home, I sat on the sofa and reflected on the day. With the exception of meeting Brenda, it was everything I'd dreamt about for months. I'd spent the day with friends, accepted each other as equals, and just been normal. It was everything and the only thing I ever wanted. It was brilliant and gave me confidence for next week when school restarts.

About an hour after I got home, Mum returned, having enjoyed a lovely day in Wigan with Patricia and Gavin.

'Here you are,' Mum said, handing over a sizeable brown-paper shopping bag; I'd forgotten about the new anorak. With trepidation, I opened it and was pleasantly surprised to find a greenish-brown Parka coat with fur trimmed hood.

I smiled. 'A Parka?' I said, genuinely impressed. I tried it on and was overjoyed when I saw it was slightly too big. 'It's brilliant, Mum!' I said and went over to give her a hug.

'Patricia suggested it,' Mum said.

'I'll thank her next time I see her,' I said, running to the back hall where our tallest mirror hung. I loved it because I looked normal, and I loved it because it wasn't too small.

'James?' I heard Mum call and returned to the living room.

'What?' I asked.

Mum was holding an envelope. 'You have a letter.'

34

Annwyl James,

Are you okay? I sort of expected another letter from you but it didn't arrive.

3 hours gap.

I can't remember exactly what I put in my last letter, but I don't think I said anything hurtful, did I? Anyway, I'm sorry if I did.

14 hours gap (overnight)

I'm now thinking you no longer need someone to urge you on; to complete your quest. If that's the case, I'm happy because it means you've told your parents about the bullying – and it also means I didn't say anything nasty. So, as far as I'm concerned, you've told your parents.

3 mins gap.

I just re-read that last bit, and I'm smiling, trying to imagine what freedom means to you and your family; I would imagine it's made you closer.

1 hour gap.

I know you won't be interested, but I've been okay. The work at the café's interesting, not because of the work, but because of the different types of people who come here. Three days ago, a man came in carrying a small case. After serving him two teas and two welsh cakes (with butter), I noticed he kept opening the case and lifting one of the cups as if pouring it in. He didn't; he just pretended to and sipped the tea himself. He did the same with one of the welsh cakes, nibbling it himself after first offering it to the case. The other tea and welsh cake were consumed normally. I told Wenna, who works with me, about him, and she told me his wife had recently died, and it was his first holiday without her. The second helping was for her! I felt so sorry for him, but he looked happy enough as he walked out after paying and giving me a small tip. Isn't that sad?

1 hour gap.

I know I told you to be selective with your letters, but after not getting them, I realise I don't like not hearing from you. I know we only met for a few minutes, but I think we share something, don't we? Anyway, there's no pressure for you to reply.

Yours Sincerely,

3 hours gap.
Love, Rhian x

I reread the letter three times. Feeling ashamed, I put it down and curled into a ball on my bed. There was a gene I hadn't considered; the selfish gene.

I pulled my knees tighter into my chest as I realised what I'd become. I was using people.

I dug out my dictionary and thought about what I was about to do. Until now, I'd used the dictionary to record what bullying meant for different words; now I was faced with putting in an entry that would record my unbullied state and what my unbullied self had become. I decided it was worth documenting so it could act as a warning. When I opened the dictionary, I saw I'd already entered a post-bullying entry when I came across the earlier entry for *DEATH*.

SELFISH: Adj
- *What I'd become during my Quest.*
- *A by-product of freeing myself from Ollie.*
- *Something I'm ashamed of having become.*

James selfishly discarded Rhian's help because he now had other interests.

James stood and looked through the window watching Peter Crabtree, whose friendship he'd selfishly dispensed with, sitting alone at his table.

Rhian's letter had upset me, but it was when I linked my behaviour to that unkind dismissal of Peter's friendship that it struck home.

I sat on the edge of my bed and glanced at the letter lying on my pillow. I remembered how excited I felt and that adrenaline rush when I read *Love Rhian x*, and that it should have set me off to immediately compose a reply. It didn't. As I reread the letter, I realised, despite the help I'd received, how cold and selfish I'd been and that I'd used various things and people as stepping stones: Fishing, Chess, Football, Uncle Harry, Dr Clarke, Maude, Doris, Peter, Rhian, Mum, Dad, and Ed. I knew I won't use them in the same way again.

I won't fish.

I won't play chess.

I'll play football on my terms.

I'll go back to treating Harry as I had previously.

I'll have no interest in the activity of our MP.

Now that Maude is going, will I ever think of her again?

Ditto Doris.

I've told Peter already that I'll be rationing our meetings.

I'd discarded Rhian because I believed I had no further need to nurture our friendship.

Mum and Dad? I'll probably start excluding them from knowing about my activities.

Ed will return to college, and I'll only show a perfunctory interest in his life.

I, I, I. It was everywhere in my head! Everything was about ME. I'm probably using Nigel and football in exactly the same way. When school restarts, will I make an effort to keep our burgeoning friendship going? I hoped I would, but seeing how I'd clearly hurt Rhian, and that Peter was too much of a gentleman to admit I'd done the same to him, I would probably drop Nigel in much the same way. I was willing to do anything to enable James Smith to reach whatever he sought, despite that selfish creature not knowing what it was.

I looked at my clock. It was almost seven, give or take ten minutes, and I knew I could apologise to Rhian in a letter later, but I needed to do something else right now. I ran downstairs and told Mum I'd be popping out.

'Isn't it a bit late for you to be going out?' She said.

The living room clock showed seven-thirty. 'I won't be long, Mum. I just need to do something,' I said, making a mental note to reset my bedroom clock when I returned.

○ ○ ○

I knocked on the door and waited; I had never been as late as this. It was Saturday; he'll be out. As I turned to leave, I heard the door open behind me.

'Goodness! Is that you, James?' I heard Peter ask.

I turned around. 'Good evening, Peter. Sorry for being so late; I was worried you'd gone out for the evening,' I said.

'Oh no, James, I don't go out until nine; that gives me ample time at the Railway Inn for my needs; come in,' Peter said and held open the door.

'No, Peter, I won't come in if that's okay,' I said, and Peter moved to the centre of the doorway, surprised I'd declined the invitation. 'What it is is I've been thinking about one of our last conversations and that I seemed to indicate we should ration our friendship.'

'I don't think you expressed it in those terms, James,' Peter replied.

'Well, whatever way I said it, I think I was acting selfishly because I was succeeding in my quest to rid my life of Ollie Jenkins, and I could now push you to one side.'

Peter looked at me with a confused look around his eyes. 'What made you think of this tonight?' he asked.

'It's a bit of a long story,' I said.

Peter looked at his watch. 'I have plenty of time until I need to leave for the Railway, so indulge me.'

I nodded, remembering I'd told Peter about accompanying uncle Harry. 'During my day trip to Wales with uncle Harry, I met a girl, and when I returned, I sent her a letter informing her about the bullying. In total, I sent two letters and received two replies, but I decided not to write the third after the last reply because by then, I'd told my parents about Ollie, and I could see some light at the end of the tunnel.'

'This is all well and good, James, but a bit Barbara Cartland. Is there a point to this?' Peter asked.

'Well, yes,' I began, feeling less confident. 'Today, I received a letter from her, asking why I'd stopped, suggesting I no longer needed her because I'd told my parents,' I said.

'Had you informed her you'd confessed to your parents in your earlier communication?' Peter asked.

'No, she worked it out because I hadn't written the third letter,' I explained.

'So, now you think you're selfish for not continuing the correspondence?' Peter asked.

'Yes, and thinking back to how I treated our friendship,' I explained.

Peter began laughing. It was unnerving, and I was glad it didn't last long. 'James, James; you've just made me very happy,' he said smilingly.

'Why?' I asked, confused.

'Because you have shown me that you are still a child,' he said, and I immediately bristled, staring at him. He noticed but continued to look kind. 'During our recent conversations, around the time of Doris' death, you seemed to converse in a very analytical way. Like an adult. I was worried about this, but here, listening to your silly concerns, I see you have a long way yet to go on the path to understanding,' Peter said calmly.

I was feeling frustrated with his reaction, that he was belittling me. 'I don't believe my reaction was childish, Peter,' I said, trying to control my temper.

'It isn't childish per se; it is simply the reaction of a child, and before you snap my head off, allow me to explain,' he said, and I listened. 'Everyone will interact with people as their circumstances dictate. You spent a day with your Uncle Harry and probably interacted differently with him that day than you usually do. Now that he isn't here, it doesn't mean you need to seek him out! He's doing what he's doing, and you're doing, etcetera, etcetera. It is the same with us. It is the same with your pen pal. It doesn't make you selfish; it makes you normal.'

'But,' I countered.

'But, nothing, James. You are probably the least selfish person I know,' Peter said, shaking his head as if disappointed. 'Why are you helping Maude? Why did you go to Doris' funeral? Why did you bother to have that conversation with me? If you were selfish, you wouldn't bother with these things; believe me.' Peter saw that I was struggling to find a reply. 'This girl, who wrote to you today, sounds very perceptive and perhaps all you need to do is write back and tell her about how you've changed. There's no need to apologise for that; you've simply been growing up.'

I'd listened intently as he spoke, and, despite storming here to confess my sins and being told I was still a child, I felt another wave of gratitude. 'Thank you,' I said and turned to walk home.

○ ○ ○

I reckoned it must have been close to eight-thirty when I took a sharp turn off the High Street onto New Road past the Post Office. As I looked across at Maude's shop, I heard a movement from my left and saw Ollie emerge through a gateless opening between the Post Office and the disused printer's building. We were about five yards apart.

The instant he saw me, he lunged. 'Come here, you little cunt!' Ollie snarled, but I took a few quick steps away from him. He stopped in the middle of the street, and we faced each other. I knew he could charge, but I was confident I could outrun him.

'It's finished, Ollie,' I said sternly.

'You think?' Ollie smirked.

'Too right it has.'

'It finishes when I say it fucking finishes, okay.' Ollie stated.

'No, it finished six weeks ago and will never start again, do you understand?'

'What I understand is that you've been snitching to Ernie's parents, and I've been grounded because of it. So it hasn't finished, okay,' Ollie said, and I could see he meant it.

'I'll tell you one thing, Ollie. If you do anything to me in school, I will hurt you. You may beat me, but I will fucking hurt you,' I snarled, feeling the same surge of anger I felt confronting Brenda.

'You? Hurt me? In your fucking dreams,' Ollie said, and as he finished, he charged forward. I casually ran away towards home but stopped when I heard him stop. I looked back at him.

'Come on, then,' he challenged, egging me to come forward with his hand. 'You don't look like someone who's going to hurt me, running away like a frightened little mouse.'

'I can't, not tonight, because I've got an important day ahead of me tomorrow,' I said.

'Oh, your football match, I forgot. Think your posh Grammar school mates will help you do you?' Ollie mocked.

I smiled broadly at this, imagining Ollie in the centre as six larger boys meted out their justice. 'They would, and they'd snap your pudgy arse in two, but I don't want them to. I'll sort you out myself in school because it isn't just Ernie's parents I've told,' I said, still smiling.

'What?' Ollie seemed unsettled with that.

'After one of the matches, I had a long chat with Jim Gym, and he was very interested when I told him what you've been doing to Ernie and me; very interested,' I explained.

'He'll do fuck all, and you know it, you little snitch,' Ollie snarled.

'Anyway, you're boring me now, so I'm going,' I said, ' but I can't wait to see you again in class on Tuesday,' I said and walked away without waiting for a reply.

35

I spent the morning of the final trying to compose a reply to Rhian's letter. It wasn't easy. Not only did I have to find the right words, but Ed and Dad kept coming into my bedroom asking if I was ready for the big match. Because of Andrew's injury, they knew there was a good chance I'd be starting, but I also knew coach Brightwell might opt for a physically stronger player to replace him.

On his second visit to my bedroom, I asked Dad if he could spare a few minutes for a chat, so he closed my door and appeared anxious as he nodded for me to start. I suppose that parents whose children have confessed to something as I had done would worry each time that child wanted a word, so I could understand his anxiety.

'Last night, I came across Ollie – don't worry, nothing happened,' I said immediately to allay his fears. 'But during that confrontation, I felt this tingling anger build up inside. I had exactly the same reaction the previous night when a girl shouted at me. I've never had that feeling before,' I said, wondering if I'd been clear enough.

Dad seemed to relax. 'It's normal, James, don't worry about it. I guess that you psychologically couldn't trigger that emotion while you were being bullied. Your bullied state allowed Ollie to do things to you that ordinary boys would react to,' he said. 'Does that make sense?' Dad asked.

'Yeah, it does make sense, Dad, a lot of sense.'

'In a way, I'm glad you felt it because I think it shows you've finally come to terms with who you are,' Dad said.

'Thanks, Dad,' I said, thinking that was the last of it.

Dad stood there looking at me. 'I hope you didn't hit that girl,' he said.

I smiled. 'No, Dad, I'd never hit a girl. But I did push her away after she grabbed me and screamed in my face to pick up her bottle of ale I'd accidentally knocked out of her hand.'

'How old was she?' Dad asked.

'It was Brenda Johnson from my class,' I explained.

'Oh, no, you did right to show you're not a pushover.'

'That's what I thought, Dad.'

He nodded towards my writing paper. 'You writing to that girl in Wales again?' he asked.

'Yeah, I received a nice letter from her yesterday, and I'm just going to update her on what's been happening,' I said.

'Good,' he said. 'It's important to have as many friends as possible; makes life interesting.' He smiled and walked out. It's amazing how Dad does that; he says something and walks out, leaving me to wonder if he meant anything else by it.

I continued writing for a bit but decided to finish it tomorrow. I could smell Mum's Sunday roast from my bedroom, and she was more than happy for us to have it an hour earlier after I'd made the request (coach Brightwell told us to not eat anything within two hours of the three o'clock kick-off). Ed, who thought he'd have a hangover, grumbled about the high noon lunch, but seeing how he'd been into my bedroom a couple of times, I suppose he wasn't as bad as he'd feared.

○ ○ ○

After lunch, I gathered my gear and set off for the ground. We'd been told to get there by two. When I arrived, quite a few people were milling around, and as I made my way towards the changing rooms, someone shouted my name.

I turned and saw Ernie with his parents. 'Hi, James,' said Ernie, 'I want to wish you luck for today, but more importantly, I'd like to thank you for what you did the other day. You didn't have to, especially after I'd told Ollie where you were that time.' His parents nodded to reinforce Ernie's kind words.

'Thanks, Ernie, but *you* didn't tell Ollie where I was; the *bullied* Ernie told him, and that's a totally different person,' I said.

Ernie smiled. 'Yeah, that's a good way of thinking about it, James, thanks,' he said. 'And best of luck, again.'

'Thank you for stopping me and saying that; it means a lot. Sorry, but I need to report in, so bye for now,' I said.

'No, no, James, you go ahead,' Mrs Taynor said. 'And best of luck.' I nodded and continued to the changing rooms. Seeing and feeling the carnival atmosphere around the ground was exhilarating, and many had gathered around the hot dog and ice cream vans that had been allowed through the old rusty double gates.

I was a part of this whole thing. It felt wonderfully surreal walking towards the changing room, knowing I wasn't on the periphery. I was centre stage!. As I strode onwards, my elevated level of pompousness crashed to the ground. I may not even be playing! I shrugged; I still loved being a part of it; playing would be the cherry on the cake.

We had been given the visitors' changing room, and I was pleased to see I wasn't the first nor last to turn up. Eric "Man-Mountain" Woolfall was in his underpants getting himself ready and beamed when he saw me walk in.

'Well, squirt, you ready for this?' He asked.

'I was born ready, Eric,' I said, pointing at my unimpressive chest with both index fingers.

Eric released a huge belly laugh, making everyone else smile along. 'You crack me up, Smithy; you really do,' he said. 'Do you know what the saddest thing about today is?' He asked.

'No.'

'Win or lose, today will probably be the last time I see your scrawny little body,' Eric said.

'Cheers, pal; do you know there's nothing better than having a teammate point out your physical shortfalls when you're preparing to look after his sorry fat arse out on the pitch,' I replied and was pleased to see the resultant smiles from around the room. However, with unexpected balletic grace, Eric jumped up, grabbed, lifted and carried me before dumping me on top of a row of lockers standing against the wall. Everyone was laughing, so I lay on my side and propped my head with my hand, my elbow on the locker's steel surface.

More of the lads were arriving and started to join in the merriment. Eric, wearing only his underpants, looked up. 'Well, squirt, you enjoying the view?' He asked. 'I bet you can see everything from there, can't you?'

I looked around theatrically. 'Yes, Eric, I can see everything clearly apart from one thing,' I said.

'And what's that then, squirt?' Eric asked.

'Your dick,' I said. Everyone just began laughing their heads off, pointing at Eric. To be fair, Eric joined in, moving his belly with his hands to look down. Eric smiled broadly and shook his head, leaving me stranded on the lockers.

'Smith!' Coach Brightwell shouted from the door. 'What the hell are you doing on top of those lockers?'

'Sorry, sir, I tossed a coin and had to get up here to find it,' I said, hoping I had some coins in my pocket if he asked for evidence.

'And why the hell were you tossing a coin?' He asked, and I wasn't sure if he was serious.

'Uh, well, coach, I was playing strip toss the coin with Eric, and as you see, I was on a winning streak, and I thought it best I get up here rather than Eric, in case the lads threw up,' I said, managing to keep a straight face, which was more than the other lads managed.

Coach Brightwell's face lit up. 'Get down here, Smith. The last thing we can afford now is for our starting right-back to get himself injured.'

I was starting the match! As I lowered myself, I felt ecstatic and almost dizzy as I made my way to my changing bag. As I passed Eric, he stood up and hugged me. I pulled away and winked, knowing I'd do everything to not let them down. As I changed and looked around at the smiling faces, it was as if I'd become immune to the sounds and experienced a wonderful feeling when I realised that these strangers had accepted me and that it was real; it wasn't fiction as I'd thought initially.

After changing, we ran out for a quick warm-up and saw that Ailsworth Pit's 'A' team was already out practising. I felt great seeing the large crowd and my fan club standing near the halfway line, opposite the two dugouts. As three o'clock approached, there was a perceivable increase in the tension as we passed the balls around.

'Team huddle,' Nigel shouted, and we all ran over, linked arms and huddled. When he was sure we were all there, Nigel spoke commandingly. 'Look, lads, they're the favourites for this, and they do have good players, but I know one thing for certain: we have even *better* players, yes?'

We all shouted, 'Yes!'

'So don't let the occasion get to you. It's a game of football, and we're better than them. What are we?'

'Better!'

'What are we?'

'Better!'

'Alright then, let's go and do the business,' Nigel concluded.

'For Andrew,' I shouted as I felt the huddle relax.

It had the desired effect, and we pulled ourselves tight again. 'For Andrew!' We shouted and broke off to face our destiny.

○ ○ ○

The match was exciting for the neutrals in the crowd, but it was very tense for supporters of both sides. Initially, I had difficulty containing their speedy winger but still managed to stop him from getting any crosses into the box. As the half wore on, I got his number and neutralised any threat from that source. I even had a couple of runs, linking with Damon and getting in some crosses that their defence, unfortunately, coped with easily. The great thing about going on those runs is they dragged their winger back with me, and I reckoned that it would affect his fitness later on, seeing he was in his late twenties. Overall, we were the better team in the first half, but they came closest to scoring when their centre forward latched on to a ball and struck it against the post from twenty-two yards. It was a lucky escape.

During the half-time interval, coach Brightwell emphasised how well we were playing and told us to continue playing as we had been. I was pleased to not be substituted but knew that could be an option for the coach if we needed to be more attack-minded.

The second half played out similarly to the first, but after about twenty minutes, they seemed to slow down, and our superior fitness began to tell. During one of our attacks, I was standing on the halfway line watching Paul putting in a cross from the left for Eddie to get his head onto it. He didn't, and their centre-half got there first, heading the ball towards my side of the pitch. I knew I'd reach it before their player and sprinted forward, got to the ball, squared it to Damon, rounded their player and charged forward. Damon saw my run and fed it in for me. As I arrived in their penalty area, I made that I was about to square it, but dummied, taking the ball towards the by-line. Their centre half, committed to the tackle, missed the ball and scythed me down. The referee had no option but to award a penalty.

I was sore when I got to my feet, happy that my shin guards had done their job, and hobbled back to the halfway line, where Eric came over and gave me a huge slap on my back. We were in the fifty-sixth minute when Nigel stepped forward to take the spot kick. I couldn't imagine how he could cope with the pressure, but cope he did, and cooly slotted the ball into the right-hand corner of the net.

We managed to hang on for the last few minutes, and the team gave a huge collective scream of delight when the referee blew for the end of the match. It was brilliant being in the middle of all those smiling faces, and we all hugged and screamed and did little victory jigs after shaking hands and commiserating with the team from Ailsworth pit. Coach Brightwell joined the celebrations and went around us individually to say well done. 'Thank you, James Smith, for doing such an excellent job for us,' he said when he got to me. I know it was a bit stiff, but I appreciated its sentiment.

It seemed to take a long time for the medals to be handed out. Eventually, after we'd all received ours, Nigel received his medal and waited for Mr Eric Lander, Manager of the new Co-op store, to hand over the Inter-Colls Trophy. Once it was in his hands, Nigel raised it aloft, and we all cheered as loudly as we could.

o o o

We all separated at the end of the cheering to seek out our families. I was so happy walking across the pitch towards my little posse of Mum, Dad, Ed, Maude and Peter. During the walk, a few team members slapped me on the back, and we'd shout inanely in each other's faces. It was wonderful. Even a few Ailsworth lads congratulated me.

It was too simplistic to say that this was what I'd striven for throughout the six long weeks, but it did feel extraordinary. As I reached my family and friends, I knew I'd be in for a fair amount of embracing and back-slapping.

After hugging my family and showing my medal to Peter and Maude, I waved to the Taynors and returned to the changing room to change into my clothes. Once showered and changed, I returned to my parents and explained the team was returning to Brinsley in two of their school minibuses. They'd arranged refreshments at the school gym, and I fancied going with them. Mum encouraged me to go, and Dad and Ed said they'd also go out to celebrate the win, despite it being Sunday. Mum shrugged and said she wanted to catch something on the TV. After sharing more congratulatory hugs, I gave them my bag to take home and joined the lads on the minibus. Dad was noticeably emotional and didn't or couldn't say much.

∘ ∘ ∘

The minibus ride to Brinsley was like nothing I'd experienced before. We chanted some well-known footballing standards and even began to sing "You'll never walk alone", a song generally associated with Liverpool, not Wigan; it was probably the only song they knew. I joined in but eased off during the high notes. I'd never seen so many ecstatic faces in one place; it was joyous.

Despite the joy, I worried about what I'd find in Brinsley. It wasn't my town, and I began to feel like a tourist, another Doug Molyneaux, and I hated to think I could be one of those. I looked around the minibus at the smiling faces and nodded; I was part of this celebration. I contributed, tried my best, and I think this bunch of players appreciated the effort. I deserved my seat on the bus and began to relax and look forward to the celebrations.

I had a brilliant time in Brinsley, enjoying the sandwiches, sausage rolls, and cakes prepared by the lads' mothers. Every five minutes or so, someone would shout "Champ-i-ons", and all of us would scream it a second time. I presumed this was what being drunk felt like seeing how Ed and Dad would loosen up and appear as happy as we were. The happiness was hard to describe and scaled new heights at around twenty-past seven when the door opened, and Andrew Scott was wheeled into the gym by his Dad; he'd been allowed home early. As we all calmed down, coach Brightwell made a lovely speech about how indebted we were for Andrew's contribution in those first tough matches and that it gave him immense pleasure to hand Andrew his medal. As the melee thinned out, I managed to get a quiet chat with Andrew to ask about the injury, and he was hopeful that he'd be able to bear weight by Wednesday when he was scheduled to see a physio. Behind Andy's cheerful façade, I could see he was hurting, both physically and emotionally.

Before stepping on the minibuses at the end of the match, Nigel and Thomas had informed me they were staying at a friend's house in Brinsley, so I knew I had to catch the last bus to Ailsworth at eight-thirty. As the clock sped past ten past eight, I thanked the coach and began going around all my teammates to thank them for making it easy for me to fit in, but I reserved my final farewell for Eric, whose company I'd enjoyed so much.

'See you then, Eric,' I said and offered my hand.

'Do you not fancy playing for us next year, then?' He asked, knowing I couldn't.

'Yeah, I do fancy it, but I'm needed in Ailsworth, I'm afraid, but thanks for everything. You didn't have to take me under your wing as you did, but I truly appreciated it. Thanks.'

'Jesus Christ, Smithy, you're going to set me off if you don't piss off,' he said. 'You didn't mind me knocking you into shape then?'

'No, Eric, I didn't mind one little bit. I don't want to be soppy, but I won't forget this in a hurry, so thanks, big man, you were brilliant.' I smiled and gave him a soft punch to his arm before walking towards the doors.

About five yards from the door, I heard Eric's booming voice. 'Before he sneaks off, let's have three cheers for Smithy.' I turned and saw everyone raise their paper cups and give me the three "Hip-Hip-Hoorays" demanded by Eric. At the end, facing my football friends with my face thoroughly flushed, I gave a theatrical bow; Peter would have been proud, and, as tears threatened to ruin my curtain bow, I walked out.

o o o

Looking out the window of the bus, I saw my reflection. I was alone again, but tonight I didn't feel alone. I knew I had friends in Brinsley, I knew I had friends in Ailsworth, and I knew, given time, I'd have friends at school. The six weeks had seemed like a daunting challenge when I set out that first Saturday morning for the Black Lakes, but here I was, actually looking forward to school with a sense of hope for the future. I smiled at my reflection because I felt pride in my achievements. I knew I could start listing what got me here, but that would be pointless. I needed to forget that now and be James Smith, an ordinary boy from Ailsworth.

When the bus arrived at Commercial Square, it must have been around ten to nine. As I waited to get off, an old couple also decided to disembark, so I waited patiently, even helping the old woman with the last step. I waved them goodbye and set off down the back alleys, wondering if I'd bump into Brenda again. To make sure I didn't, I listened before any corner to ensure there were no voices. As I walked quickly, I realised I was back in Ailsworth, my Town, and people, other than Maude's customers, would now know who I was. I was John and Martha Smith's son and winner of the Inter-Colls tournament in 1975.

After turning a left-hand corner, my head seemed to bang into something hard. I couldn't focus clearly and began staggering around, confused and feeling dizzy. I tried to focus on something but could only see flashes of stone walls zooming in and out and swirling like a kaleidoscope. I reeled sideways as my head struck something hard again, and this time I collapsed to the ground, arms around my head to break my fall. My head was swimming, but then I heard laughter, maniacal laughter. I was being attacked! I curled into a ball and felt a sickening blow to my back; someone was kicking me! The next kicks struck my arms and my shins. Then there was shouting, someone grabbed my collar, and a blow smashed into my face. I was dropped to the floor and heard more shouting, a loud crack, silence, and crying. It was the last thing I heard as everything around me dissolved into black.

The End of the Holidays

1

John Smith was sitting at a table with Peter Crabtree; three others who regularly frequented the Railway Inn were also present. John was not drunk, but he wasn't sober; he's reached the green zone, where he was no longer constrained but hadn't yet drunk enough to render his speech slurred and his thoughts invalid. He was happy.

'You should've seen him, Bert,' he said, demonstrating with his hand how his son had squirmed his way into the penalty box with fish-like agility. 'Wasn't he brilliant, Peter?' John asked, turning to Peter.

'Well, not being an expert in the field of footballing skills, I can't really comment, but he did demonstrate some form of talent at that point which led to this big oaf trying to break his legs,' Peter said, not confident he'd helped.

'He lured him in, Bert; that's what he did. Sold him a dummy and bang,' John punched his left palm, 'penalty.'

'Well, we weren't there, John, but winning the Inters is no mean feat for any team, let alone an under-sixteen team.'

John felt a warm glow of reflected glory as he remembered how well James had played. He felt guilty for not gushing to James how well he'd done, but at the time, he was finding it difficult to contain his emotions. Watching his son on the pitch, shoulder to shoulder against some men he knew had reputations for being hard, and his son never took a backward step. Even now, getting close to ten, he felt himself welling up at the thought.

Peter must have noticed. 'You must have been very proud of James, John,' he said. John nodded, unable to voice a reply and took a gulp of his beer. Peter decided to change the topic, and soon, the five friends were talking about politics.

Suddenly the door to the Railway Inn burst open, and two young men walked briskly to the bar, seemingly desperate for beer and looking extremely excited. As John and Peter looked at these men, they noticed people gathering around them and a buzz starting. No one at their table could hear what was being said, so Bert got up and joined the throng. A few of the men suddenly left the bar and ran outside. John and Peter looked at each other; something was wrong. They were about to get up themselves when they saw Bert returning. They followed Bert's movement to their table and watched as he sat down breathlessly excited.

'What is it, Bert? What the hell is all that about?' John asked.

'There's been a murder, John! They've found a young lad murdered in the back alleys by Commercial Square, but they don't know who it is.'

John Smith jumped up and ran to the bar. 'Alf, I need your phone,' John shouted. 'Now!'

Alf, the bewildered barman, dragged the phone from behind the bar and placed it in front of John. He watched, worry etched across his face as John Smith, someone he regarded as a close friend, dialled frantically. He couldn't wait for the dial to complete its anti-clockwise return before starting the next.

John held the phone to his ear. 'Ma? Hi, love, uh, has James arrived home yet?' He asked, trying to keep his voice calm. Suddenly his composure disappeared. 'What? Then where the hell is he? Has he phoned?' He realised he was worrying Martha, so he calmed himself down. 'No, I was checking because I wanted to say well done. Yeah, he's probably gone to one of his friends' houses,' he said. 'I'm leaving for home now anyway, so see you in ten minutes or so. Bye.' John put the handset down and turned to Peter. 'It's James; he hasn't come home.' As he said it, John felt he'd just said, "James has been murdered."

Peter ran back to the chairs and got their coats. 'I'm taking you home, John. We need to be there to explain things carefully to Martha.' John nodded as he put on his coat. Once outside, the two kept walking briskly, their hearts racing, trying not to believe the worst. 'Do you have a phone number for one of his teammates?' Peter asked, and John was grateful for his calm head.

'No, we don't. No, wait, I think we do. We have the number for Nigel Mannion, the captain,' John said.

'Well, we can start there, and I'm sure he'll be okay.'

John's well-trodden journey home seemed to take an eternity, but they soon arrived and walked into the house together.

'Oh, hello, Peter,' Martha said. 'Have you come to greet our little Kevin Keegan too?' She asked, smiling.

'John,' Peter said, 'why don't you make that call while I tell Martha what we know.' John nodded and went through to the hallway, closing the door behind him. He found the number that James had written in their book.

'Hello, is that Mr Mannion? . . . . It's James Smith's Dad, and I was wondering if I could have a chat with Nigel? . . . . What, oh, do you have his friend's number, because this is very important? . . . . Yes, yes, yes,' John said as he recorded the number. 'Thank you very much, Mr Mannion,' he said, cut him off and dialled the new number.

As he listened to the distant rings his call had generated, John's world slowed down. He heard Martha sobbing through their hallway door and saw distorted human figures through its rippled glass. He saw James standing in the hall, waiting outside the parlour door for the right moment to say goodnight to his father. John knew he'd been drinking and could feel its effects, but his senses were sharpening as he prepared to look after his family. He didn't want to; John Smith wanted to scream at somebody.

'Hello? Is that Mr Khan?' . . . . 'I've been given your number by Mr Mannion, and I wanted a word with his son, Nigel.' . . . . 'Thank you, I'll wait.' . . . . 'Hello, Nigel? It's John Smith, James's

Dad,' . . . . 'I was wondering what James did at your celebration party tonight?' . . . . 'The eight-thirty bus? Are you sure?' . . . . 'It's just that there's a report that someone's been found dead in Ailsworth, and James hasn't come home yet; I'm sure it's nothing to worry about; bye,' John said the last word in a trance as he cut Nigel off.

He entered the living room and saw that Peter had managed to calm Martha down. She was sitting on the sofa with Peter by her side, holding her hands. They both looked expectantly at him.

'Martha, you need to remain calm,' he began, but his wife sobbed louder. He waited for her sobs to subside. 'James should have been home just after nine, so he's late..'

'No, no,' Martha wailed, and Peter tightened his hands around hers.

'Martha!' John raised his voice. 'This doesn't help..'

'But it's James, John; our little James,' she said pleadingly, hoping he understood.

'I know, love, but we don't know what's happened. So..'

'Off you go, John. I'll stay here with Martha,' Peter spoke in the calmest voice John had ever heard. John nodded. He bent down before his distraught wife, and the pair hugged. Nothing further needed to be said, and John walked out.

○ ○ ○

Standing outside the old building that housed the Ailsworth Police Station, John saw various officers running in and out. He knew it would be busy as he pushed open the large wooden door, but that knowledge didn't prepare him for the turmoil that greeted him. It was pandemonium.

Like a statue being pushed, John moved unnoticed through the chaos until he stood before the tall ornate wooden reception desk that wouldn't look out of place in a church. He brought his palm down to ring the chromed bell. He waited, but no one came. He rang again, and again, and again, and again, as his hand became a blur and blood began to appear over the bell's domed cover.

'Whoa, whoa. Stop that: stop that now!' A flushed sergeant shouted at John. 'Can't you see we're fucking busy, pal?'

John couldn't see or hear anything but the man's voice facing him. 'My son's missing,' he said calmly.

The sergeant's expression changed. 'Could you please say that again, sir?'

'My son is missing,' John repeated.

'Shh, keep it down!' The sergeant shouted, and the milling officers focused on the calm man standing at the desk. 'Could you give me some details, please, sir?'

John nodded. 'My name is John Smith. My son James Smith, who is fifteen years old, should have been home by nine. He caught the eight-thirty bus from Brinsley and usually gets off at Commercial Square.' He watched as the sergeant frantically wrote down the details. When he'd finished, he looked up. 'It's just that I've heard that someone, someone young, has been found dead in the back alleys, and, and…' John bowed his head and began to cry.

The sergeant had sent two officers from the back, and they took John by the arms to lead him to a waiting room where they bade him sit. As the two young men stood awkwardly, the sergeant, who'd passed the details to others, came in and took a chair in front of John. The sergeant flicked his head, and the two men gratefully exited.

'John,' the sergeant said. 'Is it okay if I call you John?' He asked. John nodded and looked up. 'I can confirm that we are investigating an incident, but why would you think that involves your son?'

A sudden panic flashed through John as he considered if he'd been foolish. He hadn't; there was something wrong. 'It's just that James is never late. He told us about going to Brinsley to celebrate winning the Inter-Colls, but I phoned his friend, and he confirmed that James left in plenty of time to catch the eight-thirty to Ailsworth.'

'You said he'd get off at Commercial Square. Is that the nearest stop to home?' The sergeant asked.

'Uh, no, the Town Centre stop is slightly closer, but he told me he preferred Commercial Square because the back alleys lead to our street. We live at number five Cromwell Terrace,' John added, and the sergeant jotted this in his small notebook.

Suddenly the door opened. 'Sarge, we've got a problem at the desk!'

'Can't you see I'm busy?' He replied, frustrated that the messenger hadn't sorted it out.

'It's just there's this drunk, and he's screaming he's the victim's brother.'

'Ed!' John said

'What?' Asked the sergeant.

'That's my eldest boy, Edward. He must have heard,' John said.

'Right, get a couple of lads, calm him down and bring him here. Tell him his father wants a word,' the sergeant ordered.

'I'm sorry,' John said.

'Don't be sorry, John. You have no need to say sorry,' the sergeant reassured him.

'What's your name?' John asked.

'My name's Steve, but people around here call me Sergeant Collins.'

The door opened again, and a red-faced Ed was dragged in, resisting. The moment he saw his father, he relaxed and freed himself. John stood, and the two embraced, pulling each other tightly.

When John felt Edward had calmed enough, he asked him to sit. With father and son facing him, Steve decided to carry on. 'Edward, I know emotions are running high, but you must remain calm because that's the best way for us to know if James is involved in this, okay?' Even though he'd seen angry eyes like Edward's before, he felt he could continue. 'Right, John; what was James wearing tonight?'

Suddenly John wanted Martha to be here. 'He had, uhm…,'

'He wore a pair of blue jeans. Not Wrangler or Levi or anything, just a cheap pair…,' Edward interrupted. As Edward continued to describe James' outfit, John felt ashamed he hadn't paid any attention as his happy son set off for the minibus.

'Thank you, Edward,' Steve said as he closed his notebook. He looked at the bowed heads of the devastated pair sitting there and stood. 'I'm just taking these details to the investigating team, and I'll return as soon as I have anything for you. Is that okay?' He asked.

John looked up and nodded.

○ ○ ○

John and Edward considered any possible alternative scenarios that might exclude James from this mess, but despite thinking that James could have gone to Maude's, they knew deep inside that James was involved in the turmoil they could still hear outside their waiting room.

John looked at his watch and saw it was over thirty minutes since Steve had left them alone. In the meantime, they'd been offered and accepted coffee but were now desperate for any snippet of information. They needed to know; they wanted to know. John was pleased that Edward seemed to have sobered up but knew that was more to do with the stress and focus of their predicament rather than the natural process of sobering up.

The door opened, and the pair straightened immediately to see Steve walk back in with a man dressed in a grey suit. The pair took up chairs to face them. 'John and Edward, this is Detective Sergeant Hopkins, and he has some information for you. Please listen to everything he has to say.'

DS Hopkins cleared his throat. 'Sorry for taking so long to get back to you, but we had to check your story.' He looked at them. 'Mr Smith, I can tell you that your son James has been involved in an incident tonight. He's in a serious but stable condition in Wigan hospital….'

'What!' Edward interrupted.

'Shut up, Ed; let him finish,' John commanded, and Edward, his eyes burning, nodded.

DS Hopkins saw that Edward was calm enough. 'Right, as I said, James has been badly beaten up, and he's in the best possible place to be treated, but I don't know the details of his injuries. Another young man was also present when James was found, and that young man sadly died of his injuries.' John's head and heart were pounding, but he forced himself to remain silent as he listened. DS Hopkins continued after seeing slight nods from his audience. 'The parents of the dead lad have been informed, and specialist officers are supporting them as we speak. I just need to know if your son James had anything to do with the dead lad.'

John and Edward looked at each other and then focused on DS Hopkins. 'Who was it?' John asked.

'I'd appreciate it if you didn't spread this around because we're sending officers out to inform other family members.' DS Hopkins asked and saw them nod. 'The lad's name is Liam O'Rourke.'

2

A split second. That's what it felt like. One second I was confused in the darkness on the ground, and now it's light, and I'm in a bed. I tried to move, but everything ached. My face, sides, arms, legs, and back ached, and I could only see through my left eye. I reached up slowly with my painful left arm and felt the dressing around my eye. I began to panic.

'Try not to move, James,' a calm voice spoke. I turned my head with difficulty and saw a nurse standing on the other side of the raised cream-coloured bed rails. I tried to respond but felt restraints around my chin. 'You've been badly injured, James, and we had to operate to reset your jaw, which was dislocated. Normally we don't operate, but you'd suffered a bad dislocation.' I nodded, but even that was painful. 'You've also other injuries, so we want you to rest until we can fully assess them.' I raised my hand again and pointed to my right eye. 'Yes, your right eye has taken a direct hit, we think from a punch, and there's some damage and swelling. Initial checks in the theatre don't indicate a fracture, so we'll take these dressings off shortly for our eye specialist to assess. Is that okay?' She said, and I nodded. I then managed to get my right index finger to point at my left wrist and rotated it clockwise. The nurse smiled. 'It's three in the afternoon on Monday.'

I fell asleep.

o o o

Another split second. I was awakened when I heard voices and felt my head being gently lifted as someone raised the bed's headrest. I saw a gathering of medical staff around me.

'Hello, James, my name is Mr Wearne, and I specialise in eye injuries. I just need to remove the dressing around your right eye to examine you, if that's okay?'

I nodded.

'Please don't try to open your eye until I ask you to, okay?'

Again I nodded and immediately felt hands working to remove the bandages or whatever they were. The doctor or whatever title he had leaned in, and I felt his hands prodding all around my eye socket and eyelid.

'Okay, James, please try to open your right eye, but slowly, okay?' I nodded and began to focus on opening my eye. It wouldn't move! 'Try again, James. It will be difficult because it is swollen.' So I tried again, and through the pain, I saw a blurred sliver of light, but it immediately began to burn, so I closed my eye again. 'Did you see anything?' I nodded. 'Was it blurred?' I shrugged because I wasn't sure if it was blurred or hadn't opened the eyelid far enough. 'Right, please continue to open your eye until you know if you can see correctly. If you don't open it far enough, it will give you a false blurred image through your lashes.' I nodded and began to exercise the eye. Eventually, I could open it far enough and saw the expectant faces looking at me. If I could smile, I would have. 'Can you see, James?' Mr Warne asked. I gave him the thumbs up. 'Is it similar to before?' Again I gave the thumbs up and felt relieved when I saw them smile.

○ ○ ○

By half-past five, I'd seen three specialists, who all seemed happy with my progress. The surgeon who'd reset my jaw made me open my mouth slowly as he held either side of my face below my ears. He seemed happy and asked me to speak slowly. 'Hello,' I said. He smiled and asked me to repeat a phrase slowly. 'I want to go to the café for some food,' I said. Although it was slightly painful, I felt proud I'd managed it.

After the chin specialist (I don't know if he has a posher title) left, I felt better about my condition. I was astounded that I hadn't spent time analysing my situation as I usually did, and all I managed to do was listen to the staff and sleep. It was surreal, but normality returned when I began to feel hungry. It was past six o'clock, and I craved fish and chips, but instead of food, they gave me a large milkshake, and I had to drink it through a big straw. It did the trick, and I lay back to wait for visiting, which they said would be permissible after seven.

I sat with the headrest up, awaiting the doors to open. It seemed to be ages until I saw them move, and then my family walked in, unsure of what they would see. It didn't start well because Mum burst into tears, and Dad was hardly any better. It was Ed who came to me first and studied my face.

'Did a good job there, Jamie boy,' he said smiling.

'I know,' I replied through gritted teeth, complying with the surgeon's commands.

'Great to see you again, though,' he said.

'And you.'

Dad came to me next. 'Are you in any pain?' He asked.

'Why'd you ask that?' I asked and was pleased to see them smile. Gradually the tension and awkwardness disappeared, and we managed a general chat that included me not knowing what had happened and them knowing even less. I learnt that Peter had helped out and they were grateful to him. I then had to ask the question that had been on my mind since the moment I awoke.

'It was Ollie, wasn't it?' I asked and studied their faces for a reaction. I didn't see anything.

'No, it had nothing to do with Ollie,' Dad said, 'But we can't tell you any more than that because the police need to speak to you when we leave, okay? Believe me, James; if we could tell you, we would, but we can't, okay?' Dad seemed pained to say those words.

'That's okay, Dad; I understand.' I said, and they left after leaving drinks, sweets and fruit, promising to return for afternoon visiting tomorrow.

I was going to miss the first day of school. After all that effort, I was going to miss the first day. But it wasn't Ollie. I didn't understand. Did I just run into a mugger? As I pondered this, the door opened again, and two men in suits walked in.

'Hello, James. My name is DS Hopkins, and this is DC Clements. I need to ask you about what happened last night if that's okay?'

'It's okay,' I said, gritting my teeth.

'In your own words, I'd like you to tell me what happened,' he said, and I did just that, finishing with the crack and the crying.

'Do you know who attacked me?' I then asked.

'Yes, James. It appears you were attacked by Patrick O'Rouke. He ambushed you in the back alley off Commercial Square, and it seems his brother Liam intervened because of the brutality of the assault. In pushing his brother away, Liam tripped backwards and cracked his skull against a stone that had fallen from a wall. Liam died instantly, and Patrick gave himself up after running home to tell his parents.'

The pain in my right eye stung so badly, but I didn't want help. I *wanted* my tears to burn as I re-imagined the noises I'd heard. That awful crack and the heart-breaking wail I now knew came from Patrick as he saw what he'd done.

3

Physically, I improved quickly after the first two days and was told I would be discharged on Thursday or Friday. The police returned to ask me if I remembered anything else; I didn't. I mentioned the football match and the history between Edward and the O'Rourkes, but that had been four years earlier. They didn't bother talking with me again after Tuesday. Ed had returned to college but would return on the weekend to make sure I was okay.

On Tuesday, I asked for a mirror from one of the nurses because I needed to see what was causing my pain. My face was a mess! My right eye, which was still difficult to keep open, was severely swollen and purple, reducing the appearance of the eye to a narrow slit. I thought it was the eyelid, but on closer inspection, I saw it was the soft bit above the eyelid that had swollen. The right side of my face was all bruises, running from the swollen eye down to below my mouth. Because the blows came from the side, I still had all my teeth, but they said I would need to see a dentist afterwards to double-check. After dispensing with the mirror, I lifted my gown and saw the extent of the bruising on my abdomen; apparently, three ribs were cracked. I already knew about the bruises on my arms and legs.

I lay back and began to shiver. The bruises were the physical depiction of Patrick's hatred for a boy who got the better of him during a stupid football match. I couldn't understand how someone could be affected like that. I'd recently experienced instant rage, but a minute later, that rage had gone. I didn't carry that rage around with me for days; I couldn't. It didn't make sense. The whole episode didn't make any sense – to me.

On Wednesday, Eric, Nigel and Thomas came to see me after asking permission from Mum that it was okay. Foolishly, I cried when I saw them, but we ended up having a laddish chat about the match and how I needed to look after myself. Eric even offered to be my bodyguard. I smiled, saying I was pale enough as I was and would never see the sun again if I accepted his kind offer. It was nice to joke, and seeing them leave made me sad.

Maude visited me on Thursday afternoon with Elsie and Mum, who'd taken the day off. Elsie was initially slightly subdued but brightened up when I offered her some soft fruit jellies. As they left, Maude kissed the top of my head. 'You can't imagine what I felt when I heard the news, James. Of all the children I've known, why would anyone do this? What on earth possessed him?' She asked.

'I don't know the answer to that, Aunt Maude, but whatever it was, it must have been very powerful because it destroyed his life and his family's.'

When I was told I wouldn't be discharged until Friday, I was glad to see Dad turn up for the Thursday evening visit. After talking about how we'd cope at home, our chat seemed to falter, mainly because I wasn't engaging properly. I had something on my mind which was an obstacle to our usual light-hearted discussions.

'What's the matter?' Dad asked, probably fed up with my lack of engagement.

'It's Peter,' I said.

'You want to know why he hasn't been to see you.'

'Yes.'

'You know he's been brilliant, don't you?' I nodded. 'Well, he told me on Tuesday, when we returned from a visit, that he felt unable to see you in hospital. He didn't say why, but I got the feeling he couldn't cope with the emotion of it all,' Dad paused. 'Do you know he's told me more than once that he felt you were the most remarkable boy he's ever met?'

I smiled. 'To be fair, I don't think Peter knows many boys my age, so that's a very subjective statement,' I said, wishing to deflect my embarrassment.

'Subjective or not, the point is Peter thinks the world of you, and while he's looked after us this week, I don't think he'd cope with seeing you in here. He'd rather see you when you're better.'

I felt reassured. 'Thanks, Dad,' I said, wanting to move on. 'You haven't told me yet what you thought of my performance. All these visits and not a word about the game; I don't know why I bothered.'

'God, you're such a drama queen, James; you're almost as bad as Ed,' Dad said, and I wondered if my shocked expression would trigger further discussion. It didn't.

○ ○ ○

As I walked into our house on Friday afternoon, it seemed to have shrunk; every room seemed small and claustrophobic. After being fussed over by Elsie and Mum, I felt tired and excused myself to my bedroom. Looking around, I saw my empty football bag and the letter I'd begun writing to Rhian. It was almost a week since her letter, and I wondered if I should bother completing the reply. I reread what I'd already written and kept it, deciding it was worth finishing.

○ ○ ○

Later, on Friday evening, Ed arrived back from college. It was great talking with the three of them as they asked how I was and what I could look forward to once I was better. It all felt dreamlike, non-reality, and I wasn't comfortable; I was also exhausted.

Lying in my bed, I couldn't get Liam out of my head. I sort of understood Doris dying, but I didn't understand Liam's death. I couldn't stop crying, and whenever I heard footsteps coming upstairs, I'd turn on my side with my back to the door, pretending to be asleep. I didn't want to talk with anyone. I kept turning onto my back. I'd stare into the darkness and cry uncontrollably as I imagined Liam falling backwards and the horrified realisation sweeping over Patrick he'd just killed his twin brother. His twin brother! Because of me: because of a stupid fucking football match that means absolutely nothing in the big scheme of things.

Why is it that we, in this small town, bothered to think that the Inter-Colls tournament was anything significant? Was it a symptom of our desperation to cling to the history of Ailsworth and its decommissioned industry? I couldn't cope with the pointless loss of Liam's life and kept seeing some of the tackles, elbows, punches and headbutts men thought it necessary to administer in their vainglorious attempt to change the course of a match. I then remembered how I'd absorbed the folklore surrounding the tournament, and the memory made me nauseous. I pushed myself to a sitting position but had to swing my legs out because of the pain. I sat there with my head in my hands, still crying, but my nausea had passed. I stood, turned on the light and walked to see myself in my mirror. I removed my pyjama top and stared at my distorted face and bruised body. This had nothing to do with a football match or Ailsworth's history; this was Patrick O'Rourke. If it hadn't been the football, it could have been a political argument in a pub, or he simply didn't like how you were smiling. It was Patrick's problem.

I felt calmer after that and returned to bed. I was tired.

○ ○ ○

On Saturday morning, Ed insisted on taking me for a walk. 'Who cares who sees your face? You've always been ugly,' he said, dismissing my objection as we started. We walked all the way to Maude's, and, despite the slow pace and the stiffness in my legs, I was pleased to be outside.

'Goodness me,' Maude fussed, 'out and about already,' she said. 'Are you sure you should be doing so much, James?' She asked.

'The doctors told me to go for walks but not to overdo it,' I reassured her. It was nice to smell 'Moonwind' again and see that the shop was still tidy despite the stock being run down ahead of the final closure.

I told Ed that I was tired, and after being given a small bunch of bananas from Maude, we began an even slower walk home. When we got in, Mum took the bananas and whispered in my ear that I had a visitor in the parlour. I smiled and forgot about the tiredness.

Peter was sitting in the visitor's chair and stood when I entered. He had a cup of tea on the side table. We stood mutely facing each other, and I watched Peter's initial smile disappear as he studied my bruised face. I walked over and embraced weakly; Peter was aware of my physical sensitiveness. I sat down, and he did likewise.

'I'm sure you thought me heartless,' Peter began.

'No, I would never think that Peter, but I did wonder why you didn't visit me.'

'I wanted to, James, I so desperately wanted to, but I don't think I could cope with seeing you damaged and in an alien place.'

'Dad did say that you were finding it difficult, but I wanted to see you. I wanted to tell you I was okay, but you didn't come,' I said.

'I'm sorry, James, I really am, but you mean too much to me, and I'm not as strong as your father. I couldn't do what he did on that awful Sunday night and go to the police station while keeping it together. I would have exploded with worry. He is your father; they are your family, and they kept it together to visit you and share your pain. I'm not built that way; I'm weak, and the last thing you want at the side of your hospital bed is a blubbering mess.'

'I understand what you're saying, Peter, but I'd have welcomed that blubbering mess because I wanted to show him first-hand that I was okay,' I said.

'Physically okay, you mean,' Peter said calmly.

'What?'

'You're not okay, James; you can't possibly be,' he said. 'Your wounds may be healing, but knowing you as I do, your worst pain comes from within.'

'I, I'm….'

'You will have been thinking about poor Liam and your role in his death. You had none. You will blame yourself, but you mustn't because you were blameless. This tragic episode, and its seismic effect on so many people, came about because of a failure in poor Patrick's emotional state. This fact won't stop you from worrying, but you must, James, or your recovery will take far longer than it will for those bruises to fade.' Pater reached across and held my hand.

'I have struggled with what happened to Liam, but I feel myself improving whenever I realise that Patrick wasn't attacking me; he was attacking what he wasn't, and as such, I can't help but feel sorry for him…. Is that strange?' I asked.

Peter was smiling brightly. 'No, it's what I'd expect James Smith to think, and hearing that makes me realise that you are now on the road to recovery.'

'I also realise how Liam may have saved me from sustaining life-changing injuries or even death, and I feel a massive obligation towards him. I've turned around in my head what I can do, but his tragic death has robbed me of any options,' I said, unsure where I was going.

'Patrick didn't plan for his brother to die, did he?' Peter asked.

'No, I sensed that from the noises I heard; it was a terrible accident.'

'And Liam wouldn't want his brother to suffer unfairly, would he?'

'No, Peter, he wouldn't,' I answered. I smiled as the penny dropped, marvelling at how this extraordinary man knew more about me than I did. I decided to change the subject. 'I've asked the doctors about returning to school, but they've advised against it because of my ribs. They suggested I stay off for at least four weeks, but I'm worried about missing schoolwork and other things.'

'Surely they'll send you copies of the lessons you're missing?' Peter suggested.

'Yes, they will, but it's not quite the same, as I'm sure you appreciate,' I said.

'I do, James, but I'm sure a full recovery is preferable to being present in class, isn't it?'

'I suppose it is, but, as you know, I have another reason for going back. I must face what I've been running from for seven weeks.'

'But facing Ollie in a weakened and vulnerable condition is the last thing you need. I would advise you to listen to the doctors because any physical attack from that monster could set you back months.' Peter explained.

'I know, Peter. I'll be vulnerable for six weeks, so I will need to face him even if I do listen to the doctors,' I said. As I saw Peter thinking, I thought back to the last few nights when, after upsetting about Liam, Ollie would enter my thoughts.

'Well, James, you set out on that first Saturday to exorcise Ollie Jenkins from your life. You were on target to confront him last Tuesday, but through no fault of your own, you could not do this. Am I correct?'

'Yes, Peter, you are.'

'You set out on this journey alone, and you planned to complete this journey alone. No one helped you… ,'

'That's not true, Peter. Many people helped,' I said.

'No! Many people were present to support you, but for all intents and purposes, you would see this through alone. Humour me. James,' Peter said, and I nodded. 'Now that your situation has changed, you must change your tactics, and as far as I'm concerned, when it comes to that boy, any new tactic is perfectly acceptable,' Peter nodded triumphantly as he finished.

Just as Peter finished, I nodded my understanding. I then saw the simplistic brilliance of the man and began to applaud. 'Bravo, Peter, bravo,' I said, and the two of us grinned mischievously.

4

Rhian's first week back in school had been uneventful as she and her classmates caught up with their holiday activities and slowly reintegrated into school life. On the second week, after Rhian returned home on Tuesday, her mother handed her a letter. She smiled, recognising the handwriting, dropped her school bag in the hall, and ran upstairs to read it.

Annwyl Rhian,

I was so happy to receive your letter – I liked your time gaps. They made me laugh, but I won't copy the idea because it would be unoriginal.

You didn't say anything to upset me, but the new letter did (I'll get to that later).

Usually, I don't like a smart Alec, but I'll make an exception in your case because you were spot on. I have finally told my family about the bullying. It has been life-changing.

Shortly after returning from holiday, an old primary school friend (he's now in grammar school) asked if I'd join their under-sixteens team because they'd entered a football tournament. Although initially nervous, I've had a fantastic time getting to know their players during practice. One of them, Eric, they call him man-mountain because of his size, has taken a shine to me, and we're pretty close, but this is where your new letter gave me a problem.

When I received your second reply, I thought – what's the point in carrying on with these. I'm probably making a fool of myself anyway. I also thought I was forcing you to write stuff and that it wasn't fair for me to depend on you to dig me out of a hole – of my own making. I was comfortable with that, but your new letter greatly upset me. It made me realise how self-centred I'd been and that I'd happily dump you and your kind words when I was okay and had dealt with my demons. I did the same with Peter – not dumping him exactly, but telling him I'd be seeing less of him now I felt in control. I've apologised to Peter face-to-face, and I'd like to be able to do the same with you, but I can't.

I'm sorry, Rhian; I hope you can forgive me for being so self-centred.

Poor Doris (from Maude's fruit and veg shop) suffered a bad stroke and died shortly after. It made me think about death and stuff and brought me closer to Maude and Peter and my grandma Elsie, whom I used to take for granted.

I went to Ernie Taynor's house the other day to tell his parents he was being bullied. It was awkward because Ernie walked in, and when he denied being bullied, I asked him to remove his shirt. Oh my god, you should have seen the bruises on his poor little body. I felt sick, like I'm sure his parents felt. I hope they're coping.

I told you that confessing was life-changing, didn't I? Well, I've also chatted a few times with Ed, my brother, and it's amazing how much closer we've become.

Anyway, this letter's getting pretty long, so I'll just say that, at the time of writing, our football team is through to the tournament's final. We're playing on Sunday (tomorrow), and I'll probably finish this letter by saying if we won (or not – but perhaps I won't expand on the details if we do lose)

SIX DAYS GAP (it makes sense here)

Sorry, you probably thought I wasn't replying.

We won the game and became champions.

Before the match, I saw Ernie and his parents, and they thanked me.

After the match, I celebrated the win with the lads at their grammar school. It was great to celebrate with friends.

This next bit's weird.

On the way home, I was mugged and spent five days in Wigan Hospital.

I was attacked by a lad who I got the better of during the semi-final. He has a twin brother. This lad punched and kicked me, but I can't remember much. I've been told the rest of this by other people – As I lay on the ground, because of the viciousness of the unprovoked attack, the other twin brother intervened to stop the assault. He was pushed away and tripped, hitting the back of his head against a rock. This boy tragically died; he would have been nineteen in a month. The twin has confessed to the police.

I know the letter's a mess – I can't face tidying it up. I just wanted to let you know I'm okay and getting better every day. I'm having more difficulty dealing with that poor boy's death, but my family and Peter are helping me cope.

Rhian, I will always look forward to hearing from you. As you said, we only met for a few minutes, but I feel you've been with me through the most important six weeks of my life, and I'll never forget that. So yes, I agree; we do share something, something important that a brief meeting should never have been able to form – yet it did.

Thank you for not giving up on me.

Yours Sincerely

1-second gap

Love, James x

When Rhian didn't reply to her mother's demands to come to tea, Mrs Thomas stormed into Rhian's room. She found her daughter sitting on her bed, drying her tears. Instead of saying anything, Rhian simply handed the letter to her mother.

5

Dad and I were walking through the alleys that led to Commercial Square. I asked about the O'Rourke family along the way, and Dad gave me a concise history.

Michael O'Rourke, the father, used to be a miner at the old Flinsby Pit. Since it shut down eight years ago, Mr O'Rourke has worked as a labourer for various builders. His wife was Irene O'Rourke, and they had five children; Patrick and Liam were the youngest.

'You're walking much better now,' Dad commented, changing the subject.

'I need to,' I said, 'seeing that I'm planning to start school next week.'

'Are you sure about going back?' Dad asked. 'The doctor did recommend staying off at least another week, didn't he?'

'I know, Dad, but I need to get back because the longer I leave it, the harder it will be,' I said, stopping abruptly. 'It's just around the next corner, isn't it?' I asked.

'Yes, James,' Dad paused. 'Are you sure you want to do this?'

'I have to, Dad. I need to see the place again.'

Together we turned left, and here, where the back alley to Commercial Square crossed another, was where my life changed. I didn't look down; I walked across to the other side and turned back to reenact my journey that Sunday night. Turning left, I realised Patrick was hiding behind the wall to my right. That was how I didn't see him, which was why the right side of my face took the brunt of the attack.

Dad must have been horrified as he watched me work out where I'd fallen and as I stood, pretending to be Patrick standing over me. I took a deep breath and turned. There, about six feet away, sat a lone rock. It was gnarly and uneven, roughly three by two foot and nine inches tall. I walked over and looked down to study it, focusing on the left-hand corner where I imagined Liam's head had struck. I heard the crack again and turned to look at Patrick. I saw his face crease into terror as he realised what had happened. My unconscious body lay behind him now; it was unimportant. All Patrick could see was his twin brother and what his temper had inflicted.

I dried my tears on my sleeve and laid the single rose with the other flowers that marked Liam's sad memorial. I looked up at Dad and nodded; I was ready to go.

○ ○ ○

'Are you sure you want to do this?' Dad asked me for the second time today.

'Yes, Dad, I do,' I said and watched Dad ring the doorbell to the pebble-dashed council house. It was Thursday, almost three weeks since the attack, and we were in the large council estate built on the south side of Ailsworth.

A gaunt man opened the door and stared at us. Slowly, the realisation of who the visitors were dawned on him. 'What the fuck do you want?' He snarled through the remnants of his teeth.

I'd told Dad that I wanted to do the talking. 'Mr O'Rourke, my name's James Smith,' I began.

'I know who you are, you little cunt!'

'Who is it?' A woman's voice joined from the hallway.

'It's the little fucker who got Liam killed,' he answered. The woman joined her husband at the door and stared at me.

'I know you hate me, Mr & Mrs O'Rourke, but I've come here to tell you something about what happened,' I said.

'We know,' he screamed. 'We fucking know what happened, you little shit,' Michael O'Rourke spat.

At first, Mrs O'Rourke said nothing. She just stared at me. 'What do you want to tell us?'

'I only want you to know that Patrick had no intention of hurting Liam. It was a horrible, horrible accident, and I've never heard anything as awful and soul-destroying as the cry that came from Patrick when he saw what he had done to his twin brother,' I said, looking at them. 'That's all I wanted to say. Patrick loved Liam, and if asked in court, I will tell everyone that it was a tragic accident,' I said, staring at them to make sure they understood. They said nothing.

Dad put his arm on my shoulder, and we walked away, leaving the grieving couple holding each other in the doorway. As we closed their garden gate and turned to look back, they were walking towards us halfway up the path.

'You'll say that in court?' Mr O'Rourke asked.

'Yes, I will,' I answered.

'Despite what he did to you?' Mrs O'Rourke asked.

'Don't get me wrong, Mrs O'Rourke,' I said. 'Patrick wanted to hurt me. What he did to me was planned and vicious, but Patrick never meant to hurt Liam, not for a second.'

Mrs O'Rourke bowed her head briefly before looking at me again. 'Thank you, James. It was kind of you to tell us,' Mrs O'Rourke said, and her husband begrudgingly nodded.

'It was the least I could do for Liam,' I said and turned to walk home with Dad.

6

On Sunday, three weeks after the attack, I left home to walk to the High Street. I was excited because Mum and Dad had agreed I could go to school, despite their doubts and my inability to move freely because of the rib injuries. The eye was still lightly bruised, but most of the swelling had gone.

Nervously, I stood at the familiar door and knocked, peering through the privacy glass once more. Mr Jenkins answered, took one look at me and shouted for Ollie. I watched the familiar shape lumber towards me, his face lighting up as he recognised his visitor.

'It's okay, Dad, I've got this,' Ollie said, and his Dad walked inside. He waited for Mr Jenkins to disappear, then turned to me and snarled. 'What the fuck do you want, you disabled piece of shit?'

'I want a word with you, Ollie, before I start back in school next week,' I explained.

Ollie closed the door. 'Let's take a walk,' he said, and we set off along the pavement toward our old "football pitch".

I was walking slowly. 'Next week, I need you to keep away from me because I've still not fully recovered,' I said.

'Ooh, what's the matter; has poor lickle Shitsy's got a booboo?' he taunted.

'Look,' I said, 'the bullying has finished; it's gone. It's not going to happen again, okay? If I was fit enough, I'd fight back next week, but I can't; I'm still in pain. I'm asking you to forget about it for good, so we can continue our school work without distraction and act like normal decent human beings,' I explained. I looked into his face to see if he was taking any of this in, and all I saw was the same pathetic snarling face.

'Next week, or maybe starting right now, I'm going to show you what pain really fucking means, okay?'

'You can't do that, Ollie; it's cruel and cowardly,' I said. 'But I'm not afraid of you anymore, so you need to stop. It doesn't matter how much you hit me; I'll never listen to you again, okay?'

'Do you think for one second that I give a shit that it's cruel? And me stop? Next week your sorry ass will be back in my control, and if you don't listen, I'll hurt you so bad you'd wish you were Liam O'Rourke. Do you understand?' He shouted as we turned the corner towards the pitch.

'I was afraid you were going to say that, Ollie,' I said, looked ahead and clapped my hands.

'What?' Ollie said before looking up and seeing Nigel, Thomas and Eric walking towards us from the side of the Norweb building. They were twenty yards away but didn't speed up when Ollie clocked them, recognising Nigel and Thomas from our knockabout. 'You think you could ambush *me*, you little shit?' Ollie said and turned to run home.

'Going somewhere, Ollie,' Ed asked. He stood three yards behind us and immediately grabbed Ollie in a headlock. With a struggling Ollie unable to break free. Ed calmly walked towards the other three, who'd stepped off the pavement and moved to the pitch. I walked after them a few yards behind my brother and his writhing captive.

Ed released Ollie in the middle of our pitch, near where Nigel, Thomas and Eric stood. The four of them formed a guard around the stunned Ollie.

'Right, Ollie. I think you know Ed, Nigel and Thomas, but this impressive specimen here,' I said, pointing at Eric, 'is known as the lecturer, and he's going to teach you a lesson.'

'Wha....' That was all Ollie could say before Eric punched him on his arm. Ollie began to sob, nursing his arm.

'You won't get away with this,' Ollie cried. Suddenly he raised his head. A middle-aged couple were strolling in the road, close to the pitch. 'Help!' Ollie called, 'They're beating me up.'

The couple stopped and looked at us. 'That's terrible,' the woman shouted. 'That poor boy's been in the papers, and you pushed him over?'

'What the hell are you saying?' Ollie screamed. Gradually, I saw the realisation dawn across Ollie's face as he recognised the couple.

'It was so lucky for him that these four boys ran from the High Street to save him, wasn't it dear?' She said, in a loud voice, turning to her husband. I had to admit they were acting it perfectly.

'Yes, dear, I'd hate to think what would have happened to that poor injured boy if they hadn't saved him,' the man replied. The couple carried on walking away from us towards the high street.

I turned to them. 'Thank you, Mr &Mrs Taynor; I'm glad you saw that,' I said.

'Not a problem, James, glad to have witnessed it,' Mrs Taynor said, waving as they walked away.

I turned back to face the shocked Ollie. 'I'm going to leave you here now, Ollie, and I'll see you in school. Oh, and since Ed was behind us and heard what you planned to do to me next week, I'll leave it to him to decide on the severity of your punishment. But just to let you know, if you even so much as look at Ernie or me next week, then we'll intercept you on your way to school the next morning and do this all over again. Do you understand?'

'Yes,' Ollie sobbed resignedly.

I turned and walked away, feeling nothing but hatred for the crying boy as I heard the familiar sound that a fist makes when it connects with the upper arm.

END

Printed in Dunstable, United Kingdom